Dedalus Europe
General Editor: Timothy Lane

THE DEVIL'S ROAD

JEAN-PIERRE OHL

THE DEVIL'S
ROAD

translated by Mike Mitchell

Dedalus

Supported using public funding by
**ARTS COUNCIL
ENGLAND**

Published in the UK by Dedalus Limited
24-26, St Judith's Lane, Sawtry, Cambs, PE28 5XE
email: info@dedalusbooks.com
www.dedalusbooks.com

ISBN printed book 978 1 910213 93 3
ISBN ebook 978 1 912868 13 1

Dedalus is distributed in the USA & Canada by SCB Distributors
15608 South New Century Drive, Gardena, CA 90248
email: info@scbdistributors.com   web: www.scbdistributors.com

Dedalus is distributed in Australia by Peribo Pty Ltd
58, Beaumont Road, Mount Kuring-gai, N.S.W. 2080
email: info@peribo.com.au

Publishing History
First published in France in 2017
First published by Dedalus in 2019

Translation copyright © Mike Mitchell 2019
Le chemin de diable copyright © Editions Gallimard, Paris, 2017

The right of Jean-Pierre Ohl to be identified as the author and Mike Mitchell
as the translator of this work has been asserted by them in accordance with
the Copyright, Designs and Patents Act, 1988.

Printed and bound in Great Britain by Clays Ltd, Elcograf S.p.A.
Typeset by Marie Lane

THE AUTHOR

Jean-Pierre Ohl has combined a career as a bookseller with his writing.

He is the author of three novels *Mr Dick or The Tenth Book*, *The Lairds of Cromarty* and *The Devil's Road*, all published in English by Dedalus.

He lives in the Dordogne.

THE TRANSLATOR

For many years an academic with a special interest in Austrian literature and culture, Mike Mitchell has been a freelance literary translator since 1995.

He has published over eighty translations from German and French. His translation of Rosendorfer's *Letters Back to Ancient China* won the 1998 Schlegel-Tieck Translation Prize after he had been shortlisted in previous years.

His translations have been shortlisted four times for The Oxford Weidenfeld Translation Prize: *Simplicissimus* by Johann Grimmelshausen in 1999, *The Other Side* by Alfred Kubin in 2000, *The Bells of Bruges* by Georges Rodenbach in 2008 and *The Lairds of Cromarty* by Jean-Pierre Ohl in 2013.

"WINE! I WANT TO BE A DRUNKEN PAWN ON THE CHESSBOARD."

MICHEL OHL

PROLOGUE

Diary of Leonhard Vholes,
intended readership: none

London, 3rd March 1824

Nothing else exists apart from this hand that is writing.

Is it even known to whom it belongs? Am I a good man? Certainly not. Otherwise why would I pay a rogue such as Robert Grant? A bad one, then? Well, I do give alms of my own free will, and I am moved to tears by the death of a child.

Grant makes himself comfortable in the chair facing me. For a moment I thought he was going to put his feet up on my desk, as I'm sure he does on the greasy tables of the dives in Seven Dials. But he sees the look on my face. And then he takes a book out of his pocket. I recognise it immediately: *Du contrat social, ou Principes du droit politique* by J-J. Rousseau, citizen of Geneva. The Beresford seal is very prominent on the flyleaf and Danton's dedication covers the whole of the title page. As I drop the volume into a drawer an odd metallic 'click' can be heard.

"I thought you might be interested, in connection with the

name of Beresford…"

"Where did you steal it from?"

He sits up straight, feigning indignation. A good actor. Second-rate, but all the same…

"I didn't steal it, Mr Vholes. Someone gave it to me. In trust."

"Grant, I find it hard to believe that anyone is naive enough to entrust anything at all to you."

"Sometimes you can't choose the person you have to trust, sir."

Guile, instinct, professional know-how. Grant's mind leaps from one object to the next, like a cat after mice. It doesn't follow any rule, any general plan but, in keeping with our age, is solely led by the prospect of immediate profit. Cats are incapable of drawing up an overall plan to eradicate mice but they still manage to do that.

"Who? Where? Why?"

"I knew someone who spoke like that, sir. A guard. On the bridges. He just asked questions. And he always got a reply, some true, some false. By using his whip."

I play along with him and pretend to look for the whip. Grant is amused and raises his hand as a sign of surrender.

"In Marshalsea prison. In the cellar. An old man with a face like a knife-blade…" He thinks for a moment, then adds, "Not that old, perhaps. He goes by the name of Perkins, but I'd stake my life on it being a false name."

A debtors' prison! Can you imagine a more absurd establishment? Poor people, who are unfortunate enough, are required to pay back money they don't possess – and it's done by putting them in prison where they are deprived of all means… and what is more, they're forced to pay a daily fee!

"What is this cellar?"

"The dungeon of the old Borough Prison. That's where they put the debtors who don't even have the twopence a day to pay for a room and food: they're fed with the scrapings from the bowls until they're declared insolvent."

"But it's obvious they're insolvent. Why else would they let themselves be cooped up in a rathole?"

"I'm not the one who decides that, sir." Grant draws back into his chair and puts on a deferential air. "It's you, the legal gentlemen."

"I'm a lawyer, not a magistrate and even less the minister of justice. This man, does he have small eyes, very close? A broad forehead?"

"Very broad, given that he hasn't a single hair on his head. As for his eyes, I can't say."

"About six feet tall? His hands long and slender."

"I've only seen him lying on his mattress. His hands, yes, certainly."

"Speaking like a gentleman?"

"As for that, yes, not a man from my class. If it really is the lord in question he has come a hell of a long way down in the world… but you have clients over there, you can go and check yourself. Unless you'd rather not have a chat with him…"

Grant allows himself a brief smile. What precisely have I told him about Beresford? I can't remember.

On the opposite side of Lincoln's Inn Fields the windows of the other chambers are going dark one after the other, following some complex scheme of annihilation, sometimes vertical, sometimes horizontal, like pawns devoured by an invisible castle and bishop. Soon the chessboard is empty and all that remains of life around is concentrated in the sound of the elms rustling in the wind. But you can't make out the leaves or branches any more, just an inchoate mass that seems to be coming closer.

As far as I'm concerned, I completely lost interest in the chess game a long time ago. Since my queen was taken.

"Yes, I will go. When I've got time. What did he want?"

"Money, for God's sake! He wanted me to sell the book so that he could get out of the cellar and sleep in a proper bed, at least for a few days."

"There are two sovereigns, one for you, one for him."

"He thinks the book is worth a lot more."

"Prices have fallen. Try to find out more. Discreetly. And now off you go."

"At your service, sir."

Once I was alone I opened the drawer and took out the book. My iron ruler came out with it, as if attached to the leather by an invisible force. Strange... why the hell would anyone hide a magnet in a book?

I

Edward Bailey's Rude Awakening

Darlington, County Durham, March 1824

At the moment when the navvies reach the pond four o'clock rings from a church tower: the bell doles out the chimes slowly, grudgingly, the way one throws scraps of old meat to dogs – and, indeed, a dog barks at a nearby farm, alerted by the men's arrival. A few sunbeams weren't enough to brighten up the afternoon, and now large clouds are arriving from the west. The pond is giving off a foul stench – like the smell that clings to old clothes. The shadow of a copse of birches, very long already, runs across a strip of ground dotted with weeds, then hits the oily surface, black with no reflections, that absorbs everything.

They've been working since dawn, only stopping to eat their lunch. There are twenty of them, the oldest hobbling along clutching his ribs, the youngest still has to start growing a beard. The newcomers have no idea exactly what a 'railway' is and why they are moving along a line indicated by posts and string, flattening the humps in the terrain here, filling its ruts with earth mixed with bricks there.

The foreman, Alan Forbes, surveys his men to assess how tired they are and eventually announces a fifteen-minute rest. Those who have some tobacco fill their pipes, the others just sit down to contemplate the expanse that seems to consist of viscous oil: here and there unknown shapes touch the surface without quite breaking through, like elbows or knees under a dirty sheet.

Most of the men are Geordies but in one corner there are also three Highlanders who mostly talk in Gaelic. Coming from the south, Forbes sometimes has the impression he's in a foreign country, the interminable *aaa*s and the guttural *rrr*s seeming like a meaningless outer layer that has to be stripped off to reveal the actual words. The Highlanders, driven out by a new wave of evictions, have come south and crossed the Cheviots in the hope of finding work in the mines round Bishop Auckland, but at the moment the mines aren't taking on any more men, even though there is plenty of coal waiting to be extracted: the extreme slowness of transport by river makes it uneconomic for the owners to extract more.

"That's what the railway is going to be used for," Forbes explained during the lunch break. "To take the coal down to the sea more quickly. Then everyone will have work."

In the meantime most of his men don't seem unhappy with their lot. The work is hard but adequately paid, the foreman demanding but honest. And George Stephenson, the engineer, has promised a good bonus if they keep within the planned time limit. Travers, one of the old hands, knew Stephenson when he was a simple mechanic in Killingworth mine: "A real genius at improvising! Give him two knitting needles, a piece of string and a bedpan and he'll make you a clock."

Jim Doughty stretches and lets off a few oaths. He came from Yorkshire a couple of months ago where he'd worked in several cotton mills before the pay slumped, along with the price of cotton, while at the same time the price of bread was rising. He's a fat man, very slow with a stubborn look on his face and an expression that varies between incomprehension and mistrust. Looking for someone to talk to, he sits down beside Canning, a newcomer who is wearing a black armband.

"Where are you from?"

Canning sighs as he unlaces his boots. They were originally of good quality but the rain and the lack of care have dried out the leather; now they're too small and his ankles are swollen and hurt.

"Clitheroe," he replies at last.

"Never heard of it. What were you over there?"

"A weaver. But there's no work for me any more."

"These bloody machines doing a man's work," Doughty says, trying to sound like a man who's in the know.

Canning pulls a face. "It's not the mechanisation that's the problem. There weren't any machines in our valley before I left but the master simply threatened to buy some if we didn't agree to have our wages lowered. But even with two shillings less we could still manage."

Without them realising it a worker called Sam Davies is following their conversation.

"So what happened then?" Doughty asks.

"The master came back and told us we had to remain competitive: the men in Barrow, the next village, were working for three shillings less and he was going to deal with them alone. So we accepted."

"Accepted what?"

"The three shillings less. We didn't even go to Barrow to check up. The roads were frozen and they said there was typhoid there. But I'm sure he told them the same – that we in Clitheroe had agreed to work for three shillings less."

After taking time to think it over, Doughty understands the trick and chuckled, "My God, he really put one over on you there!"

"So what would you have done, then?" It is Sam Davies asking in a toneless voice. "You'd have thumped him, would you?"

Doughty turns to answer the challenge and opens his mouth to reply, but then hesitates. Davies hasn't said more than ten words the whole week nor done anything threatening, but there's something about him that gives the others a vague feeling of apprehension. Perhaps it's the scar that does it. Despite the cap that he never takes off, everyone has seen the deep gash running across his forehead until it vanishes under the peak, but so far no one has had the courage to ask him how he came by it, nor why he keeps on drawing letters in the soil with a stick during breaks. What is more, no one dares to laugh at his odd habit of placing a kind of kiss on the rind of his cheese before each meal. Standing up, somewhat to one side, he looks at the gently sloping edges of the pond, at the place where a bank of mud emerges from the dirty water.

Doughty decides it is safer to concentrate on Canning.

"Who's the armband for?"

"My wife."

Canning pulls a face again. He gives the impression that

he's remembering two things at once, one pleasant the other bitter, and that these two memories are pulling his lips in opposite directions at the same time.

"We closed up the house and went down into the valley, where the cotton mills are. But they only take on women down there because they can pay them less. Hattie worked for five weeks and then… she fell ill."

"Those who stayed up in the villages didn't fare any better," says Forbes, coming over to join them.

While he smokes, the foreman never stops scrutinising the surroundings, looking for suspicious movements or sounds. He knows what happened to the surveyors who went to check out the line of a future railway in Lancashire: they were given a thorough thrashing and left for dead. According to one Tory newspaper the farm workers had "gathered together spontaneously to defend their ancestral traditions." The more likely explanation is that a landlord determined to preserve the copses where his foxes had their lairs or a company with toll roads had bribed some vagrants to do it.

"I was in Heptonstall not that long ago," Forbes goes on.

"I know where that is," Canning says, massaging his ankles.

"The first person I met was a man with a huge pack of woven wool on his back. He'd sold his mule and was about to set off on a ten-mile walk to the factory. The village seemed deserted, there was a vile stench in the streets. Then I saw this lad sitting outside a cottage. When he saw me, he stood up and said, 'There's something for you inside, sir.' 'For me?' I asked. 'Yes, sir, since there's only you to see it.' It was very dark in the cottage. My father was a weaver. We weren't rich, but we had chairs, a table, beds, candlesticks, a chest of drawers for the linen and a clock. In the boy's cottage there was nothing. Dirty water was seeping up through the flagstones on the floor; it came from the river and the river… was teeming with things, the boy said. So I then asked him what there was there for me and he pointed to a straw mattress with two figures under some sackcloth on it. He told me his father was dead while his mother was still alive, though frankly I couldn't tell the difference between the two. Then he asked me for a penny."

"Did he tell you why?" Doughty asked.

"Yes, it was for his funeral club."

"What the hell is that?"

"At the Sunday school every boy gives a penny. It's to pay for their coffin when they die."

Thinking it's a joke a young lad with tousled hair guffaws. Travers gives him a resounding slap.

"From mud we come, to mud we shall return," Canning declares, as if he was reciting something.

"You mean dust," Forbes replies between two puffs of smoke. " 'For dust thou art and unto dust shalt thou return.' It's in the Bible."

"No. I know what I'm saying. Dust is dry, it's clean and it doesn't smell. That's for the rich. As for us, we're mud."

A puff of wind shakes the branches in the trees but doesn't even ruffle the surface of the pond. The old mule that pulls the equipment cart pricks up its ears. Behind the tops the gloomy mass of Wooler Manor with its ruined chapel can be made out.

"Still," Doughty finally says, "I don't see why we should have to drain this blasted pond when there's a perfectly good road that goes round it."

"It's not carts that'll have to go that way," Forbes explains, "it's wagons. The line of the rails has to be as straight as possible. Just imagine you're in the train zigzagging. Your paunch would be wobbling this way and that."

That gets a few laughs, though the tousled lad, looking at Travers out of the corner of his eye, doesn't dare join in.

"Well I'll be damned if I ever get into a contraption like that!" Doughty mutters, pulling in his stomach. "Coal, all right... beasts, if necessary... but people?! At more than ten miles an hour, or so we're told... with smoke everywhere and making one hell of a racket! If you want my opinion, it's not Christian."

"Because you, great tub of lard that you are, know what's Christian and what isn't?" mocks Sam Davies.

Forbes notices the dark look on the face of the man with the scar and sees Doughty clench his fists as well. He immediately gives the signal to go back to work. It's starting to get dark anyway, rain is coming and there's still a lot left to do. Following the foreman's instructions, the Highlanders start to dig drainage ditches while others put in drainpipes at strategic points; up to their thighs in mud, Doughty, Travers and the young lad with the shock of hair are pushing the water towards the pipes with their spades and watching the water slowly run off. Every time they take a step they have difficulty pulling their boots up out of the sludge, producing a strange sucking noise, a sort of spine-chilling plaintive lament.

"Careful where you put your feet," Forbes warns. "You don't know what there is down there."

At certain places the sludge is so thick that it just won't flow towards the drains and simply stays there, forming vast concretions like putrid molasses that have boiled over from a pan and then have to be cleaned up. Seeing this, the Highlanders start to swear and curse in Gaelic. In other places fortunately, the work is going better and soon the knees and elbows are sticking out above the sheet of mud, revealing their true nature: an overturned tree stump draped with interlacing roots, a millstone, an old shaft of holly that some boy must have thrown as far as he could, ending up with it sticking in the soil like a spear. Thanks to these marker points, the progress of the operation is soon visible to the naked eye. Relieved, Forbes can now concentrate entirely on keeping watch. A gang could well be ensconced in the woods, waiting to fall on them when it starts to get dark. He can almost see them there, hiding among the trees with their forks and cudgels, their faces set and their stomachs empty.

But out of the corner of his eye he sees Sam Davies moving along the edge of the pond, crouched down as if he was following some tracks in the mud.

"Davies, what are you up to there?"

Instead of replying, the man with the scar shouts at Doughty, who is wading along a few metres away from him, "Stop there, not another step."

With two strides Sam is beside Doughty and, pushing him unceremoniously aside, bends down: there, in a place that was under water a few minutes ago, a metallic object has appeared. While the others gather in a circle round him, he rolls up his sleeves and plunges his hands into the mud to make it flow away more quickly, revealing the dagger, then an indistinct form into which it is stuck.

"What it is?" Doughty asks.

Davies, with a look at the fat man, loosens his cap a bit. "What do you think?"

Others come to help Davies clear away the mud and the object lying on the bottom of the pond takes shape, becomes clearer until there's only one word for it:

"A corpse!" someone finally says.

The shadows of the workers stretch out over the skeleton which, by contrast, seems tiny. Sam Davies takes a piece of lace covering the bones and roughly cleans it on his jacket. "An article of ladies' clothing. Torn."

The dagger is an old weapon but in pretty good condition. The silver hilt is decorated with the design of a castle between two hills. All those who know the region turn their heads to look at Wooler Manor.

Doughty frowns. "Just a minute! That's not at all like that dump over there!"

"Shut up," Travers snaps. "You know damn all."

One of the men goes to fetch a sack from the cart, undoes the seam and lays it down beside the human remains. As delicately as possible, as if they were dealing with a newborn baby, Canning and Davies place them on the canvas. Travers wraps the dagger up in a handkerchief. All the while Forbes is examining the mud by the side of the pond, looking for whatever had attracted Davies' attention, but everything has been trampled on.

"That's bad," the foreman mutters. "Very bad."

***

Scratch, scratch!

Edward Bailey wakes up but keeps his eyes closed. He's not really awake anyway, he slips into that intermediate state, so much appreciated by lazybones and poets, in which the mirage of dreams continues along with very agreeable real sensations: the warmth of the blankets, the softness of a pillow. There's not a sound coming from the alcove where his co-tenant, Solomon Deeds, must still be asleep, fists clenched. No noise from outside, either, which is remarkable in London, even in this quiet little street; it must be early, or perhaps it's Sunday. *Scratch, scratch!* But in that case why is his landlady bringing up the kettle? And, above all, why is she scratching at the door instead of giving three sharp knocks as she usually does?

Let her scratch. Edward Bailey wants to enjoy this lazy state a bit longer and to go over all the reasons he has to be pleased with life. Twenty-five, bachelor of laws, an iron constitution, able to drink the night through and do a headstand in the morning. Drawers full of perfumed letters, his memory full of rakish episodes. But that's all over now: tomorrow – or the day after, he can't remember – a mail coach will be taking him to the awe-inspiring, wild north! Darlington, what a pretty name for a town. Castles à la Walpole, fields of daffodils straight out of Wordsworth, cliffs to make Scott turn pale, lochs where Ossian could have swum. Up there he's going to marry Miss Margaret Raffle, the most beautiful girl in the world, and become the partner of her father, a prosperous lawyer. So...

Scratch, scratch! Woofwoof!

Mrs Delaware hasn't got a dog. And she doesn't bark herself, except when we spill some madeira on 'Uncle Mortimer's table'.

Now Edward is truly awake.

"Go back to where you came from, you obnoxious beast!"

The creature outside doesn't give up, on the contrary it scratches, yaps all the more, and after a long minute of torture Edward decides to open his eyes. Yes, the old divan he'd had as a student is there, which is hardly surprising since he paid Mrs Delaware three times what it was worth when he left London. And also the ivory hand he bought one evening in a Covent Garden second-hand shop. He remembers having succumbed to an irrational compulsion: the trinket was neither remarkable nor heavy enough to serve as a paper-weight, but there was something about the delicate fingers, the realism of their articulations that had appealed to him. The hand seemed to be alive. "With all your conquests, you won't be needing it, so how about lending me it for tonight," Solomon used to joke.

But as for the rest, oh Lord, the rest...

No, Solomon's gone and it's not London any more. The little flat in Holborn has been replaced by the summerhouse at the bottom of the Raffles' park, tiny and poorly heated, but for all that preferable to the house itself. Through the window he can see that repulsive cube bought twenty years ago from a ruined squire: two storeys of boredom, two grim rows of five windows (you'd throw yourself out of all ten of them if it were possible), two chimneys stuck on either end of the roof, like two prison guards. And all that more than a mile away from the amenities of Darlington... to live out in the country or on one's estate... that gives a man status, it appears.

Now Aloysius Raffle has reached his final status – under ground, in the graveyard. Edward is the last living partner of Raffle, Raffle, Raffle & Bailey. Dead too is his beautiful mother-in-law, the wife of Aloysius. And dead – if it ever existed – is Margaret's love for Edward. And Edward's for Margaret?

Woofwoof.

"I'm coming, you misbegotten hound! Just you watch out!"

Edward gets up, puts on a dressing gown, while thinking it was absurd to get dressed for the sake of a dog, and sets off for the door. But on the way he stops at the mirror on his little dressing table. Thirty-four but looking more like forty-five, bags under his eyes, hair falling out all over the place, terrible headaches the morning after a night out – and recently that has been every morning. Where have his seductive smile and sparkling eyes gone? How long is it since he touched a woman's body without remuneration agreed in advance?

He lets in Titus, his wife's horrible mongrel. But what kind of mongrel? The offspring of a dwarf bulldog and a dropsical poodle? Of a rat and a mop? Of a wriggly worm and a bowl of mouldy porridge? You could treat a good twenty mangy dogs with all the excess skin hanging down from its belly, its neck, its chin; you could fill a bale of hay every evening with all the hair it scatters wherever it goes. In his wildest dreams Edward hands Titus over to Mr Bramby, the local upholsterer, and, a few hours later, receives a blood-stained rug in return. And to say that this four-footed abomination in a way *represents* Margaret, that it is her messenger, the last tangible link between the two of them! One of the servants has fixed a basket to its back with a leather strap. While Titus nibbles away at his slippers, Edward bends down and takes out the letter. Margaret's writing, elongated, sinuous, looks like a snake that's swallowed a spring:

You must come over at once. She is at the door!

Edward sighs. He opens a drawer and files it with a good twenty similar communications: *She's coming to get me! Don't abandon me, she's coming! My God, she has taken hold of me!* etc. Then he imagines his next conversation with Margaret. He knows her replies in advance, it's a scene from a play without rhyme or reason performed by two terrible actors:

"Edward, I beg you, don't leave me alone with her!"
"But there's only the two of us in this room, Margaret, no one else…"
"But I can see her, I can feel her, she's right next to me, she's…"

Curled up in a ball beside the hearth, Titus seems to be attempting a conjuring trick by which he'd disappear inside his own skin. Edward, too impatient to wait for this to happen, slowly creeps round the hairy clump until he can pick up the poker, that he hides behind his back. With one leap he tries to skewer his enemy, but his thrust is too short: Titus, yapping dashes off back to his mistress, leaving, on the tip of the poker, a tuft of hair like a dervish's moustache.

"Oh, Master Bailey," says Effie, the little maid he encounters on the stairs. "One of the Spalding's servants has just come by. You have to go and see Sir Walter at once."

Edward has never mastered the Darlington accent, he always has the impression people are speaking through a foghorn.

"What do you mean, at once?"

"That's what he said, sir: at once."

Under any other circumstances he would have found the tone of this summons unbearable, but he is ready to jump at any pretext to delay his confrontation with Margaret. He puts on more formal attire, takes his stick and decides to go to Spalding's on foot. In order to avoid the road and its traffic, he goes through a little wood then cuts across the fields.

Smug and sly beneath the sun, the Skerne flows down to meet him following a long detour: after spending some time wallowing among the rushes of a swamp, it has remembered it is meant to be a river and heads off south to swell the Tees. On a clearer day, the scabs of the coal mines could be made out. Before him Darlington is basking in the sun. Nine-arched Stonebridge, with its parapet split in the middle, looks like a drunk who's fallen asleep across a ditch. The bell-tower of St Cuthbert's mounts guard over this charming scene of provincial dullness.

No, there's nothing awe-inspiring or wild here. For landscapes such as you find in Romantic engravings – hills, gracefully dotted with sheep and bushes, stretching away to infinity – you have to take the interminably long road up Weardale or Swaledale. Much too far.

His imagination, the little bitch, really fooled him!

Solomon Deeds was also imaginative, but at least he made something of it, epigrams, lines of verse, five-act plays: admittedly very bad ones, totally unwatchable to tell the truth, but at least something concrete. Edward's imagination, on the other hand is not of the stuff to create works – not even doggerel verse. All it does is twine itself round reality like ivy, that looks vigorous but breaks off whenever you try to climb it. That isn't the way he's going to get back on his feet, as Doctor Trees puts it.

And there are the first houses on North Road: large and opulent but unpretentious. The Quakers set the example when they settled in this district, beyond the traditional limits of the town, and they were soon followed by townsfolk who felt constricted by the old alleyways round Market Place or, on the other hand, by gentlemen weary of the mud of the countryside. Instead of being situated beside the road, like the houses of the Quakers, Spalding's residence is tucked away behind a big garden with banks of flowers and hedges. "Here I hear about everything, straight away," the master of the house said to Edward one day. "Anyway, soon nobody's going to be living out in the country."

A heavy-lidded butler informs Edward that Sir Walter is "undergoing treatment" and puts him in the library to wait. It's not a room he knows; the couple of times that Spalding saw him previously he was taken straight into his study, but generally day-to-day business is done with Snegg. Looking round the shelves Edward can't see anything interesting. No sign of Byron, Shelley or Blake, for example, which is unsurprising given the style of house. With his finger he caresses the spine of a novel by Walter Scott, magnificent in its leather binding, but quite obviously never read, no more than the few other novels round it: Defoe, of course, and Richardson's *Pamela*. Only the books on economics show signs of frequent use.

All at once he notices, on the mantlepiece above the fireplace, the portrait of a stunningly beautiful woman: a woman of a beauty that is both disturbing and hostile, totally alien to the prosaic nature of the room and to the poor physical standards of the Spalding family. The model, with long, black tousled hair, is glaring at the painter and, through him, the observer, awestruck by such magnificence beyond reach. Her prominent cheekbones, her olive skin, her thick eyebrows and fleshy lips suggest a Latin origin, perhaps Spanish. Some filmy lace on the low neckline of her dress is still moving to the rhythm of her breathing. She doesn't look as if she's posing but as if she has materialised for just a few seconds in the painter's field of vision and it is only patient memory work – doubtless sharpened by ardent admiration – that has enabled him to reconstitute the scene. Perhaps she turned round in an abrupt movement, suggested by a slight twist of the shoulders.

"Hhm hhm. Sir Walter will see you now, sir."

Still under the spell of the portrait, Edward follows the butler up to the first floor to find Spalding in an armchair upholstered in green velvet, his left leg stretched out on a stool. There is a dressing on the big toe.

"Ah, Bailey, my dear boy. You're going to save my life. These stupid servants don't know how to tie a bandage. They pull it tight, as if I were a Clydesdale. And Trees with his ointments and foul potions isn't much more use either. Would you be so good as to take that off, otherwise my head won't be clear enough to talk to you."

As he is gradually released from his agony Sir Walter emits a crescendo of ecstatic sighs, which Edward finds a trifle too demonstrative.

"Oh the gout, my dear friend, the gout! That's what's in store for you, just you remember that. Too much meat, too much gravy, too much wine, they all say... too much of everything! But what is there to live for, then?"

The bare toe now stands proud, a monstrous protuberance attached to a tiny white foot, worthy of being exhibited in a chamber of horrors.

"It's just as I told you, Bailey, you've saved my life. There's a good samaritan behind that reprobate air. And that reinforces my opinion that you're obviously the very man we need."

Having said that, Sir Walter contemplates the ceiling blissfully, heartened by the renewed throbbing of the blood in the arteries of his lower limb. When he looks down again, his face has its habitual expression: superficial affability beneath which there appears an iron will and a great aptitude for getting what he wants out of people.

"You've heard the news?"

"Not yet."

"A skeleton. Stephenson's men have found a skeleton at the bottom of a pond."

"Stephenson?"

Spalding emits an irritated grunt. "Where have you been, Bailey? Stephenson, the engineer who's building the line. The whole town is talking of nothing but him."

"Of course, Stephenson," Edward says, vaguely recalling having had in his hands – or, to be more precise, seen pass through the hands of his clerk Snegg – a large number of deeds of conveyance transferring property to the Stockton and Darlington Railway Company. "Where was that?"

"Near Wooler Manor."

Sir Walter's meaningful silence and knowing look spark off no response in Edward. He does know the place, of course. If there is one spot in the area worthy of interest, it is surely Wooler Manor. Before he became too lazy he used to go there for walks occasionally. He doesn't particularly like the Gothic style of the house itself, a sort of imitation of Walpole's villa in Twickenham, but he does acknowledge a certain boldness in its pretentiousness and the neglect appeals to him: the ivy creates complicated designs on the façade, giving a Byzantine touch to the arched windows, the belfry and the darker turret beside it. In the neglected park common shrubs have sprung up beside august centuries-old oaks, weeds are climbing the parapets, water lilies cover the surface of the large stone basin where, so it is said, there are carp of antediluvian size. Not far away is the chapel, that is at least genuine Gothic, from the same period as the former castle. A nice walk. But he still hasn't the least idea of what is expected of him now.

"A vagrant must have drowned," he suggests cautiously.

"Huh! The remains still had some shreds of decent clothes. And then they also found a dagger belonging to the Beresfords."

A further silence. A further meaningful look. No reaction from Edward. Sir Walter rolls his eyes. "How long have you been living in Darlington, Bailey?"

"Nine years."

"My God, nine years… and one would think you'd just arrived from the moon. Nine years and you haven't heard people talking about Beresford… when not a minute passes without someone here mentioning his name! It's true that he wasn't one of your father-in-law's clients – but at least you've just met *Lady* Beresford."

"Sorry?"

"Down below. In the library."

"You mean… the portrait?"

Clearly ready to overlook Edward's ignorance – or perhaps moved himself by the beauty of the portrait – Sir Walter clasps his hands over his stomach and explains patiently, "It's my Uncle Henry who painted it. The artist in the family. After some fruitless attempts he threw away his palette and went and got himself killed at the Battle of Castlebar in a fit of pique at not having become Gainsborough… or at not having managed to seduce the beautiful baroness, who knows. Anyway, having seen Lady Beresford once when I was young, I can tell you that it's a mediocre portrait."

"Really!"

"She was a thousand times more beautiful in the flesh, but enough of that. The Beresfords hardly mixed with local society at all. Not prestigious enough in their eyes. Robert Beresford had brought his wife Mathilde back from France and they lived a reclusive life at Wooler Manor with only the Baron's younger sister, Ophelia, for company. When she died, in 1803, the situation at the manor suddenly took a turn for the worse. There was talk of arguments, even of open and violent quarrels between the couple. To cut a long story short, they suddenly left, each on their own, or so it seems. Since then it's been a lawyer in London who manages their property… yes, in London, though don't ask me why. Ouch!"

Edward looks at the gouty toe again. It seems to have become even more swollen, even redder – he felt you could almost see the pain throbbing in the damaged tissue.

"It's a real torment, I can tell you. Pour me a drop of brandy, will you?"

"So early in the day? Are you sure that's…"

"Yes, confound it, I am sure."

Imaginary or real, the effect of the brandy is immediate. Spalding resumes his contemplation of the ceiling, gasping with relief.

"Excuse me, Sir Walter, but…"

"Shh! Wait. Just wait a moment… until it has its full effect… where was I now? Oh yes – all that's none of our business, of course – people such as the Beresfords do what they want with themselves, with their time and their money, they travel wherever they like…"

"All the same, a trip lasting twenty-one years, that's not normal…"

"That's not the problem. The trouble is there've been rumours… below stairs," Spalding points at the floor. "Based on the evidence of a drunken valet and a hysterical lady's maid."

Edward grants himself a mouthful of brandy and contemplates the gouty aristocrat. "What kind of evidence?"

"The wagging of idle tongues. Beresford is supposed to have made terrible threats to his wife, then, later on, had himself driven to Durham, alone."

"Hmm. And Mathilde?"

"Disappeared."

"All the same…"

"Shut up! There was a discreet investigation that didn't produce anything unusual. Those are just rumours, I tell you, lackeys' gossip. Nowadays people will take any excuse to besmirch the noblest flowers of society. So now you'll see why the discovery of this skeleton is... inopportune?"

"Inopportune, true, but I still don't see how..."

"I must say it looks as if you can't see very much today." Without really raising his voice, Sir Walter has given the conversation a different tone, as if he had tugged at an invisible string. "Lord Glendover is in London and will not return that soon. As for myself, I'm no good for anything at the moment," he went on, pointing at his toe. "And the other justices of the peace in the district, they are available, of course, but totally incompetent. Now this is a matter that demands some skill, tact and above all impartiality. Or, to be more precise, a convincing appearance of impartiality."

Edward stares, wide-eyed. Spalding claps his hands over his stomach and goes on, after a short pause, "My idiot son admires you – because you know a few words of Latin, because you criticise the government, rail against the church and have a huge repertoire of dirty songs."

"He must be the only one in the whole of Darlington."

"Indeed. In the eyes of most people you are an idle fellow come from the capital to get your hands on an old family fortune and have a good time at the expense of your in-laws. A bit of a reprobate, as I said just now. Morally and politically."

"And you share that opinion?"

"To a great extent. But I grant that you have a certain mental agility, even if you haven't given great proof of it this morning... and sometimes, if you have to repair a piece of furniture, you need a part that is slightly twisted and therefore the only one that can take a suitable shape..."

"I presume I am that part."

"You are above all a source of problems. A dilettante with vaguely liberal ideas. A vacillating Benthamist."

"I hereby declare that I execrate Jeremy Bentham and all his works."

Spalding frowns. "Really? You surprise me. Even I don't reject everything he says. His panopticon prison, for example – there's a good idea. It ought to be put into practice, then perhaps the ex-convicts would behave better. And according to the newspaper Bentham's working on an amendment to the poor law at the moment: instead of the poor being paid to stay at home and do nothing, as they do today, they should be confined in workhouses where life would be so hard no one would want to stay there – resulting in great savings for the royal purse, and for ours! Excellent! Problem solved!

"To return to our own problem: Glendover has give me full power to appoint an assistant Justice of the Peace. If I call on right-thinking men such as Price or Paisley, all the Whigs of the county will come down on us, claiming we're trying to hush the matter up. You, on the other hand, will enjoy the benefit of doubt, at least for the time you need to make sure that the Beresford family has nothing to do with the business of this skeleton."

"And if they do have something to do with it?"

"Dr Trees will perhaps have more to tell us about that in a couple of days' time when he comes back from his blasted congress in Newcastle and will deign to examine the remains. But in any event your task will be to reconcile our sacred duty to justice with the demands of maintaining public order."

Edward almost choked as he swallowed his brandy. "What

a nice way of putting it, Sir Walter. It reminds me of the farmer who wanted to sell his laying hens while still collecting the eggs."

"Still, I know that you are capable of achieving this tour de force… in the world we live in, my friend, everything has its price…"

Spalding suddenly seems very cordial. Edward stays on his guard. "So far you have received much and given little. Look on the favour I am asking of you as a very small tax on the advantages you have enjoyed for nine years. Anyway, I'm sure that everything till turn out for the best and what you have to do will not bring a blush to your cheeks. By the way, it is Cobbold, the policeman, who will be in charge of the enquiry – under your orders, of course."

Edward grimaces. He doesn't know the fellow but he's heard people talk about him. And not to his advantage either.

"Don't worry," Spalding immediately goes on with a soothing gesture. "I know that in the past he has been rather… heavy-handed, but we do need someone we can rely on. And in contrast to him, you will have the role of the nice Justice of the Peace, close to the right people, you should be happy with that… right then. Since you accept your nomination…"

"Have I accepted it, Sir Walter?"

"Oh, come now, Bailey…"

It's no longer just cordiality, it's almost affection. Now Edward is genuinely concerned.

"Now be reasonable, my lad," Spalding says, fluttering his eyelashes like an old actress. "Don't force me to…"

A threat, however unbelievable that might seem. What on earth could he threaten me with? To withdraw his custom? That would be good riddance, Margaret has enough money for both of us. Edward prepares a haughty reply, but something makes him hold back, one of those premonitions he finds ridiculous from a novelist's pen. This isn't about Sir Walter's custom. There's something else.

Spalding closes his eyes. It's as if he's counting up to ten before he opens them abruptly and fixes them on Edward. "Keep me informed, Justice of the Peace Bailey. And, oh, before leaving would you be so good as to hide the brandy and redo the dressing? Without squeezing, of course. If my wife should find out that I've been disobeying doctor's orders she'll crush my other toes…"

Edward Bailey and Solomon Deeds: the Inseparables. Bailey, the reveller, the rake, inveterate punster, Deeds, the sensible man who only went to bed with the idea for a poem. One evening they were walking up and down Piccadilly Terrace, right next to where Byron lived, at the time when the craziest rumours were going round about the great man's private life, his relations with his half-sister Augusta, and abuse was being hurled at him in the Lords because of his liking for Bonaparte. They waited for hours to see him; they had come to assure him of their support against the vile tongues, the morality-bashers, those who envied and derided him, the warmongers, the odious Tories and the treacherous Whigs. But when his limping silhouette finally appeared, when his handsome, icy countenance passed before them, they didn't dare approach him, nor chant the special encomium composed by Solomon: "All glory to the immortal author of *Childe Harold,* glory be to his name, glory to his works and may his enemies vanish into their graves."

Under the influence of this memory, Edward walks up Northgate, then High Row. When he reaches Market Place he briefly entertains the idea of going on to Bull Wynd, the most... *accommodating* alleyway in Darlington where perhaps a charming young woman... but no. Pulling himself together, he turns to the right.

In their little apartment in Holborn he and Deeds would read Wordsworth and Scott together by candlelight, the remains of chops on the table along with two glasses of madeira, mediocre but as precious as nectar. No other sound but the crackling of the sparse fire in the grate and the music of the words in their heads full of dreams and yearning. Deeds sitting up straight in his chair, Edward stretched out on his divan. The silence and beauty of Coleridge, the calm and the passion of Blake.

He still has the books, here in Darlington, but they no longer serve any purpose. They were a canvas for his imagination, a kind of mould giving shape to his undisciplined ideas. But then they turned their backs on him. Without Solomon Deeds, without their interminable discussions, the books no longer have anything to say to him.

The Raffle Chambers, Skinnergate: as always for the last nine years he goes from one Raffle to the next. He's surrounded by Raffles: dead Raffles (innumerable), an ex-Raffle (Margaret), a stone Raffle, paper Raffles on headed documents, Raffles in paintings, Raffles on seals, Raffles in brass on the original plate for the chambers – Raffle, Raffle & Raffle, lawyers – while his own name is a negligible codicil on another smaller, more modest brass plate. 'Raffle, Raffle, Raffle' is the rhythm his shoes, bought with the Raffles' money, beat out on the pavement. Good morning Mr Raff – Mr Bailey,' the chemist says. He may have won a prize in the raffle of life, but now he's having to pay for it.

He keeps on walking – he hasn't walked so much for ages – and then something very rare happens. He starts to find it all very funny. His life. Or, rather, the backside of his life. The arse of things. As if the door of a squalid hovel had opened on a ravishing whore. He bursts out laughing, so much so that an old lady gives him an outraged look. He's still laughing as he reaches the chambers, a building of massive architecture he would have called Rafflian if the adjective had existed. Striding across the floor, deformed by the tread of millions of Raffles, he enters Snegg's tiny office, a room he much prefers to his own office for the simple reason that Snegg is there – there's nothing worse than a silent tête-à-tête with the files in the Raffles' chambers.

Snegg's office. A bastion of order at the heart of chaos. An oasis of hard-working constancy amid a desert of negligence and idleness. Everything there is classified, filed away in drawers, dossiers of all sizes or archive boxes. Once there Edward, as usual, sprawls across the only armchair, reserved for clients and, still laughing, watches the clerk going about his duties.

He is perched on his ladder so that he can reach the upper level of the archives – the oldest – then he comes down again, holding a piece of paper, slips the document into a file open on his desk and directs a quizzical look at his employer. The only odd thing about his fairly ordinary mild, round face is the almost total lack of eyebrows.

"No, Snegg, you're not dreaming. I have come to the

chambers and I am in a good mood... at least I have been for the last five minutes. On reflection, it's probably due to Sir Walter's big toe. It didn't occur to me right away, but there's something priceless about having the big, gouty, stinking, fiery red toe of one of the most important notables of Darlington under your nose, don't you think?"

"I do indeed think that in certain circumstances big toes can have great comic potential." His voice is soft, with a slightly reedy tone, but also a hint of something metallic, as if a country stream with a charming babble had been diverted through a complex maze of pipes, ducts and cascades. Even as he speaks, he continues to attend to his work and starts rummaging through an appropriately labelled box of old newspapers.

"You're quite right – again! You can laugh at everything, absolutely everything." Here Edward is more or less repeating the words from a speech he made as a schoolboy and which brought him a great success. "I'm flabbergasted at how close to each other wild delight and absolute despair are. Heads I laugh, tails I cry."

Snegg takes a carefully cut-out article, then another, and puts them in the file as well. From time to time he smiles at Edward, emitting words of encouragement or questioning grunts, like an adult who doesn't want to upset a child nor be too distracted by its babbling.

"Just a minute," Edward goes on. "When you think about it, that metaphor doesn't work! We can only see one side of the coin at a time, while with a bit of practice it's possible to imagine the tragic aspect of existence and its totally ridiculous side at one and the same time."

For a few seconds Edward watches the clerk, who is once more perched on top of the ladder, at the other end of the room this time – it slides silently on a rail – busy but always ready to take part in the conversation, enigmatic through his very ordinariness, like all the things we see everyday without looking at them properly.

"Snegg, do you think anyone from the chambers has ever been appointed a deputy Justice of the Peace?"

"Hmm. Certainly not your father-in-law." The clerk comes back to ground level, completes the file on his desk with two or three further items, finally sits down and puts his fingers together as if he were saying a prayer to his own memory. "I would have known. And little likelihood of Mr Raffle being thus appointed for, as you doubtless know, he left all the work to his brother and spent his time drinking and betting on the horses…"

"Yes. He's the only member of the family I might have felt some affinity with."

"And anyway, he probably thought 'Justice of the Peace' was the name of a cocktail or a racehorse. As for Mr Raffle, the father of the last two… well, I never knew him but it seems he was a very proud man and I'm sure that if he had had that honour he would have had it engraved on his tombstone."

Edward stares out of the window at the lowering clouds. Then he gets up. "You see before you a remarkable creature, neither a cocktail nor a racehorse but a recently appointed deputy Justice of the Peace."

"Excellent, sir."

"I suddenly feel a bizarre enthusiasm for this task. My intention is to go down in history as the most punctilious, the most scrupulous and honest Justice of the Peace there's ever been. I don't care what Spalding's instructions are, I will root out the truth, even if that will destroy the entire British social system. But..."

"But?"

Edward frowns, putting on a show of concern – all those parts he played in farces during his student days come flooding back to him. "But I'm just an incomer. I need the help of someone born and bred in Darlington, someone who knows the town like the back of his hand, someone whose profession means he knows everybody's secrets – a doctor, for example, a priest. Or else... yes, why not someone in the legal business? Someone who has his ear to the ground, whose eye misses nothing, who knows who's being unfaithful, who drinks too much, who owes money and who's lending it, who votes Tory and who votes Whig, who takes the pro-governmental newspapers and who the *Leeds Mercury* or Cobbett's *Political Register*. To put it in a nutshell: an exceptional person capable of assembling a complete dossier on the Beresford family in... let's say a couple of days." Edward emits a heart-rending sigh. "Alas, I can't really see where we'd find such a rare bird."

"It doesn't seem such an impossible task, Mr Bailey... yes, I think a man like that is available." And with a faint smile Snegg dips his pen in the inkwell, writes something on the cover of the file he's been putting together and hands it to his employer.

" 'The Beresford Affair'?" Edward is dumbfounded. "But, Snegg, how... how on earth could you..."

"To be honest, I wasn't sure, but Sir Walter's messenger dropped in here before going round to your house. It seemed unusual to me for him to want to see you forthwith and, though I can't say why, I immediately linked it to the business of the skeleton everyone's talking about. And since I had nothing urgent on hand…"

Edward can't take his eyes off the file, if only to convince himself that it really does exist. He wonders how Snegg managed to complete something so quickly after thinking of it. His own projects are no more precise than the turbulence on the surface of a river and had as much chance of completion as Titus had of winning the prize for the most beautiful pedigree dog. With him cause never led directly to effect – the mechanism must be jammed.

"It's a real magnum opus! What's in it?"

"Articles from local and national newspapers – the affair caused a great stir – various notes made by your father-in-law on the people involved, letters from Mr Dull, his great friend and colleague in Durham who looked after the interests of Lord Robert Beresford and, like Mr Raffle, had a very elastic conception of the notion of a professional secret…"

"Spalding also mentioned a lawyer in London."

"We'll come to him… your father-in-law kept absolutely all items of information he deemed useful on his actual and potential clients, their likely opponents or anyone of a certain repute and stature who had any connection at all with Darlington. He used to call it 'covering his rear'."

"I'll never have the patience to read all that."

"I skimmed through the major items just now while I was putting them together. I can give you a summary, if you like."

A sunbeam pushes the clouds aside and peers in through the window, setting the china inkwell on the desk aglow, while the brass clasps on the files, the gilt-edging of the old law books and the drawer-handles sparkle – as do Snegg's eyes at the prospect of finally exercising his faculties on an interesting task. As for Edward, he is once more in his preferred position, sprawled across an armchair, legs dangling, head back, eyes on the ceiling, waiting for what is to come.

"Beresford – as I will refer to the subject of this file: 'Lord Robert Beresford, baron', if you're happy with it – came back from France in 1794. There is no explanation in the file as to why he went there nor what he did there, though there are a couple of references to his revolutionary sympathies. But what is certain is that he brought Mathilde back with him…"

"The beautiful Mathilde."

"…so people say, and that the couple set up house in Wooler Manor with Beresford's sister Ophelia, who was only a child at the time, and lived a surprisingly quiet life there."

"Surprisingly?"

"I mean for an English noble suspected of Jacobinism, having married a Frenchwoman and with a dissolute past behind him. His mother died during the birth of Ophelia; his father disappeared in 1796 and he inherited both the title and the house. In the autumn of 1802 Ophelia fell ill. Beresford consulted a leading medical authority who prescribed a stay by the sea, in Hartlepool. But it was ineffective and the girl died the next February at the age of seventeen. Her body was brought back from Hartlepool and buried at Wooler Manor. And that's where everything gets complicated."

"Let me guess: thunder over the moors, flashes of lightning, cries, people dashing round in the dark…"

"You're not far from the truth, or, to be more precise, from the legend, since at the moment the truth is unknown. The day after the funeral Beresford prepared to leave and dismissed all the servants with the exception of the coachman and Mathilde's maid. In this he was only bringing forward a plan he had been arranging for some time, as is attested by a letter to his lawyer, Dull, and transactions designed to realise a large part of his estate."

"And he didn't want to take Mathilde in his luggage?"

"Doubtless he didn't. At least that would explain the violent altercation that woke the lady's maid a few hours later. Following the sound of the cries, she encountered Beresford in the courtyard with blood on his hands. She went to look for her mistress and saw the baron leave in his four-in-hand, driven by the coachman. Unable to find out what had happened to Mathilde, she eventually went to the police."

"Well she had to, didn't she?"

"Indeed. But the police could find no trace of Lady Mathilde dead or alive."

"Did they drag the pond?"

"Perhaps they would have if it had not been that someone formally testified to having seen Mathilde Beresford two days later in Newcastle. She had, it appears, been deep in conversation with the captain of a Portuguese merchant ship."

"That's what we call a happy coincidence."

"Yes, and it set a lot of tongues wagging at the time. The witness was an old boon companion of the baron, a good-for-nothing who was living on his wits – therefore perfectly corruptible. But the police and the magistrates, relieved to be able to file the matter, didn't look very far. That didn't stop people here wondering how Mathilde could have left the Manor alone, in the middle of the night, on foot, with no outside help and end up in Newcastle two days later."

"Those kinds of people have several carriages, horses…" Edward closes his eyes, the portrait in Spalding's library starts to come alive: in his mind's eye he sees a beautiful woman galloping along on horseback, hair flying, pursued by…

"No. Neither horses nor another carriage. In preparing for his departure Beresford had disposed of a large number of things during the preceding weeks."

"All the same… you don't leave a property such as Wooler Manor to deteriorate merely on the pretext of going off on your travels."

"Not travels, sir, a genuine relocation. From what we know, Beresford went to live in Brazil after having entrusted the upkeep of the Manor and the management of his property – or, rather, what was left of it – to a certain Leonard Vholes."

"The much-vaunted London lawyer."

"In 1803 he was still in Durham, just a young clerk of Mr Dull's – who, in fact, wrote a letter to your father-in-law expressing his surprise and outrage at such a choice. Two or three years previously Beresford had started inviting the young man quite frequently to Wooler Manor and Mr Dull wondered in what capacity. To cut a long story short, it was Vholes who shut down the Manor, merely making an annual visit for maintenance – in 1804 he bought chambers in Lincoln's Inn Fields and Mr Dull wonders where the money came from."

"Who knows? Perhaps the payment for silence? But why Brazil? A funny choice, isn't it?"

"Not for an Englishman who wants to escape the laws of his country and hide in an immense land with no connection to

Britain or its colonies?"

"Any news of Beresford since then?"

"Letters that Vholes passed on to Mr Dull, who is also one of the lawyers representing Alastair Beresford, a cousin and also the heir presumptive to the Manor should Robert die without issue. In one of these the baron says he assumes his wife must have returned to France, but nowhere does he allude to possible divorce proceedings."

"Which would be pointless if Madame is lying at the bottom of a pond."

"But indispensable should Robert desire to remarry in order to produce an heir."

"Hmm… what witnesses do we have?"

"None, I'm afraid. Friend Vholes doesn't give the impression of having a loose tongue and, even if he does know something about this affair, I very much doubt that after twenty years he will be taken with a sudden desire to reveal it."

"Well I'll still have to go to London anyway. Thirty hours jolting in a post chaise and one night with a dyspeptic commercial traveller in some hovel round Nottingham!"

"Tim Turnell, the much-vaunted Newcastle witness, eventually joined up after one scandal too many – he was decapitated by a cannonball at Vimiero. Beresford's coachman is dead as well."

"That perhaps still leaves us with the lady's maid?"

"Then we'd have to find her. Mathilde Beresford was much taken with her during a stay in the north, at cousin Alastair's place, and brought her back to Wooler Manor. Apparently the young woman went back home, immediately after the events, and no one knows exactly where. Moreover, given the circumstances we can hardly rely on the police…"

Edward sighs. His fine determination is already fading. "Dammit, Snegg, d'you think we'll ever get there? It was a long time ago. What can we do after twenty years?"

"Time travels in divers paces with divers persons."

Edward nods – it must be Shakespeare.

II

The Business with the Wheelbarrow

When he opens the wooden shutters, Solomon Deeds sees the two volumes of Wordsworth, that are visibly turning yellow and also a huge grease mark on *Tom Jones* – how could he have missed it? He decides to change his window display. But not just now. In order to enjoy a rare sunbeam, he leans back against the shop window and opens a newspaper left by a customer.

WHAT FUTURE FOR THE COTTON INDUSTRY?
From our Manchester correspondent

Gathered together at their congress, the most important manufacturers in Lancashire have discussed their views. We can only congratulate ourselves on such an opportune development, in these times when hope and concern... outstanding debates... very clear-sighted discussion... Mr Thompson, from Salford, having suggested that the workers should be guaranteed decent living conditions in order to produce a better output, Mr Gates, from Preston, replied with considerations that were perhaps less humane but certainly more pragmatic, reminding those present that "destitution drives men to work and a worker who can live on three days' wages will remain idle and drunk the rest of the week." Despite these differences in detail a great consensus finally...

"Confound it! Serve me right for reading a Tory rag. Though the Whig ones are just the same, or almost." He stuffs his pipe as he surveys the Strand.

London hasn't changed much, at least 'his' London, this limited area that stretches as far as Holborn where he studied law before taking over the bookshop when his father died. Lawyers and gentlemen in a hurry to get to the City look warily as they pass some crossing-sweepers, dubious individuals and boys in rags who ask for money. Elegant carriages coming from Piccadilly or Kensington have difficulty finding a way through the traffic. Some constables are forcing the whores towards the filthy alleyways that run down to the Thames, others keep an eye on the pedlars to make sure that, as the law prescribes, their trays do not touch the ground. The smell of dung, always the same, envelops these various little scenes in a cloud of sweet derision.

However, Deeds is aware of new forces that are having a profound effect on the capital. Horrendous waves are threatening his island on all sides.

CORPSE FOUND IN DARLINGTON
From our Durham correspondent

It is well known that the very idea of a railway and a steam locomotive arouse a good deal of superstitious alarm among the common folk and ill temper in country gentlemen, whose main concern is to avoid disturbance to their game preserves. We are willing to wager that the discovery of a human skeleton by workers digging trenches for the railway in Darlington, County Durham, will only serve to increase the resistance of both parties...

Darlington. Isn't that the place in the north where Edward Bailey went to hide himself away? Unless it was Middleton? Or somewhere else ending in *ton*.

...publicity that Mr George Stephenson, the engineer in charge of construction of the line, could well do without. However, this self-made man bears no responsibility for the regrettable array of coincidences that have turned the incident into a sensation... appalling rumours are now rising, like some ignoble phoenix, from their nauseating ashes and certain individuals are indulging in deplorable speculation as to the identity of the remains which, in a less tolerant country than ours...

What ridiculous bombast! Absorbed in his newspaper, Deeds doesn't immediately notice the young boy approaching him.

...Then there is the statement of Jean Morgan, seventy-three, unemployed and destitute, that adds to the general confusion. She swears by all that's holy that on the night preceding the discovery of the skeleton she saw lights in the chapel of Wooler Manor, the ancestral home of the Beresfords. She says she hoisted herself up onto a little wall so that she could see inside the chapel, where she claims she saw hooded silhouettes walking round and round the apse and heard strange words. For our part, and remaining faithful to the good sense and constructive scepticism that characterises these columns, we are prepared to wager that Miss Morgan's Christian name is spelt G i n. But the damage has been done, alas, and this new, even more unlikely rumour is reviving the previous one, just as a drunkard's breath will set a smouldering fire ablaze again.

"Good morning, Mr Deeds."

"Oh! Good morning, young Charley. I haven't seen you for some time, I suppose that's a good sign."

The boy gives an odd smile. He has a nice face, with fine and regular features, just his nose is a little too long, giving him a serious air for his age – eleven or twelve perhaps. At the same time his eyes gleam with a mixture of mischief and intense speculation. He's carrying an old bag on a strap slung over his shoulder and is avidly examining the window display. "Not exactly. It simply means that we haven't any more books to sell."

"I see. Your father's affairs haven't been sorted out yet, then?"

"Huh, that's the least one can say, sir. He's been imprisoned for his debt in the Marshalsea, along with the whole family."

"Good lord!"

Nine o'clock sounds from Westminster. The activity on the Strand was increasing, the coachmen's cries mingling with the more distant noise of a building site by Waterloo Bridge. Solomon moves aside a little to allow a large lady with a very small dog on a lead to pass. Ten paces away from him a street vendor surreptitiously puts the stand of his tray on the ground to relieve his shoulders – he's wearing a gaudy scarf and a tailcoat with incredible bone buttons. The constable has definitely seen what he's doing but, being well acquainted with the powerful voices and repertoire of insults these characters possess he prefers to look away this time.

"The world's upside-down, Charley. It seems that progress is on the way but none of us can tell where it's going. Before they used to tell us it was the fault of the war, but now it's over things aren't any better, quite the contrary, in fact. The soldiers who've been discharged can't find work, the bits of common land have been stolen from the countryfolk. The workers' wages and the price of flour are going in the opposite direction. The Irish are arriving en masse. And all these poor people are here in London, in the hovels of the East End or St Giles."

"And in Seven Dials too, sir. I pass through there every-day."

Deeds gives a vague nod. In the past he used to go with Edward to radical meetings at the Crown and Anchor or the White Lion. Of course it wasn't the glorious 1790s any more, when the London Corresponding Society was spreading all over the country and sending representatives to the Jacobin Club in France. The war had been partly responsible, cooling certain enthusiasms. However, in 1815 the meetings were still continuing, you would see weavers there, tailors, typesetters, booksellers, construction and road workers. They were polite to each other, didn't interrupt when others were speaking and every man, even the poorest, paid his penny contribution as he came in. Deeds had no problem mingling with *those paupers*, who were clean, courteous and attentive – he didn't feel any fundamental difference between himself and them.

But at Christmas he had gone to the East End to give a valuation of a library and there he had met a different kind of poor people who were disturbing, even for a *progressive* such as himself.

"Everything's going to the dogs, my lad, even poetry. Keats is dead, Shelley's dead and as for Byron... he's given up the muse and set off for Greece to fight with a band of brigands! But why am I telling you all this? Which school do you go to?"

The boy looks away before replying. "If my father was here, he'd say 'the school of life'. I'm working, at Warren's Blacking Factory."

Deeds knows the place, an old dump down by Hungerford Stairs that's threatening to collapse into the Thames. He goes closer to the boy and finally see his creased shirt, dirty collar and boots with the soles coming off.

"Hmm. That's not ideal for your Latin declensions..."

"True, sir. But I thank you all the same – it's because of you that I know them almost all off by heart, even if I keep getting lost in the third."

"That's the most difficult one."

Deeds thinks of Edward Bailey and his hilarious parodies of Cicero; meanwhile the boy is looking at the window display.

"The Fielding was one of yours, wasn't it Charley?"

"Yes, it's unmistakable. My little brother Frederick made that mark with a piece of bread and butter."

"You like *Tom Jones*?"

"Do I like *Tom Jones*, sir?" The boy's face lights up. Since he's rather pale it looks like a sudden feverish fit.

"Just wait a minute, will you?"

He goes into the shop and comes out with the book. "I'll never be able to sell it. Because of the mark."

The boy isn't fooled. He strokes the cover of the book and then looks Deeds in the eye. "Oh thank you, Mr Deeds, thank you."

"When you've got an hour to spare we'll get on with your Latin again."

A man is strolling along the pavement opposite with boards hanging down over his back and belly proclaiming:

Not to be missed! This evening until March 31st
THE GREAT WILLIAM MACREADY
in
HAMLET
at the Theatre Royal Drury Lane

"He looks like a sandwich," the boy says.

"That gives me an idea. Why don't we go and see that play one of these evenings? It seems that Macready is truly remarkable. You'll be my guest. It's not much fun going to the theatre by yourself."

"My cousin Lambert took me to the theatre once, in Rochester. I'd be delighted, Mr Deeds."

"Right then. See you soon, young Dickens."

***

"Did you sleep well, sir?"

Stephenson gets into the vehicle before replying; he'll never get used to being addressed as 'sir', especially when it comes from a man so little given to formality as Thornton.

"I tossed and turned a bit," he finally says as they drive away from the Company's offices – provided by one of the principal backers of the railway, the banker Pease – and set off out of Darlington by North Road. "I couldn't stop thinking about that business. It's made us lose three days already."

"That's not going to make a great deal of difference."

"In principle it won't, but who knows what the future holds. I've no idea what that policeman's doing. And this… meeting today, what's the point of that?"

"Before we go there, sir, it would perhaps be a good idea to go via Aycliffe. There's another little problem there."

"Not another skeleton, I hope?"

"No," Thornton says with a grin. "This problem is very much alive and wearing silk stockings. You'll see yourself."

"Off we go to Aycliffe, then," Stephenson sighs.

When he worked in Killingworth, the only people who were 'sir'ed were the manager of the mine, the vicar and the schoolmaster. Or then when things started to get heated on a Saturday evening in the inn and fists were clenched in the men's pockets, it was flung in their face as a kind of provocation: "If you're not happy with that, *sir*, perhaps we should go outside and sort this out there."

Now Stephenson is earning at least as much as the mine manager, is better dressed than the vicar and doubtless knows a lot more than the schoolmaster, but he still hasn't got used to the *sir*, like a pair of new shoes that haven't been worn in yet.

"In a year or two," Thornton says as they leave the town, "people will be taking the train to go to Aycliffe."

"Indeed they will, if everything goes as planned."

The Devil's Road

Stephenson watches the countryside pass by at the reassuring trot of the horse. The steady pace gives him a certain sensation of speed while still allowing him to see the details of the trees and copses, and to turn round to scrutinise a hare in the middle of a field, a mound in the distance. For a man such as himself, used to going a long way on foot, it is a priceless luxury. A luxury his father practically never enjoyed. At Killingworth his first real locomotive, *Blücher*, hardly went as fast as a trotting horse. But with *Locomotion* all that was going to change. According to his calculations, the new engine would surely reach twenty miles per hour on certain stretches of the line. Like a horse at full gallop. And after that, surely very soon after that, they would exceed forty, then fifty – it was just a question of money, of equipment, of know-how. Stephenson does wonder whether the fields in the sunshine would still be as beautiful at such a speed, whether there was a threshold beyond which our experience of the world would change, transforming the traveller into a sort of blind rocket.

The carriage slows down at a slope. How had he got this far? How had he become someone the men called 'sir'?

When he was a child the railway for the mine passed right in front of his parents' cottage in Wylam. When the coal trucks, drawn by horses, went past, he would run after them – he loved the dull sound of the axles on the wooden rails, the smell of the horses' sweat. Sometimes the driver, a friend of his father, would let him climb up beside him and he would watch the pieces of coal on the top twitching and rolling like small animals that had been startled. Everything came from that, he told himself: being in the right place at the right time. From watching the rails getting worn day after day and obstructions forming that impeded the wheels, he realised that wood wasn't the right material. Moreover the saving in time turned out to be minimal compared with the normal means of transport, which meant that another source of energy than the horse was required.

He knows his own good qualities: he's a hard worker, but isn't Forbes, his foreman, that as well? Common sense, but don't a lot of people have that too? Thus when the moment came, he chose steam instead of horses, smooth rails instead of toothed rails – people imagined they were necessary to improve adherence, but the weight of the load was enough to solve the problem of adherence, he'd realised that when he saw the horses straining in Wylam. Perhaps he's intelligent, but certainly less so than his father, who would delight the children of the village by creating stories based on *Sindbad the Sailor* or *Robinson Crusoe*. However, at the height of his career Robert Stephenson, a simple mechanic, earned no more than eighteen shillings a week – which George is now earning in one hour with his salary as chief engineer of the Stockton & Darlington Railway; and to that you have to add the patent for his 'Geordie lamp' and his share in the profits from several local companies.

The spirit of enterprise, that's what makes the difference.

Just before Aycliffe, the carriage leaves the main road for a cutting through a beechwood. The recently felled trunks are strewn all over the ground and their branches are interlaced in a parody of an embrace. Just one tree has been left standing. The lumberjacks are standing round it, heads back, staring up.

The spirit of enterprise. He's abundantly supplied with that. Every new material inspires him to find a novel use for it, every new idea demands to be implemented immediately, nor can he bear to see other ideas, born in more worthy minds than his own, being overlooked for too long. As he sometimes says with a smile, "Even a Mr Watt needs a Stephenson." However, all this does not stop him feeling terribly ill at ease among this new generation of 'entrepreneurs' proliferating in the north, covering the land with factories. Men who, like him, found themselves in the right place at the right time, sometimes talented, often lucky, but solely motivated by the desire to make their money yield a profit, not to carry out a plan. Or rather, their plan *is* to make a profit. And the much-vaunted 'spirit of enterprise' is like some divine unction, justifying all the injustices, easily washing away all the moral objections, bypassing all humane considerations. Just as in the past a nobleman could get away with anything by virtue of his rank, the new entrepreneurs only have to show *enterprise* and the sweat is transformed into wine, weariness into riches and obedience into liberty. They even have the blessing of the Church for this transubstantiation. They are the new gods.

"Mr Stephenson? Should we go and have a look?"

He pulls himself together, gets down out of the carriage and follows Thornton. He makes his way between the trunks, going round the biggest, stepping over the rest. It's something else that reminds him of Wylam, when the mine's lumberjacks had finished their work: the trees left standing were too small to make good posts. Exposed to the wind, their roots weakened and vulnerable to the rain in soil that the felling had made too loose, they were condemned to a short life. Thus the living forest was disappearing to supply the forest underground.

"Pity there aren't any birds in the mines, that would be

nice," his father used to say. "Yet there are nests there," he added with a grim look, "but in those nests there's only birds of ill omen…" He was referring to the pockets of firedamp, that the miners called 'nests' in their slang.

There is a ladder propped up against the trunk of the last beech. The lumberjacks stand aside as they approach and, looking up, Stephenson can see the silk stockings Thornton mentioned. They are covering a pair of legs perched on a side-branch. He can also see a pair of baggy knee-breeches and patent leather shoes with wide buckles such as he had only previously seen in books.

"Sir?"

The legs are softly swaying but their owner shows no further sign of life.

"Sir? Could you please come down from this tree?"

No reply. George climbs up the ladder and parts the leaves to find himself facing a little man with a powdered face, a wig and a brocade jacket with old-fashioned outside pockets. The man, in his sixties, continues to watch a nest on the next branch in which three black nestlings are squawking.

Even before he sees the little birds Stephenson had guessed that they were blackbirds from the particular way the nest was woven in a double network of large and small twigs and lined with lichen. And at the same time he imagines he can feel his father's hands under his armpits, lifting him up to see a similar nest. On fine days Robert Stephenson would take the young George into the woods after work and teach him to recognise the different species. Later he had tamed several bids, including a blackbird that would come and perch on the wooden rail of his bed. In the mating season Blackie would go off into the wood, then come back, a little fatter and – at least he liked to think as a boy – a little wiser.

"I've never seen that before," he said admiringly. "In general blackbirds use spider webs simply as trimming, but here they've used them to weave together some of the twigs. It's very clever."

"Very clever indeed," the man in silk stockings agrees, finally admitting Stephenson's presence. "That's always assuming it's not pure chance."

For a while the two men just watch the nest in silence. Then Stephenson has an inspiration. "Sir, I..."

"You're Stephenson, aren't you?"

"Yes, sir."

The three baby blackbirds stay still.

"So you're the one responsible for all this mess..." The old man nods, then abruptly holds out his hand. "Roderick Preston, squire of Aycliffe." There's no arrogance about the way he says the word *squire,* it's simply an item of information, the way they put people's height and age in police reports.

"Mr, Preston, I'm very sorry to have to tell you that this... mess has been duly approved by a vote in parliament..."

"It seems there's no clock mechanism that can resist you. Is that true?"

"...a vote in parliament on the authority of which the Stockton & Darlington Railway Company has become the owner of all the lands required for the construction of..."

"Do you think you can convince me that your company also owns the blackbirds?"

"No, not the blackbirds," Stephenson concedes, "but definitely the trees on which they happen to be."

"Bah! That's ridiculous! You seem to know about birds, so you will also know what will happen if we dislodge them now – they'll die. They're too young to accept food from us. On the other hand, if you send your butchers away for a day or two, their parents will come back to feed them, they'll put on weight, and then... two days, it's not that much I'm asking..."

Stephenson leans over the nest a little. Some significant differences between the nestlings can already be seen: the one in the middle seems noticeably more robust, it's flapping its wings and has doubtless made one or two reconnaissance flights. He'd survive, perhaps, but the two others...

"Thornton!" he suddenly shouts. "Tell the men to leave this tree standing for the moment." In memory of Blackie, he thought.

The squire gives a grunt of approval. "Mr Stephenson, the Constituent Assembly of Blackbirds of Northumberland will be eternally grateful to you. In its name I invite you to dinner on Saturday evening."

"That's very kind of you, but..."

"No buts! You absolutely have to have a look at my tourbillon watch. A Breguet, of course. Does that mean something to you? Well it's losing time. I ask you, what is there worse than a watch that's losing time?"

***

Through the trees Edward Bailey can see the muddy depression, still gleaming; several men are waiting there, beside a cart, just on the edge of the woods. The pond itself has been drained but doubtless it will be given a name that will retain some trace of it for future generations. By Brusselton there's a Gallows Crossroads, though the gallows that provided the name disappeared a long time ago. Words alone are immortal, and even then not all of those. The name Edward Bailey will not outlive the negligible quantity of flesh, blood and awareness that it designates for long, while a hundred years later lovers will arrange to meet at 'Skeleton Pond' and that will add an extra thrill to their ecstasy.

It's difficult to imagine a world without Edward Bailey, a world in which *Edward Bailey* no longer means anything.

"Believe me, Mr Stephenson, that policeman, that Cobbold, is in the hands of our enemies."

The voice is so near it makes Edward start. He hadn't seen the three men under the trees, apart from the others and less than ten paces away from him. He is reluctant to stay hidden but he also feels a shiver of excitement, as when he's dealt a good hand at cards.

"Our enemies?"

"As you well know, our enemies are the landowners who believe they have been robbed by the compulsory purchase; moreover they have shares in the toll roads. For those people the railway is nothing less than an abomination. Cobbold will grab at the least excuse to make our lives and work a misery. He's already forced a great delay on us. If there's the least complication to the investigation, he'll keep the section sealed off and we'll lose several more days, perhaps even weeks…"

"You're being too pessimistic, Forbes. I don't see how Davies' testimony can harm us. Cobbold's a policeman and like all officials he wants to mark out his territory. But in the end he'll leave us in peace. After all, it's a very old story without any connection with us. On the other hand, if he should happen to find out that we've been hiding things from him…"

Forbes shakes his head, unconvinced.

The third man remains silent, lifts the peak of his cap and watches some men on horseback approaching the drained pond.

"There they are," Stephenson says. "It's up to you now, Davies, do as you think fit."

Edward lets some time pass before coming out of the trees and following them. The new arrivals have dismounted. One of them is examining the scene while questioning Stephenson and Forbes. The other two follow them, a few paces behind.

"Beware of Cobbold," Snegg has warned him. "He comes from a humble background, therefore he's very ambitious. Intelligent. Lots of mistresses, consequently lots of support at a high level. He was the right-hand man of Deputy Constable Nadin in Manchester."

"Joseph Nadin? The man who gave the order for the charge at Peterloo?"

"He was much more cunning than that. He set up the trap for the demonstrators then got out of the business by claiming the police forces weren't sufficient. The magistrates then had no choice but to send in the military, first of all the Manchester Yeomanry, then the cavalry under Lieutenant Colonel L'Estrange. Nadin was unequalled in his ability to *create* criminals – by secreting incriminating objects in people's houses, by encouraging his informers to stir up feeling at political meetings or even by entirely inventing imaginary conspiracies."

"And you think that Cobbold…?"

"Is his worthy pupil? There's no doubt about that."

'Shame on Nadin!' the radical newspapers had proclaimed at the time. 'Shame on the butchers of Peterloo!' Sixteen dead and several hundred wounded among the demonstrators. As Thomas Wooler had recently recalled in *The Black Dwarf*, "That 16th August was a veritable carnage – carnage which allows the principal instigator to enjoy a happy retirement today…"

But Alfred Cobbold is still around. Well dressed: polished boots, black coat. A pleasant enough face, slightly running to fat, with eyes too close, a strong chin, and a fold at the corners of his mouth – is that what is called a sensual mouth? There certainly needs to be some explanation for all the conquests of this short fellow who, pot-bellied and hirsute, is neither handsome nor an imposing presence. While he waits to find out whether Cobbold is a swine, he must remember that swine often look remarkably like ordinary people.

He spends several seconds weighing Edward up, as if he was wondering which smile to make: the standard smile or the one for important occasions. The stale biscuits for the less important visitors, the cake straight out of the oven for the distinguished guest. Apparently, he decides on the cake.

"It's Mr Bailey, isn't it? I see my messenger must have failed to do his job. I wanted to inform you about this gathering but I didn't imagine for one second that you would go to the trouble of coming for such a minor matter…"

"It's no trouble at all. I just needed to get a bit of fresh air. But don't bother with me, it's your investigation."

"This gentleman is Edward Bailey, the Justice of the Peace overseeing this affair," the policeman explains to Stephenson.

"And now I'm going to talk to the workers."

Cobbold remounts to ride the few yards between him and the men – in order to look down on them? But he surveys them calmly, from right to left, with a certain affability. He stands up in his stirrups, sits back down, then stands up again. His voice is clear, strong, with a slight touch of derision. "Listen, all of you. I am Alfred Cobbold. I'm a police officer and I bite if I'm attacked… be on the level with me and I will be with you. A few days ago you found some human remains. You may have happened to notice some detail lying around that would allow us to identify them. Who saw them first."

"I did," says the man with the cap.

"What is your name?"

"Sam Davies."

"Well, Sam Davies, did your father never teach you to take your hat off to people?"

Edward watches Davies. Approaching forty, he has hard but intelligent features, with very prominent cheekbones and he doesn't look at all as if he's going to take his cap off. He looks Cobbold straight in the eye.

"My father didn't have a hat."

This comment seems to delight Alfred Cobbold. He smiles and wags his finger like a roguish old schoolmaster. "Your father was a sensible man, for I promise you that if you continue in that tone, I'll make you eat yours, peak and all. What do you say to that?"

Davies folds his arms. He's started to smile too. His workmates have their eyes fixed on their toecaps.

"I think it would be amusing to try."

Cobbold's two assistants take a step towards Davies, but

their boss waves them back.

Stephenson intervenes. "Mr Cobbold, this man has a very nasty wound on his head."

Alfred Cobbold is still smiling. There's something in that smile, not really a threat – the man's more subtle than that – but a general warning to the crowd, attached to his face like a notice on a courtroom wall.

"And where does this scar come from, Davies? Did you sleep with your barber's wife?"

"No, sir. He suggested I should but I didn't fancy her and that annoyed him."

"A witty fellow, no less! All the better. My little finger tells me we're going to meet again. Have you anything to report about this matter?"

Out of the corner of his eye Edward can see Forbes and Stephenson waiting for the reply of the man in the cap.

"No, sir. I simply saw something in the pond. Then I cleared away the mud. Nothing else."

Now Cobbold's gaze sweeps across the gathered workers from left to right again, as if to put them under his spell once more. "Very well. I suggest you choose a barber with a pretty wife next time. Mr Stephenson, my two assistants are going to go over the area with a fine-tooth comb. I will inform you when they've finished."

Stephenson is about to reply, but Edward steps in first. "Mr Cobbold, I'm surprised these investigations have taken so long to get under way. It is now three days since the body was discovered. I would remind you that Mr Stephenson is carrying out important work with the support of the authorities…"

"…which he will carry out under better conditions once the

criminals in the area have been put out of harm's way."

With a nod of the head too vague to tell precisely to whom it is addressed, Cobbold prepares to leave. But before he goes he leans down to Edward and murmurs, "Very interesting to meet you, Mr Bailey, truly. I'm delighted to be collaborating with you on this matter... for we have the same end in view, don't we? At least that's what Sir Walter thinks."

His eyes are blue with a black spot on the edge of the left iris. He sets off at a trot along the edge of the former pond. Edward Bailey shivers as he watches him leave.

Around him the men are discussing what has just happened or watching the two policemen as they proceed, with no sign of enthusiasm, with their 'investigation'. Davies, sitting apart from the others, is nibbling a piece of bread and cheese while Stephenson and Forbes are examining a plan. Waiting for the right moment to speak to Stephenson, Edward tries to remember Shelley's 'Mask of Anarchy':

> *And if then the tyrants dare*
> *Let them ride among you there,*
> *Slash, and stab, and maim, and hew,*
> *What they like, that let them do.*

Magnificent. But then Shelley wasn't at Peterloo, Shelley wasn't slashed or stabbed or maimed or hewn. And now that Edward has seen one of the actors from that drama in flesh and blood, the rhetoric of those lines seems weak with its glorification of martyrdom and naive hope of an eventual miraculous victory of Good. Joseph Nadin and Alfred Cobbold couldn't have asked for more.

Rise like Lions after slumber
In unvanquishable number,
Shake your chains to earth like dew
Which in sleep had fallen on you
Ye are many, they are few!

He likes that better. He'd like to feel he had the soul of a lion. To have his own turn at slashing, stabbing and maiming... but whom? – apart from Titus the dog, of course... Spalding? Cobbold, five years after? His common face? His common potbelly? But then where are the chains? Don't you have to find them before shaking them? And that much-vaunted dew, which...

"Oh, Mr Stephenson."

The engineer, about to get into his carriage, gives him an intrigued look. He's a man in the prime of life with an open face and long sideburns that are already turning grey. Edward feels he can detect a touch of awkwardness in his bearing, as if some internal metamorphosis had been interrupted at an intermediary stage. That attracts him to the man.

"Mr Bailey?"

"I'd like to have a word with you before you leave. With you and Sam Davies."

Stephenson hesitates for just a moment, then gives a sign to his driver to wait, calls Davies over and the two of them go to join Edward on the precise spot where the skeleton was discovered.

"Gentlemen," Edward says, "I have unwittingly committed a regrettable indiscretion..."

The blue eyes of the man in the cap subject him to intense scrutiny but with no visible animosity. Stephenson folds his arms and watches a pair of rooks that are flying over them.

"Just now, under the trees, I happened to overhear your conversation with Mr Forbes. I'm sure you know the remit of a Justice of the Peace. In this matter Mr Cobbold will act under my orders, however important he likes to make himself look elsewhere. I am the one who will make the decision to continue or abandon the inquiry. I am the one who will approve or cancel the steps he wants to take. You have absolutely nothing to fear from him."

Edward pauses as he sees the ghost of a sceptical smile on Davies' lips. But he says nothing and Stephenson encourages him to continue with a nod of the head.

"Davies, I need to know what you saw, or thought you saw on the day in question. I give you my word I will not tell anyone about it – and above all not Mr Cobbold – until some other element has come to back up your evidence."

At first nothing happens. The sun has been shining since the early morning but a shiver goes through the undergrowth, perhaps a precursor of a change in the weather; the thinnest branches bend and the wave extends to the tall grasses growing all round the old pond. Then, suddenly, Davies turns on his heels and strides off. Stephenson, unfolding his arms, watches him go, while the wind draws back like a wave.

Having reached the edge of the wood, Davies stops as abruptly as he started. Searching all round, he picks up a big stick then, dragging it along behind him to make a furrow in the mulch, comes back along the former pond. When he reaches the two men, he passes them and turns so that the furrow continues into the pool of mud. Then he takes one step back and drives his stick into the ground either side of the furrow, making two holes equidistant from it. All that is done without a word. Still silent, Davies goes off to join his fellow workers, leaving the two men bent over the strange diagram.

Edward feels a pleasant tingling down his spine. "Good lord! A wheelbarrow!"

Ten minutes later he's going back, almost running. He's in a hurry to inform Snegg. And he's annoyed with himself for not asking Sam Davies why he kissed his cheese before eating it.

III

Diary of Leonard Vholes,
intended readership: none

London, 18th March 1824

"You're costing me dear, Vholes, very dear."

I keep a pleasant smile on my face. He hasn't paid me a penny yet.

"I want to recover my property. You just have to do your work."

"You can count on me, Sir Thomas. It's only a question of weeks."

The door slams, my smile fades. I go to look out of the window.

There's a great winter calm over Lincoln's Inn Fields. And the whole of London's shivering, even with spring only three days away. The cold bites everyone equally; what isn't equal is the distribution of the means to protect oneself from it. I glance briefly at the large log burning in the grate, then I watch a starving squirrel searching for a pittance among the bare trees of the square.

I don't want to be a squirrel.

Sir Thomas' tall silhouette emerges from the building. He despatches an angry look in my direction. I exhume my smile from its coffin, just for a few seconds. Sir Thomas won't outlive it for long. Nor the lengthy, whining, arrogant, acrimonious procession of my clients. Tall and short, young and old, mainly men but a few women as well, all convinced of their right, their *birth*right – a 'birthright', that's an immense store of stolen goods where generations of lazy, incompetent braggarts have put away the fruits of others' labours. They still believe their star is in the ascendant simply because they have a name, a title and a certain number of habits that go with them: speaking brusquely to their subordinates, avoiding the eye of a beggar or criticising Whig governments.

But now there is a new, more wily, cunning breed of men who have siphoned off their money with impunity, dragging them into their schemes, taking them for a ride with their shady deals, double accounts, spurious profits and genuine bankruptcies. My clients are teetering on the edge of the abyss, but still they continue to despise, mock, humiliate those they regard as the lower orders, as if money had no life of its own but was simply a personal accessory: they might lose it inadvertently but can always find it again, at the back of a drawer or down the cushions of the sofa.

They have spent centuries stealing, killing, destroying, raping. They were all-powerful, almost immortal. And now a nameless wave is coming that will sweep them away. In France they died on the scaffold. Over here their executioner is called neither Samson, nor Rousseau, nor Paine, nor Robespierre, but Adam Smith. Their death throes will last a while longer – I give them two or three generations.

Money is not a personal attribute but a being in its own right. Not an object but a living creature. I know how to talk to this creature. I've learnt how to cajole it. With a modicum of good luck I'll save Sir Thomas this time, but sooner or later he and his kind will disappear and I will sink with them, like a shellfish embedded in the back of a whale. For I'm a parasite. I've spent almost all my life analysing the least of their gestures, secretly envying them their life of luxury, their nonchalance, their blue blood, their Gainsboroughs, desiring their wives, their daughters, their sisters, and at the same time hating them. It's too late for me to change. I am chained to the old world and when it dies, I will cease to live.

In the meantime I write these pages, hang them out on the washing-line of the years and dry them in the sun of boredom. With no proofreader to argue with me, no critic to pillory me. Edition: one copy. Title: *History of my Life, readership: myself.*

Chapter The First

*in which the author makes an effort to arouse
his sole reader's interest in events that both of them
already know in detail...*

It doubtless frequently happens that boys see their mother as a paragon of beauty. But my own such impression was supported by all the men whose heads turned as Serena, my mother, walked down the street, who gave her a radiant smile or rushed to open the door of the Durham shops. For as long as we could pay their bills, the shopkeepers would stroke my hair and fill me full of sweets just to please her. However, I much preferred to stay at home and have her all to myself. I could spend hours just watching her sew, totally forgetting the presence of Grandfather Forster. When she looked up at me, I would pretend to be absorbed in my reading. "You look as serious as a bishop," she'd say with a laugh.

If I'd been asked to describe my love for her, I would have talked about an ocean. But the greater the ocean, the more chance there is of one part or another being threatened by a storm, and that's what used to happen inside me. The waters seemed calm, a lustrous blue like her eyes, but in some dark corners of my mind waves were gathering under a heavy sky. Especially when she talked about Beresford.

"Don't worry, Leonard, he won't forget us."

I, on the contrary, did wish that he'd forget us and whole months of silence helped to build up that hope. But eventually a letter containing a cheque always arrived and then I found my mother's delight was simply unbearable.

"There you are. I told you he'd remember us."

In such moments she was like the sheet of paper I'd just thrown away. Life had crushed her mercilessly, but when she remembered Beresford she would recover some of her former fulness, just as the rough copy unfolds a little in the waste-paper basket. As soon as I was old enough to read the sums on the cheques, I started to snap back, "It's a pittance! Everything's his fault and he sends you a pittance!"

And I would follow her round the room chanting words the meaning of which I barely understood: *shame, infidelity, dishonour,* parroting them, having heard them from my father's lips, always preceded or followed by the name of

Beresford at the age when children feel that language has a kind of magic power. She, however, was simply amused at my fury, at hearing me talk 'like a bishop'.

"You'll change your tune this evening with two lovely chops on your plate."

Her delight had nothing to do with the amount of the promissory notes, she was just happy at having received a sign from the man she still loved.

Durham is said to be a beautiful city, but when you have to avoid the main streets for fear of running into someone you're in debt to, make constant detours to avoid the butcher and not answer the door when someone knocks in case it's the landlord, the most beautiful city in the world will turn into a grim place. In defence of Beresford, however, I have to admit that the post would have had great difficulty in keeping up with our rapid descent from the well-to-do districts round the cathedral to the wretched hovels on the other side of the Wear. Of all these lodgings there is one, dark and dank but still respectable, that I remember above all, doubtless because we stayed there a little longer and because Grandfather Forster was still alive at the time.

He wasn't really my grandfather, not even quite my great-uncle, just the husband of my Great-Aunt Priscilla. He suffered from a bone disease that got worse over the years while at the same time showing the symptoms of stubborn innate laziness without it being clear which of these two causes prevented him from earning a living. When Priscilla died, his in-laws allocated him a little room in their South Bailey house, "in recognition of my status as a relict" he would say with his one-toothed smile. But when my mother fell into dishonour, he quite unexpectedly took her side and was therefore banished along with her, who could have done without an 'ally' who was both an encumbrance and useless. However, Grandfather Forster was the sole remaining link with her life before the catastrophe. It was for that reason that she cherished, supported and fed him, and that was presumably the reason why, against all logic, we called him 'Grandfather'.

He would play chess on a magnificent ivory board, the only valuable object in our household. It is impossible to say precisely how good he was at the game, he was much too ill – or lazy – to go to some club and challenge others. His only visitor, a sly little man called John Daniels who gave off a strong smell of tobacco, only used the chessboard to put his pipe on.

"You were my last hope, Leonard," he told me one day when I was just ten. "When I leant over your cradle, I was already weighing up your chances of being able to move the castles and knights one day."

He also used to call me 'the Bishop' because of the chessman and my habit of pontificating that made me seem older than I really was; and when, later on, Ophelia Beresford used to call me "my dear little monk," I began to think there really was something ecclesiastical about me.

"It's your turn, Bishop. I'll let you have white."

At that time we were living in the splendid apartment on the superior bank of the Wear, at the foot of the cathedral. Our neighbours' view, that looked out over the river, must have been very pleasant, but ours, at the back of the block, was blocked off by a tracery of climbing plants and bushes that were struggling to climb the ramparts of the old town. Glimpses of the castle rock could be seen among the foliage, in places almost black, in others shining with the rainwater. Occasionally some animal would set off a miniature landslide and our windows would be spattered by pebbles.

"But you always used to play with Daddy," I said as I moved my pawn two spaces.

"Your Daddy, huh! Thick as a brick and with all the charm of a door-knob... not that Serena had any choice, poor woman... she was very happy to meet Mr Vholes after the, hhm, events... I can't say I miss the bugger, even though I imagine that for your sake he should have lived fifteen years more – and above all avoided leaving you two to deal with a bankruptcy."

His pawn moves to face mine, then I bring out my knight and my bishop. Even before I could read my own name, I knew all about castling. Later on I learnt the openings of classic games and the principal variants – which was all very convenient for my mother who was too busy stitching and sewing, patching and mending to look after me. That day I remember that it was a Spanish opening that the old man played with his eyes closed.

"Grandfather Forster..."

"Hmm?"

"What does *dishonour* mean?"

He clucked his tongue and turned to face the window. The corpse of a small rodent was decomposing between two roots; I could almost have picked it up simply by stretching out my hand.

"Errr, how shall I put it? You know your red dress..."

"My dress?"

"Yes, your red dress… the one stained with egg yolk on the front."

"But… I'm a boy, Grandfather. I haven't got a dress at all."

He frowned as he looked at me. "No dress? Are you sure?"

I was starting to feel uneasy, but suddenly he opened his mouth and burst out laughing. "Right, then. That's exactly what dishonour is, Leonard: a stain on a non-existent dress."

That day I lost the game after about fifteen moves and had to content myself with his sibylline metaphor. But there was a game the next day, then another, and amid the maze of trajectories, the web of diagonal, vertical and horizontal moves, crossing each other on the ivory palimpsest, replies to my questions finally started to take shape. Even today, when I have to resolve some problem or other, I imagine a chessboard and wait for the truth to emerge from the black and white squares, like a tune from a score.

"How much did he send today?"

"Twenty pounds. I hate him."

"Oh, come on, Leonard, he's not such a bad chap."

"Everything's his fault!"

"Now then, now then… It takes two to make this kind of mess. Your mother and Beresford were young, all they were thinking of was having a good time. Then life caught up with them… and that was the end of the fun. Things could have turned out differently, of course – for example if you'd been his son. His class of people look after their bastards, it's a question of principle. They find sinecures for them. But you arrived too late, alas, you're nothing but the son of that imbecile Augustus Vholes."

"But Beresford's rich, he has millions, he could…"

"Not as rich as all that. His father cracked down on him as well, like your Grandfather Greenfield. He sent him off to France, with a very small allowance, or so I've heard, the idea being that it would build his character. The great Louis XVI was still in one piece at the time and the revolution no more than a glint in Mirabeau's eye. Then when his father died and his son returned, with the *sans-culottes* at his heels, as you might say, Wooler Manor went to the dogs. There wasn't much left in the coffers."

"How do you know all this?"

"Johnny Daniels. He knows everything about everybody for fifty miles around." (He gave a long sigh, as if merely saying 'fifty miles' had exhausted him.) "Check. It's funny, but those revolutionary ideas don't flourish over here. Just like vines, they must need more sun…"

By then I was thirteen with a downy moustache and sometimes I could get a draw with the Philidor defence. As I was coming back from school one day a tall man with hair and sideburns that were almost red passed me on the stairs.

"That was Mr Parker, your Grandfather Greenfield's lawyer," my mother told me. "He says you can go back to the house, if you like."

The sitting-room table was covered with scraps of cloth of all shapes and sizes and different colours, as if some soft toy had moulted. Sitting at his chessboard by the window, Grandfather Forster was pretending to be asleep.

"Which house?"

"The one in South Bailey. You'll have some new clothes and you'll be able to attend a much better school."

"Will you be coming with me? And Grandfather Forster?"

"No. We'll be staying here. But you can come and see us from time to time."

"In that case I won't go. This is my house."

"This isn't a house," the old man broke in, abruptly opening his eyes, "it's a box-room, just a box for humans."

How would he have described our future lodgings?

"I'm not going," I said.

My mother nodded. I suspect she'd have preferred me angry, fulminating, revelling in unseemly words rather than calm and determined as I seemed at that point. One hour later she left to deliver a dress she'd repaired for a client and I was sitting at the chess board, eyes fixed on the squares.

"Good Lord! What d'you think you're doing?!" Grandfather Forster exclaimed, seeing me deploy my chessmen in an unusual and premature attack.

It was already quite dark, but to save money we always waited until the last moment before lighting the candle.

"I'm fed up with losing, so I'm going to try something new."

"You don't say! You're not being very consistent, Bishop. Something new occurred just now and you failed to take advantage of it."

The old man chuckled as he accepted a risky gambit. My 'combination' turned out to be just as much of an illusion as those early morning dreams when we think we've caught a glimpse of the solution to our problems. When we wake, reality takes over and the dream fades, leaving us forlorn.

"The only time I... tried something new," he went on, sweeping my bishop off the board, "my one imprudent act, in a life devoted to sponging off others and never taking the initiative, was when I defied my awful brother-in-law Greenfield and took your mother's side. And whoops! there I was rotting away in a sordid hovel with a woman – the most beautiful woman I've ever seen – already shrivelled up though not yet thirty-five and forced to mend the petticoats of old hags who aren't even worthy to iron hers... as for that lad of hers, there he is biting the hand that feeds him and seeing himself as Bonaparte. Check."

"I'm not going, and that's that."

"But it would have been perfect. Not having anything to do but to wait until you see the enemy moving towards you... That's what chess teaches us: wait, wait. Reinforce your rear... above all: no mistakes. And when you spot a breach, dash into it."

"They humiliated Mother. I hate them all."

Grandfather Forster jiggled his legs, that were stretched out on a footstool, in order to restore circulation, an operation that made him grimace with pain but did nothing to prevent him from maintaining his stranglehold on the game by threatening my queen with his castle.

"But you don't know what there is at the back of that breach. Once you're there you might perhaps, with time and patience, manage to soften Grandfather Greenfield's heart. Your mother and I would be able to return to the house and I'd be back in my comfortable bed, my dressing gown and slippers, with my little glasses of sherry..."

He glanced at me to assess the impact his proposal had made. "Greenfield's a nasty little puritan, obstinate as a mule... but that visitor today proves that he does have a heart, even if he keeps it well hidden. You know, he thought so too… he really imagined his daughter was going to marry a baron's son. And then came Beresford's decree: no, no, three times no!"

"He should have married her anyway."

"You think so?" he asked, with a glance at the window the rain had started drumming against. "Defy society? The whole world? Set out on a hand-to-mouth existence, without happiness, without distinction. The callow youth didn't have the courage. There was that stupid escapade in London when the two turtle doves did the irreparable damage. It was nothing that couldn't be repaired with a needle and thread… but the deed had been done and people knew. That wasn't such a problem for Beresford, but for your mother, alas…"

"I hate him!"

"Still? You keep harping on about that. But hatred is a poor counsellor, even if what you're looking for is revenge… *especially* if you're looking for revenge. Do you think Philidor hated Legal?"

He tried to shift his weight onto his left side. "Hey, give me that cushion there."

"They can all go to hell as far as I care," I muttered as I made my move.

Grandfather Forster gave an exasperated sigh. "Well you'll go there with them too. Checkmate."

A few weeks later, right in the middle of a Sicilian defence, he leant forward to take a piece and his heart simply stopped beating. I saw him frown and open his lips to say something, then he simply collapsed on the chessboard, his chin crashing into the ivory and breaking it, scattering pawns all over the table, with his one last tooth rolling round with them, like an intruder dressed in red at a ball of black and white ghosts. His empty eyes surveyed the battlefield, perhaps following a game against God Himself.

He was buried in the paupers' corner of the graveyard – his friend Jack Daniels dropped some ashes from his pipe on his grave – leaving mother and me to enjoy the illusory calm of life together. Though there was always someone invisible between us.

The war on the continent continued and, despite what Grandfather Forster had said, the revolution in France found followers over here, especially in London, but also in the countryside, in the mines and the naval dockyards. As a protest against the price of bread, women would stick a round loaf on a broomstick or a fishing rod and march through the streets, just as the *sans-culottes* had done with the head of Mme de Lamballe. Prophets were announcing the Apocalypse for 1800.

No one had any idea how 'all that' was going to finish, in fact no one really knew what 'all that' was. In those difficult times even middle-class women were repairing their clothes themselves, or buying them cheap from the ones made by the machines that were operating in Lancashire. The pieces of cloth on our table gradually lost their colour then became increasingly scarce – it was like a river drying up. My mother started coughing more and more and her beauty was no longer sufficient to mollify our creditors; even the most optimistic, the most smug among them came to see that they would never get more than smiles from the pretty widow. The washing line of time broke and was now hanging over the abyss; we were sliding down and continuing to fall despite trying to cling on to the knots: first of all the little maid's room in the house of Mr Jobs, the coalman, with the black dust that got everywhere, then the hovel beside a tannery on the other side of the river and finally a further hovel on the edge of town that was so cold it made no difference whether the window was open or shut. Since those days I have sworn never, *never*, to be cold again. A narrow corridor divided the cottage in two apartments and whenever I appeared there, going in or out, a four-headed hydra would appear at the door opposite ours: the Wilkins children, left in the charge of the eldest, who couldn't have been more than six, never missed anything that might amuse them. In the gloom I could make out four fringes of dirty hair, ranged according to the height of the little brats, and four equally snotty noses with the mucus dripping down from one face to the next, in a cascade that left that of the youngest covered in a uniform coating.

I thought we couldn't fall any farther. How naive! Soon there were no more knots in the line and we were going down all the time. As well as her cough, Mother suffered from chronic rheumatism that made sewing very painful. Her last customers were losing patience with her. I had to leave the seedy school where stupidity was drummed into me with all available pedagogical methods and started delivering newspapers for wages that didn't even meet the rent for our garret. And not the slightest sign from Wooler Manor. My mother didn't get any better. I wasn't quite eighteen when she started coughing blood and I was forced to undertake something I was very loath to do.

One evening I crossed the Wear and climbed the slope up to the old town. It was freezing cold. The fog had spread a layer of hoar frost over the cobbles and the buildings making the street look strange in the light from the windows. Below a certain temperature it can seem that heat never existed, that it was only a dream, a figment of the imagination from a flame seen in a picture. Half way there I passed a pedlar who couldn't get his handcart up the slippery slope: he'd simply secured his cart with a big stone and, sitting on the ground leaning back against a wheel, he uncorked a little flask as he bawled out a song. By the University three tipsy students gave me a good evening, and soon afterwards I heard them hail the pedlar: there were shouts, profanities, bursts of laughter mingled with the words of his song, the clatter of the handcart hurtling down the slope, all mingled together and muffled by the grip of the cold and the fog.

Once I was in South Bailey I slowed down. All the chimneys of those fine houses of the well-to-do were belching out smoke at full blast, which made the cold even more biting.

After having made me repeat my name three times, an old servant let me into the cramped hallway, then into a kind of office with spartan décor in which the few pieces of furniture seemed to have been selected to look less expensive than they had in fact cost. "So this is *the house*," I told myself, "the one in which I could have grown up." I sat down in a fireside chair, staring at an empty hearth, a desk with two equally high piles of paper mounting guard, a worn velvet bell-pull and a screen that hid nothing, trying to imagine my *terrifying* Grandfather Greenfield on the basis of these few clues. But instead of an old man it was one in his thirties who entered.

"Who are you?" the man whom I guessed was my Uncle William asked.

He was not at all like his sister, even though his eyes were the same colour and his face had the same general shape. But apart from those two aspects, his physiognomy seemed grotesque to me, as if some painter had tried to reproduce the beauty of his sister but, on realising his failure, had furiously slashed the canvas.

"Leonard Vholes, your nephew. The son of your sister Serena."

"But I no longer have a sister," he replied in the tone of a schoolmaster correcting an obvious mistake, "and consequently I can't have a nephew."

"It's not you I've come to see, it's my grandfather."

William walked across the room and sat erect behind the desk. "The man you call your grandfather is no longer capable of receiving any visitors."

"Is he ill?"

Instead of replying, he opened a drawer and rummaged round in it. "Not ill," he said eventually, "Just very old."

"My mother, you see, is seriously ill. She needs help."

"That is regrettable but is of no concern of the Greenfield family."

That was it. I realised that once this principle had been established, the next step would be to give me some money. As a final settlement. But then, wasn't that what I'd come for?

He picked up a pen, lifted the lid of the inkwell, wrote out the cheque and held it out to me in his fingertips. "That brings any relationship between us to an end."

I put the cheque in my pocket vowing that I would never, *never* again beg for anything.

My first idea was to use Greenfield's money to find better lodgings, but Doctor Murphy, whom I consulted, dissuaded me. There was a craftiness about his extreme affability, like that of certain shopkeepers, yet what he was selling me was his own inability to effect a cure.

"Spare her that, young man," he said. "It would be an ordeal for her. See how weak she is already and going back into the town would do nothing for her. What she really needs is Italy... make the place draughtproof, install a good stove and give her some meat. That won't do any harm."

That was done and many other things besides. My mother had a new quilt and I gave up delivering newspapers in order to stay at her bedside, only leaving the apartment to do some quick shopping. We would talk about this and that but never about the past, always the future. We ought to get away, move to Newcastle, perhaps even London. I had to study something worthwhile. At least she could think of the future, like a down-and-out who has two farthings left in his pocket and can't stop fingering them.

Murphy, as affable as ever, seemed to enjoy visiting us: he would sit down by the new stove, pink with self-satisfaction and never short of new suggestions that 'wouldn't do any harm.' Why did he spend all this time with us? Could he still see my mother's beauty, despite her wasted body and waxy complexion? Or was it the proximity of death that attracted him? Both perhaps. I sometimes have the feeling that death and beauty go together, though I can't explain that, I'm neither a philosopher nor an aesthete. What I do know is that all the things I found beautiful have been taken away from me, while the ugly things proliferate with unashamed vigour, multiplying like vermin, cluttering the ground wherever I place my foot.

My mother died at the end of January. I had enough money left to give her a decent funeral. Doctor Murphy saw to everything with his usual affability, contacting the authorities of Shincliffe parish – I could never have borne the idea of her resting in St Oswald's, close to a family that had repudiated her – but he wasn't there when the undertakers knocked at the door. No one else, I told myself, would knock like that, with one single, menacing, peremptory blow, not even the nastiest of creditors. I can still hear that blow and, looking back, it feels as if I've always heard it, even when my mother was still alive. It is in a way the acoustic background to my existence: a loud 'boom' resounding unremittingly in an empty corridor.

I went to the door.

"Mr Vholes?" said the first man, tipping his cap.

He was a stocky man with a hard face and his acolyte, who was carrying the other end of the coffin, was chewing a quid of tobacco. They brought the smell of rain and sweat with them, but also the pleasanter scent of freshly worked wood. They were wearing light-coloured coats, presumably in defiance of the stereotype.

They made their way along the corridor then into our lodgings. It took only a few minutes to lay the body in the coffin and screw down the lid.

As they left, the Wilkins' door was open and their four offspring appeared in the opening, one above the other, like mops hanging from nails at different levels. You could see, below the crop of dirty hair, their eyes fixed on the coffin. As it passed the youngest held out his hand towards the strange object invading his territory.

"You mustn't touch it!" his sister said, giving him a slap.
"Why not?"

"It's not for us. That's for dead people."

The wind ruffled the hair of the young Wilkins. If there was a draught, it meant the door to the hovel had been left open; and there, at the end of the corridor, I saw an unknown man.

He appeared to be fascinated by the coffin, almost as if he were seeing one for the first time, and seemed uncertain as to how to behave: go out to leave room for it, as logic would demand, or try to squeeze his way along between the wall and the men with their burden? But he did neither the one nor the other, he simply stayed standing on the doorstep as if transfixed. Later on I was to come to see that he could be paralysed in this way by two contradictory impulses or made, almost despite himself, to choose a third way. All in all he was both puppet and puppeteer, while at the same time observing himself in a way.

"Hey, you! There are people with work to do here."

He started at the voice of the tobacco-chewer. "Oh! I... yes, of course. Do forgive me."

He backed out over the doorstep, but instead of leaving, he leant against the house wall, eyes closed, his hands apparently kneading an imaginary lump of dough – at least that was the strange position I found him in when I came across him a few seconds later. While the undertakers were loading the coffin, an old man stopped to observe their technique; two other passers-by, on the other hand, hurried past. It was no longer raining. The hearse executed a neat turn and headed off for Shincliffe, perhaps at a slightly too fast a pace by the standards of the profession.

For his part the stranger had not moved an inch. Finally he said, "I'm looking for Serena Greenfield."

"Serena Vholes."

"Yes, Serena Vholes."

"Down there," I said, pointing to the hearse.

"Oh Lord!"

But he'd already guessed. "You must be Leonard."

"Yes. And who are you?"

"Beresford. When and where will the funeral take place?"

"At Shincliffe. This afternoon."

"I'll be there."

If you want to love or hate someone, it's best not to get too close, to keep your distance, leave everything vague. Look away when they gesture, stop your ears when they speak. Otherwise you'll start analysing every one of their actions, interpreting everything they say and you'll no longer be able to love them *absolutely* or to hate them *utterly*. You opinion will be nuanced. You'll want to see further evidence before giving your verdict, and that will be neverending. You'll get lost in what Grandfather Forster used to call the 'frills': "Don't try to understand your opponent, to analyse his style... no frills! He's there to lose, you to win. Go to it, Bishop!"

"Actually I ought to call myself Bedford," Beresford said, "or perhaps Berford, there is some doubt, from the name of my swashbuckling ancestor, who was knighted by Edward Balliol after some obscure battle against the Scots and rewarded with a fief in the valley of the Wear. In the course of the following century the fief became a barony and Bedford changed to Beresford. Thus it was enough for a hirsute oaf, who probably couldn't read or write, to strike some harder blows than the others with his mace to give rise to a dynasty."

It was the August of 1800, not quite seven months after my mother died, and we were travelling to Wooler Manor. It hadn't been the end of the world but, with Bonaparte as first consul and victorious at Marengo, the prophets of disaster were still hopeful. As for my own personal situation, there had been an avalanche of miracles worthy of the Bible. The good Doctor Murphy, after having had a few words with Beresford at my mother's funeral, had put me in touch with one of his acquaintances, Mr Dull. This Mr Dull, a lawyer, happened to be looking for an errand boy, a position which, depending on the young man's competence and ability to complete the appropriate courses, could turn into a position as clerk. Mr Dull was on the best of terms with the headmaster of a college and knew a certain Mrs Watson, who had a room to let half way between the chambers and the aforementioned college. I had of course no doubt about the identity of my *deus ex machina*, but I was still surprised to find him knocking at my door that scorching summer's day. I had assumed he would never dare to show himself openly.

"Alas," he went on, "nothing has ever happened since then to justify that stroke of fate. We Beresfords have never shown the least talent. We have no philosopher, no philanthropist, no patron of the arts, no agricultural reformer, no inventor to show. Not even a great soldier. It seems that the transition from a mace to more sophisticated instruments was beyond us... the only fame we have we owe to vice. And there has never been a lack of scandalmongers to make a mockery of the family crest."

Durham seemed far away, quivering in the heat haze, like one of those imaginary towns dotted across the background of Florentine paintings. It was hard to believe that seven months ago the water had frozen in the wash-basins in the houses.

He showed me the coat of arms embroidered on his handkerchief. "Look: that represents two hills with the first family residence in the hollow between them, up there in the Pennines. It doesn't take much imagination to see it as a... female posterior – and that, precisely, was the area of expertise of my ancestors. At the end of the fifteenth century the Beresfords, weary of screwing shepherdesses in their valley in the back of beyond, came to live in Darlington, closer to civilisation – that is closer to the brothels and courtesans, of which one, so the legend goes, persuaded my ancestor James to marry her..."

We hadn't been travelling for an hour when the mines of Bishop Auckland had already appeared in the west. Beresford's coupé, drawn by four horses, kept up a good pace on the highway. It was the first time I'd been inside such a luxurious vehicle and I relished every detail – the soft upholstery, the smell of leather – though I didn't fail to notice a certain lack of maintenance, just as the coachman lacked style. For the moment, however, I didn't ponder on this too much, I was too occupied with new sensations, quietly noting the embarrassment which Beresford was trying very hard to conceal with his endless flow of flippant conversation.

No mistakes now! Wait for your chance! Keep an eye on the opening!

The style of the manor isn't really to my taste, but it's comfortable and the chapel's worth a look. All the Beresfords lie there, even the most ungodly, even that licentious villain James. His brother Robert was prior of the Benedictine monastery in Durham and he had the unfortunate idea of holding a grandiose funeral mass for James in the chapel at Wooler Manor. Just before the service a huge oak tree that had been struck by lightning collapsed, causing the death of the prior and several monks. That was all that was needed to give rise to the ridiculous legend... from time to time, when the harvest is very bad, when the plague is raging or some war or other is bleeding the country dry, there's always a tipsy fellow who ventures to have a look into the chapel on a moonless night where he catches the ghosts of the poor Benedictines celebrating their unfinished mass...

We left the highway at Newton Aycliffe. Sparse meadows and woods, a dreary landscape. The carriage was jolting along a poorly maintained road – though nothing compared with what we had to endure a little later on the private drive to Wooler Manor. That road was in the image of the man Beresford himself as I got to know him over the next few months. Here and there attempts had been made to fill in the ruts, improve the line, clear out the brush all around, but nothing had been carried through, nothing was really effective. There were a few seconds when the track was so wide and smooth, the outlook so clear, you might imagine you were heading for a palace worthy of Palladio, then the ruts took over, the jolting started once more, quivering bushes rubbed against the axles and the coachman had his work cut out avoiding the branches of the trees.

How often did I subsequently see Beresford striding round his estate followed by an overseer with a dubious curl on his lips or a steward with a frown on his face? Beresford draining a marsh in his mind's eye, flattening a hummock with a sweeping gesture, pointing to some agricultural building in the distance that would only ever be built in his imagination. Beresford promising his farmers some amazing agricultural reform and their day-labourers a land of milk and honey, where the plough would work the land on its own, where the corn would sway gently in the breeze before tying itself up in delicate sheaves. Addressing working men as 'citizen'! Then, a few days later, this same man prostrate in his armchair, complaining of stomach ache, calling his butler a thief, his workers lazy, mulling over complicated retaliatory measures against perfectly peaceable neighbours. Then, finally, this third Beresford, perhaps the strangest of all and certainly the most disarming, who was looking at me that day, his eyes moist, his cheeks flushed with emotion.

"We do at least have one thing in common, Mr Vholes... but perhaps I might call you Leonard?"

"What thing?"

"We neither of us have any family. Your father was an orphan, the Greenfields have repudiated you. As for myself, I don't want to have anything more to do with the Beresfords."

Apart from the title, the estates, the tenant farmers, the income and a luxurious residence, I thought as the Manor came into view.

"I have seen things... terrible things in France, Leonard. And when I came back my father treated me like a beggar! I couldn't do anything for you... nothing more than what I did do."

Wooler Manor. For a long time the name had been nothing

but a letter heading to me. But the mystery of those compact syllables was now allied to a real place of an equally compact beauty that had not been spared by time, negligence and the lack of funds. And this encounter between myself and the thing gave birth to a hybrid visible to myself alone. The imposing portal surmounted by stone figures like gigantic chessmen, the many-mullioned windows, some rectangular some rounded off by elegant arches, the building's U-shape, recalling wide-open jaws, the basin in the middle with its dried-up fountain, its Saturn pitted with lichen, its exhausted Neptune leaning on two enormous water lilies – it all evoked somnolence, abandoned projects. Even in the higher parts, the triangular pediments, the forest of chimneys challenging the trees in the park, the stone seemed to weigh down like a blanket of stupor. You felt that such a place wasn't made for living but simply for sleeping and waking up, soaked in sweat from incomprehensible dreams.

We passed the basin on the left, driving along one of the symmetrical wings. Its windows were obscured by dark, heavy drapes.

"It was a real torment for me to know that you…"

The coupé stopped outside the main entrance. No footman dashed out to receive us. The coachman himself, who seemed to have lost a little more style en route, came to open the carriage door but Beresford dismissed him and we stayed, silent, in the oven that was the vehicle, he looking for words, I determined to do nothing to help him, both of us sweating profusely.

"To know that you were in need," he finally said. "I'm not lascivious like my ancestors. There have only been two women in my life and there would only have been one if, at the crucial point, I hadn't lacked…"

"Courage?" I broke in this time, looking him straight in the eye.

He started to shake his head, then changed his mind and returned my look. "True. I'm a coward. We can always find excuses for our faults: a man of a fiery temperament cannot resist his anger, nor a libertine the lure of his senses. A miser can be seen as exercising foresight, a vain man can sometimes show panache, a jealous man is partly exonerated by love… but there is never any excuse for a coward… isn't that unfair?"

To my great relief he opened the door and we got down from the carriage.

"At least I'm determined to make good my mistakes, as far as can be done. My father was incapable of managing his affairs but since he died I've stopped the rot."

'Stopping the rot,' as I later learnt, consisted of employing an even more incompetent steward than the previous one and selling off a third of the family estate dirt cheap to pay off his debts.

"In all likelihood my wife will not give me a child. I need someone with whom to share my ideas, my plans. Why not you, Leonard?"

I didn't know exactly where I was, perhaps in my room at Mrs Watson's, dreaming this incredible scene – even today, putting it down on paper, I can't really believe it. How did he dare. We were standing there, side by side, facing the Manor. The sun seemed to make the air thick, difficult to breathe and transformed every windowpane into a nimbus round the face of my dead mother, like a chalcedony cameo. How did he think he was going to make good *that* mistake? Standing still, he was silently staring at the sky and at that moment I could have grabbed his red neck, gleaming with sweat, and strangled him until he was dead. But the moment passed and a few further seconds took me beyond hatred.

After all, she had loved him. After all I was on the point of entering the holy of holies, the place where she had never been accepted.

One hell of an opportunity, Bishop! You see? All you had to do was wait.

In Wooler Manor the number of servants always seemed ridiculously small to me, given how immense the place was. I hardly ever ran into one outside meal times – and even then I always had the impression I was surprising them in some dubious activity, involved in something more or less illicit that had nothing to do with their employment. On that first day, for example, no one came to open the door for us. We crossed a hall with black and white tiles drenched in sunlight, but very quickly, going through a sequence of rooms shaded by shutters, we reached a part of the Manor that was nice and cool with a pleasant smell of old oak, plaster and lime flowers: the fragrance of Wooler Manor. Columns, columns everywhere, most of them simply decorative: either side of the hearths, framing antique statues or breaking up the monotony of a long, empty corridor. In one place there were white double doors open between two pillars and a chandelier, also white; and in the next room a precise replica, black as remorse. Then came another succession of narrower rooms with windows right at the end, looking out onto an invisible park and, on the left and right, doors giving onto further corridors out of which drifted the scent of dead flowers.

Beresford was no longer the same man. In general very gauche, with a jerky, almost mechanical gait, he now moved smoothly – like those tortoises in the tropics of which it is said they drag themselves laboriously across the shore but are transformed into graceful naiades once they're in the ocean. The Manor was his ocean, he would rove round it with a jaunty air, breathing more freely. Even his face was transformed, became less angular, more expressive.

"We – that is my sister, my wife and myself – occupy the main building, though I also have a little den in the north wing. This is the south wing, its twin, reserved for guests." We were climbing a marble staircase that made every word reverberate, giving them a strange modulation, "And your room."

I had never imagined that one day I would sleep in a four-poster bed! Its blue velvet drapes were rather dusty and suggested boredom rather than comfort, but the room was very nice with a lovely French writing desk and the French windows gave onto a balcony looking down on the courtyard and the basin. Just at the moment when Beresford was showing me the view, a chaise stopped by the entrance to the other wing. A man got out, carrying a box of the kind certain tradesmen use to carry their tools – but he was meticulously dressed and resembled neither a carpenter nor a cabinet maker. Furthermore he was familiar with the house and was clearly a regular visitor – once he reached the door he took a key out of his pocket before disappearing into the room with black curtains.

"But I have to leave you on your own for the moment," Beresford said abruptly. "Be in the little drawing room at six, it's at the end of the hall… you'll be able to find your way?"

Just as he was leaving the room, he stopped and looked at me with proprietorial satisfaction, as if I were his colt and had just won the Derby.

"I'm very happy to have you here, Leonard. Truly happy."

One hour later I was opening the door of the 'little' drawing room, that would certainly have taken ten of my room at Mrs Watson's. It had a view of the park behind the Manor and a walled garden to the south. Lit by very high windows on the park side and a glass door on the garden side, it was so long and wide it seemed to contain relatively little furniture, but I imagine that three antique dealers could have made a fortune from the sale of what was there. (Later I was shown the 'big' drawing room, an immense nave with ceilings so high that, despite the light from five huge windows, you could hardly make out the coffering, and the sound of footsteps provoked a lugubrious echo.)

Mathilde Beresford was contemplating the park with an air that suggested those dearest to her had just died a terrible death there, and Ophelia, stretched out on a chaise longue, was waving her fan, that always made me think of the wing of a swallowtail butterfly that had been tortured. In her other hand she was holding one of Mr Richardson's books but had her eyes fixed on the hysterical zigzag flight of a fly maddened by the storm. She had just said something of which I only heard the end, "…get exhausted eventually."

No doubt she was talking about the fly. But it seemed to me, though I can't say why, that behind the word there was much wider meaning that was in tune with Wooler Manor, its columns, its interminable corridors, the faded petals on its flower-pot stands. Uncertain of myself, I took one step forward.

That's it, Bishop, you're in the right place. It's your move.

But for the moment I was neither a player nor a bishop, just a pawn two women were fighting over with their looks, weighing its future usefulness according to a combination of criteria known only to themselves.

For a few long seconds they didn't respond to my 'Good evening', and I had plenty of time to observe them. My first impression of them was a joint one in that the great dissimilarity between them struck me before their individuality: it was like seeing two paintings that didn't go together at all and noting the discomfort or displeasure their combination provokes rather than their individual good or bad qualities. Mathilde was a landscape: rugged trees with twisted roots, a graveyard in the pale moonlight, a ship cast aground by the waves, a silhouette leaning over the void, Ophelia a still life. The deep black eyes of the Frenchwoman expressed an energy lacking a goal and above all a vindictive sadness: she always looked as if she were scrutinising a crowd in search of some criminal. Her beauty was of the kind that can drive a man mad and which discourages any rational reaction in advance.

Much younger but appearing almost the same age, blonde with a pallid complexion while the other was a brunette and of a ruddy complexion, Ophelia's charms were more discreet but strangely enough her physical attraction seemed stronger to me. That said, I immediately dismissed that from my mind. I was a machine of war whose purpose was to cause as much damage as possible, not a young emissary destined to become infatuated with the first female spy I met.

"Mr Vholes," Mathilde finally said in the tone of a scientific assessment.

"Leonard," Ophelia added with a mocking smile.

I felt as if I were an insect that they were unsure whether to call by a technical term or by its common name but that was going to end up pinned to the block of one or the other.

That was all for the moment because Beresford arrived at this juncture and took over the conversation until dinner. While Ophelia made the effort to deliver herself of a few pleasantries – always accompanied by an ambiguous smile – Mathilde didn't say a word and, to go by her husband's indifference, that was the usual situation.

The storm broke during the night with a torrential downpour on the roof and gusts of hot wind attacking the statues round the basin. A damp patch appeared on the ceiling of my room. The whole building was grunting in its sleep like a weary old mule.

In the morning my hosts were nowhere to be found. After looking in the small and the big drawing room, I happened to find the breakfast room where a sleepy maid served me a bowl of lumpy porridge – I hadn't been very impressed by the previous evening's dinner either, despite the splendid silverware and porcelain.

Fortunately I'd brought my travel chess set and I sat down at the window in my room.

Around ten the man with the toolbox arrived, this time in Beresford's coupé, driven by the same not very stylish coachman as the previous day. The unknown man, whose face I couldn't see because of his hat and raised coat collar, was about to take out his key when the door was opened – by Beresford himself. Then I saw that the curtains blacking out the windows were not high enough to stop me from seeing part of the large entrance hall – a precise replica, I surmised, of the one in the south wing – and, if not the library itself, a least to door to it, through which the two men disappeared.

Not five minutes had passed when Mathilde appeared in the hall, coming from the main building. She went up to the library door, seemed to hesitate for a moment, then decided to knock. Nothing happened. She waited a while, then knocked again, still to no effect. I saw her turn the handle. In vain, the door was locked. She clenched her fists, doubtless to hammer on the door, but eventually she changed her mind and left.

But while on my right Mathilde Beresford was going off into the building, Ophelia appeared on the left, at the end of the courtyard, as if in a scene long since planned. She was clearly coming from the stables, still wearing her riding clothes, holding her crop. She went into the hall and then took her turn at knocking on the library door. Was she expected or had Beresford recognised her footsteps? In any event, the door opened almost immediately. Her visit didn't last long and I soon saw Ophelia taking the same route as her sister-in-law to the main building.

This merry-go-round had certainly aroused my curiosity. After the stifling heat of the previous day, I felt reinvigorated and, above all, keen to advance my first pawns. I took advantage of a break in the rain to go down to the courtyard and, strolling round the basin before pretending to admire certain architectural features, approached my goal, the hall of the north wing. It wouldn't be entirely unknown territory since

I'd seen part of it from my room and, anyway, the two wings seemed perfectly symmetrical. Thus the room on the southern side matching the library was framed by two alcoves with an arch supported by pillars. If there was the same arrangement on the other side, I would be able to hide until the two men left, eavesdrop on some of what they said and perhaps even get a sight of the unknown man. If the worst came to the worst and I was found, I could always use my ignorance of the building as an excuse and claim I'd got lost...

My assumptions were partly confirmed: on the north side I only found one of the two recesses, the other having presumably been sacrificed to enlarge the library, but one was sufficient for me. Once in position I had all the time in the world to refine my plan.

'No mistakes, Bishop, above all no mistakes.'

The first mistake would be to choose the wrong target. As the rain started to whip poor Saturn and Neptune once more, two possible options came to mind.

Logic suggested I should attack Mathilde and the prospect of cuckolding Beresford after he – at least in my view of the matter – had cuckolded my mother, seemed very promising. But it had only taken me a few hours to see how far apart the two of them were, the contempt each had for the other. By sleeping with his wife I would doubtless dent the Baron's pride, but the wound would not go deep, I wouldn't make him suffer. But by blackening his sister's name I would be hitting his own flesh and blood. He, too, would then know what it was to suffer dishonour...

But all that was, of course, nothing but the braggadocio of callow youth, I'd already forgotten the feeling of inferiority

I'd had in the little drawing room the previous evening: from an insect my overconfidence had transformed me overnight into an entomologist... half a dozen easy successes with seamstresses had made me think I could seduce any woman at all. I thought myself handsome – two or three of those unwise virgins had assured me I was – knew I was patient, stubborn, and that was enough for me.

From time to time murmurings came from the library and some noises as well – rustling, rubbing, rattling – but none evoked an association with any known human activity. The low, grey sky, the black curtains covering the lower half of the windows meant that the hallway was semi-dark. I was squatting at the back of my hiding place and I was about to doze off on my imaginary laurels when the coupé returned. Beresford must have ordered the coachman to come by ringing a bell, or he had been given a time in advance. The noises in the library stopped; soon the two men came out, finishing a conversation.

"Don't worry, my Lord, I'm almost there." He spoke correct English but with an unpleasant lisp and a slight accent of the Levant. "I'll take that secretary to bits... I'll use the jemmy if necessary."

I just about managed to stop myself bursting out laughing – it sounded like one of those coded languages certain eccentric clubs use, I thought. But what I saw when I peeped round the pillar immediately took away all desire to laugh.

The left side of the face of the unknown man with the toolbox was that of a forty-year-old with black hair and eyes, showing a certain nobility despite his Saracen tan. But the other side of his face was completely burnt, probably by some red-hot object it had been forced down on. A puffy crease of an unhealthy yellow ran down from the end of his eyebrow to the side of his chin; the socket was covered by a kind of membrane and what was left of his lips seemed to have been sewn back together, so that his mouth could only open half way. A clear line, as if drawn with a burin, divided the Janus face in two.

The man hurried off, but while whole years of my life have been consigned to oblivion, his face keeps on rearing up out of my memory like the head of a snake from its basket.

"Of course, Newton, I have absolute confidence in you."

Beresford stayed standing in the doorway until the carriage had left the courtyard, waving twice. As far as I had understood, the conversation suggested that his visitor still had work to do at the Manor. But if he ever did come back, I never knew and no one ever made any reference to a Mr Newton in my presence.

IV

Snegg's Cousins

"Margaret…"

"Mmmmmm…"

"Oh, Margaret… Margaret

"Mmmmmm!"

The young woman kneeling down spits out what she has in her mouth and states firmly, "I'm not called Margaret, sir, I'm called Kirstie."

Edward Bailey opens his eyes and surveys the room: small but pretty with its modest furnishing, tasteful engravings, its lavatory discreetly concealed by a curtain. That's the reason why the establishment in Bull Wynd suits most of the men in Darlington, those of the middle class as well as the surrounding squirearchy, the well-to-do shopkeepers and the wealthier farmers, the engineers from the mines, the doctors and lawyers. Comfort without ostentation, forbidden pleasure without recourse to subterfuge. In Bull Wynd you avoid both the noxious stench of the sordid hovels as well as the dubious décor of the old-fashioned bordellos with their mirrors, their exotic draperies, their courtesans with their affectation of passion and put-on French or Italian accents. You can imagine you're at home, sitting by the fireside. With your wife…

"Of course, er, Kirstie, but… let's go on, shall we?"

The young woman gets back down to work.

She knows she shouldn't have protested. By paying her the men are buying above all an empty shell into which they can pour not only their semen but all their fantasies as well – a slate on which they can write a name of their choice. But it's stronger than her: to give herself to all comers, she can do that, but to turn herself into a dummy provided with orifices, no. To make up for her indiscretion, she applies herself wholly to her task. She likes this Bailey anyway. A courteous man, gentle and clean. Thin arms and legs, a slightly rounded belly. Even the others, even the most horrible ones all show some touching detail, a charming weakness during intimacy. Everything's a question of distance, she thinks, as she licks Bailey's member. Close up ugliness fades, becomes soothing. Like Sam's scar.

Her father would kill her if he were to come across her in Bull Wynd. But he'd kill her all the same if he found her together with Sam Davies, by the barn where the workers sleep. Her father who bawls out Methodist hymns:

> *O precious Side-hole's cavity*
> *I want to spend my life in Thee.*
> *There in one Side-hole's joy divine,*
> *I'll spend all future Days of mine.*
> *Yes, yes, I will for ever sit*
> *There, where Thy Side was split.*
> *Still the fountain of Thy blood*
> *Stands for sinners open'd wide;*

Now, even now, my Lord and God,
I wash me in Thy side.

The previous evening, at sunset, she and Sam had walked as
far as Wooler Manor to find a quiet spot. (She's still at work.
You have to forget the taste, the thickness of the member.
Pretend it's part of yourself that you have to recover whatever
the cost. Swallow it like your own life.) The old building was
mounting guard in the blaze of the sky. The trees seemed to
be whispering to each other. They found a hollow lined with
moss, sheltered from the wind, close to the chapel.

"Why don't you tell me?" she asked.

"Tell you what?"

"The scar."

Without a word Sam picks up a stick and scrapes away
the moss to clear a rectangle of rich earth. Then he draws
something in it. Leaning over his shoulder, Kirstie deciphers
the letters with difficulty, "Sam Dav… ies writes."

"So you know how to read," Sam says.

'Yes, I learnt at Sunday school."

"But not to write?"

"We weren't allowed to. Because Sunday was the day of
rest."

"That has nothing to do with it. It's just because they don't
want you to learn."

"Why not?"

"Because if we could, we'd write *our* history."

"Would that be very different, *our* history?'

Sam pulls up a blade of grass, raises his head and leans on his
elbow. "That would be the true history, not the one it's in their

interest to make known. What do they write, these newspapers, even the ones that claim to be defending us? That the country has never known such prosperity, that mechanisation is improving day by day and with it output... we're producing ten times more of one thing than twenty years ago, fifty times more of another, we export throughout the whole world, the landowners are getting richer, the manufacturers are getting richer, the merchants are getting richer. Everyone's getting richer apart from us. We're just as poor as we were before."

Kirstie observes him surreptitiously. Strangely enough, while this kind of conversation usually makes him get angry, he's calm, seems happy, chewing his blade of grass on his bed of moss. She wonders if it's because of her or simply because of the moss, the trees creaking quietly above their heads.

"They've swept away the last of the regulations that were still protecting us. Before the masters used to whip us, now the machines cripple us. They can't do without us, but they drag us along like balls of iron. And we're banished from the newspapers, from the books. Everything has to shine, everything has to smile. We are simply erased from the picture. If they could, they'd erase everything around us that can't be used – the trees, the flowers, the sky. All they would keep would be money and what they can produce with it."

Sam gets up, rattles the door of the chapel, that is firmly locked, then walks along the walls. (Kirstie has almost succeeded, Bailey's member now belongs to her. It doesn't choke her any longer, it tenderly fits into the contours of her mouth, her throat.)

"So it's in there that they see ghosts?"

"Yes," Kirstie says. "Perhaps they'll be there this evening.

To punish us."

"To punish us? No one has the right to punish us."

Sam smiles as he examines a particular part of the wall. "Look, that's where they got in, your ghosts. They put a ladder here and broke the window. Most of the broken glass will be inside but there's one or two bits on the ledge."

"So they weren't ghosts?"

"No, they were the most ordinary kind of men. And they were thirsty," Sam adds, picking up the neck of a bottle.

(While Kirstie continues with her task, Edward Bailey starts to groan. At the same moment there's a knock at the door. Two discreet blows at first, then three more insistent ones. Strange that Mrs Hudson, the landlady, has let someone come up as far as the room.

"Mr Bailey!"

"Oh Lord," Edward says.

Kirstie spits his semen out into her handkerchief.

"Mr Bailey? It's Snegg, sir. I'm sorry to disturb you, but it's essential you come immediately."

***

Still quite listless, Edward follows his clerk and passes Friends' House, where the Quakers meet. At the junction of Skinnergate and Post House Wynd someone hails them, "Hey, Seamus."

He's a little man with a haggard look, who is removing a poster from the door of a block of flats. He and Snegg exchange a few words while Edward, for his part, accustoms himself to the novel idea that Snegg has a Christian name.

"Mr Bailey, may I introduce you to Albert Robinson. Albert, this is Mr Bailey, my employer."

Edward scrutinises the poster, hurriedly printed on poor paper. To make up for that, they didn't stint the glue: despite the flat-bladed knife he's using, the little man isn't getting anywhere.

"It looks to me as if you've still plenty to do, Mr Robinson."

"Who are you telling," the man replies; he's taken off his cap to speak to the gentleman. "And there are some like that all over the town. It's going to take me all week, and that's for sure."

"Is it known who put them up?"

"No, sir. But if only I could get my hands on him... or I mean them, there must be a whole gang of them."

Announcement to the Inhabitants of Darlington!

Would you allow the gates of Hell to open? Would you put up with Beelzebub pouring out his foul stench over our beautiful and pious city? Corpses come out of the bowels of the earth. Poor, restless souls haunt the ancient places of worship. And what is going to happen tomorrow? What new abomination? What new subterfuge of the Prince of Darkness? There is no need, inhabitants of Darlington, to seek for what is responsible for their horrors! Every man, in his soul and conscience, could point the finger at it. The railway, that metal monster, that vehicle of the Foul Fiend will tear apart the thin curtain separating us from the banks of Erebus, dragging us all at full speed to perdition.

Further posters will follow; they will tell you how to use your justified anger.

Amen.

111

"Hmm, it's not that badly written," Edward says, "though in their place I wouldn't have used the word *Erebus*. No one will know what it means."

Cursing, Robinson gets on with his work while Bailey and Snegg continue on their way. They reach High Row and the tall spire of St Cuthbert's, still evoking Edward's memories of his wedding: old Raffle, a cock puffed up with pride strutting round among the Darlington poultry – may he rot in Hell with his digs in the ribs and 'friendly advice'! Fat Mrs Raffle looking at Edward with dismay, as if he'd been wrongly delivered in place of the real husband. Why were they happy to have a simple law student for their son-in-law, the son of an insignificant businessman? And why did they go to London to find him when all the impoverished barons of County Durham were queuing up at their door. Was it because Margaret was already suffering from occasional... 'fits'?

"Do you know, Edward," the old bag had said to him one day, "my daughter is a highly accomplished horsewoman. It's a very simple matter: she's hardly ever seen in Darlington! She's always out galloping over hill and dale, aren't you, Margaret?"

And then again, some time before they were due to return to the north, after the marriage had been decided on, "My God! I wonder how Margaret has managed to survive for *six months* without her daily ride!" Subsequently, when they were established in the North Road house, there had been no mention of going out for a ride. Margaret expressed her total indifference with regard to matters equestrian and the only available mount at the Raffles', a smallish gelding of a phlegmatic disposition bordering on paraplegia, quietly spent its remaining days in a meadow without ever seeing the least sign of a bridle, a saddle or a spur...

Grains of rice thrown on the square outside the church and trampled in the rain of an autumn morning – providing a week's food for the beggars observing the scene with a sceptical air. An interminable meal in the Nag's Head. The only pleasant memory of his wedding remains the pleasant quarter of an hour they spent together before the arrival of the vicar, sitting in the choir stalls with their sardonic misericords: on Margaret's a fawn surrounded by vine leaves; on his an old man asleep.

"This Robinson, is he a friend of yours?"

"A cousin."

Edward and Snegg cross the Market Place. Carts full of vegetables. Two market gardeners are arguing over a site in very flowery language: it looks as if they're about to bombard each other with lettuces and turnips. In various places, on the doors, on the walls, more notices have appeared that Robinson will have to deal with.

"And Mrs Hudson, is she a cousin as well?"

"Let's say the friend of a cousin."

"You have a lot of cousins. Is she the one who told you where I was on Friday morning?"

"No, sir. But it so happens that I live in Bull Wynd and when I'm heading for the chambers I pass you almost every Friday."

"You pass me? But then how is it that I've never seen you?"

In that part of the town there are several houses, that of Dr Trees for example, that date from before the great fire of 1585: red-brick walls, half-timbered above with mullions and lattice windows and on top a system of eaves and roofs with varying slopes that look as if they're telling some complicated story. Edward doesn't dislike the place: perhaps there's something good about the smell of old England after all. Anyway, there is something that tells him to hurry up and breathe it in.

"You know it's very odd," he suddenly goes on. "When I heard your Christian name just now, it was like a revelation. I've known you for nine years, Snegg and I had no idea what you were called. I suspected you had a Christian name, of course, just as I suspect you have a navel and that you eat potatoes from time to time, but that didn't interest me."

"You have lots of other things to concern yourself with, sir…"

"Which things?" Edward asks with a bitter laugh. "Drinking madeira and playing cards with idiots? Disporting myself in Bull Wynd? But Seamus, that's Irish, isn't it? Do you come from there?"

"I don't know, sir, I'm a foundling. Some Catholic nuns took me in and brought me up. They're the ones who called me Seamus."

Edward nods. He's about to ring Dr Trees' bell but suddenly halts, his arm raised. "A foundling? But then how is it that…?"

"They aren't really my cousins, sir, Robinson and the friend of Mrs Hudson."

"I see," says Edward. But he doesn't see anything at all. He stares at Snegg, trying to see behind his look, which his absence of eyebrows somehow makes opaque and fixed, while his lips, so thin they're almost invisible, seem to release every word reluctantly, like opening the cage of a bird that will never return.

"With certain people I meet, something happens. I immediately feel at ease. Those people I call my cousins."

"And the others? Those with whom nothing happens, what do you call them?"

"I don't call them anything. They're the others, that's all. You must ring the bell, Dr Trees said he wouldn't wait after ten o'clock."

Edward complies with a vague tug. "What about me? Where do you put me? With the cousins... or with the others?"

With a gesture that seems totally irrelevant, Snegg pulls his watch out of his waistcoat pocket and checks the time, watching out of the corner of his eye a small dog sniffing a dog turd in the gutter. "You, Mr Bailey, are a sheep that's climbing the hill."

"A sheep that's...?"

The door is opened by Dr Trees himself.

"And how is Margaret?"

Edward can't take his eyes off the big tiled table. The room looks like a greenhouse but doesn't contain any flowers. To make up for that, garden implements are lying around in one corner as is a plaster statue representing some Greek or Roman god that has lost its head and one of those improbable-looking two-wheeled contraptions from Germany, a velocipede. The light is harsh, pitiless, despite the rain trickling down the glass roof, making shimmering reflections in the form of wriggling worms on the tiles of the table and the beaten-earth floor.

"Not very well, Doctor, not very well..."

Very bad. Getting worse and worse. Trees nods sadly and looks round in vain for his snuff. "Believe me, my friend, she's not going to get any better. Let me place her in an appropriate establishment, with Knox in Durham, for example. She'll hardly notice the difference."

"But she has… good moments. Moments when everything seems normal."

"Pah! Now be honest – how many good moments a week? A quarter of an hour here, half an hour there… but your own life is spoilt full time."

"All the same, I'm sure they wouldn't take the dogs…"

"The dogs?" Trees says, not understanding.

Snegg takes a step forward and coughs discreetly. Trees sighs, goes over to the table and puts on his professional voice. "It's a woman. Young in my opinion. The joints are in excellent condition. At least what's left of them. Tell me now, Bailey, I didn't know you were on such good terms with Spalding."

"I'm not. I still don't understand what got into him to call on me."

"He's a vulgar fellow. He has managed to adapt to the spirit of the times but deep down he's not worth much. He complains about his gout while he drinks like a fish and stuffs himself like a pig."

A further cough from Snegg.

Trees frowns. "Not very tall, narrow pelvis."

"Dead for how long?"

"I'd say more than fifteen years, less than forty."

Edward had been expecting to see something vaguely human, not a scattering of remains. Only the skull and the thorax were identifiable to the layman – the doctor had classified the rest according to some mysterious principle, giving the whole the look of a jigsaw puzzle that had just been taken out of the box. Edward presumes the longer bones come from the legs and the arms. Eventually he manages to make out the hands."

"No wedding ring," Snegg points out.

"That means nothing," Trees says. "It could very well have slipped off when the flesh decomposed. There are various parts missing: one ulna, one collarbone, some toes, one humerus."

"Animals?" Edward suggests.

"Or they got lost during transport."

"Impossible. The foreman assured me they collected absolutely everything."

"That's not the transport I mean."

Edward and Snegg exchange looks.

"The bones are still very consistent," the doctor goes on. "It's my opinion that they haven't been in the mud more than a few days. Otherwise the damp would have made them rot and crumble. Which means they were put there recently."

The rain becomes even heavier. It's no longer worms crawling across the table but veritable snakes in a muddle of contortions. Edward's starting to get a headache, as if the flowers that are missing were still giving off a heavy, sickly-sweet odour.

"All that still doesn't help us identify this woman."

"But it does, Bailey. This woman is identified without a shadow of doubt." Trees inserts a short pause for effect. "It is Lady Mathilde Beresford. Look at these two bones. The bigger one is a tibia, the other a fibula. Of the left leg to go by the curvature. I've placed them more or less as they would naturally be. Note the white mark, visible on both of them just above the malleolus: it's the mark of a well-healed double fracture. And there, on the other leg, the same with the tibia."

"So..."

The doctor takes a large notebook with a clasp out of his pocket. "You never knew my father, Bailey."

"No, I never had that honour."

"He was what people call a doctor of the old school. Not very much formal learning, but very sure of what he did know. And a man who would not have shilly-shallied with your poor Margaret."

"Hmm, Hmm," Snegg says.

"In brief a very scrupulous man and with a neat hand – have a look yourselves."

The pages are covered in very neat, almost invisible handwriting and pencil sketches, fairly basic but well executed. At the top left of every page there is a date, a family name and an address. Then comes a description of the pathology, sometimes illustrated with an explanatory diagram, the diagnosis, the prescription. Finally, when there is room left on the page, there is a drawing portraying the patient in an often-comical attitude: a man with thick eyebrows feeling a lump on the top of his head, a woman delighted after having had an abscess lanced.

"There are more than fifty notebooks. The one you have in your hand covers a good half of 1797. My father didn't believe in theories nor in academic manuals. I imagine he wanted to bequeath me his knowledge in the simplest and most efficacious way. Ah! This one's excellent."

'17/3/1797, the Pooles, Abbey Lane. Phlegmy cough with moderate to high fever. Abundant mucus. Throat inflamed. Acute bronchitis. A spoonful of eucalyptus syrup morning and evening.' In the drawing a little boy in tears is trying to escape from two large hands that are holding his head in a firm grip while a third is trying to put a huge spoon in his mouth.

"And look here, Bailey, towards the beginning of April, I think you'll like this."

'4/4/1797, the Raffle residence, North Road. Abdominal distension. Dyspepsia. Laxative.' Edward recognises his father-in-law who, even though surrounded by a cloud representing his intestinal gases, still preserves his air of absolute self-satisfaction.

As he was leafing through the notebook a few minutes later, an intriguing detail caught his eye but he can't find it again. Then Trees takes the notebook from him and opens it on the page for the 8th of October.

'Beresford residence, Wooler Manor. Double fracture tibia/fibula left leg, just above the malleolus, also tibia right leg, resulting from falling off a horse. Reset fractures and attached two splints.'

Snegg gives Edward a questioning look and he confirms with a nod of the head: the quick sketch naturally bears no comparison, either in size or precision, with Henry Spalding's oil painting but there is no shadow of doubt that the model is the same. Her tousled hair, her perfect nose, her dark, almost furious look. Perhaps Trees toned down her cheekbones that were such a feature of the painting – at least assuming that Spalding, blinded by love, hadn't improved them. Edward prefers the first hypothesis.

"It's not conclusive," he said, "lots of people break their legs."

Trees closes the notebook and puts it back in his pocket.

"True, but the combination of the three fractures, two on the left and one on the right, is at least distinctive. In fifteen years as a doctor it's the first time I've come across that."

"And then there's the dagger," Snegg points out. "With the coat of arms of the Beresfords engraved on the handle. By the way, where is it now?"

"Cobbold has kept it as evidence," says Edward grimacing.

"On the other hand," Trees assures them, "the notebook will not go out of this house, I make that a point of honour. I've only met Cobbold once and that was enough. He's the kind of person of whom you dream of plugging his rectum after having administered an enema... if you'll allow the image, of course."

"Despite that you will be obliged to tell him what you have learnt."

"Correction, Bailey: I will be obliged to tell him what I have learnt... from examining the remains within the scope of my duty. I won't tell him about the notebook. Nor about the rest."

Edward suddenly considers the possibility that Trees also has 'cousins' and that he, without realising, is one of them. "And what is this 'rest'?"

With a sibylline smile, Trees opens a large drawer under the tiled table. "Here we have the blouse and dress she was wearing. Frayed, worn out, stained with mud. But you can still clearly see three clear tears in the two garments: one level with the cardiac muscle, two others lower down, over the abdomen."

Snegg leans forward abruptly. Edward has the impression he's trying to get into the drawer. "The size and shape of the tears correspond to a slim blade," he says.

"Yes. But there's one thing that doesn't fit."

Trees scrapes the material round the higher incision with his fingernail, removing particles of dried mud. The silk appears, uniformly yellowed.

"Look: the material is dirty, of course, but not the way it ought to be if a blade had perforated the heart. The blood would have spurted out, impregnating the silk of the blouse and even that of the dress; as it dried it would have formed a thick, very recognisable stain."

As he puzzles over this, Edward puts on a rather comical expression, not far from the one on Titus' face when he found a large lump of coal in his dish instead of meat. As for Snegg, he stares at the velocipede as if it concealed the solution to all the enigmas in the world.

"Corpses don't bleed, gentlemen," Trees says closing the drawer. "In other words: I think this woman was stabbed *after* death."

Returning to the chambers they run into Tom Spalding. His shirt crumpled, his hair tousled, eyes bloodshot, he is watching half a dozen people reading one of the mysterious posters.

"Hi there, T-teddy, there's a th-thing! The whole t-town's t-talking of n-nothing else. It's incredible how many b-bumpkins can read."

"What is really remarkable, Tom, is to find you up before dawn."

"I haven't g-gone to b-bed yet. B-but j-just look at all that, it's like the Jews of Egypt b-before the T-tables of the Law. If I was Stephenson I'd b-be on my guard or they'll be b-boiling him in a cooking pot. Are you c-coming for a quick refresher with me, T-teddy?"

"Thanks but no, Tom. My dictionary doesn't have the same definition of *refresher* as yours."

Leaving Tom to the mental torment of having to choose between the beer of the Bull and that of the Crown, Edward and Snegg go off, each of them immersed in his own speculations. Shortly before they reach the chambers, Edward finally breaks the silence.

"Friend Tom doesn't seem to be one of your cousins... or am I wrong?"

"No, sir. I think he's a very versatile young man, capable of the worst and the best, as they say. My experience is that in that case you can always be sure of the worst."

"Hmm," Edward says, thinking that the description could very well be applied to himself. "But then what was all that stuff about a sheep on a hill? Are you going to tell me what that's about?"

His clerk pauses for a moment, frowning with the part of his physiognomy corresponding to eyebrows. "It was at the orphanage. At Christmas the nuns made a crib with Mary, Joseph and the baby Jesus. Below the crib there was a hill with sheep on it, one for each of the children. When we'd done something naughty our sheep was going down. When we behaved well, it got closer to Christ."

"Ah, so that's it. I'll try to be a good boy. My ultimate goal is to become one of your cousins."

"I'm delighted at that, sir. But that was only a metaphor of course... Oh, I almost forgot. Mr Preston, the squire of Aycliffe was asking for you. He'd like you to go and see him.

Apparently it's important."

"Everything's important, Snegg. It's just a matter of scale."

***

Wooden steps supported by three posts, of which one is bent like the leg of some wading bird, go down the slope of Hungerford Stairs to the Thames. Sitting by the water, Warren's young workers are finishing their lunch, blinking in the sunlight. In front of them are abandoned boats, full of mud, and now and then a rat threading its way under the pontoon or between two bits of rubbish. Behind them the factory is asleep, slowly digesting the cries, the laughter, the bellowing of Phibes, the foreman, and the hundreds of jars of blacking that had been labelled in the course of the morning. The broad black band of the Thames refuses to shine.

"How about Dickens finishing off his story?" someone suggests.

In a trice they're all gathered round Charley, who is mentally rummaging through his stock of stories of the fantastic: patchworks derived from his reading, sewn together with the thread of his imagination. He can only vaguely remember yesterday's patchwork, but since the break lasts barely half an hour he feels perfectly capable of keeping up his improvisation until the bell sounds.

"Well then, Saladin was still trying to remember the magic word that would make the genie come out of the cave: 'Open says me!' No response. 'O pensive army!' To no effect. 'Jar of blacking, open up!' Still nothing."

As he continues his enumeration, Charley notes that each

magic word evokes a different response. At *pensive army* they all reman stonily silent while *jar of blacking* gets a few laughs.

" 'Open, O billy can!' and 'Open, O big toothless mouth of Mr Phibes!' "

Now several of the boys burst out laughing.

"Then there was a great cloud of grey smoke, like when Mr Warren chokes on his cigar, and the genie appeared before Saladin. He was wearing a striped waistcoat, a coachman's gaiters and a top hat."

"Did they have hats like that, the Persies?" one boy asks.

"We say Persians," Charley tells him. "But the genie can travel through time. Nothing can stop him coming to buy a hat in Pall Mall if he feels like it."

"Of course," a tall hefty lad with ginger hair agrees.

" 'Here I am,' the genie says. 'In the flesh... as my grandmother used to say, who had far too much of it.' "

As they gradually get the joke, or are simply carried along by others, the little workers laugh fit to burst. Words talk to each other, Charley thinks. There's a language inside language, like an underground city replicating the visible city with its tunnels and passageways. If you know the plan of the labyrinth you can pop up in people's minds at any moment and take control of them.

" 'Genie,' Saladin demands, 'you must go to the assistance of the beautiful Princess Sémirazade (saucy whistles and hands making curvaceous shapes in the air) that the vile Sultan Blifil (Boooo!) is keeping prisoner in his palace.'

" 'Immediately, Master, immediately. And even in a flash, as the executioner said as he sharpened his axe.' "

The boys, too occupied with laughing and slapping

their thighs, haven't heard the bell, but none can ignore the bellowing of Phibes, who pops out of his window like an abominable cuckoo, "Hey, you lot!"

"Close yourself, O great toothless mouth of Mr Phibes," the tall redhead whispers, setting off one last burst of laughter.

"The new delivery of labels is late. That means the afternoon is off for everyone. Unpaid, of course. Now off you all go."

A huge outburst of joy makes the seagulls take off from the pontoon, sends the rats scampering off along the cul-de-sac; the boys, still yelling, run up as far as the Strand where they separate, some heading in the direction of Charing Cross, others towards Drury Lane. Charley only stops to get his breath back on Waterloo Bridge. Free. Free, free! The word echoes round inside his skull, setting his heart beating twice as fast. There, on the bridge, his nose in the air, he feels both tiny and huge. Tiny as a blade of grass carried off by the river. Huge as a Titan whose veins are called Pall Mall. The Strand. Piccadilly.

It's only when he reaches the walls of the Marshalsea that it dawns on Charley how grotesque his situation is: he's going to spend his 'free' afternoon… in prison.

"Charles! My dear boy! The Dickens family is now complete, thank God."

John Dickens prepares to declaim something, but can't remember the verse in question, so limits himself to an embrace. The 'Guvnor', as they call him, with his curly hair and sideburns, his puffed-up chest, his expansive gestures and lips fixed in an aristocratic sneer, resembles an actor of the old school who had been handed the role of the Miles Gloriosus by mistake.

The cell – though that word is hardly ever used in the Marshalsea – contains two beds along the side walls, a table in the middle, a rudimentary washstand fitted in below the window, two mattresses on the floor, a tiny fireplace that draws badly and now seven people who would trample all over each other if they were all to follow the example of John Dickens and stride up and down the room. Sitting on one of the beds between his sister Letitia, eight, who is digging her dirty fingernails into his eyes, and his brother Frederick, four, whose snot is dripping down onto his trousers while his other brother, Alfred, two, is trying to climb up his back using his hair as a rope, Charley looks enviously at the bed opposite, where his mother and elder sister are sitting comfortably.

"Your sister Emily has passed her examinations at the music school," says Elizabeth Dickens, fanning herself with her book, *How to be a Perfect Housewife*.

"And I stuck five hundred labels on jars of blacking, with revolting glue in a foul factory," Charles retorts inwardly.

"Ladies and gentlemen," the Guvnor chinks his metal tumbler with a spoon, "I think it is an appropriate moment for a toast in the authentic tradition of old England for which the whole world envies us. Elizabeth, my dear, would you be so obliging as to slip your adorable hand down between the wall and the bed. There! That's precisely the place."

"Oh, come now, John, can we afford it?" Mrs Dickens asks, pulling out a bottle of port.

"Of course, we can. If there is, in this odious prison or anywhere else in the kingdom, someone stupid enough to claim that the Dickens family will not recover from its temporary difficulties and will not rise again like the phoenix to enjoy in full its ancestral prerogatives, let him dare to come forward, just let him dare! Something will eventually turn up, I'm sure of that, this modest amphora is merely a ridiculously small advance of the river of hippocras that will soon come flowing towards us."

Alfred has completed his ascent and now has his arms tight round Charley's neck while Letitia is exploring his nostrils with two cleverly forked fingers and Frederick is playing with the Guvnor's razor and Elizabeth, watching him with exasperation, is fanning herself for all she's worth. Charley has the feeling he no longer exists as a human being but solely as a constituent part of this noisy, swaying multicoloured mass that fills the room and goes by the name of *Dickens*.

"While waiting for the river, John," his mother says, "I have to point out that we lack certain indispensable items…"

"For example, my beloved?"

"A corkscrew."

The Guvnor is preparing to deliver a lament worthy of Hamlet when Letitia jumps off the bed and starts to stamp her feet shouting, "The Corporal, Papa, the Corporal!"

"You see, my dear," says John Dickens, "the family is never short of expedients. I'll just nip over to see the Corporal."

"Oh, Guvnor, let me go. Please!"

"No question of that, Charles," Mrs Dickens decrees.

"Oh, come now, Elizabeth. This boy needs his education. Remember, Charles: the fact that your paternal grandfather was the collaborator – what am I saying, the confidant – of a peer of the realm…"

"His servant," Elizabeth mutters between clenched teeth.

"…this fact, as I was saying, should do nothing to diminish our proverbial broad-mindedness nor our total lack of condescension towards the lower classes. Off you go, Charley, and don't forget to offer a libation to the Corporal."

It was time. Charley couldn't have stood it a second longer. He goes out onto the narrow wooden landing and breathes in deeply.

The barracks of the Marshalsea have no corridors. There are two buildings, one giving onto Angel Alley and the other onto the prison courtyard; the rooms are only accessible from two series of eight external staircases, each of which serves the three floors. The sun is shining and the usual activities of the prisoners are in full swing in the courtyard. There is talking in loud voices, walking up and down, entering or leaving the bar from which drinking songs ring out, and when a ball knocks down all the skittles there's much shouting, laughter and slapping of thighs. But there's something that's not quite right. All the bustle seems spurious, the delight put on, as if the beer served in the bar was not really beer, as if none of these people had the means to afford true laughter.

Over the wall Charley can see part of the graveyard of St George the Martyr, with turtledoves mounting guard on the gravestones. On this side of the wall a metal tube sticks up out of the ground, the sole ventilation for the cellar where poor wretches sometimes vegetate for months on end while waiting for confirmation of their insolvency. If you stick your ear to the tube you can hear strange sounds, inarticulate murmurs coming from underground – you'd say the voices of the dead. "John," Elizabeth Dickens said to her husband one day, "if your mother doesn't hurry up and die and leave us her inheritance, we'll all of us end up down there, in the cellars!"

Charley shivers, then, bottle in hand, he goes down into the courtyard and up the next staircase to the third floor and knocks on the door.

"Come in!"

Thanks to the half-pay he still receives, the Corporal has the luxury of a single room, exceedingly rare in the Marshalsea. Stretched out on his bed, arms folded under an old cape, he receives Charles with a frown.

"And what's *this*?"

"This is Charles Dickens, sir."

"Good Lord! Another one! How many are there in your family then?"

The Corporal's military voice and brusque manner contrast with his general affability. His skin is dark and wrinkled, his lips firm and there is a mischievous glint in his eye.

"Five children. Two others died."

"That's far too many! How can we get the poor of this country to see that having children is a luxury? And you are number…?"

"Two, sir. But we're not poor," Charles quickly adds.

"You aren't? Then what are you all doing in prison for debts? Are you taking a holiday?"

"My father has the habit of saying that we just happen to have got stuck in a… rut, but that something will turn up soon to put us back on the right track."

"A rut, eh?" The Corporal bursts out laughing, but with no malice behind it. "He must have kissed the blarney stone, your father, but he has a certain style. If he was a little less narrow-minded as far as politics is concerned… well then, Number

Two, I accept your existence and I will even grant you an interview. What can I do for you?"

Timidly Charles holds out the bottle that he had so far been holding behind his back. The Corporal's eyes sparkle. It's as if a sixth sense had suddenly woken up in some corner of his brain.

"Oho! A serious business."

"It seems that you have a corkscrew, sir."

"That's enough of the sir, call me Corporal. And, correction: I haven't got a corkscrew... *I am* a corkscrew!"

Without giving Charles time to wonder about this, the Corporal takes his arms out from under the cloak. The left one has been cut off at the wrist. Fixed to a metal cuff and replacing the missing hand, a corkscrew appears, ready to oblige.

"Were you frightened?"

"No, s... er Corporal. It was just a surprise."

"Why? The streets are full of one-armed men since the war."

"That's true, there are two begging in Drury Lane... but they have hooks at the end."

"Hook, corkscrew, what's the difference? If the government paid them a decent pension, they'd have nice little hands of solid gold. Come over here and put the bottle right on the tip of the point. There you are! Now turn it, pushing as hard as you can. The other way, for God's sake, the other way. Good. Now let me get on with it."

The Corporal sits on the side of the bed, wedges the bottom of the bottle between his thighs and grips the cuff with his good hand and starts to pull. After a few seconds the cork gives up the ghost with a satisfying plop.

"Perfect. Contrary to appearances, I've not entirely lost my hand…"

"My father invites you to drink to his health, Corporal."

"It's the least he can do. Get those two glasses over there and pour in enough to drink a toast to the rut into which we've all fallen. Your good health, Number Two."

Charley discovers port in two stages. First of all it turns his stomach. The alcohol leaves a feeling of fire and gall on his throat. Then it goes to his head, giving him a sudden, brief, sparkling sense of pleasure.

"Not bad," says the Corporal. I don't know how he manages to find that sort of lemonade in the Marshalsea. Good. Now let's have a chat. In general two men drinking together chat. That's what's called good manners."

"Tell me about Waterloo."

"Waterloo, of course! It's always Waterloo. On my deathbed they'll be asking me to tell them about Waterloo."

Charles takes a second mouthful. The fire remains but the gall turns to honey.

"Hey! Go easy on that port. What do you want to know about Waterloo?"

"Is it true that – ?"

"Nothing's true!" the Corporal cuts in, sitting up abruptly. "Nothing of what they tell you in the books.

He starts walking up and down the tiny room. As much to make room for him as because his legs feel a bit wobbly, Charley drops down on the bed.

"But after all it was the greatest victory for England!"

The Corporal sniggers. "Victory, defeat, they're just words people use afterwards, the way you baptise a child. But a battle is just a blind animal, with no truth, no goal, no conscience. And one shouldn't baptise animals. That's what the books don't say. They don't say that in the middle of the great battle there's thousands of little battles starting and finishing every second. And the painters portraying the scene, nice and warm in their studio, don't see the thousands of images frozen in the eyes of the dead... for me that battle isn't Waterloo, as it was called by that dandy Wellington, nor Mont-Saint-Jean, as the French say, it's Hougoumont."

"Hougoumont?"

Charles quietly drinks another mouthful as the Corporal turns away towards the door. The invasive tactics of the port have reached their third stage. A slight compression of the skull. Little bursts of pleasure-pain between his eyebrows. He has to stop himself laughing – he feels the word *Hougoumont* is the funniest thing that ever existed.

"A farm, just a farm. Hastily fortified. Situated between the two lines, but occupied by the Allies, and the place where Bonaparte took it into his head to launch a diversionary attack. I was a hussar of the Fifteenth Regiment, together with John Lange. His father was my father's employer, on a large estate near Manchester. My mother had been his nursemaid, we'd grown up together, we were almost like brothers; at least he kept on telling me he felt closer to me than to Alfred, his elder brother, the heir to the estate. John had two horses just for himself and he let me ride Duke, the one he liked less – that was why I served in the hussars and not with the footsloggers. And it's thanks to John Lange that I could take part in all that butchery without ever being afraid of dying alone, knowing that, if the great moment were to come, I would always have the eye of a friend to hold on to.

"So to cut a long story short: the Nassauers were holding the farm and we were sent as reinforcements. Only the problem was, some idiot with stripes hadn't done his homework. My brigade set off much too far to the west, against the slope, then turned off to the right, heading straight for the bulk of the enemy forces, instead of returning to the farm. Just before passing through a wood we were torn to pieces by the French artillery.

"And that," Charles said in a woozy voice, "was where you lost your hand…"

"No. Not my hand, my horse, killed by a cannonball. And I fell unconscious. When I woke I had a nasty head-wound. The centre of the battle had moved to the east, towards Haye-Sainte and Papelotte. On our side there were only the dead left. Men and horses. Apart from my friend, John Lange – I looked for him but he must have managed to rejoin our troops. The only living being with me in the woods was a Frenchman. He was called Robert Dumont."

"You… talked to him?"

"First we just looked at each other. His brigade had beaten the retreat after a pointless attack on Hougoumont. He was wounded as well, in the leg. But he still had his sabre, as did I. But we didn't know what to do. Charge each other like that, one against one? What effect would that have on the outcome of the battle? The Frenchie dropped his sabre. And so did I. And then we talked, yes, what else could we do? With my few words of French and his few words of English. Waiting for someone to come. And do you know what the remarkable thing was? In civilian life he was a printer, just like me. A

Jacobin from the very beginning, a sans-culotte, in the Pike Platoon. He'd been there at the storming of the Tuileries."

Charles, who was starting to feel drowsy, suddenly exclaimed, "A Jacobin?"

When the workers at the naval dockyards went on strike or when demonstrators demanded a maximum price for bread, the Guvnor would always say with a knowing air, 'These Jacobins are stirring the people up against us.' That was exactly what he said: *against us*. As if the Dickens had a very close relationship with the Prince Regent.

The Corporal comes over and stands right in front of Charles, lifting up his chin with the corkscrew. "I don't know what rubbish they've stuffed your brain with, but now you're a man and you have to think for yourself. The true Jacobins didn't like the war, they simply wanted to defend their revolution and their republic."

"But…"

"The stretcher-bearers found us the next morning. Dumont was taken prisoner, I never saw him again. I had a high fever, I almost died. I was demobilised and went back to Manchester. And now, when I think of Waterloo, I see two printers sitting round a fire, in the dark. I hear them talking about type and forms and Garamond surrounded by dead bodies."

"But who then?" Charles asks, trying to keep his scattered thoughts together, just as you hold the broken pieces of a vase together. "Who did it?"

"Who did what?"

"That Robert… Dumont. He wasn't the one who…?"

There's a knock at the door. His one hand on the doorknob, the Corporal gives Charles a long, hard look with a funny smile.

"Who disabled me? No, it wasn't Robert Dumont. It was my best friend, John Lange... Good evening, Mr Dickens. I'm very much afraid your second offspring is having some difficulty digesting my history lesson. His head's spinning."

***

Margaret Bailey is feeling calm, just the same as when she was little and the *other girl* was still her friend. The *other girl* would smile at her from the mirror and take the brush out of her hand to finish disentangling her hair. Then the *other girl* started coming more and more often, Margaret saw her everywhere, not just in the mirror. *She* would hide her ribbons. *She* would move her dolls. Old Dr Trees called this 'having fits,' pronouncing the words cautiously, with tact, but her mother preferred to talk of 'moments'.

"There is no *other girl*," Doctor Trees said, "you have too much imagination. "You're tired," Mrs Raffle would say, "It's because you're growing." Her father would say nothing but make the gesture of throwing something over his shoulder and stride off.

Trees prescribed camomile tea, boiled vegetables and warm baths, Mrs Raffle made her lie down after every meal, Mr Raffle advised her to forget about it – but none of these measures prevented the *other girl* from appearing more and more often, from crawling inside her skin, from trying to cry through her lips. Then there was Halnaby. Then her parents died and the *other girl* more or less never left her.

But today Margaret has heard Snegg's voice. She likes Snegg very much, she's always liked him. It gives her the strength to get up, get dressed, go down to the drawing room and say something nice to Edward. To take up her embroidery again after a month's break.

Bother! She's just put in three red crosses, while the dog's collar ought to be blue. And Titus' eyes are red too. Start again.

"Just listen to this, Snegg," Edward says, giving the newspaper he's reading a contemptuous slap. " 'According to reliable information that has been reported to us, the last crusade of our great national bard is turning into a masquerade...' The bastards!"

"Mr Bailey, I've never understood why you buy the papers of your enemies."

"Because it stirs my blood. It goes on: 'One of these famous *Philhellene* volunteers, having recovered his wits and his common sense, has just returned to London and given us a tragicomic account of Lord Byron's *epic*...' "

The needle in Margaret's hand freezes.

" 'So there are our heroes, rotting away for several weeks beside a lagoon, forced to fraternise with a squad of many-coloured Greeks: sinister militia, alcoholic tribal chiefs, and 'democratic' swordsmen. The air down there is unhealthy, the miasma from the lagoon supports an army of mosquitos – certainly the most well-organised and ruthless army of this campaign with no battles... moreover the Turks might not even have to fight, leaving the task of decimating their pathetic adversaries to various exotic diseases...' "

Margaret starts: the needle, slipping, has just stuck in the pad of her forefinger. There's a drop of blood. More red.

"How appalling!" Edward exclaims. "To mock courageous men who are risking their lives for an ideal like that!"

"True, true," his clerk says, watching Margaret out of the corner of his eye. "But does England have any lack of causes to fight for? Why go so far away?"

"Don't start reasoning with me, you know it gives me a headache. All that I can see is that... Good Lord, I missed the last paragraph: 'According to our informant, Lord Byron himself is seriously ill with marsh fever.' I don't believe it. It's a lie put about by the Tories! 'He is already suffering from an infection contracted in Venice or Naples, and his weak constitution...' Don't you feel well. Margaret?"

She has stood up abruptly, her embroidery slipping down to her feet. Her face is ashen and for a few seconds all that can be seen is the whites of her eyes. Edward leaps up.

"My God, Margaret, we'll take you to your room."

"No, everything's fine. Just a dizzy spell. It's late. I'm not used to staying up like this any longer. I need some sleep, that's all. Good night."

"Good Lord, what can that mean? Every time I mention Byron's name, she starts. And she's a woman who's never read a line of his."

Soon the Raffles' clock strikes midnight, the ash tray is full, the bottle empty. Edward has smoked too much, drunk too much Madeira and he can hardly see Snegg in the cloud of smoke from the cigar he's just put out: his mind is both clear and surrounded by blackness, like a tiny match that only shows itself being consumed. Hanging in their frames on the wall, the Raffles look down on him out of their bulging eyes.

"To sum up: someone dug up a skeleton and, after having slashed it a few times with a knife, transported it in a wheelbarrow to a place where it was bound to be discovered. Why?"

"So that it would be found, of course," says Snegg, waving away the last clouds of Havana. "And to hamper those who find it."

"True. And that's what did happen. And those damned posters are all over the walls of Darlington. It looks like a put-up job, but then…"

Edward breaks off, thinking he heard a noise from the room above, Margaret's bedroom. But no, everything's totally silent. The ridiculously red-embroidered replica of Titus on the floor is showing its teeth.

"And at the same time it's not just any old skeleton. It's that of a woman who disappeared twenty-five years ago, under suspicious circumstances. So we have to assume that those who staged this macabre event know a lot about the mystery of Wooler Manor, or want to make people think they do. That they want to disrupt Stephenson's work and *at the same time* attract attention to a possible crime. Now there are reasons of chronology that tell us that there can be no connection between those two elements. And then, why those dagger thrusts? Who could have any interest *today* in reviving the theory that Mathilde Beresford was murdered?"

Snegg shrugs his shoulders as a sign that he has no answer to the question. Grandfather Raffle, the one who played the horses, stifles a yawn.

"And then there is Trees' notebook. An idea crossed my mind while I was holding it in my hand. It was a very unpleasant sensation. A bit like hearing a knock at the door and then finding no one outside. Or going into a shop and not being able to remember what it was you needed to buy."

"You can borrow it from the doctor, then it'll come back to you."

"But I don't even know what I'm looking for. Perhaps it's just my imagination playing a nasty trick on me"

His clerk makes a steeple of his fingers and stares at the fire for a good while. He almost looks as if he's trying to persuade it to blaze up again. And, anyway, it suddenly seems to feel warmer in the room: the fiery potential of the madeira has just made itself felt in Edward's stomach.

"Let's put conjecture aside," Snegg says abruptly, "and follow the threads we do have. In my opinion a trip to Bishop Auckland is imperative."

"The mines?! Huh! Why should we go and waste our time there?"

Snegg gives his employer an indulgent look. Edward's interpretation is that his sheep has tumbled down its hill a little.

"You remember the Beresfords' coachman, Mr Bailey…"

"The one who's dead? Why? Have you brought him back to life?"

"Not exactly, but…"

"Then what connection does this have with the mine?"

"Don't people say that you have to dig deep to find the truth."

V

The Joanna

The office of Edward Pease, principal shareholder in the Stockton & Darlington Railway Company, gives an impression of opulence. Even though he's a Quaker, it is clear to see that the banker appreciates elegant objects: plaster busts in the classical style representing people Stephenson cannot identify, finely worked consoles supporting exotic plants the engineer doesn't know either and, above all, expensive armchairs such as the huge example facing the desk. Stephenson would never have thought a single posterior could fill it entirely until Gregson enters the room.

"Do sit down, Mr Gregson," the Quaker says.

But Mr Gregson doesn't sit down. Frowning and pursing his lips, he scrutinises Stephenson from head to toe.

"A word first. Is it not the case that you have registered a patent for cast-iron rails and that you have shares in Mr Losh's company that makes them?"

"That is perfectly correct."

Gregson rolls his eyes then quickly takes out a handkerchief and pats his forehead, though that seems to be more of a tic than necessitated by sweat.

"Then why come to me, thus losing several hundred pounds?"

Stephenson wiggles his fingers to calm the irritation that has taken hold of him. He reminds himself of how his father used to talk to animals, especially to the neighbours' vicious mongrel that would bare its teeth: in a calm, steady voice and a little more quietly than usual.

"I think that malleable cast iron produced according to Birkinshaw's patent is superior to my own, Mr Gregson, and you are the only person who can supply it to us in sufficient quantity."

His words seem to take some time to get through to Gregson, who weighs them at length as if he had a highly sensitive pair of scales in his inner ear. Then his face gradually relaxes and he gives a sigh such as the vicious mongrel did when it went back into its kennel; his legs manoeuvre his posterior into a suitable position and he drops into the armchair, causing it to emit a squawk. Pease looks away.

"So that's it! I assumed it was an underhand trick, but it isn't. You're simply… honest!"

He pronounces the word with amazement, like a mushroom gatherer finding a very rare species.

"It appears that you're not a Quaker, like our friend here. He has a nose for business."

"There is nothing that forbids earning money as long as you obey God's commandments," Pease rejoins.

"Of course, of course… but still, what a lot of bankers you have in your congregation!"

"You mustn't forget that many other professions are

141

forbidden to us."

"Now then! I know what the situation is. You refuse to take oaths… but that's convenient for you, isn't it? It allows you to exercise your talents… a bit like the Jews."

Pease, flushed with anger, rummages round among his papers. Gregson leans forward, bracing himself on the armrests. "Right then," he says, visibly satisfied with the preliminaries, "let's get down to business."

Stephenson looks at Pease, who flutters his eyelashes encouragingly.

"Our project, Mr Gregson, goes beyond anything that has previously been done in railway development. Not only will the Stockton to Darlington line facilitate the transport of coal to the sea, which was our principal objective, but it will also make an impression on the wider public by being the first line carrying passengers. We have already built the first railway bridge in the world, across the Gaunless, and the two inclines at Etherley and Brusselton will themselves be technical marvels that no one was even dreaming of just ten years ago. For my part I believe that innovations should contribute to the good of all, not simply to the enrichment of certain…"

Gregson sniffs impatiently, his eyes flitting one way then the other. Stephenson has to force himself to go on. "The possibilities for passenger transport are infinite. A line between Manchester and Liverpool is already being envisaged. Thousands of men, whose horizon was limited to a few hills, will be able to discover the world around them. Families that are separated will be able to get together again. My father only saw the sea two or three times in his life, even though we lived just a few miles away from it. With the railway I…"

"All that is well and good, Stephenson, but at the moment the two of us are here: you to place an order and me to satisfy it, making as much money as possible in so doing. Pease?"

The Quaker has calmed down. He holds a sheet of paper out to Gregson, who raises his eyebrows and gives a long whistle. "One thousand five hundred tons! You will have them. In three months time."

"There's no hurry, Mr Gregson," Pease interjects. "We will only start laying them…"

"Hush, man. Now is the moment when economic conditions are favourable. There's no work, the men are starving. They're ready to slave away for half a potato, but once the imbecile owners of the mine understand the godsend the railway will be for them, they'll start taking men on again and wages will rise in all areas of business, it goes like clockwork. Here is what I propose: fifteen pounds a ton, payable on delivery in three months' time. You do have the money, Pease, that I know. Which do you prefer: fifteen pounds in three months, or thirty, perhaps even forty, in the autumn?"

It's Stephenson's turn to flush. He's about to reply, but Pease beats him to it by a whisker. "That's a very generous offer. Fifteen pounds a ton. I think Mr Gregson is making a great effort to accommodate us and his offer deserves to be considered seriously, don't you agree, George?"

George respects Edward Pease, his judgment, his honesty, his work ethic. But the word 'generous' sticks in his throat. The Quaker rolls his eyes at him and he knows what that means: 'Be reasonable, George, the viability of our project is not assured. You're the visionary, I'm the financier. Let me finance your project in my own way.'

How would his father have reacted? Robert Stephenson systematically refused all promotions, avoided all honours: the position as head mechanic as well as that of secretary of the miners' Friends Society and even the schoolmasters' invitation to talk to the pupils about ornithology. George always thought he was too modest, frightened of responsibility, but now he's suddenly wondering whether it was part of a simple but effective strategy to retain his freedom, devoting his evenings to his family and his old copy of *Robinson Crusoe*, his Sundays to the birds of the surrounding area and, above all, never coming into contact with people of Gregson's kind.

Gregson looks back and forth between Pease and Stephenson with a smile on his face. "We can meet later to sort out the details. I've found my old friend Cobbold again. As you will know, we both come from Manchester. I'm staying in the town for a day or two, come and join me in my hotel."

"Tomorrow," Pease tells him. "I'm sure everything will be in order by tomorrow."

The business settled, Gregson relaxes. Now that he's eaten up all the flesh, gnawed the bones down to the marrow, he feels like amusing himself with a few tufts of hair fluttering in the wind. Pursing his lips slightly, he subjects the engineer to careful scrutiny.

"You've never been tempted by politics, Stephenson?"

"Never."

"Pity. Well-to-do people would vote for you because your projects are making them even richer, ordinary people because you come from the same background. I could get you elected on any ticket you like, Whig, Tory or even fairground barker if that appeals to you."

"I like things that are well made, Mr Gregson. Politics is a profession I know nothing about."

"Pah! In the old days you perhaps needed a certain skill. You had to keep the poor in their mud and, above all, to persuade people like us, the creators of wealth, to surrender the fruits of their labour to a load of corrupt idlers. But today everything goes smoothly. The entrepreneurs are working for their own benefit, the old propertied classes leave us alone on condition we don't touch their income, nor their estates, nor their game preserves and that we offer them juicy shares in our enterprises. As for the poor, it's their own fault if they remain poor – of which you yourself are living proof. The market manages the world for us. All the politicians have to do is simply to vote for the measures that favour their own affairs."

In support of this feat of reasoning Gregson performs a lively minuet with the carefully manicured fingers of both hands. Then, with an 'oof' worthy of a lumberjack, he hauls up his hindquarters into a vertical position. "Oh! Before I forget. I met one of your lads on the site. Tall and skinny with a cap and scar across his forehead."

"Sam Davies. I'm thinking of making him foreman of the second squad."

"Get rid of him."

Stephenson tries to catch the Quaker's eye, but he's never seemed so absorbed in his paperwork.

"And why should I part with one of my best workmen."

"Because he's dangerous."

"In what way?"

Gregson turns his back on him and hands on knees leans forward to examine one of the plaster busts. For a few seconds all that is seen of him are his buttocks topped by a tuft of grey hair.

"I belong to the Manchester Yeomanry. If Colonel L'Estrange hadn't put several spokes in our wheel with his tuppeny-ha'penny military principles we'd have made mincemeat of that radical vermin. Alas, things being the way they are, a lot of them escaped, and I'm sure your Davies was one of them. That fellow is a time bomb. In you own interest I will speak to Cobbold about him – he'll know what is to be done."

"I can do without the help of Cobbold, Mr Gregson. I appreciate your concern, but…"

But the discussion is over. Without turning round Gregson sketches a vague gesture as a farewell. He opens the door and, without closing it, starts to negotiate a tricky bend on Pease's staircase, that emits a shriek under his weight, as did the armchair previously.

The Quaker finally looks up. "Don't say anything, George, I know what you're thinking. I don't like him either, but in business there are rules that have to be respected. As long as private interests do not run counter to the general interest…"

Stephenson doesn't reply. But he would very much like someone to give him a clear, precise definition of the general interest.

"I'm keeping Davies," he says, picking up his hat.

***

It could be a religious procession but there is no priest leading it. A march past by demonstrators, but they keep their lips tightly shut. The resurrection of the dead, since they come up out of the ground, but they hardly seem to be alive. A few seconds ago the steam engine that operates the cage emitted a terrible wail and, as if that was the signal, they emerged from the pit in single file, slightly bent, even the children. They're covered in coal dust. The rain trickling down their faces doesn't really clean them, it leaves them daubed in soot and grime. It also covers the surroundings in a thin, sticky film, dulls the outlines of the slag heap, splashes down on the wooden rails where the last cart is slithering along, pulled by four black snorting horses, their blinkers looking like giant glaucomas.

"It's a spectacle that ought to be shown to those who glorify British industry. Let them see something of what the greatness of our Empire is based on," Edward declares.

"Mines have existed since the days of Classical Antiquity, Mr Bailey. In Laurium the miners rarely survived more than a year…"

"But they were slaves, Snegg."

"…and here, in Bishop Auckland, they've been extracting coal since the seventeenth century."

"My answer remains the same. For the powerful men of the time, slaves, serfs, weren't full men. They sent them to their death without batting an eyelid, then replaced them like changing a drive belt. But it's 1824 now."

"Slavery still exists in some of our colonies…"

"And it's a disgrace! But not in England. These men are Englishmen, born free like you and me. They have the right to a decent life. Not to mention the children…"

"Coal is useful for society, someone has to go down there to get it. Clearly it's a pity it doesn't grow among the daffodils in the meadows..."

"Are you trying to provoke me, Snegg? Playing the devil's advocate, is that what you're at?"

The jet of steam has hardly stopped than a few rooks, in search of warmth and an observation post, come down to perch on the funnel of the engine, where they peck at each other greedily. Inadequately sheltered by the hood of their carriage, the two men slump back into their damp seat. It smells of wet leather, weariness and discomfort.

"The devil hardly needs an advocate, alas. I'm simply trying to weigh up the pros and cons. I will simply mention that Duddle's firm installed a coal-burning stove in the chambers last week because you thought the open fires didn't give off enough heat. That this morning you probably ate bread made from flour ground by a steam-driven machine – therefore fed by coal, the same as the one that grinds the barley for your whisky..."

"I don't drink whisky, I prefer madeira."

"The Portuguese wine-makers keep their madeira heated for three months, that's what gives it its special flavour. I assume that nowadays they use coal for their ovens. Moreover I have to remind you that during the nine years we've been acquainted you've never expressed the slightest reservation about the extraction of coal and I had to drag you here – against your will because mines, as you said, were 'dirty and stinking' and that you 'had no business' to be there."

They look at each other, which is made difficult because of the rain dripping down off their hats.

"All right, Snegg, you win. I'm a filthy little egoist with a big mouth but small in all other respects... but that doesn't mean..."

The miners have come out of the gate and, passing some twenty yards away from their carriage, start walking up a steep path that leads to the village, grimacing from the effort. Some are shaking from a hoarse cough and stop every ten steps to get their breath back. The children, their little faces blurred and daubed with black, look like old men. Some seem to be smiling, but that's only a chance result of the layer of coal dust drawing their lips up. At the top of the rise the shacks of the village still seem very far away. There is a line of them stretching along a curve of the track, all the same, like the rings of a large snake.

"That doesn't stop me finding the sight... harrowing."

"Harrowing, yes," Snegg agrees softly. Then he gestures in the direction of one of the miners. Edward wonders how he could identify anyone beneath these anonymous masks, but that is what he did. A young man slowly peels off from the procession and walks over towards them. Like all the others he has a haversack slung over his shoulder with his pickaxe and his spade.

"William."

"Mr Snegg."

"It's been a hard day, I'm sure."

"Na worse nor yestreen."

"Fire damp?"

"Nay. Aw'm kep'n ma fingers crossed."

"What is it you do? Do you cut the coal?"

"Aw divvent nae mair. Wi' a' the hewin aw dislicated ma shoalder. Luckly th'owerman laikes me. He's put me tae work on toap."

Edward stares at him, wide-eyed.

"That's good. Is it up there?" Snegg asks.

"Nay, in th'aald village. Yon road there on th'rait. But sin her uncle died aw dinna think Jean's rait in the heid nae mair."

"We'll try to make do with what's left to her. Thanks, William."

The young man goes back to join his workmates and while Snegg steers the carriage onto the rutted track, Edward huddles up in his corner even more. "I didn't understand a single word of your conversation, Snegg! I could have been listening to Chinese."

"It's the pitmen's dialect, sir."

"Then how the hell did you come to understand it?"

"Because I was a miner myself for a few months. I was ten years old and..."

"Ten?"

"...I'd just run away from the orphanage."

"Why ever did you do that?"

"Well... how should I put it? I was what they call strong-minded."

Snegg, inscrutable, concentrates on driving. He avoids the deeper ruts and from time to time gives the horse a word of encouragement.

"I wanted to see the country... at least I saw what was underneath it. The children are very useful in the mines. In the first place they have good sight and then they can worm their way into the narrowest staples.

"Staples?"

"Secondary galleries that are dug for prospecting, or to link the principal ones. That was a long time ago – Stephenson hadn't yet invented the Geordie lamp."

"Just a minute! Not so quick. What's a Geordie lamp?"

"A safety lamp that doesn't make the fire-damp explode. But in my day we only had ordinary oil lamps, sometimes even simple candles. At the least escape of gas you were blown up."

"And was that George Stephenson? The man making the railway?"

"The very same. Thanks to that lamp several lives are saved everyday. I remember that almost all the miners used to keep a lucky charm in their pocket to protect them against rockslides and firedamp explosions: a rabbit's foot, a medal, a piece of cloth. Anything. The lucky charm often became their surname. They would call each other 'Rabbit's foot,' 'Cloth' etc. As for me, I had nothing of the kind, so they called me 'None'."

The old village appears beyond a grove of trees, a group of six or seven ruined houses surrounded by brambles; it's doubtless a quarter of a mile away, but the grey sky, the heavy rain falling with the regularity of a cascade make it difficult to estimate the distance. The horse can hardly drag the carriage through the dreary mud and soon a pile of branches blocks the way.

"One day when I was crawling along an exploratory gallery looking for a new seam, a voice sounded behind me, 'None, where are you? The foreman wants you.' "

The two men get out of the carriage and start to clear the way. The cold of the rain seems to creep straight into their bones, their clothes are stiff and heavy, and Edward wonders what he's doing there. He also wonders why some boys of ten are crawling through the darkness thirty feet underground while others are quietly learning their multiplication tables in a nice warm classroom. Why the George Stephensons are trying to improve their lot while the Edward Baileys spend their time drinking madeira. Eventually he wonders what the little fellow with no eyebrows is made of as he watches him throw away the huge log he couldn't even lift an inch himself.

Before getting back up onto the seat Snegg, transformed into a rain-statue, pats the horse's neck.

"I guessed what it was about and tried to hide at the end of the gallery, but they found me and hauled me, struggling, back up into the open air by the seat of my pants. I blinked to clear my eyes and saw Mother Mary in front of me, the head of the orphanage. She took out her handkerchief to wipe my face. 'Yes, that's him,' she said to the foreman before giving me the worst slap I'd ever had with the back of her hand. Gee up, my lively, one last effort."

"And... where did you meet your, er, cousin, Jean Morgan. Not down the mine, surely?"

"No, in the Methodist chapel."

"Methodist? Weren't you a Catholic?"

"The nuns in the orphanage were Catholic, but I left them for good when I was thirteen. I'd been told that the Methodists' faith was more concrete, more rational, so I thought I'd try it. Now I'm neither one nor the other. I've become 'None' again."

"You're an agnostic. Like me."

"I'm afraid so. Jean Morgan doesn't have that kind of problem. She's a Joanna."

"Sorry?"

"A disciple of Joanna Southcott."

"That madwoman who claimed to be the mother of the future messiah?"

"The Joannas didn't think she was mad because she

predicted the war in Spain. At the age of sixty-four she became pregnant with no human intervention and was delivered of a divine baby called Shiloh, but an angel took the child away from human sight… at least that's the story the zealots tell."

When they reach the old village the two men have to clear their way through the brambles again. They head for the one house that is still more or less standing. Its sole window is covered by a sheet of crimson cloth replacing the broken panes. A trickle of grey smoke comes straight out of a hole in the roof.

"Before she died a few days later, Southcott sealed a few other prophecies in a box that could only be opened by the twenty-four English bishops gathered together in conclave."

"That won't be happening soon, in my opinion."

"True. According to certain followers she set the arrival of the New Kingdom for 2004."

"Not so, Snegg. The New Kingdom's here already. People are wrong to believe the world is trotting along in the same old way, without any significant change, when in fact everything has changed. It's no longer parliament that's in the driver's seat, it's the City speculators with their debts and their top hats. And in the state carriage a huge safe has replaced the King of England. It'll take us a lot farther than 2004, believe you me."

"Doubtless, sir. Regarding Jean Morgan, let me talk to her. We mustn't rush her if we want to learn something.

The rain suddenly stops, as if it was curious about what was going to be said in the hovel.

Snegg doesn't dare knock at the door in case it collapses. He simply pushes it and it opens with a creak to reveal a small, square room with a floor of beaten earth and, at the centre, a puddle caused by the rain. In a dryer corner the Joanna is sitting on a stool beside an empty rocking chair. She's wearing a white hat with a wide brim, a white, dirty, shapeless dress. She's as old as a much-read Bible: dog-eared, crumpled and torn but still respectable. At the other end of the room a pile of branches and planks on the ground is slowly burning down, giving off acrid smoke only a small part of which escapes through a hole in the thatch. The rest fills the room and makes their eyes sting.

"Do you recognise me, Jean?"

"Of course, I recognise you, Seamus, even if you haven't got much hair any more. But you still have a bit more of that than eyebrows."

"That's not very difficult. Less difficult than finding you. Fortunately I happened to run into your nephew. Your former neighbours thought you were dead."

The old woman nods. Her pupils are faded, almost milky, but there's still a spark shining inside, like a pearl forming inside an oyster.

"They're the ones who are dead. All the unbelievers are dead. Seamus, this is my husband Charles. I think you've never been introduced."

Edward starts to look round for Charles, even though he knows he won't find the least trace of him, but then the rocking chair suddenly starts moving. But, after a moment of panic, he sees the string in Jean Morgan's hand,

"Pleased to meet you, Charles," Snegg says with a bow in the direction of the empty rocking chair, "And this is Mr Bailey."

"I know. Joanna speaks to me, here," she points to her stomach. "I hardly get out at all any more but she keeps me informed about things. Do you still go around with Wesley's henchmen, Seamus?"

"No, Jean, Methodism has lost all attraction for me."

"I knew that too. But that's not the case with the owners of the mines and the mills. Lots of them are converting to it. A religion that advocates frugality, work and obedience – what a godsend!"

"But the Established Church is not to be outdone," Snegg says with a smile. "According to a certain Reverend Paley, the rich are very unhappy because they don't know what to do with their money and their freedom. The poor, the people who are slaving away, don't know how lucky they are."

A strange sound that must be a laugh comes from Jean Morgan's throat and Charles' chair rocks two or three times as a sign of agreement.

"Seamus, do you know why the Established Church, as you call it, refuses to recognise Joanna's miracles? Because she promised victory to the weak over the strong, the triumph of the victims and the defeat of their torturers. There's a programme to get their backs up. So you've come to tell me you're prepared to espouse the true faith…"

"Well, I…"

"Of course, you aren't," Jean crows. "I know why you're here, Joanna told me. You've come to talk about the chapel at Wooler Manor and its damned ghosts of papist monks, haven't you?"

"People hardly had any choice at the time," Edward says, forgetting his promise. "Everyone was papist."

The old woman gives him a long, hard look. He could swear that the pearls in her pupils have just got bigger, that they are hardening and turning into black diamonds.

"If you had come to ask me to baptise you, my lord, I would make you lean forward, I would grasp your private parts with one hand and give your backside a thrashing with a stick. That's the way Joanna did it."

Edward begs Snegg's pardon with a look. His clerk, in return, glares at him.

""You can do us a great service, Jean," he says. "You have to tell us exactly what you saw and heard."

As if by magic a little flask of brandy appears in his hand. Jean holds out hers, uncorks the flask and takes a good swig.

"Don't think you've bought me, Seamus."

"Of course not."

"Anyway, I foresaw that I was going to recount it."

"Thank you, Jean. Thank you very much."

"It's good, your booze. Better than what Withers brought."

"Withers?"

"Lord Glendover's estate manager. He bought me."

The two men give each other a look.

"He was a friend of Charles'. From time to time he would come by to give me a fowl. Two weeks ago he came to see me, saying he wanted to show me something. Something strange, he added, and he didn't know what to think of it. We got into his carriage and went to the Manor. Night was falling and I immediately saw lights in the chapel. 'Listen carefully,' Withers said."

"And what did you hear?"

"Voices. People singing in Latin. Withers made me climb

up a ladder and through a broken window I saw three or four people in black robes with hoods doing things round the altar."

"Things?"

"Papist business: kneel down – up you get – walk down the aisle – kiss the crucifix. After a while the singing stopped, the candles went out. Withers took me home. He talked fast, as if he was in a hurry to seal a deal. It was an ill omen, he said. Someone from the law ought to be told, but he had his situation, his reputation to remember. He wanted it to be me who spoke."

"So what did you do?"

Jean takes another swig. Under the effect of the alcohol the look in her eyes has calmed down. But the simple fact of knowing the pearls are there, hidden away in her oyster-like eyes, makes Edward uneasy.

"I asked Joanna for advice. That's what I always do. She told me it was all the business of unbelievers. Gentiles settling scores with each other. That if God wanted to send a sign he would use a flood, a plague or a heat wave. And then the monks were singing out of tune. And I'm sure it wasn't really in Latin, they were just adding an *um* or an *ibus* to the end of the words. But Joanna ordered me to do what Withers said and to accept his two sovereigns. She authorised me to drink a half sovereign. I have to keep the rest for the Great Moment. To pay for my journey to London when they will open the box that will amaze the world. Will you come too?"

"Yes, and that's a promise. If the twenty-four bishops of England decide to open the box, I will go there."

"But perhaps we won't ask them what they think, Seamus. Perhaps we'll open it ourselves…"

Snegg acquiesces with a vague gesture, his eyes fixed on the fire that has almost gone out. From time to time a drop drips down from the roof, making an unpleasant hissing noise as it hits the embers.

"There's another thing I want to ask you, Jean. Charles was in service with the Beresfords, wasn't he?"

"Yes, for twenty years. Groom, coachman, handyman. Until they left."

"Precisely. It's their departure I'm interested in. It seems that that evening he took Beresford to Durham. Beresford alone."

"I can't remember any more, but I'll ask him."

The chair starts to rock, creaking, and for a few long moments it is the only sound in the room; Jean listens to it, nodding. "Alone, yes," she eventually replies. "It had been agreed on the previous evening. He took him to Durham and dropped him outside a hotel, close to the coaching inn."

If he'd intended to take the mail coach, Edward wonders, then why not Darlington, that was much nearer. Because no one would know him in Durham, they would lose track of him there. Like all liars, Tim Turnell had perhaps been inspired by the truth. He did encounter a Beresford on the quay in Newcastle, but Robert, not Mathilde. Beresford knew Turnell very well, was familiar with his dishonesty, his money problems, and in a flash must have had the idea of the false witness. Yes, that made sense. Edward tries to catch Snegg's eye, but he's still concentrating on Jean.

"Did Lord Robert say anything to Charles?"

"Not a word. Not with the weather there was that evening. It was pouring down. Lightning fit to tear the sky apart... a porter came to take his luggage, Beresford disappeared into the hotel and that was that. Charles spent the night in Durham, with a cousin of his and when he got back the next day all hell had broken loose. They were looking for Mathilde. Hey? What's that you said, Charlie?"

The rocking-chair ploy, visibly well-rehearsed, is repeated. Edward raises his eyes to high heaven.

"He says Beresford killed his wife," Jean reports, after a theatrical pause to wet her whistle with brandy. "The two of them hated each other. He killed her and hid the body somewhere. All by himself, or with the Egyptian."

"The Egyptian? Which Egyptian?"

Jean is swaying a bit on her stool but she's still talking fluently as if the alcohol were a river and her words boats carried along by the current.

"People called him that. Or Burnt-face, because half of his face was all red. He came to Darlington several times. He slept at the inn and Charles would go to pick him up in the morning to take him to the Manor. He would spend hours locked in the library with Beresford. Joanna didn't like the Egyptians because of what they did to the people of Israel. And black magic. They invented black magic. I saw him once – Burnt-face. I'm sure the devil looks like him."

"That's not very much to accuse someone of complicity in a murder, don't you think?"

Jean nods and closes her eyes. Then she sits up, seizes Edward's hand and looks at the lines. "You have a dog, my lord."

That is not a particularly great feat of palmistry: Titus had rubbed himself up against him that morning – not out of affection but to spread his old hairs all over him. There must surely still be some on his clothes.

The old woman takes his other hand. "You will cry when he dies."

"No chance, dear lady!" Edward guffaws, "The day he dies I'll put on my best suit and go out to celebrate."

"You will weep for him," Jean Morgan insists without blinking an eye. "It will be in September."

"Lord Henry Glendover! A big fish…"

"Very big," Snegg agrees.

The two men climb up onto the driving seat. It's raining again, though less heavily than before: a dreary persistent drizzle continues to cover the back of the horse with its layer of cold wax while the ruts in the track are overflowing, miniature lakes ruffled by the wind.

"It's logical," Snegg goes on. "He's invested a good deal of his wealth in the development of the Tees. The toll roads bring in a decent return. For him the railway means a clear loss."

"All the same… it's difficult to believe that a man of that status should resort to a stratagem…"

"…worthy of Lewis' *Monk*? True, but it works, doesn't it? They've already lost precious time for laying the rails. In the town the posters are doing the work. They say a stock of sleepers mysteriously caught fire last night."

"Oh come now, their cause is lost in advance. Stephenson has the law on his side."

"Yes, but in the eyes of the old-style aristocrats like Glendover the law is nothing but a pointlessly pettifogging version of their own rights, that can always be simplified with money or force. Doubtless all he's trying to do is to gain time. I imagine he's already pursuing his intrigues in the Lords to get a vote that will be favourable to him"

"Do you think Spalding has a hand in the business?"

"Certainly not! He's far too crafty for that. He got rid of his shares in the Tees Canal Company ages ago. And, as I'm sure you know being a lawyer, he's just joined the Society of Railway Investments of Pease and the other Quakers."

Edward smiles inwardly. The allusion to his own negligence is a jewel of Sneggian irony. And then a provincial clerk, an orphan and self-taught, who can quote Lewis, is not something you find everyday.

"Gee up, my lovely, off we go."

The track is too narrow to turn the carriage, but there seems to be a place a bit farther along where they can manage it. The horse keeps trying to avoid the brambles and the wind is blowing the rain into the driver's face. Edward observes his efforts with the admiration of the uninitiated.

"But that doesn't help us make any progress with the *other* investigation," he says. "The one we're really interested in. A macabre piece of theatre, yes, ghosts of monks, a skeleton… and why that particular skeleton anyway? The graveyards are full of them. Where did they find it before taking it to the pond? Why start the old Beresford business all over again? What interest can it have for those plotting against the railway? It's certainly damning for Lord Robert but… and then what about the story of the Egyptian. I have to admit that there is something about your friend Jean but… can we believe anything an old sot says?"

"I'd go even farther, sir – can one believe anything a

rocking-chair says!"

Once they reach the clear space, Snegg performs a perfect turn and they set off back down the track.

"You know about horses," Edward says abruptly. "Why, in your opinion, would a mother want people to believe her daughter is an accomplished horsewoman? That's what my future mother-in-law told me when I met her in London, that Margaret was out for a gallop everyday."

"Well, mothers do like to deck their daughters out with all possible talents, even those they don't possess."

"A poor answer. Try again."

Working with Snegg, Edward is gradually coming to be able to interpret the most subtle play of his very subtle physiognomy. He can read embarrassment in an infinitesimal creasing of the lips, an inward debate in a flutter of the eyelids.

"It can happen," Snegg says, looking the other way, "that women who go out riding frequently rupture their er... hymen through the rubbing of the saddle."

"So...?"

"So horse-riding can be an excuse, cited to make people believe the young woman is still... intact."

Margaret. Margaret's beauty beneath a cupola of rain. *Intact*. He can't touch her but he sees her stretched out there, before his eyes, floating amid the squalls in a state of perfection that cannot be of this world. It's a Margaret who doesn't really exist. A dream or a nightmare Margaret.

"I would have bet on it!"

"Indeed, you seemed to have known the answer already," Snegg says with a touch of hoarseness in his voice which for him takes the place of annoyance.

"That's not what I meant. I would have bet that you were going to use the word *intact*. You're the kind of man to use the word *intact* instead of a *virgin*."

"So what?"

"So nothing. You're right, *intact* is nicer."

As they go through the abandoned village again they see Jean standing by the side of the road waving to them. "There's one thing I forgot to tell you, Seamus Snegg. About the monks."

Her dress must have originally been very stylish – a summer frock, perhaps, or one for special occasions – and her hat is elegant. Suddenly Edward is aware of her bare feet, very white where the mud from the road isn't sticking to them.

"Yes, Jean? The monks?"

"I listened very carefully to them and I noticed that one of them had a problem. When he sang with the others, everything was normal. But when he pretended to be praying, he couldn't do it."

"Why not?"

"He stammered."

VI

Diary of Leonhard Vholes,
intended readership: none

London, 15th April 1824

Mr Robert Grant has just left the chambers and I am enveloped in the stench of the Marshalsea. I'm not talking about body odour – Grant stinks of sweat, grime and cheap gin like all his fellows – but about a kind of moral odour, that of hope lying forgotten in a cupboard, dignity stagnating at the bottom of a drain, beauty ravaged by the pox. That of our world.

"What is it that brings you, Grant?"

"It's the old gentleman, sir. The one in the cellar."

"What about him?"

"It's my opinion that he's not very well."

"What makes you say that?"

"His cough. He's coughing like mad. And when he breathes, it's as if he'd swallowed a whistle."

"It's the job of the doctor to evaluate things like that, Grant, not yours."

"True, sir. But the official prison doctor only comes twice a month. We could bring in another, but we'd have to pay him, of course. Or perhaps…"

"Or perhaps what?"

"Or perhaps… let nature take its course."

There, he's said it. Now he sits there waiting, arms crossed. In the nearby chapel a tyro organist hits a dissonant chord.

"Go and see Dr Skimpole," I said opening my purse, "and take him to see the sick man."

"You don't want to come and see for yourself?"

Beresford pale and distraught, watching my mother's coffin pass. Or standing by a window at Wooler Manor, surveying the night.

"As soon as I'm able. By the end of the week, I'm sure. Oh, and Grant," I add a sovereign to the money on the table, "treat yourself to a good meal, to celebrate the arrival of spring. We never know how much longer we have to live."

Every year I head off north to go to Wooler Manor in June. I'm under no obligation to do so but I pay people up there who, though not resident on the estate, carry out repairs when they become necessary. And this pilgrimage has become the most important event of the year for me.

In 1815 I left London three days after Waterloo – the celebrations were in full swing because the news had just arrived. Children who hadn't gone to school, the crowd gathered along the Mall all the way down to Buckingham Palace, the drunken revellers bawling out songs from their obscene repertoire, improvising confused variations to the glory of Wellington. In a dismal mood, made worse by the hubbub and the unusual heat, I took the mail coach in order to get out of London as quickly as possible in the belief that the North would at least provide some calm and more pleasant weather. But it didn't. The rumour was always a few hours ahead of me and everywhere, from Luton to Northampton, from Nottingham to Leicester, there were the same festivities as in the capital: the same bibulous racket, and that kind of animal jubilation combining the patriotism of the rearguard – the last refuge of a scoundrel, according to the good Doctor Johnson – the need to drink oneself into oblivion and the relief of the coward. And the same heat, all the way to Leeds, to Darlington.

Night was falling when I reached the Manor and, as I was wandering round the empty corridors, past furniture covered in white drapes, the clouds gathered outside the windows and then there was a rumble of thunder – as there had been at the same hour thirteen years ago.

The memories of that strange night came flooding back to me with such force and wealth of detail, that I ran my hand over my head to reassure myself that my bald spot was there, proof that the years really had passed. Yes, henceforth I could be called the 'little monk' with that tonsure and that little blond lock, like a leaf of Virginia tobacco. In the hall I looked round. The chessboard tiles, crossed by the grey shadows of the clouds, seemed to have come alive and for a chess player it wasn't difficult to see the two pillars framing the fireplace as two kings, face to face in an eternal check.

England woke from three long nights of celebrations with a hangover to make Falstaff go green with envy and the unpleasant feeling that nothing had changed. As for me, in that huge deserted building, I…

But there I go, getting the chronology all mixed up!

True, I know it off by heart and no one's going to read it. But does the cook burn the dinner when he's going to be the only one eating it? Does the cobbler leave the ends of nails sticking through inside his own shoes? I owe it to myself to get a certain amount of coherence and a certain amount of style. It's *absolutely* necessary for me to take control of this hand that is writing of its own accord. Become young again, Leonard, recover your hair and your illusions, even if you've never had much of either, and go back to 1802.

Applying the pragmatism of Grandfather Forster, I decided not to waste time speculating about the mysterious Mr Newton; at most I kept in mind – like a move made impossible for the moment by the presence of an opposing piece – the idea that it might be useful to have a look round the library one day, and I didn't have long to wait for that, anyway.

In the course of several months I had become a regular guest at the Manor. However, the word *regular* is not quite appropriate, since the rhythm of these invitations, even though it seemed to accelerate imperceptibly, was completely unpredictable. The procedure, on the other hand, always remained the same: I would receive a letter at the chambers and the next day Beresford's coupé, the coachman and his tin flask would appear at my door. So I wasn't given the time to accept or decline the invitation and, exasperated by this method, I twice in a row sent the carriage back without excuse or the least explanation. But these refusals did not prevent a further letter from arriving. Dull appeared to have been informed of my absences, even before I told him, and he never made any objection despite the fact that they took no account of workdays and weekends – I could be summoned on a Monday and only return on Thursday evening, depriving my employer of almost a whole week's work, but that had no effect on my salary nor even brought me the least frown.

Beresford always greeted me with a start of astonished delight, as if he had nothing to do with my arrival at the Manor. We would exchange a couple of bland remarks, then he would quickly steer the conversation to his sister, "You know that Ophelia swears by you," then disappear with a wave of the hand and the air of a busy man. But all that his 'business' consisted of was long afternoons by himself in the library or vague expeditions to the outlying parts of the estate, looking for a blocked drainage ditch or an old ruin that could perhaps be restored for a new tenant. He would generally return late in the evening, muddy, weary and in a foul mood, without having found either the ditch or the hovel.

Even more bizarre was the way in which the length of my stay was decided. The first letters fixed it in advance, but later I learnt to interpret the least change in Beresford's attitude, the vaguest of allusions to 'poor Mr Dull' and the 'innumerable' files he had to deal with, as a hint to leave at once. I took this chaotic succession of summons and dismissals with good grace, even finding in it the spice of adventure and a pleasant distraction from the boredom of life in Durham. The Baron never again spoke of 'making good his mistakes' – in his eyes the privilege of being invited to the Manor seemed sufficient compensation. And we were far from 'sharing his ideas and plans,' that he had talked about on my first visit, unless the plan consisted of an abortive attempt to have a picnic on the banks of the Gaunless and the idea a vague exchange of views on Cromwell.

My function, if I had one, could be summed up in three words: to amuse Ophelia. No one had asked me to do so, but everything encouraged me to: Beresford, who often left us alone together, the young woman's beauty and my own ulterior motives. She adored riding. I had my first success with her despite myself by falling off my horse in all imaginable ways: backwards, sideways and over the horse's neck. I was happy to go along with all this, exaggerating the somersaults, the rolls, getting up again stoically and inventing philosophical maxims for each further attempt. She found all that so funny that, even after I'd acquired the rudiments of horsemanship, I still let myself fall now and then, just to set off her laughter. In such moments she seemed to be only ten years old, the age when little girls clap their hands as they watch the clowns.

One day, out of curiosity I feigned a heavier fall and then pretended to be unconscious. While I was lying there in the moss, eyes closed and motionless, I heard her cry out, run over and kneel down beside me.

"No, not now! Not now!" she muttered, patting my cheek.

Opening my eyes, I saw an anguished expression on her face, quickly replaced by her habitual cheerfulness. "My poor little monk is definitely too clumsy," she mocked. "What he needs is a pony – or a rocking horse."

She went on in that tone, but I'd seen what I'd seen.

As a reward for my equestrian exploits, she agreed to be initiated into the mysteries of chess.

Of chess!

I think that in my place Grandfather Forster would have gone mad: while I was explaining things, she stared at the board with a sulky expression, giggling at the names of the pieces, arguing about the rules even before she'd learnt them. Then, while we were playing, she would yawn pointedly, moving any pawn to put an end to a game she knew she'd already lost. Then, suddenly, for no obvious reason she would become interested in the pieces on the board – an avid, disproportionate interest – and since I myself had relaxed my concentration, I had to gather my thoughts quickly to counter her plans. Defeated, but only just, she would bite her lips and look at me with an odd combination of pique and enthusiasm.

In general we put the chessboard on a Venetian table of lacquered wood decorated with a mythological scene. What I most recall about it was a dubious figure on my side of the table holding in each hand half of a broken hourglass. At his feet the sand that had trickled out formed a little mound from which emerged the crimson head of a sort of insect or crustacean. Ophelia would stretch out along the interminable red bench she was so fond of while I sat opposite her in an ordinary chair. She would always complain that the board was too far away and I had to more or less attach the table to the bench, thus leaving me looking straight down on both the board and her and sometimes I would slowly survey her from one extremity to the other, from her toes imprisoned in silk stockings to her hair, which she kept short, in curls under a red-and-white bonnet. Her elbow reclining on a cushion, her eyes level with the chessmen, she watched them from so close to that she started to squint.

Sometimes Lady Mathilde would come and join us in the middle of the afternoon. Sitting at a table at the other end of the room, she would start a game of patience, only to give it up almost immediately, go and stand by the window and spend hours contemplating the same rectangle of the neglected park – but sometime I would chance to catch her gaze fixed on us. Ophelia used to call her the Castle, not because she was tall or massive but because of her posture rooted to the spot in the corner of the room – as she happened to be on the day Beresford decided to show me the book.

I can see it now, as I write these lines, lying there open on the table. Dog-eared. The leather sticky, the spine missing. Stains on the title page, a concave depression on the edge where something damaged it. More stains. And then the smell – a fetid, human smell. My metal ruler moved a few fractions of an inch and stuck to its back.

"Oh, Leonard! I absolutely have to show you my Rousseau."

"Oh, for pity's sake, Robert!" Ophelia protested. "How many decent people went to the guillotine because of that book?" Dragged out of her daydream, Mathilde went back to her card table and started to shuffle the cards compulsively.

I knew enough French to spell out, *Du contrat social, ou Principes du droit politique* by J-J. Rousseau, Citizen of Geneva. Even then, in a reasonable state, the book seemed unremarkable to me, its simple sheepskin binding wasn't improving with age. But the reason for Beresford's enthusiasm lay doubtless in the inscription on the flyleaf: 'À mon cher ami Paul Moulton, J-J. Rousseau.'

"Just a minute," Beresford said as I made to hand the book back to him, "You haven't read the most interesting bit. There, on the title page. There's another inscription."

I am rereading it at this very moment. Regular handwriting, plain, hardly corresponding to the impetuosity that is part of our image of the man – except for the tail sloping forward on the end of each word: *'À mes chers amis Robert et Mathilde et avec la bénédiction du cher vieux Jean-Jacques, Georges Danton.'* There too a tail prolongs the end of the last *n* of Danton but then it curves downwards in a vast swirling flourish.

"You will now see why this is the showpiece of my collection?"

"Your collection?" Mathilde swept the cards off the table with the back of her hand. "You're forgetting that that book belongs to the two of us."

"But of course, my dear, everything that belongs to you belongs to me and vice versa."

"It seems to me that I have an even greater right to that book than you."

"True, I can't deny that you knew Georges before me…"

Ophelia gave me a quick glance. Even if I couldn't understand a single word of the conversation, I could feel the tension rising in the room and I was expecting Mathilde to erupt in fury. But that didn't happen. After a minute she simply said, "I would like to be able to have a look at the book whenever I feel like it."

"And what prevents you from doing that?"

"Your library. I don't have access to it."

"Wrong. I've had to make certain improvements but they're all finished today, so I'm inviting you all to a kind of… inaugural visit."

Ophelia having refused with a sardonic pout, Mathilde and I followed Beresford.

The library smelt new and that was all that could be said for it. If the extreme cold of the big drawing room could be explained by its size, that of the library was deliberate, the product of long deliberation. The few pieces of furniture had been arranged with obsessive care: four armchairs placed precisely at the four corners of a quadrilateral in the centre of which was an empty table. Painted a sickly green, the north and south walls, containing respectively the windows and the door, lacked any paintings, curtains, drapes or any other ornament. Outside, a poorly maintained lawn only went as far as the fringes of a birch wood. The serried ranks of the trunks with their dense foliage formed a sort of oppressive lattice, through which the last scraps of sunshine filtered to die on the dark-oak parquet floor.

At one end of the room a gigantic tiled stove went up almost to the ceiling: it imitated the architecture of a two-storey house with a roof in the form of a pagoda. At the other end was a wall of books: the stove and the library faced each other like two duellists, motionless in the gloom.

"It's the perfect place to preserve the books," Beresford said. "They don't like the light and that's never strong here, not even in the midday sun. They are also afraid of both the heat and the cold. The stove is far enough away from them but maintains an equal temperature."

I went over to the books. Arranged precisely in order of size, most bound in the same leather, they looked firmly stuck to each other, as if they belonged to a single being, constituted a single body. A kind of unified matter, compact and interdependent, secreted by the room itself or perhaps by some spell cast by its main occupant. Instead of being drawn to the titles, the eye slid from one to the next without being able to fix on any. You felt as much like taking down any one book from the shelves as detaching a rib from a decaying corpse.

"There, my dear," he said, replacing the Rousseau on its shelf. "As you can see, there's no risk of our joint treasure coming to any harm."

Mathilde, chin raised and a fiery look in her eyes, tossed her head and turned on her heel. Hardly had she left the room than Beresford, who a moment ago had seemed so proud of himself, dropped into a chair giving a long weary sigh.

"There you are," he mutters, "We fight like cats and dogs. In France I've seen friends kill each other, men send their own brothers to the scaffold... but they at least were fighting for ideas and their names will go down in history. While this battle..."

I had an idea going round at the back of my head, otherwise I would surely have asked which battle he was talking about, why he was fighting it. Night was falling fast. Beresford sketched a gesture of lighting a candle.

"We're fascinated by the unknown... but it's just a distorting mirror. The temptation is to dig a hole inside yourself and simply disappear into it."

In the gathering darkness I made as many mental notes as possible: the gaps between the windows and the walls, the number of beams in the ceiling. While pretending to examine the books, I measured the width of the room: twelve paces. My estimate was that the room was twice as long as wide. No recesses, no passageways; it formed a perfect rectangle.

I waited a little while longer but Beresford, sitting there in the darkness didn't seem to have anything more to say. As for myself, I'd already decided to explore the bric-a brac in the south wing, in the room corresponding to the library.

"They used to be my mother's apartments," Ophelia had told me. "Today they're used as lumber rooms. There are broken battledores, rickety chests of drawers, old toys – I hate the place."

Once I had walked round the Manor on the south side, as far as the old kitchen garden, below the windows of the room in question, but that part of the ground was slightly lower and I hadn't been able to see anything, even standing on tiptoe. As for the door, it was always locked and how can you ask for the key to a room where you've no business to be?

I didn't achieve my goal until September, during that ridiculous Peace of Amiens, which both sides used to dress their wounds and refurbish their weaponry. There was also a kind of truce in operation at the Manor. For some time the Beresfords had deigned to speak to each other in a friendly manner. Mathilde, having brought back from a stay with their cousins in the north a certain Emily, a spruce lady's maid of sixteen who seemed to amuse her, was in a good mood. She talked to us about Paris, about picturesque places or interesting people, never about political events. Sometimes she would even agree to a game of whist. Then Robert would have a bottle of Moët champagne opened (miraculously his father had had several cases sent just before the wars began) and we would settle in the little drawing room, the ladies on the bench and we men opposite in low armchairs. With the help of alcohol it was easy for me to get Ophelia to laugh, which pleased Robert. In return I placed my skill as a player in the service of the Frenchwoman; we would win four out of five times against the brother and sister and Mathilde liked nothing better that to taunt her husband by announcing our winning number of tricks in a loud voice.

At those times we were almost like a real family… it took an effort for me to remind myself what Beresford had done to mine.

One evening, after having drunk four or five glasses of champagne with the others, I was staggering off to my room when I saw lights on the other side of the courtyard. From the place where I was, on the ground floor, all I could see above the black curtains was the upper part of the vestibule of the north wing. From the reflections on the ceiling I deduced that they came from a candelabra with three branches; to see who was carrying it I had to get higher up, to my room on the first floor from where I could look down over the curtains. But just as I was about to do that, another, smaller light appeared, probably that of a single candle.

During the whole day there had been a storm rumbling in the distance, without ever breaking. Suddenly huge drops of rain started to fall, fat, oily single drops and, opening my eyes wide under the influence of the champagne, I witnessed a strange and magnificent play of light. That of the candle was coming and going round the other comparatively large one, like a flickering moon round its sun; both of them, diffracted by the rain, covered the ceiling with a marvellous iridescence, merging then separating according to some complex choreography. By now the rain was falling heavily, the drops hitting the windows with an insistent, metallic sound. I could have imagined myself dead, lashed by all the whips of hell – perhaps the other inhabitants of the Manor were dead as well, perhaps it was their souls I could see dancing on the ceiling. But all at once they disappeared. Coming back to the real world, I realised they must have gone into the library.

I then decided to do what I had been starting to do a couple of minutes ago: to try and open the door of the lumber room. It had become an almost mechanical gesture: two or three times a day I would try my luck, hoping one of the servants, who came from time to time to deposit some new relic there, would have forgotten to lock the door. Because of a certain play in the mechanism, the door gave the impression it was going to open. I became exasperated by the false hope this gave me, only to be dashed by the sound of the bolt hitting the striker plate and the annoying feeling of resistance; I couldn't help thinking of Ophelia, of her encouraging signs that never led anywhere.

But on that stormy evening the door wasn't locked. I remember the delightful frisson I felt when the door creaked open.

Keeping my hand holding the candle stretched out, I took a step into the room and, impelled by a flash of lightning, the various shapes of the discarded furniture seemed to come hurtling towards me, enveloped in shrouds. The barrels of the firearms and the blades of old rapiers mounted guard and, sitting on a shelf between a skein of wool and a set of boar's tusks, a one-eyed doll was staring out at the night.

I was about to venture a little farther into the shambles when a noise made me hurry out of the room and return to my observation post facing the interior courtyard. The storm must have been right above the Manor. There were so many flashes of lightning, so dazzling, so close to one another, that the image of the last one stayed on my retina until the next one came; the fountain, the stone slabs, Saturn and Neptune seemed to be immersed in a milky and unhealthy dawn light. The door to the vestibule of the north wing was flapping in the wind and I heard another noise that was receding – perhaps the staccato drumming of the rain on the ground but more probably hurried footsteps. No one came to close the door, and after a while I returned to the lumber room.

There was no question of pacing out the room as I'd done in the library, the floor was too cluttered, and I had no desire to draw attention to myself by breaking some piece of china or accidentally producing a squawk from an out-of-tune spinet. But once my eye was accustomed to the shadows and the disorder I could set about making a fairly precise estimate of the length and breadth. I was helped by the measurements I'd made in the library. I checked my calculations ten times over, counting the beams again and again, multiplying the short distances I had been able to pace out by estimated factors and squeezing my way through to one corner of the room and, using an arquebus as a gauge, I measured the distance between one of the windows and the corner of the wall.

Everything brought me to the same conclusion: the library and the lumber room both had exactly the same surface area. But there was one thing that didn't fit: two alcoves, one on either side of the lumber room – just one on the right of the library. What had happened, in the north wing, to the space corresponding to the second alcove? Some kind of storeroom? But there was no door or window into it. Why?

While, having put the candle down on the corner of a table, I was thinking about the implications of my discovery, the rain intensified but the lightning and thunderclaps became less frequent. Some fifty yards from the house a low ruined wall still marked the boundary of the old kitchen garden, then the ground was covered in sphagnum moss as far as that pap fringed with beeches that the locals called Aycliffe Hill. No one ever took the risk of venturing out into that peat-bog. Through the curtain of rain a dark shape could be made out on the right, close to the wall – a copse of freezing, shivering willow trees.

It was over there that something or someone briefly appeared in the gleam of a distant flash of lightning: a light-coloured shape that I continued to see moving even after the lightning, while the leaves had gone dark again.

That evening Ophelia had been wearing a white dress.

I decided to open the window, which necessitated a brief wrestling bout with the jammed mechanism and the frame swollen with damp. When it finally gave way and I could lean out, everything seemed normal. The rain was splashing on the stones of the wall, the willows were shaking their head in all directions, like horses refusing to be mounted. Nothing else apart from the wind. But just a moment ago hadn't I heard someone crying? Groaning?

If that was true, the wind covered the lament and the rain washed away the tears.

"Me? Outside in the middle of the night?" Ophelia said with a hoot of laughter the next day. "In that pouring rain? You must be mad Leonard. You know very well that I'm afraid of thunderstorms."

That was true. However, by the evening she was shivering with fever and the following day Beresford had his friend Dr Thorne, a specialist in chest diseases, come all the way from Hartlepool. The Baron had already mentioned to me a hereditary weakness from which their mother and grandmother had died, but Thorne was reassuring and diagnosed mild bronchitis.

We spent the three following days in the little drawing room, reading and playing chess. Once more at daggers drawn, Mathilde and Beresford were nowhere to be seen. Ophelia had a tendency to drift off to sleep and at such times I would leave the room quietly and wander round the corridors where invisible draughts would lift the gauze curtains: it was pleasantly boring, rather like swimming in a warm stream, in the shade of the leaves, and I had no desire to do anything else. One morning, however, I found a note that had been slipped under the door of my room:

The carriage will come for you at ten o'clock. B.

So far he had never dismissed me in this way. But I managed to bottle up my fury and, after having put my things in my bag, I went down. Mathilde was just coming out of the little drawing room when I got there.

She squinted and jerked her chin at me, and having thus paid me her usual respects, she muttered, noticing my bag, "So you're leaving us. Just when I felt like a game of whist."

"You husband is very probably tired of losing."

"He always was a bad loser."

The Frenchwoman made a pout that was both ironic and tantalising that she appeared to reserve for me alone, gave another jerk of the chin and left at a brisk pace.

"Do you know that Robert wasn't her first husband?" Ophelia said out of the blue as soon as I came into the room.

Immediately I sensed there was something unusual, something forced in her attitude. She gave the impression that she was only talking about Mathilde to let off steam or to avoid other topics of conversation.

"Her father was a crooked banker or speculator, or whatever... when business was bad, he would sell off one of his daughters to replenish his coffers. At my age, or even a bit younger, she was forced to go to bed with a man of fifty! The old man died in her arms, it appears. The poor woman thought she was free... unfortunately, by then her father was bankrupt again and, looking for another solvent son-in-law, his eye fell on that awful man, that Danton. I've seen portraits of him, you'd think he was some kind of animal, a bull crossed with a pig! He'd just become a widower himself and was mad with grief... he even went to dig up his wife's corpse to embrace her one last time!"

She gestured for me to sit on the end of the bench. Her feet were brushing against my thighs and she did nothing to avoid them.

"At first Danton seemed interested... he even made her father a loan... but then he went off to inspect the armies in Belgium and when he came back he met another woman and married her. He never asked for his money back... but according to Robert..."

I saw her eyes shining as she searched for words. "...he had already been compensated in a different way..."

"Sorry?" I had, of course, understood what she meant.

"My God, Leonard, don't be so stupid. He'd taken advantage of the situation!"

"You mean... like your brother with my mother?"

181

She shrank back for a moment. Then, pushing herself up on one elbow, she held out a hand towards me. It was a very strange gesture, neither an abortive slap, nor a restrained caress, nor an invitation to lovemaking. At the same time she looked me straight in the eye, without irony, without coyness, as if she were turning to me for some crucial decision. I blushed and, ill-at-ease, held out my own hand. She gave it a squeeze and placed it on her chest.

Now then, Bishop, you wouldn't happen to be falling in love, would you?

"We'll talk the next time," she said, letting go of my hand

But there was no next time. A servant came to tell me the carriage was waiting.

I never saw Ophelia again.

As my comings and goings established me as a special guest at Wooler Manor, Mr Dull's attitude towards me changed: he no longer entrusted any important task to me and spoke to me in honeyed tones full of hidden meanings: "You see to the Hutchinson marriage contract, Dant. We can't trouble Mr Vholes for such a minor matter..." My colleagues in the chambers also made me pay for my connections with Beresford by excluding me from their jokes, meals they had together and birthday drinks. That didn't bother me much, to be honest. I saw Durham, of which I knew every nook and cranny, as a cardboard setting: nothing really happened there, the hours stacked up one on top of the other like a house of cards, which the oblivion of sleep blew down every evening. When I happened to find myself in a street where I'd once lived, I felt nothing, except perhaps a vague impression having long ago read a scene in a novel that was set in a similar place; even my most significant memories – my meeting with Uncle Greenfield, the death of my mother – were being obliterated in my memory like a parchment eaten away by acid.

Nothing existed apart from the Manor and its inhabitants. "We'll talk the next time," Ophelia had said in that autumn of 1802 and I lived in the expectation of a further invitation from Beresford until that December day when I finally saw, in a bundle of papers brought by the postman, the Baron's notepaper, handwriting and seal. I spent the whole day expecting to be summoned by Mr Dull, starting every time he put his head round the door – but it was always Dant, Church or Ballimont he called for, never me, and when our eyes did meet I seemed to see in his a kind of malicious satisfaction. In the evening I couldn't stand it any longer and went to see him.

"I believe I saw some letters from Wooler Manor in the morning post, sir."

He lifted his pen an inch or two from the document he was working on, but didn't even look at me. "So what?"

"I thought Lord Beresford might have mentioned a book by Montesquieu he was going to lend me…"

This time he did raise his head and looked me up and down with an expression of profound contempt. "I don't know if you realise, Mr Vholes, how extremely fortunate you have been these last few months. You have spent half your time in one of the most prestigious residences in this part of England, rubbed shoulders with some of the great and the good, dined at their table, emptied their cellar, shared in their family life… and you owe all that not to your birth or your talents but to the generosity – or should I say the unthinking extravagance – of an exceptional man. And I believe that henceforth his Lordship has more important things on his mind than a nobody such as yourself."

He was so irritated that when he tried to put his pen back in the inkwell, he slammed it down on his desk, covering the blotter in nasty black streaks.

"Henceforth? Is it the health of Miss Ophelia that…"

"Just go away and do what I pay you to do. If Sir Robert had wanted to keep you informed about such matters he would have done so already…"

I took my coat and hat and left the chambers without a word.

It was impossible to get to Darlington by the mail coach before the next day. And rubbing shoulders with the great and the good had not, alas, made me a rich young man – I very quickly saw that any kind of vehicle, even one without a coachman, was well beyond my means. I found the solution at the back of some stinking stables where horses for hire were rotting away where they stood: Bucephalus. With its moth-eaten coat, its tangled mane, a kind of stoical renunciation in its eye, the beast seemed in such a hurry to leave this world that it was exhibiting its skeleton in anticipation. It could trot along for twenty minutes only to halt at the body of a dead rabbit, gripped by I know not what interior debate. The ride would have taken four hours for an average rider on an average mount. We took six. Even with the saddle the skinny beast's spine was still chafing my backside horribly.

Unfortunately the weather got worse and I arrived at the Manor exhausted, frozen, bruised and dripping wet. Young Emily appeared somewhat embarrassed to see me. As she helped me out of my sodden coat she confirmed that Ophelia had fallen ill again. Called urgently to attend to her, Doctor Thorne had quickly managed to bring her temperature down but had then insisted on taking his patient back with him to Hartlepool so that he could watch over her convalescence.

"Since then his Lordship has slept very little and hardly eaten a thing. Fortunately I believe he got some good news this morning."

"Where is he?"

"In the library, as usual, but…"

I immediately hurried off to the north wing. After having knocked three times, I took a deep breath and turned the handle.

Lord Robert was just putting a book back on a shelf and yet he started as if he had been caught in some reprehensible act. He was pale, badly shaven, slightly distraught.

"What are you doing here? Who let you in?"

Recovering from his surprise, he gave me an odd smile then sat down at the table he'd pulled over close to the tiled stove. "Of course. I should have realised. You've come for news. There's nothing to worry about, Thorne has done a good job. But it's the climate here, Leonard, it's not good for her."

Hardly had he sat down than he got up again and went over to the window. Everything he said took time to come out, as if he had to listen for an invisible prompt or go over instructions he'd noted down somewhere.

"Sun and moderate warmth, that's what she needs. Southern Europe is being ravaged by war, our colonies are in the hands of corrupt governors or slaveowners. I've thought about Brazil. A new country on a new continent. They say that

Rio de Janeiro is one of the most pleasant cities in the world and, according to Thorne, Portuguese doctors are excellent."

"But the journey…"

"And there's not only the physical aspect. I think that the spectacle of a couple such as Lady Mathilde and myself is having a disastrous effect on my sister. The sooner that farce is over, the better. I will leave with Ophelia as soon as Thorne thinks it reasonable."

"Oh come now, that's impossible. Ophelia and I…"

"My decision has been taken, Leonard."

Everything was going too quickly. I couldn't believe what I was hearing. And never before had Beresford shown himself to be so determined, so peremptory in my presence.

"I don't know what wild dreams have got into your mind," he went on in milder tones and taking me by the shoulders. "Perhaps you have misinterpreted the marks of affection I've shown you… but you have to face facts. For Ophelia you will never be more than a good friend. Go to bed now, I've work to do."

Once out of the room I swallowed my anger and took stock of the situation. It was all over: from now on there would be nothing to tie me to Wooler Manor any more. As I made my way to my room the building was pressing itself against me like a whore: I breathed in its fragrances, I caressed its body. And they were going to tear me away from all this! Whatever the cost, I had to find a way of coming back, there must be one. I felt myself filled with irrational energy and optimism.

Memory can be deceptive: if you make too great a demand on it, it curls up like a snake tormented by a stick… but I would swear that at that moment my future life spread out before me in my mind, precisely in the way it was really to happen: I saw myself riding in a carriage past Neptune and Saturn, getting out at the steps, walking down the corridors, a heavy bunch of keys attached to my belt, giving orders to the charwomen, the decorators and glaziers. And I also saw myself in London, thinking about the Manor in the same way that Alexander, it appears, dreamt over the maps of his own empire. I saw myself as the majordomo of the palace, which is what I was effectively to become.

Going into my room I sensed something unusual but nevertheless I started to get ready for the night, not bothering to light the fire out of laziness. I was already down to my shirt when I heard a voice declare, "You're sleeping in the bed of the Young Pretender."

I gave a start before going round the winged chair by the window. Mathilde Beresford was sitting there. "I'm talking about Bonnie Prince Charlie – the Young Pretender, that's what you call him, don't you? He spent a night here a few days before Culloden."

'Your husband never told me about that," I said, quickly getting dressed again.

"The Beresfords regard history as a personal possession – and one they don't share."

I liked that comment. It reminded me of the blasé and condescending tone in which Ophelia, seeing me look for the signature on the portrait of Beresford's father, had said in passing, "Reynolds."

"You know, all the friends of my father were members of the National Convention and regicides. Round the dinner table at home we would spend our time cursing the aristocrats...

and here I am married to a baron in the land of William Pitt. But do come closer, I'm not the guillotine, you know."

She was wearing a sea-green silk negligee, very chaste if you ignored the fine lacy borders.

"He's just humiliated you," she said.

"I don't know what you're talking about."

"It's written all over your face. You're trying hard to appear inscrutable, Leonard Vholes. You may knit your brow and frown, but in fact you're the most transparent person I know. I can't understand why we two haven't become allies."

"Allies?"

"Of course. To impose our will on them, for I'm sure that's what you want to do. But in fact it's them who are using us."

"No one's using me."

She burst out laughing, then shook her hair, suddenly pulling her legs up under her chin. If she'd wanted to entice me she wouldn't have behaved any differently.

"Beresford uses everybody. When he arrived in France, he thought he was Tom Paine. He wanted to meet the leading lights of the Convention and Danton was the most brilliant, the most magnificent of them all. So he used my father and me to get to him… the fact that at that moment I was Danton's mistress – oh, I'm sure Ophelia will have told you about that in detail, at least in what she believes to be the detail. So that didn't bother him at all at that time, he was even proud of it! You almost thought he was about to proudly reveal it to our guests: 'Did you know that Mathilde, my wife, slept with Danton?' But that was before…"

"Before what?"

"Before he saw that the revolution was a serious matter, not the latest fashionable game. And before fear made his blood run cold. Generally cowards flee at the first sparks of the blaze, or the first explosion… but he's not like that. He gets as close as possible to the inferno, the shooting, he stands on tiptoe the better to see the danger. And when he realises what it is he's paralysed by fear – he's no longer a man, he's nothing."

I suddenly found myself comparing her ankles with Ophelia's. At the same time slimmer and sturdier, they suggested shapely legs and voluptuous thighs. Far from taking offence at my scrutiny, I think she enjoyed it. Despite the chilly air in the room, beads of sweat began to form on my brow and my temples started to throb.

"Robert didn't see anything coming. The more dangerous things became, the more he stuck openly to Georges, Desmoulins, Hérault and the rest… when a friend of my father's came to tell us that the officers of the Committee of Public Safety were coming to arrest us, I saw with my own eyes how he wet himself. He just stood there, wringing his hands. I found his lack of reaction more disgusting than the smell. A few days beforehand my father had advised me to make preparations for us to escape. I'd found two chimney-sweep's outfits in an old-clothes shop as well as some old equipment. I had to dress Beresford like a child, cover his face in soot, take him by the hand and drag him out into the street by the back door. Now I regret it. We would have had more dignity dead than alive.

There was a silence, the candle started to flutter.

"What do you want of me, Lady Mathilde?"

"Above all that you don't get any ideas into your head. It's winter. I hate this country, I'm living with a monster and I'm almost going mad with loneliness… but not enough to throw myself into the arms of the first man that comes along, even if he's sleeping in the young Pretender's bed. Something's going on but I'm being kept out of it and I hate that. I'd give anything to know what's happening…"

"I don't know anything at all. I can't help you."

She gave me a long, cold look. Then she stood up at last. "Perhaps I've overestimated you after all. You're nothing much more than her little lapdog. You perform your tricks and she claps her hands. All you need now is the collar and a ribbon in your hair."

She would hardly have been back in her room when my decision was made: I was going to go to Hartlepool in the morning.

VII

The Egyptian with a Bun on his Head

George Stephenson looks through his magnifying glass. Everything quiet inside. No suspicious noises. No unnecessary movements. The balance wheel and the escapement of the watch are turning perfectly in their casing. The wheels are engaging with one another: you were tempted to say perpetual motion.

Just as in Wylam, in the Stephenson's whitewashed cottage, sheltered by the privet hedge and the little green door with the knocker that never worked, his mother Mabel would be doing the housework or cooking, while he got down to working out the sums Mr Cowans had set. A little after six his father would come home and give Mabel a kiss on the forehead. Then, while waiting for dinner, he would sit down at the table and work on his current project: generally some item for the birds, a perch, a feeder that gradually released the seeds so that the birds didn't eat them all at once. From time to time he would look up and give George a smile; occasionally he would motion him to come over and assign him some simple task such as planing a piece of wood until it fitted into its slot. George would stick his tongue out as he worked, which made both his father and his mother laugh. Then they had dinner. Robert would always compliment Mabel on the meal, especially when it was a rabbit she'd cooked. Afterwards he would read a passage from *Robinson Crusoe* out loud, often one he'd read before – the meeting with Friday: *He was a comely, handsome fellow, perfectly well made and, as I reckon, about twenty-six years of age.* The scene seemed to replicate itself infinitely. At least that was what George thought at the time.

Breguet 1811. He had never seen a tourbillion watch before. Faithful to his own principle, he *feels* the watch before understanding the principle on which it works. He knows that gravity is the enemy of watches, and he senses that the tourbillion movement serves to compensate for the effects of that, to distribute them equally over the whole of the system, to draw them towards perpetual motion.

Towards but not *to.* Perpetual motion is an illusion. Otherwise Mabel Stephenson would still be there turning over the rabbit skin, the red and viscous glove that is only used once, and Robert making the bird-feeder. As for George, he would know of no other sums than those of Mr Cowans. He wouldn't have hundreds of men at his command, a deadline to meet, financial backers to keep happy, a 'vision' to realise.

Something has gone wrong. As with the Breguet watch of Mr Preston, whose invitation to dinner he has finally accepted.

The squire's study is a museum devoted to the passing of time: a grandfather clock with weights shaped like pine cones; another from which a harvester with his scythe over his shoulder emerges every fifteen minutes; above the face of a French clock a chubby-cheeked cherub is holding a curved trumpet to his lips; dozens of watches, kept in display cabinets, are all working and all show the correct time, like torn-out hearts beating in unison, gold or mother-of pearl circles carved out of the recesses of time. But none of them are as modern, as sophisticated as the tourbillion watch lying in his hand.

"Well, do you think there's something wrong with the tourbillion?" Preston asks.

"No, I don't think so, which is a good thing because I'd have great difficulty repairing it. Have you opened it recently?"

"Everyday. I can't help myself, it's too beautiful."

George surveys the squire with his wig and brocade coat, lost in the century of top hats and steam engines. He looks like Robinson Crusoe's father as he appears in the first engraving in his father's book, telling his son not to *precipitate himself into the miseries which nature, and the station of life he was born in, seemed to have provided against...* amid this cavalcade of hour, minute and second-hands, all heading for the future, Preston alone remains stationary.

"I can see that, but you shouldn't do it with your pipe in your mouth."

He hands Preston the magnifying glass. "The tourbillion itself is protected by the casing. No dust can get in. But look there, on the outside of the casing, there's a minute particle that's causing friction and obstructing the second-hand. I think it's a bit of tobacco. Have you a brush?"

Preston opens a drawer. Seen through the magnifying glass the instrument looks like a giant's weapon, capable of putting all the grains of sand in the universe to flight. George manages to capture the shred of tobacco in the bristles of the brush. The two men contemplate the mechanism in silence. Nothing obvious has happened, but they're breathing more freely, as if time itself had returned to its normal course.

"We'll have to wait a while to be sure but, yes, I think that's all it was."

"And how much does such a repair cost?"

George feels indignation rising in his throat. He remembers the look on his father's face when Mr Cowan wanted to give him two shillings for repairing the bolt on the classroom door.

Seeing his expression, the squire stares, wide-eyed, and makes a soothing gesture. "I like to know what men's work costs, that's all. You know why our world's going upside down?

Still a little on his guard, George shakes his head.

"A man's skill is sacred; its price should be engraved in marble. But today it's the market that determines the price! If a man is hungry, he'll be paid less than if he has a full stomach. If two tradesmen offer the same service people will invoke the principle of competition to make them lower their prices. Nowadays you're not simply buying the service, you're buying the man. And that at the lowest price possible!"

Preston puts the watch away and takes George over to the window. "Look at that park. You won't see any French-style flowerbeds nor great fountains."

Indeed, it's a very ordinary park: old trees, a lawn with a path across it leading to the small pond.

"That's not to say that it's not well kept. The trees have been growing there since time immemorial but the undergrowth is cleared away. The lawn is where there used to be a small clearing, no more, no less. The gardener is the son of my father's gardener and he can live a decent life on what I pay him. If the price of bread goes up, so do his wages. When there are broken slates on his house, I pay for the necessary work. When he's sick I take on an assistant until he's better. And I refuse to let those gentlemen in Manchester tell me that I must let the 'invisible hand' do its work."

George doesn't know what the 'invisible hand' is, but he very well remembers Gregson's – soft and sweaty. Outside a cabriolet can be seen next to the pond. A little dog barks, setting off a furious response from Preston's hounds. The moon is shining. Had there not been a slight rise in the land topped by a privet hedge you could have seen Wooler Manor on the other side of the river.

"Off you go! Fetch!"

Woofwoof. Do you really think I'm an imbecile?

Dogs don't talk, of course, but you'd think they could.

Edward watches the water close over the stick and is forced to recognise that his stratagem was singularly lacking in subtlety. And all dogs can swim anyway, even Titus. He wonders why Margaret had so unexpectedly given him the task of looking after the mop on paws. To thank him? But why for God's sake? To punish him? Yes, that must be it. As if she needed to give him additional punishment. As if *she* wasn't punishment enough already.

Woof woof woof.

When we get back to the house I'll make it clear to her that you tried to drown me. That will mean the end of the last bit of affection she still feels for you, that tiny offshoot of love that has lost all its leaves.

His investigation. He must concentrate on his investigation.

Your investigation? Woof woof. Don't make me laugh! It's not your investigation, it's Snegg's. He's the one pulling all the strings. What initiative have you taken since the very beginning, eh? What ideas have you contributed?

Edward closes his eyes and concentrates on Doctor Trees' notebook, trying to recall for the hundredth time what it was he saw in it. That might give him some ideas. He's already gone back to see Trees to have a look at the notebook. In vain.

You see? You're no use at all. Not even for clearing up the business in the chapel with Tom Spalding. As if there were dozens of stammerers in the region. But you're afraid Tom is hiding something from you. You're afraid because, despite his stupidity and total lack of moral sense, he's the nearest thing you have to a friend.

He decides to leave the carriage by the pond and to go on foot along the avenue that leads to Preston's house. It's a compact mass, everything about it totally *necessary*. No frills: no eaves, no pointless portico. He wonders how beauty can spring from such a lack of aesthetic concern – for in its own way the house is beautiful, like a child's drawing, like a cornfield. Titus is furiously nosing round in the undergrowth, trotting along under the ferns. He waddles past Edward, then suddenly gives a squeal of terror: in the gloom of a huge kennel two hounds are rattling the rather fragile bars that keep them back from the visitors. Their muscles stand out, the slobber is dripping from their lips and their wild eyes are already devouring the limbs of the ridiculous mongrel that is polluting their hunting grounds. Edward suddenly feels greatly drawn to the German mastiffs.

"Brute! Braggart! Sit!"

The squire is waiting for him at the top of the steps. He's said to be eccentric. To Edward he seems unbelievably real. A vigorous handshake, very blue eyes, a candid look, almost more than he can bear, a deep, uncompromising voice. He wears the disguise of an old fogey straight out of Fielding like a challenge.

"This is embarrassing, Mr Preston... I meant to come at a more suitable time."

"No, no, it's perfect. You'll stay for dinner, of course. In fact you've no choice, we're just about to sit down to eat."

The dining room is also very *real*: it's a place to eat, not a fashionable showcase à la Raffle, where you display your silver and china. Stephenson, sitting up straight and looking slightly ill-at-ease, greets him. Strangely enough, Edward also feels awkward surrounded by this total lack of artifice and ulterior motives, this authentic example of English hospitality, as if he had no right to it, or carried within himself some impurity, a poison of which a single drop would cloud the most limpid waters.

But fortunately there's some madeira – excellent! – and while the cook unceremoniously sets down before them a huge soup tureen giving off a delicious aroma of vegetables and bacon, while the squire, between two scoops of the ladle, launches into a dissertation on the future of the railway, Edward manages to relax and, ignoring the baleful presence of Titus slumped by the fireplace in a cascade of scruffy hair, fixes his eye on Mrs Preston. For, against all expectation, there is a Mrs Preson: she's twenty or twenty-five years younger than her husband, who's approaching sixty. She's wearing neither a pannier nor stays, nor powder in her hair but a simple high-waisted dress that is still in the best of taste. With her shy smile, round cheeks, pink complexion and wide, slightly wondering eyes she's as beautiful as Chardin's *Girl with Racket and Shuttlecock*.

"Stephenson," the squire declares, "I don't want to disparage your achievements – they're remarkable. But your locomotive won't solve any problems, it will simply shift them elsewhere. Misery will spread as quickly as joy, with suffering in its luggage. Not to speak of our beautiful countryside you're going to ravage."

"That's unfair. We chop down very little."

"It's still too much for our mutual friends, the blackbirds…"

"In general we build the line across wasteland, uncultivated fields of no interest."

"Of no interest, you say? Fallow fields are scraps of poetry you'll be gobbling up, patches of dream you'll be trampling over. Soon there won't be a square foot of land to feed our imagination. It used to be man guiding the plough. Now both man and nature are coupled to the same yoke – and it's called profit!"

Preston concentrates on his food for a moment, but he soon goes on again with the same persistence he showed in scraping out the bottom of the soup tureen. "Now take steam: it was supposed to relieve humanity of all its burdens. But everywhere it's developed I see nothing but pale faces, hollow cheeks, falling wages, jobs cut."

"That's not the fault of Mr Watt."

"I give you that. It's the intentions of men that's in question or, to be more precise, of certain men. In their hands the effect of the technical marvels is like that of the torturer's iron maiden. They crush people more effectively. Why do you think they

198

finance your project? Out of philanthropy? To save the world? Of course not. Because it's profitable for the moment."

Edward looks round the room in which every object has been chosen with good taste. A pretty, dark-wood rustic sideboard – Mrs Preston put her embroidery down on it. Over the mantelpiece is a slightly melancholy hunting scene showing two young lads with well-filled game-bags walking along side by side in the twilight: the shimmer of the fire illuminates and obscures them alternately. By the window there's an upright chair with an embroidered cushion. A few old rifles in a display case. He suddenly feels a desire to go to Stephenson's aid, not out of conviction but jealousy pure and simple. Because he suddenly can't bear the quiet happiness of the squire and his wife.

"Are you trying to make us think that progress is responsible for all the evils, Mr Preston? That beforehand everything was for the best in the best of all worlds?"

"You haven't been listening properly, Bailey. All I'm saying is that it is the same destitution under the veneer of novelty. But while in the past you could legitimately turn to those responsible and, if necessary, cut off their heads, today they're trying to make us think that it's the common interest that is going to triumph, that individual greed will give birth to collective well-being and that starvation, illness and death are mere jolts on the road to the glorious future. There's no one to take responsibility any more, all we have is that invisible hand I was talking to Stephenson about just now."

The cook reappears carrying a masterpiece of roast beef that Edward can already feel melting on his tongue. At that point Mrs Preston guffaws – for Edward her absence of propriety is charming. He recalls Margaret who was perfectly capable of bursting out laughing in the theatre during the death of Macbeth. A long time ago,

"Now then, my dear. Have you found a fault in my reasoning?"

"No, Roderick, it was just that… I was thinking about Miss Austen and the inconveniences Mr Stephenson's invention would have caused her."

"Gentlemen, I have to tell you that Miss Austen is my wife's spiritual adviser. She could have chosen worse! She's a hundred times better than John Knox or Savonarola. But what inconveniences, my dear?"

"Well, for example," there's a glint of Austenian malice in Mrs Preston's eye, which delights Edward, a man who never managed to finish *Sense and Sensibility*, "Marianne would have learnt much more quickly that Willoughby had seduced Eliza and Elizabeth discovered Pemberley much sooner. So Miss Austen would have had to revise her plots."

Preston nods his approval. "Just don't go thinking my wife is a scatterbrain. She has very sure judgment. There's nothing to match a great, beautiful novel. I've read the philosophers but nowadays they send me to sleep. I would willingly give up all their quibbling for Gulliver's stay in Laputa."

"And what do you make of the poets?" Edward asks with a vague thought of Solomon Deeds.

"You can't trust them. They're only writing for other poets, their acolytes, their devotees, people who are like themselves. Even when undergoing the most violent access of altruism, they're still whining about themselves. Novelists are more sincere, they don't conceal the fact that they're trying to appeal to us. And they're more determined, more stubborn. More patient."

"Byron made the House of Lords tremble! And even today he's still risking his life for freedom!"

"Poets lack neither style nor courage, but they're always acting in accordance with the personal myth they've created for themselves. I'm sure someone's told you about the masked ball in Halnaby Hall."

A distant alarm bell sounds inside Edward's head. "All I know," he replies, on his guard, "is that Byron spent his honeymoon with Annabella Milbanke there."

"But your wife was there as well. Me too, with almost all the young people of the surrounding area: Young Glendover, Tom Spalding and his poor sister, who caught her death of cold – a devastating attack of pneumonia. It was freezing cold that night and we were all shivering in our fancy dress. Oh, how stupid of me! That will be why Margaret's never spoken about it to you. Miss Spalding was her best friend, it must be a terrible memory for her…"

Edward frowns and concentrates on his roast beef.

"It was both an audacious and pleasant idea," the squire goes on. "To the horror of his father-in-law, Byron had invited people of all conditions: aristocrats, landowners, farmers, shopkeepers, lawyers and even a few workers from the mines and stable boys. Each one of us was sent a parcel containing the disguise to wear. I was lucky, I was a Roman senator, your wife a Renaissance page boy, if I remember rightly… but imagine how Glendover felt when he had to dress up as a beggar, with old clothes and shoes with holes in them, while one of his valets was strutting round as Henry VIII!"

"But why accept such a humiliation?" Stephenson asks in astonishment.

"Curiosity, my friend. For people such as Glendover Byron was the devil incarnate... but, as everyone knows, you get ten times more fun in hell than in paradise. Only the party fizzled out. True, there was excellent stuff to drink, served by gladiators. The orchestra played waltzes – at the time they were still seen as having a whiff of the devil. And the disguises caused some delightful cases of mistaken identity. But Byron and Isabella remained invisible and around midnight we all went home. The lackey put on his livery again, his master took up his silver-topped cane. A ball can never make good the injustices. A white plume can never dissipate the smoke from the factories."

In the ensuing silence, George Stephenson keeps his eyes fixed on the dark rectangle of the window, where perhaps his locomotives are driving past only in his eyes and the cook, with less and less ceremony, almost drops a gigantic chocolate fudge cake on the table. Fortunately that's the end of the meal, otherwise she might well have served the following dish on the floor. But as soon as he's taken one mouthful – delicious – Edward pardons her bad manners. For a few minutes all that can be heard is the sound of spoons on china. Then Preston wipes his mouth.

"Gentlemen, I tell you that we will need our best writers to become aware of the rut in which we are stuck. And those who put pen to paper must themselves be children of that rut, with dirty hands and fury in their hearts. The profit fever is far from abating. If we don't look out, it will turn into a religion. There's no greater fanatic that a pragmatist."

***

Stephenson puts his hand close to the bars, slips it through a gap. Edward, who is watching from the drawing-room window, is amazed to see the two hounds rush over, pushing and shoving each other – not to bite it but to let themselves be stroked. They stretch out their necks and lick the hand greedily, emitting little grunts of affection and pleasure.

"He's met your dogs before?"

"No, never," Preston replies. "When he arrived, they barked as usual. But then he said a few words to them and that was it. Dogs can sense goodness. And strength."

Now the imposing silhouette of the engineer is moving away down the avenue.

"He's a remarkable walker," the squire adds. "Pease told me that for their first meeting he came on foot from Killingworth – forty miles! At that time he was already an engineer, he could have done the journey more comfortably… but he doesn't like to go to expense, it seems, at least for himself. And what's more he used the journey to get his first bearings. Since he was a bit muddy after going all that way, the Quaker's servant assumed he was a beggar and shut the door in his face. He simply sat down on a big stone across the road, staring fixedly at the house, and after an hour Pease eventually noticed him… I was quite a walker myself, in my younger days. Before I got the rheumatics."

Stephenson is already by the pond. He goes round it to the right and disappears into a copse. As for Edward, an idea has suddenly buzzed across his mind, a mental bee, impossible to grasp…

"It's no use him walking fast and far, alas, he'll never shake off all the profiteers who're already sticking to his coattails. All those blasted speculators who…"

"Roderick, poor Mr Bailey has had to listen to you preachifying during the whole meal… refill his glass and get down to the point…"

Edward wants to kiss Mrs Preston. Not only is her melodious voice a delight, not only is she sparing him a further disquisition, but he also owes her a new glassful of this Portuguese nectar.

Having poured the wine, the squire goes to stand by the window. "I won't beat about the bush, Bailey. We hardly know each other, but…"

"Excuse me, but you said something about rheumatics just now. What exactly?"

Baffled, Preston looks at Edward, then at his wife. "I said I have the rheumatics, like all old people. What has that got to do with…"

"Nothing, nothing, do go on."

"Hmm… so, we hardly know each other but I have great regard for your clerk, Seamus Snegg and he says you're an honest man."

Another cousin. Edward wets his lips with the madeira. "Yes, doubtless. Incompetent, debauched, lazy, capricious… and honest. I spend other people's money, but I don't steal it."

"I know. You're not a paragon of virtue, but my instinct rarely fails me. I have something to say. Something I've kept secret for almost twenty years. Today seems the right moment for it. Do with it whatever you think best. Keep it in mind or forget it, use it or don't. At least we won't be the ones to prevent justice being done."

Edward is starting to find this preamble rather long and wonders when Mrs Preston will leave them together so that the real confession can start. Her hands are moving to and fro over her embroidery and the exercise, so hard to watch when Margaret is doing it mechanically, seems to him now to be exquisitely delicate.

"You know what's on the other side of the pond?" Preston suddenly resumes after having stared out into the night for some time.

"Wooler Manor. You go along the edge of the park when you come here. Did you use to see a lot of the Beresfords?"

"Of course not. I was as chary of the son with his protestations of liberalism as of the father, as Tory as a prize pig. But on the evening of the… disappearance, it was at *my* door that Lady Mathilde's lady's maid came knocking…"

"Oh yes, the lady's maid…"

"It must have been at one in the morning, perhaps a little later, when…"

"Excuse me again, but I know that already."

"But you don't know everything she…"

"That, alas, is only second-hand testimony. As long as we haven't found the lady's maid herself…"

"Let me finish a sentence, for God's sake!"

Wound up, like the springs in his watch, Preston leaps forward to plant himself in front of Edward. The comings and goings of Mrs Preston's fingers over her embroidery – *shoosh shoosh* – the faint rustle of the linen, evoking the sound of a naked thigh on a sheet, take on a very slightly reproachful tone.

"Why do you think I asked you to come, Bailey?"

Edward looks at the squire and the squire looks at his wife, who is looking at Edward, who opens his mouth wide. Mrs Preston puts her needlework down on her knees, smiles and nods her head, as does her husband, and Edward as well who, still not knowing what is going on, proceeds by unconscious imitation. Titus hides his muzzle under a paw in dismay.

"Oh my God!" Edward finally blurts out, suddenly seized by the truth. "But how the hell…?"

"Bear with me, my lad, and listen – though clearly those aren't your favourite pastimes."

The girl with the shuttlecock is still smiling. Under these conditions Edward is ready to bear with anyone until the end of time.

"Lady Mathilde noticed me in Berwickshire," she says.

"At Alastair's place – the Beresfords' cousin," Preston adds. "He's the one who will inherit Wooler Manor if Robert dies without issue."

"She thought I was lively, resourceful and… pretty." She blushes charmingly. Edward is captivated.

"But if she persuaded me to go with her, it was above all to annoy my previous mistress, Alastair's wife. At the time I didn't realise that, of course, I was only sixteen – just as I didn't see the darker side of her character. Her beauty was almost unbelievable. For me she was a real goddess who was going to let me discover a whole world of marvels. I certainly didn't expect to end up in Wooler Manor. Lord Robert and Lady Mathilde had made a good impression in Berwickshire, but as soon as we set off back they started behaving towards each other in that… strange way, that I saw ever after."

"They argued?"

"Not exactly argued, no. They challenged each other. Often one or the other would refer to a far-off event, mention the name of a person or street, sometimes a date… and that with a bitter smile, a nod of the head suggesting that the other had behaved badly then. A book was also often discussed. I didn't know that Rousseau was a writer, at first I thought they were talking about some object or other brought back from France."

She blushes again. Quietly the *shoosh, shoosh* starts up once more.

"But they never raised their voices to each other, there was never a direct confrontation. Robert would make a cutting remark, Mathilde would take it without a word, but one hour, or one day, or a week later she would retaliate with a below-the-belt remark from her own arsenal. Wooler Manor was the ideal place for that kind of sick game."

"What do you mean by that?"

Mrs Preston purses her lips a little as she tries to clarify her thoughts. "Well, at that time I hadn't read *Northanger Abbey*, of course – it hadn't even been published… and, anyway, I couldn't read…"

A further blush, a quick glance at her husband, who flutters his eyelashes almost imperceptibly.

"But when I went to the Manor I was hoping to find that kind of romantic decor in which your imagination can wallow, peopling it with ghosts, fairies, imps and passionate lovers… quite the opposite to what I found there. I somehow had the impression that the air was heavier there. That when something fell on the floor it made less noise. To get the same effect as elsewhere – tidying up a cupboard, ironing clothes – you had to make ten times the effort. Things resisted you. Over there the bubbling ferment of my youth stopped. Movements got stuck as if in a spider's web. And in the middle of the web was Ophelia. Or perhaps Ophelia and her brother. Or perhaps all three together."

"Emily, do remember that Mr Bailey is conducting an investigation. He wants facts. Like Mr Bentham."

So her name is Emily.

"But it's so difficult to explain – that feeling that one of the three was pulling the strings in a puppet play… except that it was never the same one, that each of them could go to sleep as a puppeteer and wake up as a puppet…"

She gives Edward a questioning look and he nods emphatically, not particularly enlightened from a practical point of view, but totally charmed by the metaphor from a poetic point of view.

"Of course, of course, Emily, but please let us now focus on the events – you know very well which events."

"Yes, you're right, Roderick. I suppose I have to talk about that night that has been so much talked about…"

"Go a little farther back, it will make understanding the events that much easier."

"Back to the death of Ophelia, perhaps. I think the brother and sister adored each other. They could have acrimonious arguments but they were only surface ripples, down below the depths of the lake remained calm. And I think that his wife and his sister detested each other. But there, by contrast, the surface appeared calm, the depths tumultuous. When he heard that his sister was dead Robert literally collapsed. I heard him howling like a dog."

"Where was the young woman buried?"

"In the chapel crypt," Preston says. "It was Robert who insisted on it. Since the trouble with the oak tree that was struck by lightning the Beresfords hadn't used it at all."

"Mrs Preston, people say that even before that Lord Robert had it in mind to leave his wife and travel. Is that correct?"

"Yes, I think so. The death of Ophelia will simply have brought the matter forward. But it was a complete surprise for my mistress. She was told about it the day after the funeral, a few hours before he left."

"What really happened that evening?"

"There was a first... scene between them at the end of the afternoon, in Lord Robert's apartments. I was in the pantry, one storey lower, but I still heard the sinister howling I told you about... then the silence... and then cries again, but this time from my mistress. What shocked me was not how loud they were but their nature. She kept on and on repeating the same word, which I couldn't understand, and always with the same intonation and without pausing for breath. Then nothing more. From the stairwell, where I was standing, I heard her go down the corridor and slam the door of her room. When I knocked a little later, she brusquely told me to go away. 'I want to sleep,' she said. Let me get some sleep.' I didn't dare say any more and I never saw her again."

"But, from what I've been told, in the courtyard later on..."

"Forget what you've been told," said Preston, breaking in. "You want something new? Well this is, entirely. It's the first time Emily has told what happened from start to finish to anyone but me. In the middle of the night the police pestered her with questions to which she was in no state to reply... two days later, just when she was recovering, Tim Turnell made his statement: they wanted to tie up the matter as quickly as possible and didn't bother to question Emily a second time. After all, she was nothing but a lady's maid."

"I didn't see Lady Mathilde in the courtyard, Mr Bailey, I heard her... I was woken by their voices a little after midnight. I'd been dreaming about their previous dispute and it took some time for me to realise they were actually down below, outside."

"What were they saying?"

"All that I could really make out was Lord Robert saying, 'You wouldn't dare!' and Lady Mathilde replying, 'Yes I will. I'll do it!' After that the sound of hurried steps, then nothing. Why were they out there, in the cold? The skylight looked out onto the roof and I couldn't see anything apart from the beam of a lantern moving up and down. I hesitated for a long time but eventually I left my room, in my nightdress. At Wooler Manor the servants' quarters were in the attics of the north wing. There was no way down to the upper floor of the wing, even less, of course, to the ground floor where the library is. To go to and from our rooms we had to go along an interminable corridor which went to the main building after numerous twists and turns. But at the beginning of that corridor there was another skylight from which it was easier to see down into the courtyard. That's where I went and I saw Lord Beresford."

"How long did it take for you to get there?"

"A quarter of an hour. Perhaps a little less."

"So what was Beresford doing?"

"Nothing. He was sitting on the steps, his head in his hands, rocking back and forward. Then he got to his feet, picked up the lantern and used it to light the lock on the door to the north wing. He opened it and I could see that his hands were covered in blood."

"Are you sure? Couldn't it have been the reflection of the lantern."

"I am sure. Later on I saw the blood on the door handle."

The girl with the shuttlecock has disappeared, caught up in the torment and passion of a darker picture: a Fuseli or a Delacroix. Or perhaps it's Edward looking on her with a different eye. Now she belongs half to reality and half to *the story*. And now he's no longer listening to her, he *sees* her running back to her room, hastily getting dressed, leaving again. Outside the wind is blowing. Emily is turning all the time, to the left, to the right, going down a few steps then up again without any obvious reason, as if the architect, weary of room after room in a straight line, had decided to amuse himself. Edward had never been there, but he can hear the creak of the floorboards, smell the stale air, the dust, and keeps on the heels of Emily, who is running in front of him all the time, eventually emerging on a landing in the main building.

Edward has never been there either, but what he has heard about the Manor surreptitiously mingles with the memory of his cousin's dolls' house: he sees rooms that are both vast and tiny at the same time and he has the impression that if he stretched out his hand, he could grasp Emily with two fingers, move her from one corridor to the other, from one floor to the other, just like a doll dressed in cambric, *shoosh, shoosh*. As if he, Edward, were the puppeteer.

The madeira's excellent, really.

Emily goes round Mathilde's apartments, then Robert's, calling out, looking everywhere, without finding or seeing anything – but then she does. From a window she sees the coupé arrive from the stables, a carriage as black as a hearse, as long as death. Edward can feel her shiver. She hesitates a moment and then starts going down the main stairs. A glance out of the bull's-eye window: Charles Morgan, the coachman, comes out of the north wing carrying various items of luggage and piles them up on the roof of the carriage.

On the ground floor Emily goes through the little drawing room, then the big one, then the former library, where no one ever goes: empty shelves, dust, a large window with dirty panes where she stands. It's started to rain. Morgan has just climbed up onto the box; a few moments later Lord Robert appears, dressed in his green greatcoat – the one he calls his 'French manteau' – and the tricorn hat Mathilde detests. Of course, he's too far away and it's too dark for her to be able to make out his face, but she knows he's looking in her direction.

With a volley of oaths Morgan sets the hearse going. The other servants were paid their wages the previous day and left immediately – apart from the cook, but on hearing the howls of the first argument, she packed her bags and left, saying, "It's no longer a Christian house, here!" So Emily is alone in the Manor. Alone with, perhaps, the corpse of her mistress.

Shoosh, shoossh.

Suddenly she has the feeling the building is entirely hostile: an animal crouching in the darkness. No question of spending the night there, nor even of going back for her coat and hat, her old shawl will be enough for her and she puts it over her head. She mustn't stay alone. She must run, run to the nearest neighbour.

"A little later Emily was knocking at my door," Preston

says, taking up the story after a silence. "Mrs Wellcome looked after her while the police searched the Manor."

"Did they search the surrounding woodland? The chapel?"

"Yes but it was too superficial, I'm afraid. When the investigation was closed, Emily went back to her parents in Kelso... where I decided to go hunting during the next season."

"And the next. And the next. You were as patient as Colonel Brandon, Roderick."

The girl with the shuttlecock is back. Her happy husband devours her with his eyes, leaving only the scraps for Edward.

"Her father said we didn't belong to the same world," Preston says, "her mother that she was too young, her brother that I was too old and her grandmother that such things 'weren't done'. In one sense they were all right, but... we went ahead all the same. There, you know everything."

"Err, no, Roderick, not yet... if Mr Bailey would grant me a few more seconds."

Edward is happy to grant her them.

"While I was putting my memories in order so that the story could be as clear and concise as possible, something came back to mind. It's doubtless of no importance but... it's just a strange little detail that that happened a few weeks before my mistress disappeared, after Ophelia had left to be treated in Hartlepool. A letter arrived at dinner time and I was the one who took it to Lord Robert, to whom it was addressed. Although the day was chilly and windy, the dining-room windows were all open – a whim of Lady Mathilde who was always 'suffocating' in the Manor. 'Oh, that Vholes again!' the master said as he unsealed the envelope. Then his face contorted, went the colour of the tablecloth, white that is, livid. 'What does he want,' Lady

Mathilde asked. 'Er news… of Ophelia,' the master replied, stammering. Then he stood up and tried to stuff the envelope in his pocket. But he was so distraught that what was inside fell out and the draught blew it across the room, right to the place where I was standing. It was a page torn out of a book. An engraving. Lord Robert hurried over to pick it up, but I had time to see it."

"Was there anything written on it?"

"Yes. At the bottom. Doubtless a title and then the name of the artist. I saw the letters of my first name: Emily."

"And… what was the engraving of?"

"A stone statue. Decorating the door to a tower. Or perhaps a lighthouse. A person with a bare chest, male but wearing a kind of skirt… and a funny hat in the shape of a bun on his head. At the time I'd never seen anything like it, of course… but today I'd say it was perhaps… an Egyptian."

Edward swallows and looks for his glass which, fortunately his host has just refilled one last time.

Shoosh, shoosh.

A dog that can talk, rheumatics, a squire who marries a lady's maid, blood on a door handle… and now an Egyptian with a bun on his head. It's rather a lot for one evening.

***

He's crawling. He's crawling along in the gallery pursued by Mother Mary. *None* Snegg! Are you proud of your nickname?" She's whispering in his ear. "God – none, faith – none, hope – none. Is that what you want?" The taste of soil in his mouth, a strong smell of gas and incense. At every intersection he sees, trembling in the polluted air of the mine, the *face* of one of his dead workmates. Medal, who used to frighten him by making animal noises. Rabbit's Paw, who was lame and had survived one firedamp explosion, but not the second. And above all Halfpenny, his best mate, the one who was a few body lengths ahead of him in the gallery that day.

Snegg wakes with a start: *clack*. Someone's tapping at his window and he lives on the second floor!

At first he doesn't move – the noise must have been part of his dream. Or it was the rain. In his bed, eyes half closed, he recalls another noise: the detonation muffled by the lack of air and the narrowness of the passageway, a sort of croak preceded by a joyful *pshiiitt*, like rockets going up on Bonfire Night. Down there, in the bowels of the earth – they deserved the name because they'd just swallowed up Halfpenny and digested him in a vast semi-organic, semi-geological contortion while a wave of fetid earth was rolling towards None. But *just before* the wave covered everything, just before the tiny support posts that make the galleries look like models and give children the impression they're taking part in some macabre game, for a fraction of a second the air turned into a mirror and Halfpenny was reflected in that infernal glowing mirror. Halfpenny looked at him one last time. It was his face, but entirely devoid of substance, his face *minus* the flesh. That is what haunts None Snegg: the *faces* of the dead.

Then everything faded. Someone was tugging at his feet. One support, stronger than the others and far enough away from the explosion, had held. "You were lucky, it was just a little blast," the foreman assured him later on. All the same, it was big enough to suffocate a child. But he, None, was unharmed, apart from that oddity, that striking detail, that sort of tiny curse at which the lads lowered their eyes and nudged each other with their elbows: not a single hair scorched, no burnt skin, but no eyebrows any more.

That's where Death placed its lips on him.

Clack!

This time he's sure. Someone has thrown something at his window. He's about to go and check when he's pulled back by the elephantine Mrs Carroll, his landlady, who is climbing the stairs and making a racket. "God in heaven, I've had tenants for forty years but I've never seen the like!" She knocks on his door and plants herself on the threshold, cheeks red, arms akimbo, nightcap all askew, her right foot tapping the floor. "Two in the morning, Mr Snegg! And there's that... that ladies' man hammering at the door and throwing stones at the window demanding to see you. You, Mr Snegg, you, so... calm, so punctual, so reasonable! Get rid of him. And that at once."

Snegg finds Edward Bailey in an extraordinary state. Not drunk, even though he's doubtless had a few glasses, but muddy, dishevelled and talking volubly, trying to explain a thousand things at once and brandishing a book or a notebook. After a long palaver with his landlady, Snegg manages to get him allowed in, "A quarter of an hour, not a minute more!" and sits him down on a chair.

"Sorry, I'm going to ruin your reputation."

"I haven't got anything of the sort, Mr Bailey. On the other hand, I do like a good night's sleep and I think that Mrs Carroll..."

"Of course, of course but... it's very important. So

important that I woke Trees as well... look."

"The notebook of Trees senior... well?"

"What can we read on the page for the 5th of January 1798? 'Pains in the joints, Unable to bend knees. No treatment.' And have a good look at the top of the page, Snegg: a child's face, smiling! You see?"

"Yes."

"Children don't get the rheumatics! That is to say that Trees' sketches were not necessarily of the patients themselves but those in the household that interested the doctor from an artistic point of view. And you realise what that implies?"

"Yes."

"That the skeleton found by the workers doesn't *have* to be that of Mathilde Beresford... now we know that at the time there was another young woman living at Wooler Manor..."

"Yes."

"If you say 'yes' once more in that blasé tone of voice, I can assure you that I'll go and hammer on your Mrs Carroll's door and demand a cask of madeira and two whores to finish off the night. Good. It's out of the question to inform the police about all this at the moment. Tomorrow I'm going to do what I ought to have done ages ago: get into the chapel at Wooler Manor...."

"No."

The lawyer, staggered, stares at his clerk. "What do you mean, no?"

"I will not allow a respectable Justice of the Peace to play at burglars and risk being caught on someone else's property. Mr Cobbold and all the other Tories of the region would be beside themselves with delight! I am the one who will go to

Wooler Manor."

"But what difference will that make? If you're caught there they'll immediately make the connection with me."

"The difference is that I won't be caught. I know the area much better than you. I will go at night, using a roundabout route on footpaths. I know how to sneak inside. It's the best solution."

Edward is about to reply, holds his breath then gives a long sigh. He's just noticed the deal cupboard without doors serving as a library. Having also spotted an open book on the table, he's wondering whether he will ever again be able to win over those strange beasts of leather and paper, that are giving him the cold shoulder at the moment.

"You're right, I'd probably mess everything up… anyway, why insist on undertaking anything, eh, Snegg? Why not make do with just turning the pages of a book? By the way, would you have anything about Egyptian statuary in your library?"

VIII

Yorick's Skull

"You were there, eh, Davies?"

Canning and Darwood start to put away their equipment while Hope, his fat buttocks settled comfortably on the deck of the bridge, his legs dangling down, observes Sam as he inspects the pillar nearest to the bank. Close to Darlington the railway will have a fine stone bridge; but in this out-of-the-way place that even the anglers avoid, cast iron will do. Ash-grey, the iron absorbs all the light, but the sun still gives it a sort of granular varnish which, lower down, mingles with the reflection of the Gaunless. In the language of the Vikings it appears that Gaunless means 'useless river'. Today it is quietly lapping the piers, but in the winter so much snow had fallen that the waves swept away the first bridge, designed by Stephenson himself – there is still wreckage from it littering the bank and several deep gashes can be seen in the stone of the abutments. The engineer spent two sleepless nights devising a more solid one with a fourth span and reinforcement under the deck, taking, against Pease's advice, the extra cost of the reconstruction out of his own salary. The new piers look like splayed insects with very thin legs, and the remains of their predecessors, rusting in the water or distorted close to the bank, like dismembered corpses of the same species. Now just the riveting has to be finished, the four of them will be enough for that in the morning.

"I'm sure you were," Hope insists. "A lad like you just had to be at Peterloo."

Sam Davies jumps nimbly from one little cement island – the girders of the base are embedded in them – to another. He has been put in charge of the team, because he's the only one to have worked on metal structures, just as he's also the only one who knows how to rivet. He can hardly remember all the trades he's worked at: he has been involved in so many things that people suspect he keeps adding to them when he makes a list and he even begins to doubt his own memory. Day labourer, of course – everyone has been that at harvest or fruit-picking time. But also stonemason, construction worker, mechanic. He knows how to shear, card, spin and weave wool. He spent three months down a mine. As a docker in Sunderland and Newcastle he got drunk in the sailors' dives and slept several times in a penny hang, standing up in a cellar with dozens of others, simply leaning on a rope that the tenant took down in the morning: "That's enough shuteye, you lazy lot!" Then, in great confusion, everyone would collapse onto the beaten-earth floor that stank of urine. But he's also known proper beds, with clean sheets, and had real jobs properly paid, in well-kept premises, like that brickyard where he was in charge of deliveries without ever making a mistake.

The worst of all is not having to work hard or being hungry, it's being unable to keep his memories in order, the way the rich folk can, those who have a neatly arranged life with an education, experience, a goal. Their memory is a sunny house where you can go easily from room to room; his is chaotic, a dusty lumber room where faces, experiences, dreams, sorrows and pleasures are piled up to the ceiling. Pen, paper and ink, that's what he'd need to make an inventory. And then some time.

"And what do people like me do, in your opinion?" he finally says without looking up at Hope.

"They refuse to lie down. They fight. D'you know why I wasn't seen at Peterloo? Because I was in the clink. Rawfolds, that means something to you, I imagine? The attack on Cart-right's mill?"

The question is directed more at Canning and Darwood, rather than Sam. The two men pretend they haven't heard.

"I was there. I charged with the army of General Ludd. We didn't want to hurt anyone, just smash the machines."

Hope sings a few bars:

Let the haughty the humble no longer oppress
Then shall Ludd sheath his conquering sword

"But some bastard spy had informed on us. They were ready and waiting inside. With pistols, and muskets. And a cannon as well, so it seems, even though they didn't use it. Two of our men got killed, Booth and Hartley. I liked Booth very much. He was wounded in the leg. A doctor tried to save him by amputating it. I remember it was in the snug of an inn and people were coming and going to have a look, with mugs in their hands, as if was a music-hall act. Eventually Booth died and that was when I opened my big mouth…"

"For a change," Darwood mutters as he finishes stacking their tools in the cart.

"I said the people who'd done that were scumbags. And one of the drinkers, who worked for Cartright, recognised me. He testified that he'd seen me among the attackers at Rawfolds but that I was unarmed. They couldn't hang me, but they gave me seven years in jail."

No one can see Sam where he is at the moment and he takes advantage of that to remove his cap to feel the last rays of the sun on his head. His scar itches a bit but it's not unpleasant. At night, on the other hand, it feels tight, stings and burns as if the devil were pouring molten lead into it. He can't get to sleep until the early hours and has difficulty waking up afterwards. Not only does he wonder where he is – that's normal, he's been in so many different places – but, what's worse, he doesn't know *who* he is. The blood is flowing and throbbing against the edges of his scar. It feels as if he's in the penny hang, just after they've undone the rope, half unconscious from falling down and crawling round among other bodies, unable to tell where his own starts or finishes, whether this arm or that leg belongs to him or not. "That's enough shut-eye, you lazy lot."

Sometimes he dreams that he's lying in the dust of St Peter's Field, his eyelids stuck together, his nostrils blocked by a thick mixture of blood and cheese; and when he wakes up he wakes to the awareness that he could have died on that August day of 1819 and that since then his existence has been a flurry of blind, incoherent steps in all directions, like the shoots from the stump of a dead tree. If he doesn't open his eyes at once, the scene continues to play out before him with remarkable precision. He can smell the gunpowder and horse dung, he sees again the big top hat rolling along, blown by the wind, the banner-bearer from Middleton stretched out on his back, unconscious, his cut-off hand lying beside him. He hears two of the Yeomen approaching, "Well, just look, isn't that a nice little radical's hand?" "Keep it as a souvenir. In my opinion it's owner isn't going to need it any more."

"Are we going to get on with it?" says Darwood impatiently.

There must have been informers at Peterloo, at least one per committee, there were others in Lancashire, when the weavers met, breaking the laws on associations: some were very clever and never unmasked, others less so and in front of them they would talk about non-existent 'comrades', or secret meetings that were always cancelled at the last moment. But a spy as conspicuous and bungling as this Hope... a big mistake on the part of the police.

Too big?

A little hampered by the sunlight despite the peak of his cap, he scrutinises Hope intently; he doesn't look as if he's stupid.

"Seven years! You don't know what that means, seven years behind bars... I got out three months after Peterloo, otherwise I wouldn't have missed it, that's for sure."

Canning picks up a piece of twisted iron and throws it away, startling a huge grouse that shoots up out of a thicket and flies off in a flurry of wings.

"That's all past history, that is," Darwood growls. He's already sitting on the cart, the reins in one hand, stick in the other, while the old horse nibbles at one last strand of clover. "Things are different now."

"That's what you think. But I say everything's still the same. Everyday the bosses are getting richer and poor fellows like us are getting even poorer. Even Stephenson, whose boots you lick just because he's 'one of us'... for the moment he needs manpower but once his blasted railway's finished, who'll be out of work then, eh? I can tell you now, he won't be 'one of us' then, not likely! Don't you agree Davies?"

In the course of his tirade, Hope's voice kept getting shriller; he waved his hands about to emphasise his argument and you could see they were trembling a bit. Now he's looking at Sam, exasperated.

"I'm going, says Darwood. "Are you coming too?"

Sam gives Canning a questioning look; in reply he lowers his eyelids slightly. "No, you go by yourself, you'll have to bring the cart back anyway. We'll stay here and chat for a bit."

Canning throws another piece of iron, just to see if there's another grouse there, but this time nothing comes out of the bushes; it's a pity, the rays of the setting sun would have made the bird shine like a comet. The creaking and bumping of the cart can be heard long after it has disappeared round the corner; they feel the noise of the harness is pinned to the sky and silence will never return. But it does and a large drop of sweat slowly drips down Hope's forehead.

When he gets to the farm, Darwood sees Kirstie standing in the middle of the yard.

"They're coming," he says in kind tones before she can even ask.

She nods her thanks and watches him as he hands the cart over to the farm boy and heads for the farthest-off barn. It's huge and almost empty at the moment, with a scattering of straw in which hedgehogs are hiding here and there – they come across them now and then trotting along by the thin wooden walls; when they tease them with a stick, they let out an unpleasant cry, a sort of ridiculous, sickly wail. Darwood, climbing the ladder, is approaching the monumental roof timbers a bat will occasionally fly out of. He's hurrying because the light's soon going to fail.

The hay-loft covers half of the barn. The previous week thirty men were sleeping there, but most of them have now made their quarters farther south, along the future line, beyond Aycliffe, and of a common accord the last four occupants have spaced out their straw mattresses as far from each other as possible – a free and much appreciated luxury.

Darwood heads over to his own mattress, slips his hand into a tear in the sacking and takes out, together with some straw, a sheet of paper. He goes over to the corner where Sam Davies sleeps, picks up the bundle of clothes he uses as a pillow then holds his breath for several seconds, listening for noises from the farm. He unties the string, rummages round inside the bag and almost immediately finds a little tin box. Inside: a worn pen, an almost empty bottle of ink, old newspapers of which all the margins and other empty spaces are covered in tiny handwriting. He adds the sheet of paper he took out of his mattress to them, closes the box and replaces the bundle.

They have no lamps or candles. There's no possibility Sam will open the box before the morning.

And tomorrow everything will be settled.

***

The hall is teeming with very busy people: some enter or leave with bundles of newspapers, others move packages of all sizes around according to some mysterious plan. A boy scarcely ten years old, red nosed and face covered in snot, is ceaselessly climbing up and down a ladder, catching books and putting them in compartments. Outside, in Fleet Street, groups are forming and dispersing, laughter bursting out at the window with the caricature, the same one Solomon Deeds and Charley Dickens were looking at just now before going in:

Rejoicing at the Palace! the title declares. *Distinguished guests such as Intolerance and Injustice are expected (subject to confirmation, these two eminent figures having much to do in France, in Prussia, in Russia and all the other great kingdoms of the universe).*

George IV, a chubby face with a silly smile surmounted by a mass of ridiculous ringlets, and his prime minister, Lord Liverpool: big nose, floppy lips and tied up in a tattered dress dragging along the ground and nibbled by courtiers with poodle heads – are clearly recognisable in the roles of the married couple.

Inside it smells of wood and ink, a bit like Mr Warren's office at the blacking factory, but without the stench of mildew, and with an additional metallic trace suggesting cleanliness, neatness, competence.

"But where exactly are we?" Charley asks, as a newspaper vendor crosses the hall with elastic steps, dumps his unsold copies in an already overflowing basket, drops his receipt in a simple open iron box, replies to a mute question from a little man in a black apron, "Nothing dodgy about it, Lenny, it was just small beer today," and goes across to join two other young men sitting in a corner trimming piles of paper with a guillotine.

"In the Temple of Reason," Solomon replies. "That's what I call the Honourable Richard Carlile's shop."

"A bookshop?"

Charley has just realised there are also customers moving about among the employees of this bizarre place, even though he finds it difficult to distinguish the ones from the others in the constant swirl of bodies, nor to work out what is for sale and what has already been sold. An old man squatting down is going through a shelf of books with a fine-tooth comb, a woman is examining a large portfolio with an expert eye – and it seems that here and there transactions are carried out acrobatically: the old man, for example, stands up holding a book, notices a very busy kind of assistant running past very close to him, grabs him by the arm and slips a coin in his hand. A few seconds later the coin lands in the still open iron box, while the lad who threw it there is already on his way, caught up in a new furious occupation.

"A press room as well," explains Lenny, the man in the black apron, who has come over. "A library. And a printing office of course."

"And what's that for?"

Charley is eyeing a pile of abandoned newspapers – *The Republican* – and immediately chews his lip, aware that he's said something stupid. Why can't spoken words be erased? But the two men seem to have taken his question seriously.

"It's for changing the world," Lenny finally says.

Two open doors give access to two other rooms at the back.

In the first men sitting round a big table are looking through newspapers while others are talking animatedly. The smell of ink and metal comes from the second, where the printers are at work: the atmosphere there seems as studious and considered as it is bustling and hectic in the main hall.

"An excellent engraving in the window," Solomon Deeds says. "One of Cruickshank's?"

"No," Lenny replies. "Apparently the fellow's not doing any more political cartoons."

"Who's it by, then?"

"By me."

"Capital! I'll take a batch at the usual price."

"At a lower price. I'm not Cruikshank yet. Have a look at the latest edition of the newspaper, you'll like it: there's an unpublished poem by Byron."

"Seen it. And the books, anything new?"

Charley takes a few steps away, attracted by the ballet of the printers. He thinks of the Corporal, "We work like the spider weaving her web, in silence and very quickly." Wearing a funny bonnet with a pompom on top, the typographer selects the letters from a kind of tray with compartments; his somewhat slack, flabby face contrasts with the assured precision of his movements. You almost feel it's his own physiognomy he's composing, carefully selecting each trait from an infinite assortment. Behind him another worker is spreading ink over the form with a roller. Seeing Charley, he gives him a friendly wave, as if he'd known him for ever. He's also wearing a hat, but tighter and without a pompom, like a baker's.

Out of the corner of his eye Charley can see that Solomon and Lenny are talking about him – at least he's just read the word *Marshalsea* on Solomon's lips.

"That your father," a voice close to him asks.

"Sorry?"

The boy must be about the same age as him. With very short hair and grey trousers he's occupied arranging fascicles – not quite books but thin bundles bound by a simple piece of string.

"Solomon Deeds, is he your father?"

In a flash the Guvnor's florid features appear in Charley's mind's eye and he can hear his baritone voice, that always becomes a bit throaty at dramatic moments, "By all that's holy, my son, let's leave this establishment as quickly as possible… it's a veritable haunt of radicals!"

"Not at all, he's just a friend."

The boy nods. "He's well known in the shop, he's a good customer, he's reliable."

"Do you work here?"

"Of course, isn't that obvious."

"And what's that you're sorting out?"

"Chosen extracts from important books. Paine, Rousseau, Cobbett. It's less expensive that way, you see, for those who aren't well-off. And when the books have been banned, they're easier to hide."

"Have you read them?"

"Of course."

"Lenny's your boss?"

"No, that's Richard Carlile."

For a few seconds the boy watches Charley to see that this has the expected effect. Then he says it again, pronouncing each syllable separately. "Richard Carlile. He was at Peterloo, you know."

"And where is he now?"

"In prison, of course."

He has incredibly delicate features, a very small nose, like a fragment of sugar candy, and two bright eyes coming and going between Charley and the piles of fascicles – he's taken up his work again. The door out into the street never stops opening and closing, nor the restless jingling of its bell – *dingaling, dingaling* – as if an invisible goblin were prodding it with the tip of its finger, driving it mad. Ignoring the racket, the workers in the print-room continue with their tasks.

"His wife went to prison, his sister went to prison – he does a quick calculation on his fingers – plus George, who was here before Lenny, and Robert, who was here before George. Joe Watkins added it all up once: taking all of them, including the vendors, they got a hundred and fifty years."

"Be doo, I'll go doo brison whed I'b growd up," the boy with the red nose says from the top of his ladder, just as he might have said, "I'll be the king and marry a beautiful princess."

"No you won't, Tom. When you're grown up there'll be no more prisons," the boy with the pretty face says, with a wink to Charley. "But then… what's your name?"

"Charles."

"And mine's Mary."

"Mary?"

Of course! He should have guessed. The bright eyes are looking at him, amused, and he feels himself blush – more than blush, he's gone bright red, his skin goes thick, puffy, stretched over his face, as if it had been larded with a strip of bacon. Fortunately Deeds is waving him over, for it's too much for him, the stampede all around, vendors being called and not answering, the constant ringing of the bell – *dingaling, dingaling* – his heart pounding and that… that something throbbing between his legs, question mark, signalling impending danger.

"Of course, Solomon, you'll have all that tomorrow. Tell me again – what play is it you're going to see?"

"*Hamlet*. At Drury Lane."

"Oh! Oh!" Lenny waves a finger, "there might be ructions."

The fresh air outside does him good. It's a lovely early evening, "Ah, spring at last!" Mrs Dickens had declared the other day, like a customer whose order has arrived late. The colours in the sky over the Thames clash – a playground for the amateur painter, a vast palette on which the red and the yellow are streaming towards the blue of the night.

"As long as our play doesn't get messed up," Solomon says as they leave the Strand to go down Aldwych.

'Change the world,' Charley wonders how you can change the world when you're immersed in it. When you don't have an overall vision, nor an external fulcrum. The world seems to be perfectly *full*, like that shop window on the corner of Catherine Street with so many pairs of gloves packed together that you can't imagine there are enough hands to put them all on, or like that cab that is discharging a swarm of young girls chaperoned by a fat black bumble bee with a jabot outside the theatre.

Solomon hurries along, smiling with pleasure. Three street lights are shining between the columns of the portico; behind them the impatient members of the upper classes – some genuine lordships flanked by young French-style dandies or disciples of Brummell – are gathering en masse, while the more modest impatient theatregoers stand around in the street or finish off their glass in the Nell of Old Drury across the road.

The world is full to bursting, it fits perfectly up against its outer walls. There's no space available for what is better or less good, there is only that which is. But then why isn't everything exactly in its place? The Corporal's hand at the end of his arm and the corkscrew in the sideboard drawer; Charley at school, absorbed in his Latin declensions and Mr Phibes in prison for having thrashed a boy who upset the glue until he bled.

Fully in the light, at the centre of the portico, a group of infantry officers – gilt epaulettes on red jackets, blue trousers, purple belts – rattle their swords and hone their swaggering looks on a passing beggar. Jostling in the foyer, at the ticket offices then on the stairs.

"Sorry, Dickens, but my purse can't afford the stalls."

Everything he was told by his father – that he would complete his studies brilliantly, that he would find lucrative work and end up buying that fine house on Gad's Hill down by Chatham – all that was wrong. Perhaps it's not the Guvnor who's mistaken but reality itself. Perhaps reality has left the main road and got lost in an insalubrious back alley infested with rats. You can't go back. You can't change anything.

But why change things? Isn't this magnificent? Incomparably more beautiful than the theatre in Rochester. Three balconies rise up above the stage; Solomon takes Charley up even higher, to the gallery. The gas lighting pours over everything, chasing the shadows down under the stalls.

No mistake is possible: in this clarity brighter than the sun itself everything is clear, everything is true! The heavy red curtains are quivering over the stage, as if a fire-breathing monster were champing at the bit in the wings. The stalls gently sway to the rhythm of courtesies exchanged from one row to the next, while livelier currents animate the balconies and, above all, the gallery; people upbraid each other, congratulate each other, friends call out to each other from one end to the other, like travellers on two ships separated by a stormy sea.

The infantry officers go down the aisle; seen from above the plumes on their cylindrical headgear look like darts stuck in the board in a public house, or a champagne glass on a tray. They bring with them the dust of Salamanca, the smell of powder of Vitoria, the blood and the triumph of Waterloo. A clicking of heels, eyes fixed, jingling of metal. One of them steps over the low wooden partition of the orchestra pit, goes straight up onto the stage and, hand on heart, starts singing *God Save the King*, while his companions with sweeping gestures try to get the audience to join in.

"They're at it again!" Solomon says. "Just the way they did during the war. Those who refused to stand up were regarded as Jacobins or spies for Bonaparte who had to be reported to the police."

The people in the stalls obey grudgingly, doing little more than move their lips. The people on the balconies stay seated and keep their hats on, while those in the gods shout nonsense and thump the floor with their feet louder and louder until the whole theatre is in joyful pandemonium while the officer on stage is bellowing his lungs out in vain and his companions, furious, put their hands on their swords as if Napoleon's

Imperial Guard had come back from hell.

But just as the noise reaches its peak, the curtain rises and Hamlet appears – or at least the actor who is to play him, black tights, black cape – and his name passes across the rows in a murmur, "Macready! It's Macready!" Charley thought he'd be older. He has curly hair, the look of a child shocked by some injustice, a medal swinging round his neck. Unsheathing his tin sword, he surprises the officer, who beats a hasty retreat – there is applause, the gods laugh fit to burst – then he slowly surveys the audience, row by row, first the stalls, then the boxes, finally the balconies. And the feet stop pounding, voices die away, like candles snuffed out one by one. And, with a mysterious hissing noise, the lights go out, the medal hanging round Hamlet's neck ceases to shine as he disappears, backing out behind the red curtain. Then the curtains slowly part to reveal, in a dim light, the ramparts of Elsinore, where the ghost is about to appear.

Charley adores this moment. He watches the immense shadow of the ghost rising on the pasteboard firmament and quivers with delight when Bernardo exclaims:

"Looks it not like the king? Mark it Horatio."

"Most like: it harrows me with fear and wonder."

***

"...with fear and wonder..."

Unless it's 'with wonder and fear.' Snegg can't remember. Why the hell is he thinking of *Hamlet*? The shadows of the tall trees are tossing and turning in the gale, swaying from side to side, cracking and creaking, like orators hurling abuse at each other. The ladder he borrowed from his cousin Robinson along with the cart seems solid enough. Lurking in the distance is the mass of Wooler Manor, the whitish flesh of Neptune bathed in a dirty yellow pool of moonlight and, right in front of him, the chapel with its gaping cracks, its sides eaten away by ivy and its wheezing tower.

"Seamus Snegg, known as *None*."

He hides the cart in a thicket a little farther on, pats the horse's neck, whispering a few words in its ear, then attaches the lamp round his waist and checks that the object lent him by cousin Leigh is still there in his belt, drags over the ladder and leans it against the wall, under the broken window. One last look round – no one. A gust of wind flattens the tall weeds along the track. You'd think you were at the end of a vast emptiness, beyond all human habitation, and yet you must be able to see the lights of Darlington from the top of the tower.

He climbs up, wriggles through and, despite the narrow opening, manages to get the ladder inside. The lamp he's just lit reveals thick walls, a low vault, a few lines of worm-eaten pews and a stone altar in the middle of the chancel. A jumble of memories comes flooding back: a pigeon-infested barn where his Methodist friends used to pray, the Catholic chapel of his childhood with the confessional like a cage with three seats. And the embarrassment, the unspeakable embarrassment.

He hesitates, but then he descends slowly, walks up and down the slabs, examines the rows of pews. It's twenty years since he set foot in a church or chapel. The same questions are still there, with or without pigeons, with or without confessional, but 'None' Snegg has no desire to hear them. He goes over to the chancel – the crypt must be below it.

Yes, there are the steps behind the altar. "Your 'I don't know' isn't enough, Seamus. You have to choose. God exists or He doesn't, it's the one or the other." He goes down two steps, changes his mind, goes back to the ladder and hides it as best he can behind a pew. "Don't you feel you want all this to have some meaning? Don't you want our life here below to have a purpose?"

"The Beresford Crypt." A good title for Mrs Radcliffe. He holds out the lamp, revealing four rows of shelves right round the room. Funerary décor. Recumbent statues. Bas reliefs. Scenes of hell and paradise on the stone sarcophaguses. All those derisory attempts to clothe the nudity of death, to fill out its desert. To judge by the names and dates, the deceased have been arranged in 'order of arrival', starting with the top row from left to right, then the next etc. Just the way Snegg puts the books away in his library as he acquires them. Thus James Beresford – the licentious, scandalous James, 1447-1495 – occupies, right at the top left, the equivalent place to that of *The Imitation of Christ*, his first book, a prize from the orphanage. And the coffin that is of interest to him – the last by date, right at the beginning of the third row – corresponds to Holbach's *Christianity Unveiled*, found a few months previously in the attic of one of his 'cousins'.

"Your position's untenable, Seamus. However many 'cousins' you may gather round you, without Him you'll always be alone."

He takes the time to read each name but instead of imagining the tribe of Beresfords it's his comrades who died in the mine that he sees – their *faces*. He doesn't believe in ghosts but he does believe in the *faces*. Those that slip into the shadow of the mind. Those that settle on his thoughts.

He's soon gone right round the crypt and reached the last coffin.

Ophelia, our beloved sister
1786-1803

He'd forgotten her Christian name.

"You idiot!" he tells himself out loud. "That's why you were thinking of *Hamlet!*"

There's nothing to suggest the lid has been moved recently, but there's mud on the ground, hardly dry. And a brown stain on the lid of the coffin. It could be blood. Whose blood?

As a child, so as to stop himself being afraid of graveyards, he used to tell himself that the tombs were empty. Now, of course, he knows what is inside the tombs, he knows the gravedigger's song from *Hamlet:*

> *A pickaxe and a spade, a spade,*
> *For and a shrouding-sheet;*
> *Oh! a pit of clay for to be made*
> *For such a guest is meet.*

But this coffin here, this very coffin…

He slides the lid aside, holds the lamp over it and bends down, very slowly.

This same skull, sir, was Yorick's skull, the king's jester.

No skull. Nothing. The coffin's empty. Snegg puts the lamp down on the floor, leans back against the coffin and thinks.

Why Ophelia Beresford? Simply because her coffin was the most accessible, the only one on the third row so the least high up and, moreover, closest to the door. There must have been at least two of them. Doubtless more, to go by the footprints. Racked with remorse and shame, trembling as they were about to desecrate the grave? Or too drunk to realise what they were doing? Or uncaring, ready for anything to pocket the promised reward – for he refuses to believe anyone could do this just for fun. But why be shocked? How important was it that the bones should decay here or elsewhere? She was dead, there was *already* nothing in the coffin. That's what the philosophers Snegg admires think, the atheists, the agnostics, the free-thinkers. Life, then nothing. *To sleep, perchance to dream.*

"So you don't believe there's anything after death? Is that the way it is, Seamus?"

He never saw Ophelia Beresford but he imagines her *face*. Big eyes. Long hair floating on the water, as in Shakespeare: *Her clothes spread wide and, mermaid-like, awhile they bore her up, which time she chanted snatches of old tunes...* perhaps it was *they* who were singing old tunes – doubtless drinking-songs – as they removed the corpse and carried it away. Or perhaps it was a guilty silence, the creak of the wheelbarrow, whispered words, quick, quick, let's get this job done, not think about it any more.

Snegg inspects the interior of the coffin again and finds a scrap of white cloth.

They would also have had to plunge the remains in the mud, immerse them in it, to be sure that only the railway workers would discover them. And then complete the macabre fabrication with... the dagger! Where did they find it? Who plunged it in? Seamus can *see* Ophelia now, stretched out on a sofa in Wooler Manor, the day she fell off her horse, while Trees senior set her three fractures. And then later, on her deathbed, carried off at seventeen by her illness, pale, hair stuck down by sweat, her huge, glassy eyes fixed on the void.

"But where is it, this *void* you French keep going on and on about? Just look out of the window – I can see nothing there but life... life and the fullness of God."

He can feel his old enemy, anger, rising. It's been a long time since he saw it. But here it is, back from its terrible campaign, having thrown oil on all the flashpoints in the world, having suddenly remembered the humble existence of Seamus 'None' Snegg: it only has to blow gently, for the embers smouldering under the ashes are many. Thousands of abandoned children. Hundreds of others dying in the mines. Priests of all confessions promising you the moon to keep you quiet. Philosophers of all hues encouraging you to riot from the calm of their studies. Those who knock you senseless with their faith and those who bludgeon you with their doubt. The death of a child of seventeen. And then to finish off, to make this great swamp of scandal and turpitude, this cesspit of perverse passions and perverted reason overflow, they seize the mortal remains of this child and desecrate them by slashing them with a knife! *Too much of water hast thou, poor Ophelia, and therefore I forbid my tears; but yet it is our trick, nature her custom holds...*

Noises.

Snegg is almost relieved. He'll have a person he can vent his anger on. Or persons. He puts out his lamp. The voices approach, two or three. Happy, tipsy and heading for the chancel. He takes cousin Leigh's pistol out of his belt, silently climbs the first few steps and, twisting his neck, he can see them: three men with their backs to him. They've pulled a pew out in front of the altar and sat down on it as if they were in the inn, drinking straight out of the bottle, each in turn tearing bits off the carcass of a chicken and eating them with their fingers before throwing the bones over their shoulders.

No grave robbers, no great macabre scene today, just a routine to frighten off idiots: lights and Latin gobbledegook in the haunted chapel. Or perhaps they were just looking for somewhere to enjoy a quiet drink?

"*Vinum me transveho,* Tommy?"

"A-m-men.*"

Snegg goes back down a few steps then, very slowly, goes back up, making sure his boots ringout on the stone. When he emerges, the three fellows turn to look at him. One of them drops a chicken leg that splatters on the ground, another tries to put down the bottle without taking his eyes off the terrifying apparition and misses the table: the glass smashes, spreading red wine and a heady smell. The third has his mouth so wide open, he could doubtless swallow the pistol.

"Well, I'll be hanged."

"All in good time, young man," says Snegg.

***

Edward looks at them, one after the other. Edward Lister, the Casanova of Darlington, Stephen Teasdale, a veritable encyclopaedia of dirty songs and, of course, Tom Spalding, the most voluble stammerer in the north of England. There are so many memories tying him to this infernal trio: sarabands of clubs and spades, pirouettes of pretty faces, infusions of gin, decoctions of beer, tisanes of madeira, gourmet dinners and morning hangovers. All three from good families, with no idea of how money is made but past masters in the art of spending it, with all the maturity and intellectual insight of a five-year-old but perfectly capable of constructing six-storey houses of cards or beating anyone at darts after having imbibed a pint of whisky – and the only citizens of Darlington to have welcomed him with open arms.

From the way Snegg, leaning against the door, is staring at them, you can work out that the sheep have no chance of eventually reaching the crib.

"T-Teddy, I kn-now it's rotten… b-but we really h-had n-no choice."

"No choice!" Edward replies. "Is that all you have to say? No choice? Anyway, have you ever chosen anything in your whole life, Tom? Apart from the colour of your wine, that is."

In order to keep his hands occupied, Edward furiously pokes the fire that has just been lit, but doing that means he has a formidable weapon in his hand that makes the culprits lined up in front of him look like three unfortunate chickens about to be skewered. The Raffles on the wall can't believe their eyes: Snegg, the discreet, level-headed Snegg, is also armed, the butt of a pistol is sticking out of his pocket.

"That's all because of the Italian, that Viglioni," Lister reflects mournfully.

"Huh! An Italian with a Cardiff accent!"

"He robbed us blind, all three of us."

"I told you two to be on your guard, for God's sake. You could smell the swindler a mile off!"

"That's true," Teasdale, the least well-off of the three and also the least featherbrained of the three, says. "but we thought we could catch him out. That we'd be smarter than him."

"Smarter, Steve? My God have you three ever managed the feat of being smarter than anyone at all?"

"N-not th-that I kn-know," Tom Spalding admits.

"What exactly happened?"

"Well," Lister replies, "the Italian, or Welshman if you like, seemed very understanding. He told us there was no urgency and just made us sign some IOUs. But then he went and sold them to Lord Glendover."

From up in his frame the defunct Uncle Raffle wonders whether this Lister is any relation of the Gerald Lister who used to drink brandy by the basinful.

"How much?"

"Tom and me almost two thousand each, Steve a bit less."

And that Teasdale, could he be the son – or grandson – of the famous Percival Teasdale, known as Double-Six?

Edward looks up to high heaven. "But what on earth did you do to lose so much?"

They give each other questioning glances and shrug their shoulders, hands wide, as a sign of powerlessness.

"Was it Withers who approached you?" Snegg, who has remained silent so far, asks.

"Yes. He was the one who set up the deal. We just had to do Lord Glendover a little favour and the debts wold be forgotten. We just had to put a spoke in Stephenson's wheel – he was nothing but a Jacobin disguised as an entrepreneur, he said."

(At that Edward sniffs noisily). "And he suggested the trick with the chapel."

"That was quite convenient. We've been going there since we were kids to be left in peace."

"All we had to do was to make a bit more noise and light than usual."

"But the skeleton? Whose idea was that?"

"Withers again. It seems he'd already asked some lads to do it, but no one would."

"We have to admit that he manipulated us pretty well," Teasdale admits. "He really buttered us up, telling us we were clearly strong-minded, far above ridiculous superstitions. He said, 'A skeleton's just a skeleton.' "

"What's imp-portant is the s-soul and that's up th-there with the All-High."

"And the dagger?" the clerk asks, continuing the interrogation. His lower lip is trembling slightly.

"That's nothing to do with us!" Lister protests. "We found it with the skeleton… between its ribs."

"We'd n-never have d-done something l-like that!"

"Did any of you cut or scratch himself during the operation?"

"No. No one."

Three good-for-nothings, three grubby brats of thirty-five. Like Edward. Except that he has an itchy splinter to deal with: Margaret. She sent for him not long ago. Her door was moving, it appeared. *The other woman* was trying to get in. Or, rather – in a grotesque variant of her usual delusion – *the other woman was the door,* changing for a few seconds into a reflective, almost liquid surface you could put your hand through. "Then, all of a sudden, it turned back into wood. Just imagine if Titus got stuck while he was trying to get through!" "It would be too horrible, my dear! We'd have to cut his suffering short."

He goes over to the window, staring at the condensation of his breath.

"Right then. Snegg will draw up your depositions. You'll come round to the chambers to sign them, but they'll stay there. For the moment. And don't let me catch you with a card in your hand, even just to play patience. Off you go now. And hold your tongues for the next few weeks."

Snegg stares, wide-eyed but doesn't say a word. The culprits neither. Their relief is visible, their shame as well. Just as they are about to leave – Snegg moves away from the door at the very last moment so that they have to endure his reproachful look for as long as possible – Tom Spalding turns back to Edward.

"You'd b-better be on your guard, T-teddy. I heard the p-pater talking to Cobbold. They d-don't want you to nose around the Beresfords too much. And they've got s-something in hand. Something they c-could use against… you."

"What could they have against me?"

Tom Spalding shrugs his shoulders and follows his cronies out. Silence. Raffle House absorbs the sound of their steps. The house has already absorbed many other things that it will never give back to Edward: freedom, the joy of living, calm, confidence – and the real Margaret, the one whom he knew briefly in London who was amused by everything. Raffle House is like a stomach that is trying to digest him all the time. One part of him would like to accompany the three good-for-nothings, stop at the first inn and drink, drink until even the idea of thirst has disappeared from the surface of the earth.

With regret, he breaks off his contemplation of the soothing void of the night and turns to face his clerk.

"Oh, no, Snegg, for pity's sake spare me the big scene with the Commendatore. What should I have done, in your opinion? Throw them in jail? It's Glendover who ought to be in there and that will never happen, as you well know... and then," Edward realises how weak an argument it is, but makes it all the same, "they're not really bad fellows..."

"Neither was Tamburlane. He loved his dog and gave him the bones of his enemies to gnaw."

"Huh!"

Edward flops down on the divan and immediately shoots up again; a forgotten needle has punctured his backside. He cautiously runs his hands over the cushions, stretches out on it from one arm to the other – something he would never have dared to do in front of one of the Raffles – and contemplates the ceiling, above which Margaret is asleep. Then, stroking his chin, he starts humming an old nursery rhyme he thought he'd forgotten.

"Mr Bailey?"

"Hmm?"

"We have to take certain decisions."

"Of course, of course..."

"Summon Withers."

"Absolutely."

"Make it clear to him that the secret is out. That all action against the railway has to stop. Mr Bailey? Are you listening to what I'm saying?"

" 'Corpses don't bleed. That woman was stabbed after she was dead.' That was what Dr Trees said, wasn't it Seamus?"

'Seamus.' He'd risked it for the first time and it produced little effect.

"Yes, sir, but…"

"Edward, for pity's sake. Call me Edward. And allow me to summarise the situation as you've taught me to do. Firstly: it's Ophelia's body and not that of Mathilde that the railway workers found in the pond. Secondly: her corpse was found by chance, which means the Beresford affair has nothing to do with Lord Glendover's little tricks. Thirdly: I watched our three rogues very closely, and I believe them when they said the dagger was already stuck in Ophelia's heart. What we must do now is to find *why* the body of this poor young girl was stabbed and then we will doubtless have solved the Beresford mystery."

Edward gets up and strides up and down the room, dazzled by his own reasoning. In a few seconds his mood has changed entirely.

"Since you are prepared to believe what these three rogues told us, er… Edward, remember what young Spalding said. People in high places don't like the idea of you stirring the ashes of the old affair…"

"Exactly! If I needed further motivation, that's it. Dash it all, a bit of enthusiasm at last, Seamus. A little elation and poetry!"

Snegg gives a start.

"Yes, poetry! There's poetry in crime! Don't you feel you'd love to know what extraordinary passion could prime the arm holding the dagger? What occult poison was running in its veins. That's an enigma that's far, far more exciting than the one we've just solved."

"Perhaps, but it's Glendover's actions against the railway that concern us here and now, while…"

"Occult! Perhaps that's the direction in which we ought to be looking… an Egyptian statuette, rumours of black magic… everyone knows that black magic comes from Egypt. Perhaps it's a sort of rite, the meaning of which escapes us… and then there was that strange visitor at the Manor, the man with the Levantine look, an olive skin… an Egyptian? If we're lucky he might still be alive… if only we could track him down, learn his name, know where he lives…"

"John Newton, 6, Palace Green, Durham."

At this point in the conversation Edward's striding up and down has brought him back to the sofa again and he collapses onto it with all his weight.

"Ouch! Damned needle!" (His clerk carefully clears his throat.) "What new marvel is this, Snegg?"

"I'm quite happy with Seamus, now that I've got used to it. The arrival in these parts of a swarthy individual, a 'darkie' as they call them here, is still sufficiently rare to stick in people's minds, even twenty years later… especially since Newton had a face that was… unforgettable, Horribly burnt. Al Carr, the landlord of the King's Arms, remembers him very well and he kept his register scrupulously."

"Does he remember anything else?"

"The man wasn't the chatty type. He stayed in Darlington twice. As the Joanna told us, Charles Morgan went to fetch him, took him to Wooler Manor and then took him back home afterwards. It was generally thought that, despite his surname, he wasn't a… 'Christian'. There were books lying around in his room, written in Arabic, according to Carr, and full of diagrams and strange drawings. Rumours were flying around at the time… people were talking about pagan rites, black magic…"

"That's what Jean Morgan said as well. When were you thinking of bringing me up to date?"

Pure Sneggian play with his non-eyebrows. Edward is annoyed with himself for what he's just said.

"Carr spent the winter with his sister, in Hartlepool, his clerk says. He came back yesterday. This morning, as you know, I went to Durham in an attempt to sort out the dispute over the Haworth will…"

"Haworth, hmm, yes, of course…"

"And I went past the address I'd been told – a certain John Newton does still live there. My evening has been a little bit… full, as I'm sure you'll agree. I was waiting until we were alone together to tell you the news."

Edward goes over to his clerk and places his hand on his shoulders. "Seamus, never forget that basically I'm just a scoundrel, like Teasdale, Lister and Spalding. There, I've said it! Now I think that courageous confession deserves a glass of madeira…"

IX

Peterloo

Shoosh-shoosh, The needle comes and goes, gigantic. Edward can't see it but he can hear it, and he feels the shiver of the cloth it's moving across and back, below, above, for he *is* the cloth. Or, rather, *he is the embroidered design.* Every time it goes across, the touch of the needle gives him hope, joy and the burning sensation of love. Every new stitch invents a little more of him, at the same time crucifying him, wrapping him in his linen shroud. He's waiting for deliverance, the climax of pleasure, the peak of pain when all the stitches have been embroidered and the needle will pierce his heart, at last.

Shoosh-shoosh, shoosh-shoosh. The needle is approaching.

But who is it holding the needle? To whom does this continent of a face bending over him belong, this ocean of a look enveloping him in a warm and gentle swell? These finger-rivers whose quiet pressure he can feel, long snakes lashing, thrusting, sliding, caressing? Mrs Bailey or Mrs Preston? Margaret or Emily? As long as it's not Lady Mathilde…

And he, who is he? What design is he about to become? He'd like to lift up his head and have a look at his body, but the tambour hoop keeps him under constraint, quartered, the needle pierces him, he can't move. Every time a fingernail-lake rises above him, he tries to see his reflection in the lustrous pink curve, or in the polished white of the half-moon – but in its incessant to-and-fro the mirror now captures the light that blurs the reflection, now goes into shade that obscures it.

Shoosh-shoosh.

If a sworn representative of Reason, in a grey apron, glasses on the end of his nose, hair cut to stubble and boredom in his buttonhole, were to come and tell him, "Stop running away from reality, Mr Bailey. You're not an embroidery design, you're a lawyer in Darlington. At the moment you're in a Bull Wynd brothel, in the hands – or, rather, lips – of a young woman whose lingual dexterity and palatal charm you will remunerate at the set tariff of one crown." If that were to happen, he would shake his head vehemently – though he can't shake it at the moment – grab the killjoy by the collar – does he have hands? – and throw him out.

But suddenly the fingernail is no longer a mirror, it's a shield in which he is contemplating his future defeat – Edward wants to be vanquished, he wants it with heart and soul – and finally he sees himself as he is inside himself: outlined in dirty grey thread, his eyes bloodshot, his paws misshapen, the skin of his belly hanging down to the ground, his muzzle grubby and sly: a nightmare of an embroidered dog.

Titus. He's Titus.

A dog? Doesn't matter. The ugliest, most disagreeable dog in the world? He couldn't care less. All that he wants is the needle in his breast: oh let it come, let it impale him, he'll roar with pleasure and that won't be long either, things are moving, he's going to, he's going to…

Not immediately. The young woman has stood up, wiping her lips with her hand. He recognises her, it's Crissie, or Kirstie, or I don't know who, the one who wants to be called by her real name. The first time he didn't see how pretty she was: a Grecian face, taut, determined. Byron would like her, there's no doubt about that…

"Well, er… Chrissie…"

"Kirstie."

"…Kirstie, what's going on?"

She remains silent, motionless, while Edward's member is throbbing. Like a litter of kittens tied up in a sack, the pleasure is writhing but can't escape.

"Is there a problem, erm… a financial problem?"

"No."

"Good, because…"

"You're a justice, aren't you?"

He sighs softly. "Of a kind, yes…"

"Then you have to help me."

"To do what."

"To put right an injustice."

***

Following the instructions he was given, Stephenson goes along the back of the town hall, then through a carriage entrance into a yard with uneven paving stones. Though the rest of the building is brand new, this part gives the impression of not having changed since the time the Stuarts were there. From the other side of a high, grubby wall comes the stench of meat and vegetables from the covered market, the distorted sound of voices, steps, items being chopped up and carts moved. It's as if the sole function of the yard where Stephenson is standing was to serve as a sound box for the invisible market hall.

Anyway, this wasn't how he imagined the offices of the police in Darlington. But for the moment nothing can spoil his good mood, neither the sordid surroundings, nor the drizzle spattering his hat or the prospect of confronting the arrogance of Alfred Cobbold. He has just been to the factory in Forth Street, Newcastle, where his son Robert showed him the plans for *Locomotion*. The appearance of the engine will be like that of its 'ancestors' in Killingworth: two vertical cylinders driving two axles by a system of horizontal connecting rods. But what fascinates George are the tiny improvements, the details invisible to the layman, the fuselage of the boiler, the wheels that are both elegant and compact, the polished, finished impression the whole made. That's the kind of thing that really interests him: the details, the fine-tuning. And to know that it's his son who is the creator of this marvel fills him with pride, with quiet jubilation such as he felt so often during his own father's time in Wylam.

As well as the detailed plans, Robert has painted a watercolour, purely for decoration, in which the colours are used to suggest the nature of the materials: the varnish on the boiler cover, that looks like a gigantic barrel on its side, gives the deep black of the cast iron a soft gleam. Beside this perfection poor old *Blücher* is nothing but a prehistoric monument. It seems strange to him that such a concrete, tangible object, belonging to the limited technical world, can at the same time be a work of art arising from the joint dream of a father and his son.

A little door opens and a podgy hand beckons him in out of the rain. Going past a window covered in wire mesh, he enters a kind of narrow, low-ceilinged office, at the far end of which is Alfred Cobbold.

"Would you be good enough to close the door, Mr Stephenson... you wouldn't think it was spring, would you?"

The room, almost as shabby as the yard outside, despite a few more valuable pieces of furniture, is like a laboratory for the most awful olfactory combinations: the stench from the market spreads there, even though the door and window are closed, mingling with the aroma of urine and faeces. However, the setting does nothing to disturb the self-assurance of the policeman.

"These small towns, my friend," he says, putting his hands apart in a resigned gesture. "They've nothing to offer people such as us. No comfort. They stink and then we're bored as well. Stand at the least crossroads in London, Manchester, Newcastle and in an hour you'll have enough material for a novel. But here... you feel time passes more slowly... no, it's worse than that: you feel it doesn't pass at all."

George is about to smile – he who grew up in a tiny village and finds Darlington decidedly too busy. But then he notes that 'us', tying him to the policeman: 'people such as *us*'. He doesn't want to have anything to do with that *us*, any more than with that *us* of Gregson's. *Us* should be reserved for members of the same family, or for those who work together to construct something with their hands and their intelligence.

"I'm here for two things," he says tartly. "The authorities have sanctioned the construction of the Stockton-Darlington line. Parliament passed a motion supporting the project. Consequently you ought to do your utmost to allow me to complete my work. Yesterday a group of men threatened my plate-layers once again. The last time that happened I gave you some clues to find these troublemakers and you've done nothing. Mr Pease is writing a letter to the Home Secretary."

Cobbold, his hands folded over his mouth like a monk, calmly accepts this and raises an eyebrow for the next item.

"And then you're still holding Sam Davies. I need the man. Four days locked up for an argument among workers seems a bit long to me."

"Hope came out of it with three broken ribs, a black eye and a smashed jaw. If all the arguments between workers ended like that you'd have no workforce any more, Mr Stephenson…"

"But you released Canning… why not Davies?"

Cobbold gets up out of his armchair. He clicks his tongue, but it's not clear whether it's in irritation or simply a nervous tic. He goes past George with a calming gesture and stands at the window. He looks out through the wire mesh, hands behind his back, going up on his toes, then back down again four or five times, as if he were practising doing points.

"I can't fulfil both your requests at once, Stephenson."

"Why not?"

"Because Davies happens to be one of those troublemakers you were complaining about."

George starts. Outside the rain is pouring down the black wall and washing out the gaps between the slabs.

"I don't believe a word of it."

"You don't?" the policeman replies, turning round. "I know from a reliable source, corroborated by several witnesses, that he was involved in Luddite group in Leicester in 1811."

"He was just a boy at the time…"

"…and that subsequently he was at Peterloo, among the most radical demonstrators."

"So what? Today he's my best worker, the most conscientious, the most efficient."

Cobbold's chubby face looks as if it had just received a blessing, divine benediction. He opens a drawer in his desk and brandishes a sheaf of papers as if they were the Tables of the Law.

"This is what was found under Davies' bed. I think no more need be said."

They are the kind of tracts that are circulating everywhere in Darlington, in Stockton, even as far as Middlesborough: *The railway is the Devil's road… one locomotive running, a hundred carters out of work… Stephenson is working for the bosses.* They're counting on fear and incredulity, distorting the facts, contradicting each other: a pack of lies.

Stephenson shakes his head obstinately. "That doesn't prove anything. Anyone could have hidden them among his things in order to incriminate him. Perhaps that man Hope… you know very well who had this drivel printed: Lord Glendover and a few other Tory landowners, and you're trying to make me think Sam Davies is both a dangerous radical and one of the henchmen of the Tory extremists?"

Alfred Cobbold puffs out his cheeks and blows a vulgar raspberry. "I'm not a politician, Stephenson, I'm only interested in facts."

"I'm not a politician either, I simply want to get my employee out of prison. I need to speak to him."

"Of course, tomorrow morning. At visiting time."

"Visiting time…"

The two men look each other up and down, Cobbold with a little amused smile, Stephenson making an effort to stay calm.

"Tomorrow morning," he finally says. "I'll come with a lawyer."

Through the mesh the policeman watches the engineer stride off, then he crosses the office, opens a panelled door and goes down a narrow staircase where a warder with a face like a fish is dozing.

"He's been scribbling rubbish on the walls again," the man says.

With a jerk of his chin Cobbold gets the bunch of keys and goes along a little corridor with two doors. The first is open and the cell empty. He unlocks the second and sees Sam Davies stretched out on a straw mattress.

"Everything all right here, Davies?"

No reply. The wind bursts in along with the sales patter of a greengrocer in the market.

"Rather chilly, isn't it? Fortunately you've got your hat… you can catch a cold through your head, as my mother used to say."

Whistling a few bars of a rousing song, Cobbold goes over to the wall, scrutinising the saltpetre, stands up on tiptoe and comes down again, two or three times. Then he performs a little chassé to the right and continues his scrutiny.

"What did you do that with?"

The prisoner doesn't open his mouth, he just holds out his right hand, the nails of which are covered in a white deposit and bleeding here and there. Indeed, there is more 'rubbish' – that is to say inscriptions – than there was the previous day. At first they're not noticeable, just shallow streaks on the surface of the saltpetre; it's only when you look from close to, as Cobbold does now, that you can make out cracks and other scrapes, and eventually decipher them.

" 'Sam Davies is alive'... well done, my friend, very true. And... well, look, here's the corollary: 'Sam Davies *wil* die'... Perfectly true, apart from the spelling. Now let's see if our philosopher has thought about my little proposition?"

Still not even the hint of a reply, but Cobbold doesn't take offence, on the contrary, he looks as if he's enjoying himself.

" 'What is *writen wil* not die.' Excellent, excellent! Oh, Sam, if you'd work with me, you'd be beyond suspicion. The best informer that ever was seen. All the game you'd catch for me. A veritable industry it would be. I was almost disappointed to trap you so easily, you know, I thought you'd be a much tougher nut to crack. But then perhaps you deliberately got caught. Perhaps you've had enough of being Sam Davies. What I'm suggesting is that you should change your life without the others noticing, wouldn't that be ideal?"

"And you?"

"What about me?"

"Have you never had enough of being yourself?"

"But I'm not myself. I'm no one. I'm a function, that's all. I have to make sure the world keeps turning without a hitch. That events don't leave too deep a trace and that fundamentally tomorrow will be the same as today."

"That's a trade, is it?"

"Of course. Otherwise I wouldn't be paid to do it."

As he wipes away all the inscriptions, Cobbold's expression darkens. " 'They are *powerfull* because they can write… sometimes I *woud* like to become a book.' " It's as if he's suddenly seen their import, revealing a violent attack against himself. He looks at the man with the cap and goes on in hurt tones.

"You've said it yourself. Look here: 'Even those who *writes wil* die.' So why this determination to leave a mark, eh, why? Why this pride?"

Sam turns away. Cobbold gives a long sigh, looks round the walls one last time and leaves the cell, throwing the keys on the table in front of the warder.

"This prison's a real pigsty, Posthill. The bedding's teeming with vermin."

"I cleaned out a cell thoroughly only yesterday," the fishy man says, rolling his eyes. "I'll move old Scarface tomorrow and…"

"That's not enough. Everything has to be whitewashed again with quicklime. First thing tomorrow I'm going to have the prisoner transferred to Stockton."

"Stockton? But why not put him instead…"

Having seen the look in his superior's eye, the warder stops short.

***

"A pint of beer, Grant, and… how old are you now, Number Two?"

"Twelve."

"Hmm. A pint of beer and a lemonade."

The refreshment room in the Marshalsea is dark and damp.

Behind the counter, which consists of a plank on huge barrels held together with hoops, Grant fulfils the order. The Corporal grasps the handles of the two mugs in his one hand and goes to Charley who is sitting at the table closest to the bar.

"It's an eternity since we saw each other, my lad."

"I can only come on Sundays, and last Sunday you… weren't well."

"Drunk as a lord, you mean. That's the best thing you can do in the Marshalsea – get thoroughly drunk. And yet things do happen here… children are born, from time to time. People die in all possible ways. Of apoplexy, heart attacks, from falling off a chair, from choking themselves on a potato. Or simply from old age. I saw one prisoner try to kill another by hitting him with a skittle. Two or three years ago a religious crank called Fairbanks got up on the roof and started bawling out that he would be the next King of England under the name of Melchisedec! They eventually got him down and sent him to Bedlam."

The old soldier takes a long draught and gives a satisfied sigh. "So, you still want to know what happened to my right hand?"

"If it's… no trouble telling me."

A further draught. The Corporal squints as if trying to focus on a distant object.

"When I got to Lancashire," he says after a short pause, "I hoped I'd find my family, my friends, my house… but my father had died by then. My mother, too ill to keep her position as cook at the big house, was living in the town with her sister. And everything seemed strange to me. The weeks continued to pass. People went about their imperturbable daily routine.

I felt like grabbing them by the shoulders and shaking them; yelling at them that this just wasn't possible! That you couldn't simply go on as if all that had never been – the cannonades, the hand-to-hand with bayonets, men's guts sliding down onto the ground, arms and legs flying off. But I had other concerns. I had to find work by hook or by crook. It wasn't easy. The big printing firms had bought steam-driven presses that I didn't know how to operate. The smaller ones had shut up shop, like my former employer, or weren't taking anyone on. There were a few independent papers but they couldn't afford the tax on the press and so had to remain clandestine. You had to be resourceful. I saw people drop a few coins through a cellar window and get a few crumpled pages in return that seemed to come up out of the ground. Cobblers used to sell papers by hiding them in shoes. Some would slip banned publications inside the front page of the *Times* or the *Leeds Mercury*. Eventually I found a position with the *Manchester Observer*, a new opposition newspaper. The magistrates kept a close eye on it, but the editor, James Wroe, had a certain amount of luck and could afford to pay the taxes. He was the man who made me see that my first impression was mistaken: times had changed. Destitution was getting worse. Injustice was flaunting itself. Starvation was becoming a national sport. No one believed in campaigns of violence, as they had at the time of the Luddites, but…"

He taps his head with his corkscrew.

"It was there that it happened. Inside people's heads. The radicals had lost the armed conflict, they wanted to win the war of ideas. And it worked. Their ideas were gaining ground. They no longer frightened off the moderate reformers. The

Whigs started to see them as acceptable allies, numerous and determined enough to bring the government to its knees and also easy to control once the moment had come... at least that's what they thought.

"That led to the idea of a large peaceful assembly through which the movement would demonstrate its strength while respecting the law. Wroe and others formed an organising committee and invited the great Henry Hunt. On August 16th all the societies in Lancashire were to send a delegation to St Peter's Field. It would be a triumph! We'd demand parliamentary reform, universal suffrage, the repeal of the Corn Laws and thousands of other things. All calmly, decently, respectably. At least that's what we hoped."

From time to time debtors would cross the little room to replenish their glasses, but they didn't stay – they went back to the common room where the card games were in progress. Even if there was no written rule stipulating it, the four tables of the bar were reserved to certain distinguished residents. The Corporal was one of them. Before going on he looks at Charley.

"As you're twelve now and are a man, you've the right to know the truth. And I'm going to tell you that right now: ideas aren't enough. In France Voltaire and Rousseau weren't enough. It needed brave people to roll up their sleeves and storm the Bastille."

Charley remembers an engraving his father had shown him: wild-eyed people with twisted mouths and wearing bizarre caps carrying the head of the governor of the Bastille on the end of a pike. He'd had nightmares about it for weeks because of the word *governor* – he could see his father's head floating in the air, his lips uttering inaudible words.

"Have you seen a boxing match? When one of the fellows is knocked out the referee stops the fight. They throw a bucket of cold water over the loser to wake him up, and the winner shakes his hand. But in real life there's no referee, no bucket of cold water and people don't shake hands. It's a fight to the death. While I was working for the *Manchester Observer* I couldn't stop thinking about John Lange. I wanted to share these new ideas with him. He was rich, of course and I was as poor as a church mouse. But he was a Liberal and we were foster brothers – and brothers-in-arms as well. When you're fighting side by side you're not interested in who earns ten shillings a week and who has a thousand-acre estate. Officer or not, you often eat the same grub. The only demarcation line between men is that separating the dead from the living. I wrote him enthusiastic letters, going on about the great project of the gathering and was surprised not to receive a reply.

"One Sunday, not being able to stand it any longer, I borrowed a horse from James Wroe and rode out to Salford where the Langes lived. Now listen carefully, Number Two: there's nothing more pleasant that riding across the countryside, thinking of nothing. But the countryside wasn't the countryside any longer, cotton mills were sprouting everywhere and the simple smell of the horse reminded me of the war. John wasn't at home and neither his father nor his elder brother William would see me, assuming I was going to ask for something. The estate workers I met, all newcomers, refused to answer my questions. Duke, my favourite horse, was still there, tethered in a meadow, old and sick. I started to cry on the way back.

"Fortunately I had things to do. The 16th was approaching. In the evenings I would give a hand to the group of old soldiers who were to act as stewards. We had to make the arrangements for Hunt's arrival, sort out the question of precedence between him and the local figures such as Samuel Bamford, select the assembly points, supervise the making of banners – one for each delegation, Middleton, Oldham, Rochdale, all of hand-woven silk, embroidered with gold thread – unmask Nadin's spies and, above all, see to it that everyone could get to St Peter's Field unhindered, without any vindictive slogans or pointless provocation. Wroe, having seen that I was good at compiling reports, gave me the task of writing an article describing the preparations for the demonstration. It was marvellous to take the letters for it out of the case to set my own words, not those of other people, and then to see them printed on the page. But I made a mistake, one terrible mistake."

"What?"

The Corporal nods grimly. Voices can be heard shouting out in the courtyard, cries echoing. An argument. He doesn't pay any attention to it.

"Every word counts, you just remember that, my lad. Words are there to serve us but you have to rule them with an iron hand, otherwise they'll turn against you. During July we got the more active members of the delegations together to teach them how to march in step and hold their banners high. Everything had to be orderly. The text of every placard had to be approved by the organising committee... I remember one that set quite a lot of people's teeth on edge: 'Equality between men and women!' We wanted people to know that we weren't a horde of beggars and down-and-outs but a well-organised group following a very precise goal. In order to describe these preparations, I could have used the word *rehearsals*, that would have been perfect, since we wanted to put on a show of our strength and impeccable discipline. Only I chose the word *manoeuvres* and James Wroe approved it… you realise what that means? *Manoeuvres* belongs to the military vocabulary. Now none of us had any kind of weapon at all, not even sticks, contrary to what was said afterwards. But everyday Nadin, the Deputy Chief Constable, made the magistrates read the *Manchester Observer* and every evening the magistrates sent a copy to the Home Secretary, Lord Sidmouth. And they found it easy afterwards to justify their decision by talking about our 'manoeuvres' and claiming they believed we were organising an uprising.

"So on the 16th of August, when tens of thousands of people found themselves stuck between the buildings along the waste ground of St Peter's Field, when Hunt in his white hat climbed onto the platform to speak to the crowd, the magistrates, stationed in one of the nearby houses, decreed a state of emergency and sent word to the Yeomanry. You know what these yeomen are, Number Two?"

Proud of his knowledge, Charley replies at once, "They are volunteers of respectable standing who maintain public order when the police force is insufficient."

"Good Lord! What a pretty little parrot. I could be listening to your Tory father!"

Charley feels a blush spreading over his cheeks, while the Corporal gives a bitter laugh.

"The Yeomen are smallholders who are ready to do anything to defend their prerogatives. Servile towards the powerful, pitiless towards the poor. The powerful they respect because they only acknowledge force. The poor they hate because they feel them close, hanging onto their coattails. Their grandfathers or great-grandfathers had been poor in the past until a piece of good fortune or a trick helped them get their heads above water. And they don't want to go under again. They'll ride roughshod over anything – or anyone – that threatens to pull them back down. And that's exactly what they did at St Peter's Field, literally. The magistrates' orders were to arrest Hunt, Bamford, Wroe and all the rest, then to disperse the crowd. But how could they disperse the biggest assembly in the history of England – sixty thousand at least, gathered in a tiny rectangle of a few acres, hardly able to breathe in the suffocating heat, crushed up against the platform on the north and against the buildings on the other three sides? They simply rode into them, Number Two, clearing a bloody path. With their sabres. I saw the shoulder of Thomas Redford, carrying the banner of Middleton, split in two like a log. They hacked down women, trampled over children. And shouting out insults all the time. 'I'll give you your reform! There you are!'

"And the worst thing about all this, my lad, was that these people *knew each other*! It wasn't the English or the Prussians against the French, it was farmers against their ploughmen, the millowners against their hands, craftsmen against their employees. I heard an old woman near me cry out, 'No, Tom Shelmerdine, you're not going to hit me. I suckled you!' But the said Tom Shelmerdine did hit her. Another yeoman almost knocked me over as he was galloping towards a man who was carrying a big cheese on his head, for the idea was to finish the assembly with a picnic. 'You filthy striker, is this *radical* enough for you?' the yeoman said, slashing him on the head, his sabre going right into the cheese. I don't know whether the fellow survived it. Some people did manage to escape in the alleyways or hide in nearby houses, but most just stood there, stuck to each other. The wounded didn't even have room to fall down, they simply collapsed onto their knees like suits of empty clothes. Just as I picked up the Middleton banner the hussars of the Fifteenth Regiment arrived to give assistance to the yeomanry. The Fifteenth! My regiment!"

He gets up and, with a nod, asks Grant to refill his mug. He pays and empties it in one draught, standing at the counter, then goes back to the table.

"The hussars were using their sabres as well, but I don't hold it against them. It hadn't rained for days and the trampling crowd, the galloping horses had raised a huge cloud of dust. They could hardly see anything at all. They'd been told it was a pitched battle with allies on one side, enemies on the other, just like at Hougoumont. So they did their job – before realising it wasn't a battle but a massacre. The massacre of Peterloo, that's what it's been called since. The hussars know how to go about it. They keep a tight hold on their mounts. They're soldiers, not butchers. They weren't there to settle personal scores, they spared the women and children, and those who were trying to run away, concentrating solely on those they saw as a potential threat: those who faced up to them carrying banners. You can unseat a horseman with the pole of a banner. And that's why John Lange chose me – and he was quite right to do so. In his place I would have done the same. He suddenly appeared out of a cloud of dust. Magnificent. His uniform impeccable. His shako nice and straight, his dolman in place, wearing his regulation cape despite the heat. He evaluated the situation with a single glance, took the right decision in a fraction of a second. Thought there was no point in chopping me down – I had no weapon. The only danger was the banner pole and thus the hand that was holding it. I will never know whether he recognised me and I don't want to know. He dealt with the danger while causing the minimum of damage. If I'd been riding beside him, I'd have said, 'Well done, John,' and he'd have given me a wink.

"One hand. What's one hand compared to the four million who died in the war. Nothing. Anyway, the extraordinary thing is that it disappeared. When I regained consciousness, some fellows where heaving me up onto a stretcher. Strangely enough, I didn't feel that bad. Just a cold feeling at the end of my arm. I realised I'd lost the hand when I tried to lift it up to wipe my brow. So then I looked at the ground all around. There were dozens of hats, big hats, little hats, a lot of white top hats like Hunt's. You'd have thought a hatter had spilled his load. And then banners torn to pieces. The laurel branches the delegations were carrying. A cheese cut in two, hair stuck on the crust with blood. A watch. But not my hand. I asked the surgeon for a corkscrew instead of a hook. I could use that."

The argument outside has stopped, the laughs and the noise of the skittles has started up again. Swaying a little, the Corporal goes for a refill: his mug's almost empty by the time he sits down again.

"There were sixteen killed at Peterloo," he says, looking Charley in the eye. "Fifty thousand at Waterloo. They said that those sixteen helped to promote the Cause. Poets wrote about them. One day perhaps, there'll be a museum at St Peter's

Field. But for the sixteen dead it's all over. If I could go back, I wouldn't be satisfied with just writing the word *manoeuvres*, I would carry them out. I would distribute rifles to the lads. As for myself, I'd go and get my sabre from the bottom of its drawer. I don't know if that would promote the Cause, but I would fight. Against the yeomen. And against John. In a fair fight."

Charley, who has just accompanied a rather tipsy Corporal back to his room, sees Robert Grant, the barman, out in the courtyard. The man has put on a Wellington beaver hat, a frock coat in coarse woollen cloth, like a coachman's, with a huge ladle sticking out of the pocket. He looks like a man with a walk-on part kitted out by a deranged dresser.

"Hey, lad, how'd you like an extra lemonade, eh? I don't know where that snotty-nosed urchin Benny's got to."

Grant gestures with his thumb at a huge cooking pot he's put down on the ground and which it appears he can't lift himself.

"Yes, sir."

Charley isn't specially fond of lemonade but he doesn't want to miss the opportunity. After having found a lamp, Grant takes one handle of the pot, Charley grabs the other and off they go. They walk along by the kitchens, passing on the way a large dirty dog lying down that watches them with a blasé air. Then make their way round a mountain of rubbish bins giving off a foul stench – that coming from the pot is hardly more appealing and reminds Charley of the glue at Warren's factory. They turn to the right, between the back of the kitchen building and the outside wall; the passageway gets narrower.

"You're shorter," Grant says when they get to another door. "I'll go down first. Otherwise we're going to spill everything."

So that's it – they're going to the cellar! But when the door opens, Charley starts regretting his curiosity: a flight of steps, gleaming and sinister, goes down into the darkness. The lantern that Grant lights seems to be feeling the wall like a cautious finger, then shoos away the darkness in front of it as they start down on the stone spiral staircase.

"Watch where you're putting your feet, lad. It's as slippery as lard."

There's some liquid slapping underneath the lid of the pot. After every step they've gone down, something hard hits the metal, doubtless a bone floating in the soup. The descent ends in a corridor that leads to an immense vaulted cellar closed at the end by a big curtain, Charley can now see the point of the beaver hat and the greatcoat. It's icy cold down there. Compared with this place, the Dickens' 'cell' is almost like a luxurious boudoir. Straw mattresses lined up along the wall. Candles placed on the floor. No furniture. Most of the detainees are lying on the mattresses, arms crossed.

Grant and Charley put down the pot by the entrance. Immediately the men rise and form a long queue before them. They're all skinny, filthy, as if they'd been standardised by their wretched condition. Hollow cheeks, shining eyes, backs bent.

"So there you are, Grant, we thought you'd forgotten us."

Each of them is holding his bowl, doubtless not washed since the last meal. There are two men who haven't moved; sitting on the ground they are concentrating on a little travelling chess set.

"Dai, sei finito, lascia…"
"Non ci penso proprio!"

In the queue a man with a round face and glasses like the bottom of a bottle smiles at Charley. They had once talked to each other in the courtyard while the Guvnor was playing skittles.

"Yes, my lad, it's the Tower of Babel in here. More the cellar of Babel, actually. Those two are Italian. There's Frenchmen, Dutchmen. And then the Irish, of course."

"The bloody Irish!" Behind the man with the glasses a tall, skinny man with bad eyes spits on the floor. "It's because of them that wages are going down. They arrive by the boatload and sell themselves at any price, leaving no work for the rest of us. It's their fault if we're stony broke."

Grant starts serving up, at the same time repeatedly glancing up at the ceiling as if he was expecting something. Working both swiftly and precisely, he pours out the viscous broth, that has indefinable things floating in it – like a puddle colonised by tadpoles. There's no pushing and shoving; despite their hunger, no one's in a hurry to devour the mixture. Once they've been served they all go back to their mattress and start eating in their corner.

"Oh, you and your Irish, Blake!" a bearded man in a cap at the back of the queue retorts. "Don't make me laugh. During the war I was apprenticed to a clothier. At the end of seven years I would have had a trade with guaranteed wages. But the old regulations have been abolished and I was replaced by a lad of eleven at two shillings a week. The Irish have nothing to do with that! It's the ones who vote for the laws and those who profit from them who're responsible."

"Now then, no politics down here." Grant, about to empty his ladle in the bearded man's bowl, halts. "You're in no position to bite the hand that feeds you. I'm giving you this for free and don't you forget it."

The man with the beard is careful to wait until he's been served before replying. "Biting the hand that feeds us would at least provide us with some meat – more than is in your soup, anyway."

While the others burst out laughing, Grant swears and summons his assistant with a harsh "Psst". They pick up the pot and go farther into the room. It's odd, Charley has the impression they're going down, but there's no slope. The air thickens. The cold is not just biting, it weighs them down. They pass through a broken door; the smell leaves no doubt as to what is beyond it. As they proceed, Grant fixes his eye on a mattress where an immobile form is lying close to the curtain. The sounds seem to be distorted, the detainees' conversations slide along the walls, like the brush of an insect's wings.

"The women really ought to be served first, shouldn't they?"

"You haven't understood, my lad. We do it deliberately. That way they get the marrow and the pieces of vegetables that stay at the bottom."

They put the pot down just in front of the curtain. With his ladle Grant taps a tin box hanging from the curtain rod as a bell.

"Miss Carp?"

"Coming."

On the other side the women start moving; on this side the man stretched out prostrate on his mattress still hasn't moved an inch. Grant surveys him while he's filling all the bowls that appear and disappear through the curtain. The soup is starting to congeal as it cools down and Grant has to shake his ladle several times to empty it; almost solidified, the contents are deposited on the side of the bowl like a pile of dirty snow at the foot of a tree.

"Nothing to report, Miss Carp?"

"No, nothing apart from the madwoman who won't stop bawling."

"What is she saying?"

"How should I know? Between two fits she spends hours staring at the ceiling… Oh, it's very jolly, I can assure you."

Hand after hand appears, holding the tin bowls. Thin or thick wrists, young or old, blue with prominent veins or smooth and white like marble. Fingers reddened with the cold, twisted with arthritis. You could imagine there was only one person behind the curtain, spending their time forging different hands in order to get multiple helpings. A single protean being, suffering from monstrous hunger, utterly greedy.

The ladle scrapes the bottom.

"Ite missa est," Grant proclaims.

Giving Charley a look, he drops the ladle in the pot and goes over to the sleeping man.

"Hey! Mr Perkins!"

Nothing happens. The man is lying on his belly; Grant shines his lamp on him, making his bald head gleam.

"Perkins?" A man nearby, a wrinkled old man, sits up on his mattress. "He told me he was called Stone."

"And me Roberts," says another.

Grant shakes the sleeper by the shoulder, but nothing

happens. He kneels down and turns him over on his side. Before even his face appears, the stiffness of the body leaves no doubt.

"Oh Lord," says Grant.

"That's why he wasn't coughing any more," the little old man says, looking at the corpse with fascination, a twinkle in his eye.

His forehead smooth as a sheet, his lips pursed in an imitation of modesty, his eyes both myopic and lost in the distance. An empty shape that appears to be waiting. Charley's also looking at him. And he remembers. The woman who lived nearby in Chatham. Her four dead babies. Wrapped up, in a row on the sideboard, while the Guvnor was trying to calm down the mother, who was breathing very fast, like a little dog and started to howl again once she'd got her breath back. Four of them aligned in a row in an infinitely patient and absurd attempt to combat the uniqueness of death. But death is not unique and single, it is nought. "Now listen, children," the teacher used to say at primary school, "nought is not a number like the others, it absorbs all the others like a sponge. Multiply it by a hundred, a thousand, a hundred thousand, a million, the result will always be nought."

Suddenly Charley understands. Now that he's deciphering the mystery of nought, his legs start to tremble in panic while a cold hand grasps his heart. A dead man in the cellar, four on the sideboard in Chatham. Sixteen at Peterloo, fifty thousand at Waterloo – and it still all adds up to nothing.

***

Edward comes out of Owengate and contemplates the towers of Durham Cathedral standing out against a leaden sky. Opposite are pretty houses where officials of the diocese or distinguished professors live; behind their sober printed cotton curtains Edward could envisage a medieval scene with half-undressed monks and nuns or, on the other side of the red door, two courtesans making a fuss of a pot-bellied man who's just taken his mitre off.

He has a smile at this little image, but a clearing of the throat from Snegg, who is standing outside the red door below the curtained window, calls him to order, for it's here that they have work to do, at 6 Palace Green. Flowers of all colours make a harmonious show in the garden: mauve geraniums, yellow and red poppies, pink peonies, white mock-orange climbing up the wall, pushing its avid tongue up to the first floor. So many species Edward would have great difficulty putting names to them – apart from the syringas, Margaret's favourite shrub – but he appreciates the picture they make. Unless he employs a gardener, Mr Newton will not have the time to enjoy lengthy meals or to dally with girls in the alcoves. And from the information Snegg and Edward have acquired, that is all the better for him, since the girls charge pretty high prices.

After having glanced at the impeccable lawn and the clover, of a pink rivalling that of the poppies, Snegg pulls the bell-cord and at once, like a mother St Bernard responding to a call from her puppy, the great bell of the cathedral rings out. Edward can feel the ground vibrating under his feet and he puts his fingers in his ears – he had a bit too much madeira the previous day again – and so can't cover his face with his hands at the same time, which he would have liked to have done, despite all courtesy, at the appearance of Mr Newton.

For some seconds, though it seems longer, while the great bell is conscientiously trampling on the smallest fragment of silence, there's no point in speaking – and anyway, Edward, fascinated by what he's seeing, would find it difficult to bring out a single word. Even Snegg, the imperturbable Snegg, has gone pale. Finally the bells fall silent, Edward's ears stop ringing and his perception returns to normal. But the face is still there, half dead, half alive: during all the din Newton's single eye did not blink once.

"Excuse our intrusion, sir... I am Edward Bailey and this is my friend, Seamus Snegg. Could you spare us a minute?"

The man turns on his heel before he's finished the sentence. Which could mean as much a peremptory dismissal as a casual acceptance; but since he leaves the door open behind him, Edward and Snegg opt for the second and follow him across a tiny hall, go down a corridor and enter a little drawing room with several views of the Nile and the pyramids. Apart from that and the shelves of books in Arabic, everything there is very English, impeccably tidy and clean. "You could eat off the floor," the late Mrs Raffle would have said. Trinkets on the mantelpiece, a quilt on the sofa, a bunch of flowers. Miss Austen's heroines would have felt at home here, Edward thinks or, rather, Miss Austen's heroes – despite the care taken over the décor, there is still something clumsy, something crudely symmetrical about certain details that suggests the absence of a woman in the household.

A bachelor who loves his flowerbeds and is obsessive about order – simply banal. But when you have a face like that, does the word *banal* mean anything any more?

They're standing up, face to face. Newton observes them closely but Edward, despite summoning up all his courage, is still examining the details of the motifs in the tapestry and the cracks in the ceiling rather than returning his look. Then, unable to control his nerves, he goes over to the window. The back garden is as fragrant as the one at the front.

"I just love mock-orange," Edward says. "Aren't they also called *Philadelphus*?"

Alas, this botanical erudition has no effect on their host whose face, or to be more precise the living part of it, remains impassible.

"Mr Snegg and I have a keen interest in Egyptian antiquity," Edward goes on.

Silence.

"Someone in Durham happens to have mentioned you to us, Mr Newton."

Still no reaction. In a sense that is fortunate, for that 'someone in Durham' is purely imaginary and could have led to an embarrassing question.

"Thus it is that, doubtless very presumptuously, we had the idea that…"

"Which doubtless explains the mock-orange."

Newton has no accent, neither a foreign nor a local one. The part of his mouth that can still move has to make terrible efforts to compensate for the immobility of the other part, but paradoxically the voice that comes out is pure, crystalline: it gives the impression of being a thought become sound with no intermediary.

"Sorry?"

"Your interest in that shrub. It must come from your passion for Egypt."

Edward hides his embarrassment by pretending to examine a portrait hanging on the wall – it's of a middle-aged man with a learned air and a prominent nose. What should he do now? Pretend to understand the allusion? Launch into a eulogy of the famous mock-orange of Egypt, which, of course he has never heard of before. Suddenly, and miraculously, however, the echo of the word *Philadelphus* awakens a memory. He sees Solomon walking up and down in their little flat in Holborn, shocked by the vitriolic tone of an article on Byron. "Oh for God's sake, why do they keep going on at him like that? Even if he did sleep with his sister, aren't great men above the law? Didn't Ptolemy Philadelphus marry Arsinoë? Out of the corner of his eye Edward notes the title identifying the portrait as that of Doctor Robert Newton. It is also the name of three volumes on a shelf close by: *Funerary Rites in Ancient Egypt. The Magic Cult of Amon Râ. Religious Organisation under the Lagid Dynasty*.

He turns round, a broad smile on his face. "Who can be unaware of the least detail about Ptolemy Philadelphus after having read your father's books, Mr Newton?"

Snegg's mouth half opens. Didn't they agree to say as little as possible. To let their 'client' talk as much as possible. But Edward's remark seems to have achieved its aim. Newton breathes in deeply, nods and invites his visitors to sit down on the sofa, choosing a simple armchair for himself.

"My adoptive father, to be precise… you must excuse my distrust, but unfortunately lots of people ring my bell just to… see the monster."

The three men's knees are almost touching; now there's no escape for Edward and Snegg. They have no choice but to look. On the left: firm, dignified features, a slightly olive complexion makes him seem a touch exotic. And on the other side of the ridge of the nose a reptilian chaos, a dessert of porphyria, a swamp of dead skin in which all expression gets stuck. Suddenly the veil of horror tears and they really *see*. The face and the *face*, Snegg thinks. The reflection, the precipitate of all dead beings, indissolubly attached to the image of life, like the two sides of a coin. But that can't be, life and death are mutually exclusive. Except in the imagination…

Except by imagining a principle, a place, a substance which would envelop them both together, a power on which both the invincible darkness and the inextinguishable light would depend, a being who… 'Oh do stop beating about the bush, Seamus,' he tells himself, 'what you're trying to describe has a name: God! Are you frightened to say it?'

There, in the little Durham drawing room, facing a human landscape that even Hieronymus Bosch couldn't have thought up, Seamus Snegg has the feeling of being very close to God. Not the God of the Papists, nor of the Anglicans or the Methodists. His very own God. The God of None Snegg. As for Edward, there's one thing he realises: you mustn't lie to a man like that.

"Mr Newton, I feel ashamed of myself," he abruptly declares. "Not that we are the kind of sick people you've just mentioned… but nor are we," he glances at Snegg, "specialists on Ancient Egypt. We just thought that it was a pretext that would prevent us being turned away. What brings us here is something quite different. We come from Darlington where the memory of your… services is still very much alive."

Another silence. Edward and Snegg peruse their toes.

"Darlington," Newton finally says in a toneless voice, before becoming a little more animated. "That's where I ate the best meat pies in my life."

"At the King's Arms, I'm sure," Snegg says. "Unfortunately there's a new owner."

"What a pity."

For a good minute the Egyptian remains motionless, looking out of the window. It's difficult to say what's going on behind that forehead divided in two by a bluish strip. Suddenly he comes to a decision. "A cup of tea, gentlemen?"

He disappears into an adjoining room, leaving the two others to recover from their surprise.

"So you would like to call on my services, then?" Newton goes on, raising his voice to make himself heard from the kitchen.

"Indeed. Lord Beresford couldn't praise you enough."

"Is that so? I'm flattered… Alas, however, you've come all this way for nothing, it's a long time since I played on the anvil."

On the sofa Edward and Snegg exchange questioning looks.

"But don't you worry, gentlemen, we'll find a solution… though true craftsmen are rare there are still one or two on the market… anyway," he goes on, appearing in the drawing room carrying a mahogany tray and a tea service of which Jane Austen herself would have praised the china, "I'm glad the misunderstanding between us has been cleared up. In general my first impression is the best and you seemed two perfectly decent fellows to me."

He fills three cups, but instead of sitting down he goes to stand in front of the portrait of Dr Newton and subjects it to a long contemplation.

"He adopted you… in Egypt?" Edward asks somewhat tentatively.

"Yes, in Cairo. I was ten and I was a real good-for-nothing. I can't remember what theft it was for which they threw me in prison when… oh do excuse me, gentlemen, you haven't come for that. I'm an incorrigible chatterbox."

"We've all the time in the world. Do go on."

"Well then, they threw me into a cell with other street urchins like me… around the prison there were hovels piled up one on the other, despite all common sense, with walls of cob, adobe or planks that caught fire easily. One evening a lamp knocked over by a drunk set off an immense fire that quickly swallowed up the whole area. The door to our block was kept shut by an old padlock; our warder tried to set us free but the lock just wouldn't work and after two or three attempts, seeing the flames approaching he abandoned us. A lock! I almost died because of a defective lock, you realise? Eventually the roof collapsed, trapping me under the debris with the right-hand side of my face squashed down among the embers on the floor. But some of my comrades, who had greater luck and agility, managed to rescue me. They pulled me out of the rubble and I was taken to a makeshift hospital set up on the banks of the Nile. There some nurses and two or three doctors made an initial selection according to the seriousness of the injuries. I was perfectly conscious despite the pain. I heard everything that was said. 'This one's dead,' one of them said, bending over me. 'But he's breathing, groaning,' another protested.

'Not for long,' the first one replied. 'And that will be the best thing for him.' He settled the argument by dumping me among the corpses."

Newton tells his story slowly, in an even voice, almost like a schoolmaster. Eventually he sits down and wets his lips in his tea before going on.

"I've thought a lot about what those men said. It's odd, but obviously…" he takes another mouthful and puts his cup back down with a deep sigh, "obviously, although still alive I was no longer *viable*. Not just because of the seriousness of my case but also because I no longer had a… human form. I might as well have been thrown on the scrap heap. With the dead."

Instead of keeping his eyes fixed on the intact part of Newton's face, Edward forces himself to look at *the two together*, thinking about those men Solomon told him about in a letter, walking the streets of London stuck between two advertising boards. Two words keep on echoing inside his head: *Ptolemy Philadelphus. Ptolemy Philadelphus.*

"I often think about the extraordinary good fortune I had that day," Newton goes on. "Yes, good fortune. Doctor Newton was staying in Egypt at the time, with his wife Emily, to continue his research. Having heard there was a fire, he went down to offer his assistance to the rescuers. And it was there that he found me, in the middle of the corpses. 'You moved one of your arms,' he told me later. 'At first I was horror-struck. Then I realised there was someone alive *underneath*. And I felt great joy.' He organised everything – my admission to a proper hospital, my convalescence. And when they went back to England they took me with them."

Suddenly Newton starts chuckling. "I can still remember

the day when he asked me what trade or profession I'd like to learn… 'Father,' I said, 'after what has happened to me do you think I really have a choice?' He stared at me and gave me a long look before bursting out into laughter."

Edward and Snegg also stare and exchange signs of complete incomprehension.

"But let's get down to your problem. If you're simply looking for a good craftsman, go and see Sotheby in Stockton and tell him I sent you. He's an expert with locks. But if you want something original, as at Wooler Manor, then I'm afraid you'll have to go as far as Newcastle. You'll find Pullen satisfactory."

"We're looking for someone capable of… repeating your feat," Snegg suggests cautiously.

"Feat, that's a bit too much and first of all we must give Lord Beresford his due: for every achievement of that kind you need an ambitious partner. Having seen the pyramids from inside I can guarantee that without the pharaoh's exorbitant specifications his architects would have racked their brains much less! And then their skills would never have developed so rapidly nor subsequently, our modest discipline…"

'But what discipline, for God's sake?' is Edward's silent scream.

"To seal the tomb of an emperor or to create a lock worthy of the name, with the appropriate key, comes down to the same thing: to produce something *secret*, that dimension without which a man would wither away under the looks of his fellows."

In order to support this declaration Newton turns his head away slightly so that only his good profile is shown to them, just at the moment when Edward and Snegg finally understand.

"That is true," says Snegg. "And... in the specific case of Wooler Manor, how did you go about it?"

The locksmith's eye gleams with excitement. He lifts the lid of a little desk and goes back to his guests with an inkwell, a pen and several sheets of paper.

"Very simply, that's always the best way. Lord Beresford wanted to have a secret closet accessible from the library where he could keep his most valuable papers in a safe place. I went for the classic solution of a detachable section of books mounted on a door and I ordered this device from a cabinet-maker I knew, insisting that he cover the back of the other sections and the door with the same panelling; thus even if someone should look behind the books they would never suspect there was a door there."

Newton skilfully sketches the installation: the panelling, the books, the opening to the secret room. Then he takes another sheet of paper.

"The principal difficulty pertained to my own skills: I had to find a system to open and close the door that was totally invisible. Neither lock nor key, of course. There should be no noticeable hollow or raised surface that might be spotted. This is how I went about it."

Neither Edward nor Snegg can understand a single word of his explanation. The bolts, latches, tumblers, striking plates, hinges and other plates seem to bear no relation to the bevelled rectangles, the spirals, the half-moons that appear from his pen, they seem rather to designate fabulous beasts or to belong to the rituals of a vanished religion.

"But all that's nothing. The finishing touch, of which I am

very proud, is the trigger for the mechanism. I can tell you the principle but I doubt whether even Pullen, who is the best between Berwick and Manchester since I retired – Newton modestly lowers his only eyelid, while half of his face blushes – yes, I doubt whether even Pullen is capable of applying it. That is why I run no great risk of being plagiarised. You, Mr Snegg, you strike me as being very resourceful, so how would you go about it?"

"Well, for example... I would have chosen knotted panelling and hidden a push button in one of the knots, after having stained it the appropriate colour..."

"Not bad, but not perfect. A trained eye could spot the trick."

"I give up."

"Really? Here's a clue: what's better to keep the secret than a force... that isn't visible?"

"Magnetism!" Snegg exclaims, getting an enthusiastic response from Newton.

"Exactly! I used two Wright magnets in the following way: one on the library side, located in the spine of a book, the other in the secret room, controlling the bolt. At that point a hole had been made in the plaster partition and the wood of the panelling hollowed out so that only a thin layer was left. All you had to do was to push the book to the back of the shelf: the two magnets attract each other, releasing the bolt and allowing the door to be opened. Lord Beresford could go into his secret room, close the panel behind him, lock it with another bolt, operated manually, and go about his business undisturbed, then come back out and seal the entrance by replacing the book."

"Remarkable, Mr Newton, remarkable," Snegg says. "We

will contact Mr Pullen without any illusions. However good his work, I'm sure you are head and shoulders above him. And I'm sure that our documents are much less important than those of Lord Beresford…"

"It wasn't just about documents, Mr Snegg, there was the secret… the secret itself. Sometimes the hiding-place itself is more important than what is hidden."

Snegg considers this surprising aphorism then, as they're taking their leave he slaps his forehead as if something has just occurred to him. "Oh, I almost forgot. I would very much like to have a look at your father's books before we go."

"Of course."

Newton quickly gets down all the volumes and places them in front of Snegg, who is very careful in turning the pages. "Magnificent engravings…"

"By my adoptive mother. As you can see, she signed them with her maiden name: Emily Grant. She could have been a great artist."

"Indeed. And this Ptolemy you were talking about…"

"Ptolemy II Philadelphus. In many respects he was more Greek than Egyptian. There's the chapter my father wrote about him. And here's our Ptolemy himself in all his splendour."

Snegg discreetly gives Edward's arm a nudge and he looks over his clerk's shoulder.

"This statue decorated the lighthouse of Alexandria, but alas it has disappeared. Mrs Newton made the drawing using the accounts of several writers from antiquity, including Strabo, I think, and following other, well-known portraits of the pharaoh: sculptures, mosaics, coins. Beside the statue of Ptolemy there would doubtless have been one of Arsinoë, his sister, who became his second wife... as you will know, in Greek *Philadelphus* means 'loving one's brother or sister'. And that wasn't something shocking at the time – incest was practically a constituent part of the dynasty..."

"Do you think this portrait of Ptolemy could be confused with that of another pharaoh?"

"That's hardly likely. His hat is quite distinctive. And you can clearly see the lighthouse behind the statue."

"Was this book available twenty years ago?"

"Of course. My father had it published in 1785. But why do you ask?"

"Simple curiosity."

Edward glances round the garden where a pair of nightingales are frolicking noisily. A statue against a tower. Or a lighthouse. A 'bun' on its head: *Ptolemy Philadelphus*. Precisely the engraving described by Emily Preston.

X

The Black Drop

Edward wakes up with his throat burning, his nose blocked and his head transformed into a gong – what time is it? Dull, damp light is coming in through the windows, like that shining in a cow's eye. He caught a cold the previous evening and that's not surprising. The sun, that was pouring its rays so generously down on Mr Newton's garden, had refused to accompany them beyond Elvet Bridge. Thick clouds, like a pack of black dogs, followed them along the river and then 'someone up there' had amused themselves by slitting water-skins over their heads. The ditches were overflowing, the track under water. And to think that mouldering at the back of a shed was a comfortable coupé, the padding and gilding of which reminded him too much of his father-in-law's. When he got home he would have been happy to huddle up in the summerhouse, but three broken gutters had transformed the place into an aquarium. As for sleeping by himself in the so-called friends' room again… no, yesterday evening that had been beyond him. That left just the Raffles' abominable drawing room and its awful sofa.

A bottle of madeira, emptied as medicine, is lying on the

carpet. Edward frowns, trying to remember word by word his astonishing conversation with his clerk: "I was struck by Newton's remark, Edward: that it's not *what* you're hiding that counts most, it's the very idea of a hiding place. In France the Baron probably came close to death. And his marriage was a fiasco. Two attempts to escape from himself, two failures. Isn't is logical to see him withdraw into his manor, then into his library, then into that secret room…"

"…where he committed… with his own sister!"

"That's what Vholes suggested. We have no proof."

"But if it is true?"

"So what? The pharaohs saw incest as the acme of purity… and I have heard it said that your dear Byron…"

The carriage lamps were tossing in the wind and the rain diffracted their light into hundreds of fireflies, a procession of hobgoblins or the funeral of an elf. In these ghostly surroundings Snegg looked different from his usual self. Rather than a provincial lawyer's clerk, he looked like an ominous coachman from one of the tales of Hoffman.

"Hmm. That doesn't tell us what game Vholes was playing when he revealed his suspicions to Beresford, and that in a pretty theatrical manner: was he trying to blackmail him? Push him to the limit? Who stuck the dagger in Ophelia's corpse? And what happened to Mathilde?"

"We should let things settle a bit, Edward. Let the story come out of its own accord."

"D'you know what, Seamus? This evening I've got the impression that the world is upside-down. I'm assembling the facts, I'm clinging on to reason and you, you're the one going off at tangents. And now you're dreaming, eyes wide open!

What's happening for God's sake?"

"Well, something of you is rubbing off on me and vice versa," Snegg replied, taking his eyes off the road. "We're becoming cousins."

His headache gets worse. He manages to get up, though with difficulty and over there, on the other side of the room, stuck in his father-in-law's letter-rack he sees the envelope... Oh for God's sake! How many times had he demanded that the mail be left in a simple and accessible place, on the hall table, for example, and not on this writing desk where, every evening, Mr Raffle would scribble away at his plans for the Raffleisation of the universe?

It comes from the elder Spalding:

Bailey, break off the investigation immediately – everything has been settled. Spalding.

His headache had gone, or was at least no longer the most pressing of his concerns. Anger functions as energy, indignation as balance. Wasting no time on thought, he grabs his still-wet coat, glances at the clock in the hall – it's six – and goes out just in time to see the sun rise, a sullen clown, between the trees. So that's what dawn is. Not one he's familiar with, neither that of the revellers coming out of the brothels and pissing under the street lights nor that of the poets, where elves and fauns wake to disport themselves in the dew; it's the real dawn, dreary, icy-cold, the dawn of the poor who have to drag themselves out of bed, hastily swallow their gruel and run down the road to throw themselves into the arms of the ogre that is devouring them all: work. On his shoulders he can feel the weight of all the thankless tasks he's managed to avoid more by luck than by his merits. But there's no question of him giving up this one that will perhaps restore his dignity.

He walks as he's never walked before.

Now he's on the steps of Spalding's house. He knocks but no one answers. So – what on earth has got into him? – he turns the handle, sees that the door is open and goes in. Facing him is the heavy-lidded butler coming down the stairs holding an empty tray. Somewhere in the house a clock strikes the half hour.

"Sir... what are you doing...?"

Edward cuts him short, brandishing the crumpled letter. "Sir Walter's expecting me."

Then he goes up the stairs four at a time, has no problem finding the door, from behind which comes the cheerful clink of cutlery and china, knocks and enters without being invited in. The gouty justice, napkin round his neck, is facing a hostile army composed of chops, kidneys, livers, black puddings, sausages and beer: everything that is forbidden by doctor's orders. Tomorrow, or perhaps even this afternoon, he will be howling with pain, his toe swollen like a puffball.

"Oh, it's you, Bailey. I didn't think you were such an early riser. Have you breakfasted already?"

Edward doesn't reply but puts the letter down on the table, smoothing it out with the palm of his hand.

"Yes, I'm glad that's over with," Spalding splutters, his mouth full of liver and gravy.

"What is it that... *achoo!*"

"God bless you. You know, you don't look very well..."

"What has been settled?"

Sir Walter sighs, reluctantly puts down his fork, wipes his mouth and puts his hands together like a canon. "You can read, can't you Bailey? It's written down there: everything is settled. The train will run. Glendover got nowhere in London, so he's giving up. He even tried to join the Railway Company, but those idiot Quakers didn't want him as a partner. They've no sense of humour."

"So what?"

"So what? Are you doing this deliberately? If Glendover withdraws, then everything's in order again; there'll be no more incidents and Stephenson will finish his line in time."

"And what about the incidents that have already taken place?"

"Such as?"

"Sticking up posters and distributing pamphlets inciting violence. All kinds of intimidation…"

Spalding goes back to his plate and starts an attack on the right wing of the black pudding.

"Beating people up. Destroying… *achoo*… public and private property. Desecrating a tomb."

"Oh! That's all been sorted out as well. The skeleton was that of a woman called Mary Bayles. She went mad in 1799 and kept on running away from her son's farm. One day she disappeared. She must have lost her way in the dark and drowned. The Bayles' farm is quite close to the pond; the size and the fractures correspond – she kept on falling down."

"Why did these people not come forward sooner?"

"Bayles died in Spain. His wife remarried and is living in Newcastle. Cobbold heard about it from a neighbour he happened to be questioning."

"Why wasn't the pond checked at the time?"

"How should I know. Perhaps they didn't really want to find the old madwoman."

"Old? Trees was inclined to think it was a young woman…"

"Trees isn't the only doctor in the county," Spalding replies, attacking the chops. "Cobbold had another come from Stockton."

"Without informing me?"

"And where can one find you, Bailey? You're never at home nor in your chambers. Instead you're off to abandoned villages, boozing with old women and… I can hardly send someone to fetch you from Bull Wynd…"

"Well, well, Sir Walter, are you having me followed?"

"Don't be ridiculous. Everything gets known round here. You just have to gather up the tittle-tattle with a spade and sift through it."

Sir Walter attacks the chop right down the middle. There's nothing left of the sausages or the chicken livers.

"And what do you make of the piece of cloth with the Beresford monogram?"

"Huh! All the great families pass on their old clothes to the poor…"

"And the dagger?"

"The dagger. Oh, now I remember," Spalding picks up a toothpick, "there was something about a dagger at one point… but it was mislaid, unfortunate, I know, in the course of the inquiry. I gave Cobbold an official reprimand."

"Mislaid? A major piece of evidence? But that doesn't really matter, a good twenty people must have seen it."

"Which proves nothing. Someone could have stolen it then

thrown it in the pond. And then, what looks more like a dagger than another dagger and a coat of arms than another coat of arms?"

All at once Edward feels ill. He pulls up the chair Spalding offered him when he arrived and drops into it heavily.

"You can't do this, Sir Walter."

"Do what?"

"Twist the truth this way and that. Eventually it's going to break."

Spalding empties his glass with several long draughts of beer, then looks over his clean plate, the empty bowls and dishes. Finally he looks back at Edward.

"I keep on hearing about this article called the truth, Bailey," he says, settling down in his armchair and wrinkling his nose in a bizarre way, "but I never find it on the shelves. In general I'm told it's out of stock and I've come to believe it just doesn't exist, but if you want to try to convince me of the opposite, well go ahead, I'll give you, hmm, five minutes."

The light, now brighter, seems to balk at shining through the windows, that look as if they've been coated with the white of an egg. Edward feels like a mouthful of beer. Like several, in fact. Nevertheless he speaks without pausing, without hesitating and without omitting anything. He tells the truth, the whole truth and nothing but the truth, but he has the impression that the words change their nature, hardly have they left his lips, as if contaminated by some foetid air. Spalding listens in silence – you could almost believe he already knows it all off by heart. From time to time he looks down at the table in case another enemy contingent should appear.

"You've finished?"

"Yes, Sir Walter. Of course I have no intention of mentioning the names of those who desecrated the tomb of Ophelia Beresford…"

Spalding nods his head slowly then stands up. Despite his age and his corpulence, he's an imposing figure. There's something of a retired centurion about him: his paunch sticking out but with broad shoulders and heavy fists.

"I'm not going to allow your story to become reality, Bailey. Not to protect my son, he's a good-for-nothing and a few months in a cell would do him the world of good, but because it's not the right story. Look," he goes back to the table, picks up his empty beer mug, lifts it up until it's level with his eyes, which he screws up, mimicking the concentration of a soothsayer, "this is my crystal ball. Let's just imagine for a moment what would happen if I let you go ahead."

There's a knock at the door, doubtless the butler who wants to clear the table, but a grunt from Spalding is enough to send him away.

"Now let's see… Beresford convicted of the murder of his wife hanged with a silken rope… or, what is more likely, condemned in absentia, stripped of his title and his estate… hurray, justice has been done!"

"Oh, but who is this I see arriving from Berwick on his ugly little horse? Alastair Beresford, his cousin. The one who will inherit everything. You know him? No? How can I describe him… compared with him our old rogue of a Glendover would be taken for a friend of the common man, a veritable archangel of compassion. I have seen round his estate – it's the Middle Ages up there. People are whipped, starved, humiliated and they doubtless still practise the *droit de seigneur*. But these people have a thick hide, they're almost Scottish, whilst down here… Alastair would like to apply the same principles at Wooler Manor and the region would be torn apart within a few weeks. Huh, you'll tell me, we'll calm these rebellious farmers and smallholders with the sword. Very well. And if the Whigs protest in the Commons the only result will be a couple of columns in *The Times* and that doesn't bother me at all… only… only there's something else. Look there, right at the bottom…"

Spalding sticks the glass right under Edward's nose.

"Glendover, the leader of the Tory Party accused of being a saboteur and a troublemaker! His candidate loses credibility a few months before the elections. Now it's the Whigs who are unleashed. They'll blow on all the smouldering embers they can find and demand more democracy, that rattle they're waving anywhere and everywhere. The Radicals, believing they have support, will go on strike and be out in the streets. They'll send in the troops again… and it'll all end in a massacre, as at Pentrich or Peterloo. And do you know what's the funniest thing? The Whigs will lose the elections – I don't like them but I can see that their defeat would be harmful to business. And why will they lose? Because the good citizens, agitated by all this violence, will choose a Tory more Tory than Glendover to restore order in all the bedlam… perhaps even Alastair Beresford himself. Shall I go on or have you had enough?"

He pours out the rest of the jug and swallows it in one gulp. There's a little bit of froth on his lips that he wipes off unceremoniously on his sleeve; at that moment he's more of a trooper than a centurion. But there's no relaxation of the look he has fixed on his visitor, lashing him like a whip.

"You're not going to get me like that, Sir Walter," Edward says, standing up. "For the first time, perhaps, I can see a task through and I will go right through to the end. And, anyway, I'm not the only one involved. You can't get rid of the truth by silencing just one man."

"That remains to be seen. Anyone else?"

"Doctor Trees."

"Huh! A country doctor. Notoriously incompetent... we can put up with him."

"My clerk, Snegg."

"Snegg? He's a loyal man. He won't do anything that might harm the reputation of the Raffles." Spalding puts heavy emphasis on these last words.

The reputation of the Raffles. That means Margaret's, the last surviving Raffle. Edward pales. He can see himself in this very room bandaging the stinking, swollen toe.

"I warned you, my lad, accept it."

Sir Walter goes across the room and to stand in front of a picture that he takes off its hook – Edward feels he can recognise the vigorous if slightly approximative style of the famous Uncle Henry, the man who painted the portrait of Mathilde Beresford. But this time his model is just a stout woman squinting at the ceiling, her unlikely hat in the form of a linen basket threatening to collapse. In the wall behind the picture is a little safe that Sir Walter unlocks.

"I couldn't let you – the spark, yes? – loose in this powder keg without having a hold over you in one way or the other." He takes out a large, well-filled envelope and rubs it with his forefinger, making a sound that grates on Edward's ear. "I thought we might come to some tacit agreement… something elegant, do you see? But if I have to dot the i's and cross the t's…"

The letter changes hands.

"When my daughter died, I cursed the whole world, Bailey… the whole world! First of all your wife, since she was the one who had persuaded Mary Ann to attend that grotesque masked ball. Then mine for having authorised that catastrophic outing. The absolute idiot I have for a son: he was supposed to chaperone his sister and he didn't even think of putting a stole over her back when it was freezing cold! I cursed us, all of us fathers, even though I was in Manchester myself on that evening… we're guilty because we didn't manage to hold our children back. They came running when Byron, that unworthy and scandalous Byron, whistled… like dogs running off through a hole in the fence. And why? Because they were hungry while we were fattening them up like princes? No. Just out of curiosity. Out of boredom. Is it my fault that comfort and security are boring?"

It's odd to see this man, who knows all the tricks of the trade, is ready to make any kind of compromise, quivering with indignation, to see him sincerely, profoundly shocked by something.

"When the letter arrived, Mary Ann was already delirious… pneumonia. High fever. Two days later she was gone… it was only after the funeral that I found the envelope and had the idea of opening it. I needed an explanation for all that… what you have in your hand and can retain is only a copy, of course, but here on the original you can still see the marks of my tears.

Tears of rage! I kept it to myself. Out of friendship for your father-in-law." (How, Edward wonders, can you be the friend of a man who almost dislocates your lungs when he pats you on the back and whose favourite word is *'undisputedly'?*) "Today I'm not using it *against* you; on the contrary, I'm preventing you from making a serious mistake. Perhaps you would be stupid enough to scupper yourself, to destroy your situation and make your life in Darlington impossible... but I refuse to believe you would coldly bring disgrace on Margaret. I'm not blackmailing you, Bailey, I'm saving you from yourself."

"You're too kind," Edward mutters as he starts to read the familiar script on the pages.

Dear Mary Ann,

They're refusing to let me see you! Your father says it's because you're ill, but in fact he's always hated me, as I well know. I didn't want to leave a message. If you're reading these lines it's thanks to Tom – at least he likes me.

The first thing I did after I woke up the day after Halnaby was to burn my page's costume in the hearth. To throw it away, to tear it up wouldn't have been enough. For when I put it on, I became the other woman, I immediately felt her slipping inside me, becoming me. It's something terrible that no one can understand. But at least you believe me, Mary Ann.

It wasn't me, it was the other woman who drank three glasses of port and danced five times with Ralph Lister! It was the other woman who was reflected in the waxed parquet, I was just the reflection with the twisted legs, an undesirable twin kept under the ground. I was the one looking desperately for you but it was the other woman *who, when I finally saw you in the middle of the crowd, slipped behind the screen instead of running over to join you.*

There was a door there and then a corridor that was very dark and very cold compared with the ballroom. However, there was a faint light at the end, it was a bluish red. The other woman *went on and came to a smallish room with a low ceiling and a fire in the hearth; the sole pieces of furniture were a worn sofa and a little table. You could have thought it was a box room hastily made up for a less important guest. And that guest could come back at any moment, someone had just put a log on the embers.*

It was the other woman, *Mary Ann, who stretched out on the sofa, despite all propriety, but I was the one who fell asleep from exhaustion and when I woke up, Lord Byron was there.*

I recognised him immediately from the portrait you cut out of a newspaper: curly, almost frizzy hair, lips well-defined with a touch of satisfaction, eyes full of irony. I didn't think he was really handsome. Just strange with a sort of slightly weary ardour. He closed the door, but the music from the ball could still be heard; it came in waves of sound and went again, like the sea breaking on the shore.

When he called me 'young page' I didn't know whether he was joking or really took me for a boy, so I looked down at my disguise and then the other woman *woke up and threw me out of my body, just the way you throw out a tramp. But I stayed in the room. I was the mist on the windows, the dust in the joins of the parquet, a fly on a candlestick. At times Lord Byron's voice came from nowhere, at times it whispered some absurd words in* the other woman's *ear: "By common accord we ought to decide no longer to live in this world. Send a letter to the owner. Hand in our notice, that's what we ought to do." Or then just single words.* England. Stupidity. Elbe. *Then this other sentence, uttered across an immense space, "A gypsy predicted that in nine years I would return to my country."*

For one moment he disappeared and the next he was there, you could feel his heat, his fingers on…

Oh, Mary Ann, I swear it wasn't me who gave way to him. It was the other woman!

Edward can't read any more. He puts the letter down on the table, stands up and looks out of the window, watching the butler with the heavy lids who, transformed into a gardener, is tearing up weeds from a flower bed and throwing them away in the dull light.

He feels like trapping Spalding's toe between two wedges and hitting it hard with a mallet.

"There are two things I demand…"

"Be reasonable, my lad… you're in no position to negotiate anything at all."

"You like negotiating, Sir Walter, it's your favourite pastime. And then, with a spark… anything can happen, can't it?"

Spalding looks him up and down for a moment, then mutters, "Go ahead, then."

"I never want to see Cobbold again. If he gets in my way again, I can't say what I might do."

"Request granted… and even anticipated. Do you think I like him? He's been useful to me now and again but in the long term he's a potential danger… fortunately I managed to persuade Gregson to offer him a position in Manchester. His resignation has already been received."

"He arrested a certain Sam Davies. One of Stephenson's workers. The man has done nothing, He must be released at once."

"What makes you interested in that scum?"

"Doesn't matter. It's just my condition."

"Agreed," Spalding says after a short silence. "I'll send someone to the town hall in a moment."

Edward starts to go down the stairs at the very moment when a cleaning woman, armed with a feather duster and a rag, opens the library door. In the gap Mathilde Beresford appears – at first the folds of her dress, then the lace of her bodice, then her eyes which, by a trick of the light, seem to follow him as he crosses the hall.

"I'll see this through to the end," he promises the French-woman.

***

The cart slowly slides along between the dirty blanket of the sky and the dreary mattress of the flat, wet fields. No trees, no buildings. Posthill, the prison warder is driving; he seems ill at ease and keeps glancing back, embarrassed, to where Sam is sitting behind, wrapped in an old shawl, his ankles shackled and his hands tied behind his back. On the seat opposite is a man called Drake with a long, angular face and holding a pair of pistols across his stomach. It's cold, but at least it's not raining, and that is a good thing because the torn hood over their heads is no protection for anyone. Behind them the bell-tower of St Cuthbert's can still be seen, hazy in the distance. In front of them, nothing. The track cuts the flat landscape in front of them in two as far as the horizon.

Sam hasn't slept. Despite failing to see any point to it, he continued to scrape away at the saltpetre, covering over and blurring older scribblings, each new word consigned to the coffin of the night, until his fingernails hurt too much. Then he stretched out on the straw, hands under the back of his neck, waiting for dawn. The sore ends of his fingers remind him of the time he worked in the brickyard. He also remembered his time in Lancashire and the bales of cotton he would load after it had been ginned and his method of counteracting fatigue: you could almost have said the bales became less and less heavy as the day wore on, which brought him appreciative glances from the foreman – the glances of a slave-driver. But in his mind there was something that wasn't working: the lighter the bale seemed and the quicker he loaded the cart, the darker, deeper became the anger in which he enclosed himself. Going to the meetings of the Society in the evenings, talking with the others, shaking hands, shouting threats, nothing brought any relief. It had become a personal matter between him and the bales of cotton. The more he carried, the more there were. Even the foreman was starting to find that odd, the silent frenzy, the struggle that was lost before it started.

Drake is whistling as he caresses the butts of his Purdeys. Something is being burnt to the south, wisps of black smoke are twisting and Sam watches them as they disappear, sucked up into the empty sky.

One day he couldn't lift a bale. Not a single one. The foreman couldn't believe his eyes: to see this strapping lad, tough, strong as an ox, on his knees when faced with a measly bale of cotton, unable to move it an inch when the previous day he'd shifted almost a hundred! As if the bale contained an anvil. As if his muscles had turned into cotton. The others stood round in a circle, unable to understand what was happening; at first they assumed it was a joke – but he wasn't that kind of fellow – then wide-eyed, flabbergasted at the extraordinary turn of events, until the foreman yelled at them to get back to work. Sam had stayed there, alone, leaning against the bale that no one dared touch.

"You look to me as if you need a good nap," said the man who swept up all the fibres on the floor. But Sam wasn't sleepy.

"Hey, Posthill," Drake said, "you're going to have to stop. I haven't got rid of all of yesterday's beer yet."

The driver looks round. "Are you sure? We're almost there."

"Of course I'm sure. What's got into you?"

Sam shifts to relieve his aching back and watches the quiet to-and-fro of the pistols, rising and falling to the rhythm of Drake's breathing. If he hasn't slept it's not because of his memories nor his fingernails that were burning, but because of what Cobbold said.

So why this determination to leave a mark, eh, why? Why

this pride?

"There, that's a good place."

"Are you really sure you…?"

"Stop here, I tell you!"

The coppice appears before them, hidden until the last moment by a long band of mist floating above a ditch. Silver birches. In the village where Sam grew up some of the old folk used to call them 'reading trees' because of their bark covered in grey signs, like the letters of an unknown alphabet. Slipping his pistols into his belt, Drake jumps down. Whistling all the time, he urinates, then buttons up his trousers and looks at Sam.

"By Christ, that does you good! You don't feel like joining me?"

"Stop it! He hasn't been drinking beer."

But Sam has already accepted the suggestion with a nod and Drake gives Posthill a nasty look. "You mind your own business and go and undo him. After all, we can't stop him having a pee."

Leaning back over the bench, Posthill undoes Sam's ankles then his wrists. As he goes about this he checks that Drake can't see his face, then puts his hand on the prisoner's shoulder, to attract his attention, rolls his eyes and shapes his lips into the word 'no'. Sam shows no reaction.

Perhaps you've had enough of being Sam Davies?

In order to unbutton his trousers, he has to drop his shawl, and that gives him an idea. He decides to put it into action when he's getting back up into the cart: he'll throw himself onto the ground and slip between between the wheels, then head for the coppice. It's a bit far to go but at least he'll be under cover for the first few steps, until Drake can get round the cart with its tarpaulin cover. He'll have a bit of a chance. A tiny bit.

And his luck seems to be in: the mist is spreading visibly. You could say the air is thickening, sticky with the smells of mud and earth, with something of the sea about it, too: the Tees estuary is only a few miles away. When he's finished Sam has a look at the two pistols pointed at him. Buttons up his trousers, and sets off back to the cart – Drake, a slight smile on his lips, keeps his eyes fixed on him – walks along it as if to get to the back seat, drops his shawl. As he bends down to pick it up he sees a mouse between the wheels; he stares at it for a moment before falling down on his right shoulder and going into a forward roll. The sound of the shot is deafening and makes the horse neigh and the mouse run off at top speed. A shower of stones rains down on Sam, bruising his face while the smell of powder, its searing heat, that missed him by less than an inch, reminds him of Peterloo. But he feels strong and clear-headed; it's as if the gunshot had shaken off the torpor of his imprisonment, made him himself again. Without losing a second he stands up and, bent down, starts to run towards the fog and goes into it with the pleasant feeling he's becoming invisible.

All of his senses are taut, expecting the second shot.

The birches rise in front of him, the 'reading trees', incomplete, as if they're half erased by the mist, but he can already make out some long bark parchments covered in shaky writing and – incredibly – he can read them, yes, he can decipher them, or he would do if he stopped running and took the time. But right in the middle of his flight, the letters that aren't letters, the words that aren't words make a sentence and whisper it in his ear. And it's a marvellous sentence. He'll never be able to write anything so beautiful.

It's an odd idea, but he plays with it, turning it this way and that inside his head, for despite all appearances, he has the time; he has just realised that the time between the two shots is immense, that you can swim in it like a limitless sea, lose yourself or take refuge in it. Everything around him suddenly seems clearer, not just the sentence written on the birch bark but also the one meandering through the moss at the foot of the tree from which he's just a couple of steps away – it's an ideal place, as soft as you could wish, he ought to bring Kirstie here. He can hear cries, the vestiges of another world: the shouts of Posthill, Drake's boots making the spongy soil creak. Another mouse – unless it's the same one? – stands on its hind legs, perfectly vertical, as if its terror was a stick it had swallowed.

As he goes through the coppice Sam is in raptures. There aren't just a couple of phrases and sentences but hundreds, thousands, running round in all directions, up into the sky, down to the ground, lining up above and below the horizon. He's on the point of entering this living book, throwing his arms wide to plunge into it, but suddenly the pages are covered by a flood of red ink.

Sam falls to his knees, He has just enough time to realise that the ink is coming out of his mouth.

XI

With an Open Mind

Grant lifts up the blanket and takes a step back. Bannister, the director of the Marshalsea, waits for a few seconds, then asks, "Well, Mr Vholes?"

The room is used to store dirty linen. Big baskets are overflowing with sheets in the half-light of a basement window. At short notice they'd made room to put the corpse on the table. The floor is littered with brushes and towels, giving the impression of a makeshift arrangement that doesn't go very well with the presence of the dead man.

The director clears his throat with a discreet cough.

Leonard Vholes has already been through this scene: just now, in the cab. When he crosses rivers he often imagines strange premonitions, as if the bridge – even Blackfriars Bridge with its nine stone arches – symbolised the fragility and vulnerability of mankind.

There was also a bridge in Hartlepool or, rather, a footbridge crossing a stream that went into the sea a little farther down. And on the other side was the clinic of Doctor Thorne; high walls surrounded the park, but Leonard could see Ophelia

307

through the bars, walking up and down on the arm of a nun. Ophelia's pale face and round stomach. Why did he never go across the footbridge?

"Mr Vholes?"

He wavers a little longer, then says, "That's him. That is Robert Beresford."

Bannister nods. Grant has already started to replace the blanket when Leonard says, "I'd like to see the place where he died."

"The cellar?" It is clear that the request makes the director uneasy. "Why not, if you insist. Grant will show you the way."

"That won't be necessary, just tell me how to get there."

***

"I wonder where Snegg's got to," Edward says.

"Indeed," Doctor Trees replies, "he's not normally late. But anyway, shouldn't we wait until night has fallen?"

Edward looks from left to right. Stretched out in the mist wreathing round them, the wings of Wooler Manor look like a beggar's arms. Nothing can be seen of the main building. The first touches of twilight are infiltrating the cotton-wool fog like drops of coffee in a cup of milk. Even their voices sound as if they're affected by the wisps rising from the ground.

"We're not running any risk in this peasouper. What did you find out in Hartlepool?"

"Thorne's establishment has a new owner, but it still exists, you know, and it's remarkably well run... it would be ideal for Margaret... hmm. To be brief, my friend Bowlby cannot remember any female patient by the name of Beresford, but there was a certain Miss Clarke who clearly came from an excellent family and about whom Thorne was both very cautious and very evasive. The dates, the physical description, a very characteristic scar he saw during an examination of the young woman's leg all tally. The young woman suffered from pulmonary disease, but above all..." Trees, embarrassed, looks at his fingertips, "she was pregnant."

"Died in childbirth?"

"Yes."

"And the child?"

"Died as well."

"And that was perhaps all the better for it," Snegg breaks in. "I'm sorry I'm late, but my cousin Wells was held up by a client."

He wasn't there and then he suddenly appears, as if the fog had woven out of its own tendrils a perfectly acceptable Seamus Snegg, hardly paler and only a little more disembodied than the original. In his hand is a ring big enough to go round a cow's neck and holds a multitude of clinking keys; on his back he's carrying a bag that seems to have a heavy load.

The three men head off for the north wing at a good pace and as they approach the door indicated by Mrs Preston, Edward's impatience grows. While Snegg, bending down over the lock, is carefully looking for a key that fits, he feels quite aroused – as if Lady Mathilde, her bodice undone, her hair all tousled, had come down from the painting and was waiting for him behind the door.

At the fourth attempt Snegg manages to engage the bolt.

"I came here once when I was a young lad," Trees recalls. "It was in this room that the old lord saw visitors of lesser importance. He would sit there, at a big table in that corner, and the people had to remain standing before him…"

But now the room is empty. They can't see a thing because of the drapes over the high windows. All around them is the characteristic stale smell of uninhabited houses, a distant whiff of tobacco. Snegg is nosing around everywhere. Outside he spent a long time examining the three stone steps, now he's slowly walking right round the room in search of God knows what – not of the door to the library, he saw that straight away. Having finished his inspection, he goes over and opens it without difficulty.

"Before we go in, gentlemen," Edward says, "might I remind you that nothing about this expedition must ever come out. We are here for the love of truth, but if we do discover it, we will never be able to reveal it, alas."

Trees and Snegg agree; then they go into the room, followed by Edward. Inside the windows are blocked by planks of wood. To their right a shiny cyclops with an improbable hat is slumbering; facing them they can make out an amorphous, hostile mass.

"Would you give us some light, Doctor?"

Snegg hands Trees a lantern and a flint and steel, that he takes out of his bag; then he dips his hand back in and shows them two bizarre, very compact instruments about the size of a horse's bit. When the lantern is lit the light shows that these are dark black. Looking up, the three men see that the cyclops is nothing but a rococo stove of repulsive ugliness, and the hostile mass an alignment of books without the least gilding nor the variation in height and thickness that make the charm of libraries.

"My God!" Edward exclaims, that reminds me of the registers in the chambers. Are you going to review all these little soldiers with your bits of scrap iron?"

Snegg goes over to the books, magnets in his hand. "That will not be necessary if my theory is correct."

"What theory?"

"Would you bring the lantern over here, please, Doctor."

Trees does so, revealing the sole discrepancy in the impeccable order of the shelves: an empty space between two octavo volumes. At the top the books touch but a narrow gap at the bottom suggests a volume had disappeared. Snegg opens the adjacent books: they are *Discours sur les sciences et les arts* and *L'essai sur l'origine des langues* by Rousseau. He puts them to one side, the wider space allowing them to see the panelling behind the books. He inserts one magnet – nothing happens – then the second.

Click!

It's a thin, insignificant sound: a tablet dropped into a pharmacist's dish, two glasses that hardly touch for a toast for fear of breaking the crystal. But there is also a brief visual effect. Something seems to have moved or, rather, shivered, before standing still again. Snegg takes the magnet from the back of the shelf – *click!* – then inserts it again – *click!* He points to a section of the shelves.

"There. Push."

Edward does so. The section drops away from them. He's assailed by a vile stench but ignores it because what he can see is fascinating. In the circle of light from the doctor's lantern his student room has appeared. Disordered. Dusty. An exact copy of his old divan, that at the moment is getting damp in the

Raffles' summerhouse. Two shelves with books put on them any old way, sometimes on top on each other, sometimes back to front. A hearth with a kettle on it. A bundle of clothes. A single slipper. But the most remarkable thing is the little knick-knack on a table beside the divan: *his* ivory hand. Exactly the same! To go by what he can see, Lord Beresford could have been one of his friends with odd ideas, steeped in poetry and the gothic novel, spending most of his time reading or daydreaming without in the least bothering about the practical details of living. His own double in a way.

Then he remembers what probably happened on the divan and blushes.

"Well I'll be damned!" Trees exclaims. That room and the library certainly weren't occupied by the same man!"

"In one sense you're right," Snegg says before suddenly exclaiming, "The lantern. Shine it on the back of the room!"

At that very moment Edward is stroking the ivory hand with the tips of his fingers, but he pulls them back immediately: the hand isn't made of ivory and it's as if it had just squeezed his heart!

"We can't leave her in that posture!"

"Leave *her*?" Trees, kneeling beside the skeleton, gives Edward a cautious glance. "Besides the clothes, that are incontestably masculine, I note the narrow pelvis, the prominent arch of the eyebrows, the steep slope of the forehead and the projecting mastoid. There's no doubt that it's a man. And I also note there," he points to a fracture in the top of the skull where a few hairs are stuck in a clot of dried blood, the sign of a pretty violent shock… "connected with the brown stains I can see on the divan cover…"

Snegg come closer, nods and mutters, "With an open mind…"

"Sorry?" Edward says.

"The blood. What a stupid mistake!"

"What d'you mean, the blood?"

It's as if Snegg is looking right through his employer – that he's talking to a quite different person hidden behind him. "I didn't follow Descartes' advice, unfortunately."

Bailey and Trees exchange glances. "Descartes?"

Pale and earnest, Snegg takes the lantern from the doctor and spends a long time examining the floor, where there are more dark stains, and the edge of the detachable panel that has been scratched in several places. He then inspects the papers scattered over the floor and in one corner find a little attaché case that is open and contains other documents.

" 'We must seek the truth with an open mind, free of all preconceived ideas.' And I did the opposite. I started out from the opinion that the blood seen by Mrs Preston on Beresford's hands was that of Mathilde…"

"So did I! It was obvious!" Edward protests.

"Did we go through the evidence with a fine-tooth comb? Was it the result of logical reasoning? No, it has been imposed on us. A preconceived idea is precisely what it is. The blood on the hands of a man suspected of murder can only be that of his victim, can't it? While there never was a murder."

"But then whose blood is it?"

"Beresford's own."

"And that man there?" Trees protests. "He hasn't been murdered?"

"Another preconceived idea, doctor. A skeleton is found prostrate, in a sinister place, with a split skull and we immediately think of violence and therefore of murder. There certainly was violence, but not the violence you're thinking of."

Edward clicks his fingers. He too has now understood.

"Mrs Preston's testimony," Snegg goes on, "that of Newton, the state of Ophelia's corpse, the blood stain I saw on her tomb, the things we have discovered this evening… it all fits together. We don't know who revealed the nature of the relationship between the brother and sister to Lady Mathilde. Perhaps the mysterious Vholes, putting his threats into practice. Perhaps Beresford himself, out of defiance or despair, perhaps even both. We don't know how far these revelations went, either – as far as the child that was born dead or not. But then here are numerous facts we can use as markers and follow them in our imagination."

That is something Edward is capable of.

He can clearly see Lady Mathilde crossing the courtyard, with no coat on, hair dishevelled, beautiful as one of the Fates and with a dagger in her hand. Beresford appears on her heels. *You wouldn't dare!* Oh yes, of course she'll dare. She remembers Danton, who used to dig up corpses out of love – she will do the same, but impelled by hatred. The Manor, like a big cruel cat playing with a mouse, stretches out its paws to hold her back; in front of her is the chapel, a nightmare reaching up into the sky. She opens the door, strides up to the altar, goes down the steps into the crypt and finds the coffin. Using all her strength, she tries to swing the coffin lid round and there she is: the woman who stole everything from her.

She is surprised by the sight of death and no longer knows why she is there. But the sound of hurried steps reminds her and just as Beresford appears, she strikes the corpse for the first time.

"He tried to stop her, which led to a scuffle beside the tomb. Perhaps he slipped, or threw himself to the ground to avoid the dagger. However it happened, his head struck the stone and he probably remained unconscious for a few minutes. We see him again a few minutes later, where Mrs Preston saw him from the skylight: sitting on the steps we came up just now with a cut on his head. Pulling himself together, he goes in and opens the library door with his key. Earlier on he'd left his coat, hat and gloves there in preparation for his departure. But he also has to wrap up his most precious possession: the letters from his sister, that you see over there. He operates the mechanism, goes into his secret room and closes the panel behind him."

Edward continues to imagine the events but is having a hard time of it. He sees Mathilde running off through the woods, panic-stricken, leaving her husband for dead in the chapel. He sees Mrs Preston, the girl with the shuttlecock, going through room after room, looking for her mistress. Then Mathilde again, who no longer knows where she's running. The stones on the path are hurting her feet in their thin-soled slippers, the brambles scratching her legs, the trees rushing towards her – the sky trembles, now it's raining, it's cold. She realises she can't escape like this, on foot, with no coat, and goes back to the Manor. Saturn sighs, Neptune sniggers. The shadows slip round her, the rain is spattering on the paving, soon to be eclipsed by another sound: that of the wheels of a horse and carriage. Mathilde has the time to disappear into the north wing, but that's precisely where the carriage is heading, stopping by those steps. She catches a glimpse of all the trunks in the gallery and, turning round, also sees that, unusually, the library door is open.

"Everything happens very quickly. Mathilde has just desecrated a tomb and, she believes, accidentally killed her husband. She has only one thought in her mind: to leave the Manor and hide somewhere... and there before her are the simple means of doing so comfortably. There's still a little light left in the library with its wide windows. She sees Lord Robert's things and, without further thought, puts on his coat, gloves and hat. As she's about to go, she remembers the book by Rousseau, to which she is very much attached; she grabs it, taking with it the magnet that operates the mechanism of the panel. This time she really does kill her husband but without knowing – she's buried him alive!"

"Perhaps he was already dead," Trees breaks in. "Even if the abundance of blood can be explained by a cut to the scalp, I would describe the fracture of the skull as very serious. If there really was a loss of consciousness in the crypt, it would indicate concussion and possible internal bleeding. In such cases the patient can regain consciousness and go about his business, then collapse again fifteen minutes later and this time for good, struck down by apoplexy."

Snegg has put the bundle of letters down and is now holding a small piece of metal.

"Unfortunately for him, death didn't come so quickly. In my opinion he attacked the panel and worked on it for a long time with this paper knife, until it broke, then with his fingernails. I wouldn't swear it but from the shape of the bloodstains, I think he went back and forward between the door and the divan several times, at first on his feet, then perhaps crawling, before falling down between the table and the couch."

"In that case he would still have been alive when the police came to check out what Mrs Preston had said."

"That's almost certain. But the men would have just had a quick glance at the library and Beresford could well have fallen asleep from exhaustion or fallen unconscious again. He will never have known that rescue was within earshot. A nasty end…"

"…for a nasty man," Edward says. "So this Mr Vholes wasn't aware Beresford was dead."

"No, but he has taken advantage of his disappearance to produce forged letters from Brazil to stop Alastair inheriting… but why? That's what remains a mystery. It's ages since the estate brought anything in, Vholes hardly ever comes up here and from what I've heard, he paid for the most recent maintenance work out of his own pocket."

Before leaving the room, they have one last glance at the remains of Beresford, that they've put in a more dignified position on the divan.

"And we still don't know what happened to Lady Mathilde."

"That is not quite correct, Doctor," says Snegg as he locks the panel with the magnet. "It is possible to follow her movements as far as Durham, where Charles Morgan dropped her off, still in the belief that it was Robert, and then to Durham docks, where Turnell saw her two days later. Did she manage to get back to France via Portugal? At this point we're leaving conjecture for the realm of fiction."

That is a border Edward can cross with ease. While the

shadows cast by the lantern chase each other across the ceiling, the fresh air of the open sea drives away the noxious air of the Manor. A ship smacking into the waves. Standing at the prow, still dressed as a man, Mathilde is staring defiantly at the horizon.

"In the middle of a war? With her French accent?" says Trees. "In my opinion she never managed to leave England, nor even the region either. Once she'd exhausted the cash that was in the luggage she'd be entirely destitute. Perhaps she's doing the cleaning in a Newcastle brothel at this very moment."

But Edward doesn't even hear that. He's entirely wrapped up in his fantasy of Mathilde, the beautiful Mathilde of the portrait, taking off her hat and throwing it into the sea, revealing her long black hair to the amazed sailors.

***

"Cosa vuole questo qua?"

"No lo so e me ne frego! Gioca!"

Studying the pieces on the board, Leonard Vholes reconstructs the course of the game. An Italian opening without doubt. Exchange of knights. Black castling on the king's side.

'Try to imagine a creature who would be to man what a man is to a pawn... it keeps on moving you around, Bishop. Quietly, from one square to the next, as far as the one you're on today. And you have no more chance of getting away from it than the marionette has of strangling the showman with its strings.'

The cellar is almost silent. The detainees, slumped down

on their mattresses, are reading newspapers several months old, staring at the ceiling, or chatting in low voices around guttering candles. Going past the Italians, Leonard easily finds what he's looking for farther down the room: an empty place right at the back, close to the curtain. The straw mattress the corpse was lying on has already been burnt. There's nothing to see there. Just to be sure, Vholes pokes around a bit, watched by a bearded man whittling a bit of wood with his penknife.

But what is he actually looking for?

There's something waiting for him down here, in the cellar. He's known that since a moment ago even if he has no idea what it is.

'Now let's make things clear: that famous cosmic chess-player is nothing but a monkey that spends most of its time scratching its armpits and giving inarticulate cries. From time to time it leans over the chessboard, strokes a pawn – that is to say, a man – with its hairy fingers, then scratches and squawks even more. But sometimes, seized with inspiration, it picks up a piece, holds it up in the air for a while, examines it from all sides, then replaces it at random. Sometimes beside the chessboard. And there's no counter-attack to that move, Bishop.'

The unknown man didn't look at all like Beresford, even if Death had stuck a disdainful mask over his face. Where had the man come from? Had he even known Beresford? By what chain of events had the Rousseau book come into his hands. If Vholes took his time replying, it was because he was weighing things up. Was it better for Beresford to be alive or dead? And eventually his answer was: dead.

"Vedrai! Scacco matto in tre colpi!"

"Ma vai al diavolo..."

Everything will be more straightforward from now on. The Manor will pass to the legitimate heirs. As for himself, Leonard... how he's longing to send all his clients packing. The hand writing his story will put down the pen and will finally be able to tear apart the spider's web of memories and dreams that still tie him to the past. He will retire somewhere. No one will ever hear of him again.

There's groaning that grates on his nerves coming from the other side of the curtain. A long lament. At first he thinks it's inarticulate before he realises the words are in a foreign language. And, although he doesn't speak the language, he is familiar enough with it to understand the meaning.

"Mon livre! On m'a volé mon livre!"

"There she goes again," someone mutters.

Leonard goes to the curtain and grasps a fold, but then stays there, transfixed, under the attentive gaze of the bearded man, who has stopped whittling his stick

"Je veux mon livre!" the plaintive voice goes on, setting off a concert of protest from the other side of the curtain. The bearded man gets up and goes over to Leonard; his black eyes are a bit wild and he has a v-shaped cut on his chin.

"It's French, you know. I can understand a bit, I spent a year in Boulogne. It's the old madwoman who's been here a few months now. She's saying someone's stolen a book."

Leonard nods. A pin has pierced the wine-skin of his memory and recollections come pouring out, thick and warm as blood, making the whole world round him sticky. He lets go of the curtain and gives the bearded man the same wild-eyed look.

"Mon livre! C'est tout ce qui me reste! Danton me l'a donné, oui, Danton! Qu'on me rende mon livre!"

"If you want my opinion…" the bearded man says.

But Leonard Vholes has already gone. As if pursued by a ghost he goes up the stairs four at a time and crosses the yard at the same speed, head down, eyes fixed on the ground. He doesn't see the warder, who opens the door for him, nor the young boy sitting in a coffee room on the corner of Chapel Court.

Charley, for his part, did see Vholes and was struck by the way he walked and his fixed look. He'd make an excellent character in a novel, he thinks. One of those silhouettes appearing round a street corner and saying a few pointless words – one of the small fry, without whom Don Quixote, Tom Jones and Roderick Random would hardly stand out at all. Then, off you go, exit Mr Vholes. Perhaps he'll turn up again in another episode.

While waiting to go back to the Marshalsea, Charley sips his coffee, nibbles at his roll and thinks of the face of the dead man in the cellar. He stares at the twilight piling up on the other side of the window. And there, right under his nose, is that inscription: *COFFEE ROOM* in capitals that he reads back to front: *MOOR EEFFOC*. In a moment the roll goes sour in his mouth. A fly tickles his ear but he hardly feels it. It's not London around him any more, he's gone through the mirror, reached another country, *the land of EEFFOC*. The country of children's nightmares. The realm of rats and the destitute. The province of darkness.

He waves his hand to drive the fly away, but it isn't a fly, it's a steel hook at the end of which is the Corporal with a grin on his face.

"Well, well, you don't look as if you're pleased to see me."

"Oh I am, of course… but how is it…?"

"You can say what you like about the Guvnor, but he's certainly not an old skinflint. With the money from his brother…"

"Uncle William's given us some money?"

"That he has! As an advance on the inheritance from your grandmother. And your father's used some of it to pay my debt. 'Our friendship, Corporal, born in the shadow of poverty, will soon blossom under the sun of prosperity.' That's what he said."

"And my family?"

"Don't worry, they'll be free as well tomorrow. The Guvnor simply promised to stay for the final of the skittles. And I don't think you're going to be in the blacking factory for long either. But there still remains one problem to sort out."

The Corporal sits down, frowns and pushes Charley's cup away with his corkscrew.

"Which one is that?"

"I haven't a single penny so… I hope your pockets aren't empty. Because, you see Number Two, you don't celebrate your freedom with a cup of coffee."

Epilogue

27th September 1825

This time, that's it, the great day has arrived.

The foreman, Alan Forbes, contemplates the long line of vehicles coming from Darlington, the barouches of the masters and the carts of the farm labourers all mixed up in a democratic chaos – not to forget several stagecoaches chartered for the occasion. Coming to meet this caravan is another, lesser, one from Bishop Auckland weaving its way towards Shildon. Lots of people are coming on foot, along the ditches, young people talking excitedly, older ones more reserved, their snack in a bag across their shoulders. Work in the fields will have to wait; the mines are closed for the day, shops as well, but not the inns. No one wants to miss the event. In the middle of the crowd the trumpets and horns of the fanfare are practising a few scales while the drummers are warming up their wrists.

The previous evening Forbes and Withers, Lord Glendover's estate manager gave each other a very cool greeting. They hadn't been seen together at the Crown for twenty years. They'd been friends back then, sipping their pints at the bar, listening enviously to the parties that were in full swing in the saloon bar on the other side of the corridor. And it's to that very place that the barmaid took them. Two sets of antlers were eyeing each other across the room, like a pair of earthenware dogs. A man dressed in the latest fashion pursed his lips as they approached: John, Lord Glendover's son. On the table in front of him was a jug of wine and one glass. He didn't invite them to sit down.

"This must remain a secret," he said brusquely, after having taken a mouthful of wine.

"There will be people all along the line, your lordship," Withers said. "the people are bound to realise that…"

"But I want them to realise, you idiot. What I don't want is to have them taking bets before the race. It's a matter of honour."

Honour? After all the dirty tricks his family had been up to?

"The train will leave from Witton Park, won't it?"

"Not exactly," Forbes explains. "The wagons will be hauled up the Etherley Hill first, then up Brusselton Hill."

"Hauled up. How? By horses?"

"No, by a fixed steam engine at the top of each slope. Once they're back on the flat, the wagons will be joined up to the locomotive."

"The race could take place on that section, between Shildon and Darlington," Withers suggested.

That was Alan Forbes' chance. He seized it, heart pounding. "Forgive me your lordship, but there will be a lot more people between Darlington and Stockton."

"Hmm," Glendover looks from one set of antlers to the other, "that's quite possible. The road goes alongside the line at Whiteley Springs, doesn't it?"

"Precisely, my lord."

"And there I'll almost be on my own estate. My presence there will seem fortuitous, which will be all the better for the lesson I'm going to teach them."

Whitely Springs! Forbes had to restrain himself so as not to show his delight.

"If I remember rightly," Glendover went on, "the road bends to the south level with a little wood. I'll wait there under cover and come out of the trees when the train arrives. It's a half-mile straight to the tollgate, which will make a good finishing line."

"Which horse will you be riding, sir?"

"Balios, of course. He's never been beaten. And a washtub on wheels is not going to be the first. Right then, gentlemen, we're in agreement? Half a mile to Whitely Springs, from the edge of the wood to the tollgate?"

Whitely Springs. Forbes has been dreaming of it all night. Full of confidence he heads off towards *Locomotion:* to someone unfamiliar with steam engines it would look like a monster, the offspring of copulation between wood and metal. The hands are polishing up the boiler, the cylinders and the connecting rods for one last time. Everything has to be shining, for the sun's going to be out. Notebooks on their knees, bookmakers are taking bets – not on the race with Balios, but on all the rest. Will the monster be able to pull the twenty or so wagons that have just been hitched on behind it? Two to one that it will get stuck on the rails, like an old mule on a steep track. Will it at least manage to get as far as Darlington, or will it explode with its inventor and his henchmen, sending a shower of scrap iron and flesh to the four winds. A few birds of ill omen have put their money on that eventuality and are sitting well away, on a hillock.

With an expression on his face as if he'd got out of bed on the wrong side, Stephenson greets Forbes with a jerk of the chin and dismisses the hands with their rags. He bends down to inspect one of the horizontal connecting rods – the most fragile one – that drives the axles; from time to time he glances over his shoulder, as if he was hoping to see his son Robert Junior at his side – he went to Colombia two months ago. An unpleasant memory comes to him: a fire-damp explosion at Wylam, men being carried out on stretchers, women crying and children running over, wide-eyed and open-mouthed. And another: his father, Robert Senior, blinded by a jet of steam, sitting at a window contemplating the empty air. "I can't see the birds any more, my son. And I can't hear them either. I'm not just blind, I'm deaf."

Mixed in with all that were the strange observations of Roderick Preston. Against all expectation the squire of Aycliffe had accepted his invitation to the trial run that had been held the previous day between Shildon and Darlington. Without making the least ironic comment or expressing any reservations at all, he had taken his seat with Edward Pease and his three sons in the covered carriage with carpets and padded armchairs, that the Stephensons called *Experiment*. He was the only one who didn't start at the whistle from the boiler. During the journey he watched the landscape in silence, nodding from time to time, as if he was satisfied and also a little surprised to find the important elements of the landscape in their right place.

"Why is there that noise, Stephenson? That *cling-clang, cling-clang?*"

"It's the wheels when they go from one rail to the next. However perfectly we align and rivet them, there's always a little gap."

"A gap, really?" Preston seemed to like the idea. "We're not travelling in space, Stephenson, but in time, it's towards the future that you're sending us, for better and for worse... that's the end of our hymns, our national anthems. Your *cling-clang* will be the marching song of mankind. So be it! But we must never forget the gaps!"

Satisfied with his observation, Preston resumed his contemplation of the landscape but when they reached the bridge of Bonomi stone he abruptly leant over to Stephenson: "Strange that all this should come from you... from you of all people..."

"Why? How do you mean?"

Leaning back in his chair, Preston shrugged his shoulders. "I don't know. Just an impression."

Stephenson's still bothered by this conversation and the sight of that enormous, alas only too recognisable posterior trying to pull itself up into the covered carriage is not the kind of thing to put him in a good mood again.

"Oh, Stephenson, you'll have to see to it that there are wider doors in future. For a while I thought you were going to put us in those bone-shakers back there."

Gregson is alluding to the twenty-one coal wagons fitted out with farm benches that will be carrying the second-class passengers. Making one last effort, he manages to get into the carriage where there are already several gentlemen in black coats and suits.

"But where's our favourite Quaker?"

"One of Mr Pease's sons died last night. The whole family is in mourning."

"All the better! These dissidents know how to run their businesses, I agree, but they make my skin crawl with their blasted…"

"May I introduce you to Jonathan Backhouse and Thomas Richardson, both fellow Quakers with Mr Pease."

"…their blasted sanctimoniousness." Gregson finishes his sentence unflustered. "A very good day to you, gentlemen. And friend Cobbold? You haven't happened to see him, have you? It's strange, I was supposed to meet him here."

George looks away and contemplates the flood of humanity climbing into the uncovered carriages. The Company's employees, recognisable by their blue armbands, are trying to check the tickets but there aren't enough of them and the fare dodgers have no problem slipping in behind their backs. There are six or seven people on benches intended for three, or they simply sit on the sides, legs dangling down; crammed full like that the carriages end up looking like millipedes or human bunches of grapes served up in wooden bowls. In the one for the musicians cymbals and trumpets are blooming in a bed of hats.

"I'm talking to you, Stephenson!"

"There's no Cobbold on the guest list."

With a mocking look Gregson takes a card out of his pocket. "*Invitation for two.* Isn't it normal that the chairman of Gregson Foundries should be accompanied by his head of personnel?"

"Cobbold is a murderer, Mr Gregson and you should be

ashamed to have him among your collaborators."

The two men look each other up and down. At the back of the carriage the other passengers remain silent.

"Well now!" Gregson says, "What a fine riposte! And there was I telling you that you ought to go into politics."

"Enjoy the journey, sir. I wish you a good day."

Gregson's voice pursues Stephenson as he walks along beside the rails: "Murderer or not, since he took up his position there hasn't been a single day's strike…"

When Stephenson joins Forbes, young Hackworth and the driver on the footplate, *Locomotion*'s safety valve opens, releasing a jet of white steam and a shrill wail that sends all the crows and blackbirds for miles around flying off in panic. A few young kids jump down off the wagons without further ado and run off.

"Ready, Alan?"

"Ready, sir."

It's eight o'clock. Pulling a convoy more than a hundred yards long and weighing ten tons, with at least three hundred and fifty passengers on board, *Locomotion* moves off, cautiously but with dignity, like an old rambler setting out on a long walk.

Cling-clang!

***

It's a very odd day, Alfred Cobbold thinks. In the first place it's far too warm for the end of September. And then…

The ex-policeman stands on tiptoe, two, three or four times, scanning the four points of the compass, searching the crowd of caps and toppers, bald heads and tousled manes for the pretty little blue hat. Not to be seen.

"Hey, sir! A meat pie?"

"No thanks, lad."

Two men from the slaughterhouse in their aprons are running towards the railway, shouting, "They're coming! They're coming!" And, indeed, the staccato *cling-clang* is approaching, accompanied by a musical potpourri distorted by the wind and the distance, by increasing clamour and a sort of spasm that is gripping the public, sending them hurrying towards the line. Cobbold instinctively crosses the bridge against the flow of bodies, noticing as he does so several people on the top of the tower of St Cuthbert's watching the scene through opera glasses.

Once across on the other side he continues his search for the little blue hat.

This is very unusual. He knows he's attractive to women but not to the extent that one completely unknown to him should make eyes at him like that. A streetwalker, then? If the Darlington whores are discreet, as in all small towns, some more shameless ones might have come from Newcastle at the prospect of good business. No matter. It's better out here than in the 'wagon' getting his coccyx bruised and having to put up with the 'bag of piss and wind', his own private name for Gregson. Then he vows to himself that he'll spend the whole day looking for the little blue hat if he has to. At least it'll help to pass the time.

For Alfred Cobbold can't stand it any more. He's had enough of Manchester, Gregson, the smoke from the furnaces, the infernal heat coming from the foundries, the big office smelling of leather and wax polish, the factory in general, that vast pandemonium where men always seem to be carrying out incomprehensible tasks. His own work is a piece of cake. Who would dare to set up a picket line when that meant you went straight to prison? Who would take the risk of losing their job with the price of bread rising and unemployment on the increase? They don't need him to maintain order, it maintains itself. Faced with the prospect of watching their children die of starvation the rebels mend their ways, the agitators calm down, the loud mouths are kept shut, the conspirators are given the cold shoulder. That's the 'invisible hand' everyone's talking about. Invisible like the chain that takes the workers from their dingy hovels to the stinking factories in the morning and back home in the evening – if one of the machines hasn't crushed them in the meantime.

Once, just once since he left the police, Alfred Cobbold had felt his heart beat more strongly with both excitement, a sort of hunger with no object, and a tiny shiver of fear – precisely the mixture that has sent him searching for the sweet little face he glimpsed in the crowd. The previous December a tall, quiet-looking fellow had appeared in front of him.

"You're Mr Cobbold."

It wasn't a question. He didn't reply.

"You know that there's a lot of people here who were at Peterloo, sir?"

"And what is that to do with me?"

The man shrugged his shoulders. "I don't know. It was just an idea I had. Everything's quiet here, but people haven't forgotten. That's what I wanted to tell you. People haven't forgotten."

Cling-clang! After having crossed the Skerne by the new

stone bridge to the north, the long mechanical caterpillar, ignoring its venerable nine-arched ancestor, chugs its way along the outskirts of the town and disappears to the east, letting off two jets of steam. People are applauding, going into raptures. But isn't that the little blue hat over there? Crossing Market Place, he goes into the town, empty but for a few cats and abandoned streamers. The silence gradually takes over from the clamour, like blotting paper absorbing ink, leaving the streets to the sun and the wind. Even though he only spent a few months in Darlington, he is suddenly overcome with nostalgia, as if he was returning to the scene of his childhood. No, it isn't that, it's the little blue hat that is tantalising him. And there is its owner, standing at the corner of a street, Bull Wynd, to be sure she hasn't lost her client – for there's no doubt about it now, she's a professional, however, they walk on past two or three 'disreputable' buildings, Cobbold following the young woman with some difficulty now since, knowing she's hooked him, she doesn't bother with making eyes at him any more and starts to walk even faster.

Then she heads off down an alleyway or, rather just the space between two buildings with piles of logs, broken wheels, old pots and pans.

"What, here?" Cobbold grimaces at the stench of urine and never-emptied dustbins – but at that very moment his arousal stretches the cloth of his trousers and, like a compass of flesh, directs him to the bottom of the cul-de-sac, where the young woman is leaning against a wall in a recess. Even prettier than he'd thought!

The Devil's Road

***

Cling-clang!

The spade makes a sharp noise like a shriek as it's shoved into the pile of coal. The little crystals start and bounce and tumble down, just as they did in the carts at Wylam that young George was sometimes allowed to ride in. But at Wylam it was the smell of horses – powerful, musky, earthy – that dominated, while today the cast iron and steel give off an odour of overcooked leg of lamb, of a forest baking in the sun. And every time the driver opens the door of the boiler for another shovelful, George can feel the breath of hell on his cheek.

As they go into the bend, he sees the tall silhouette of an old man that reminds him of his father: standing aside from a group of farm workers, in a worn serge shirt, arms crossed, legs firmly apart. Robert Senior used to stand like that, thirty years ago, facing the owner of Wylam mine. "Come on, Stephenson. I know that you disapprove of the activities of these hooligans who want to tear the country apart…"

"Indeed, sir."

"So why won't you give me their names?" Arms crossed. Chin raised. At the time his eyes, still undamaged, were fixed on the mine-owner, unblinking.

"It was dark, sir. I couldn't see their faces."

Locomotion is just passing the old man and George twists his neck to see him for as long as possible, but it is getting more crowded beside the line and, as the train reaches the edge of a wood, a rider suddenly appears out of a thicket. Immediately a group of farmers start clapping and shouting encouragement in suspicious unanimity.

"Who's that?" Hackforth asks as the musicians, in the carriage behind the footplate, start to play *The Miner's Revenge* for the umpteenth time.

Taking advantage of the straight line of the road, his mount, a black thoroughbred with glints of blue, outstrips *Locomotion,* that is still working its way round the bend. The rider, with his impeccable top boots, tight trousers and round hat, seems to have come straight out of a picture by James Seymour. Curious, Forbes watches him go.

"The Honourable John Glendover," Stephenson replies, his eyes fixed on his foreman. "It looks as if he's challenging us. Is there something you've heard about, Forbes?"

The pile of coal continues to groan at each shovelful; the lumps roll down to the feet of the three men and on each of them George sees, shining as in a mirror, his father's face.

"Er, yes, there is, sir. 'They have to be taught a lesson.' But you wouldn't have wanted to know about that."

"And if they're the ones who're teaching us this lesson, what are we going to look like?"

Cling-clang!

Now the road and the railway line are precisely parallel. Gathered between them like a long worm between two sticks, the crowd doesn't know which to follow: the locomotive spitting and whistling or the rider cracking his whip.

"It looks as if the horse is tiring," says Hackforth, the young engineer, taken on to replace Robert Stephenson Junior, has long eyebrows, curved like large commas. "We're gaining ground."

Forbes shakes his head. "Those nags can keep going ten times longer without slowing down. No, we're going to have to accelerate."

Of course. George remembers this section now, he even surveyed it himself. He also remembers the equation in the physics book lent him by the chief engineer at Killingworth. Two per cent. A gentleman on horseback or in a carriage wouldn't notice that kind of slope, but a farm labourer ploughing, a woman coming back from the washhouse or a plate-layer would. All effort made takes its toll: pain, tiredness. But now the slope is in their favour; it doesn't make a great difference for the horse, but for a convoy that probably weighs eighty or even ninety tons... it's like a giant pulling it on as hard as he can!

Glendover's whip, Balios' legs can do nothing against the laws of mechanics.

"We're winning!" says Hackforth, delighted.

Indeed, the toll-bar is approaching and *Locomotion* has a comfortable lead. The farmers and farm workers who were cheering Glendover must have been generously paid, for the crowd as a whole seems to be clearly in favour of the iron horse. As the lead widens, the clamour increases: jokes aimed at the rider come thick and fast, and a small boy, perched in the fork of an oak tree, bares his buttocks at him before making a prudent escape. Hats start flying up in the air like champagne corks, the drum-rolls get louder and louder, people are applauding, whistling and a tall, red-headed boy stripped to the waist is waving his shirt in salute of the winner.

With a furious tug of the reins, the Honourable John Glendover turns Balios onto a nearby lane and disappears. *Locomotion* continues on its journey to Stockton where, it appears, tens of thousands of people are waiting. Soon it will go much farther, Stephenson thinks, as far as the coast, and he imagines it travelling across the moors – *cling-clang!* – making a triumphal entry into Middlesborough, then running down the Tees estuary and on to Redcar, to Saltburn, then halting at the one force in the world that can still stop it: the sea.

"And they're winning too," says Forbes, pointing to the people, who are waving and shouting. "It's not everyday you can bare your arse to a lord's son."

***

Kirstie leaves the stone bridge the train has just passed, makes her way onto the road and walks alongside the green and marshy banks of the Skerne, with a few alders here and there. The crowd is dispersing in all directions. It's difficult to make progress, the verge is narrow and the way is blocked by a cart with a broken axle. There are too many vehicles of all kinds and too many people on foot. Kirstie passes a drunk asleep against a tree; a tall man leading a donkey by the reins on which an even taller woman is mounted, pushed past her without saying sorry, and it's at that moment that she notices Edward.

It's more than a year since she last saw him. Of all the men who came to Bull Wynd, he had the softest stomach and he always said, "Thank you, miss," when she'd finished. Kirstie remembers the previous spring, a Sunday in April: Sam stretched out in the grass, hands behind his neck – his stomach was hard and hollow as the font in the church. Then that other Sunday when he didn't turn up. And the pain she felt when she heard what had happened.

Kirstie stays behind the donkey, she doesn't want to embarrass the lawyer. Together with a small group, including a very pretty lady, he's trying to cross the road to get onto a path on the other side that goes into the woods. The lady shivers when a cloud blots out the sun. Perhaps Kirstie's father was right after all: it was all going to end in rain.

It was also raining on that day. She can see Blake again, the little bank clerk. The little squeals he made as he lay with her. His smug air and his cigars, supposedly 'a gift from the Company'.

"Incredible!" he'd said. "Two gentlemen who came to blows. Bailey must have seen Spalding go into the bank. He'd followed him and grabbed him by the collar."

At this point in Blake's story, there was nothing to say that the dispute had anything to do with what had happened to Sam. However, Kirstie had felt ill-at-ease, bothered by the smoke from his cigar he was blowing in her face.

"Bailey was screaming, 'You're nothing but a liar. A liar!' And the other man went bright red, jammed up against the wall. 'But I'm telling you it was too late! They'd already left.' According to the manager, they were talking about the attempted escape by a prisoner on the road to Stockton that went wrong. The lawyer finally let go of Spalding and went out without saying anything more. It took almost half an hour to get the old man back on his feet again, with a large glass of brandy. He kept mopping his forehead and after each gulp he would moan, 'Oh my God! Oh my God!'"

An attempted escape that went wrong. Those few words became a maelstrom with Sam at the centre, the axis round which it whirled and it took Kirstie a whole year to get out of it.

Edward Bailey came to Bull Wynd the morning after the scene and then a couple more times, but Mrs Hudson has instructions to say she's not there. Too many memories to deal with.

Today it's different. There's something she'd like to share with him.

They still can't move; the man leading the donkey is swearing at the carter. The lawyer has finally managed to get onto the road and is trying to squeeze past the cart that's stuck. He's even more puffy faced than she remembers and he's lost some more hair. Little Blake had kept her informed, explaining who stole what and who had bought whom in Darlington, made her aware of the constant underground hustle and bustle, the perpetual background noise that is called 'business'. She knows that Spalding has withdrawn his custom from Bailey, and was quickly copied by several influential families. That Bailey had had to mortgage Raffle House, but that then the Railway Company entrusted him with several important transactions and that the Quakers swear by him.

"He missed his vocation, it's not a lawyer he should have been but a barrister. He actually brought one in to defend the people living along the river in Great Burdon against Cross, and paid for him out of his own pocket. They're starting to call him Robin Hood…"

Finally three men lift up the cart and put it on the verge. Before setting off again, the donkey drops a whole dollop of manure that Kirstie just manages to avoid, by stepping to one side, which brings her closer to Bailey. All at once she feels a desire to be with him in the Bull Wynd bedroom again, to listen to him muttering nonsense while she helps him to an erection.

Blake has no need of that treatment, he has an almost permanent hard-on, and always takes her twice in succession. Between the two couplings he tells her all the gossip – who's turning a profit and who's in the red. Which important people his master is having dinner with.

"Mr Gregson's arrived. From Manchester. With Cobbold."

"Cobbold?"

"Yes, the former policeman. He's Gregson's assistant at the moment. They've come to see the train."

Two steps more and and the donkey stops again, blocked this time by a wheelbarrow that has just shed its load of biscuits and meat pies. Kirstie deliberately stumbles and drops her bag right in front of Bailey. He blushes, helps her to her feet and picks up the bag in which she's hidden the little blue hat. He's certainly seen the blood on the hem of her dress. Sam often used to make fun of her when she claimed she could 'say things with her eyes' but she looks straight into Bailey's: she wants him to know what happened a short while ago by Bull Wynd. Tell him that Cobbold has paid the price.

Bailey flutters his eyelids, nods to her, then goes to join his friends on the little path. Kirstie, for her part, looks up at the sky, then hurries off to the log cabin where she'll be able to put on her everyday clothes again.

***

"All the same!" Doctor Trees says. "Progress will eventually benefit the most destitute, it's only logical."

"Oh yes," Squire Preston replies, "fortuitously. Just as the flour falling out of a poorly tied sack benefits the weevils."

"But to spin out the metaphor," says Snegg with one of those sounds he makes in his throat that recall laughter as much as sobs, "you need to imagine weevils forced to grind the wheat for starvation wages..."

"...and then to pay through the nose for the flour," Mrs Preston adds in her quiet voice.

Following Edward, the group returns by the way they came. Dense and very dark, the wood bordering the Raffle property smells of humus and the rain that is arriving from the east. Two hours ago, excited by the event despite themselves, they had been talking enthusiastically. The creak of the connecting rods, the hiss of the steam, the screeching of the rails and the crowd, the dissonant music all around had made them pensive, taciturn.

"Have you ever met Alastair Beresford, Mr Preston?" Edward eventually asked in order to break the silence.

"No. For him I'm just small fry, and I very much doubt whether his wife would want to take tea with her former lady's maid. His estate manager, on the other hand did come to see us. He's a very sociable man, unlike his master. Especially after a couple of glasses of brandy. He told me something odd that Alastair's masons discovered about the secret room. The one that had the skeleton."

"Oh yes, the genuine remains of Beresford," Snegg said in pensive tones. "Unless the genuine ones are those in London."

"Alastair couldn't care less which are genuine and which are false, since he won't get a second inheritance. But in that room no one knew about, and that remained sealed for twenty years, they found..."

"What, then?"

Preston pauses in order to keep his audience on tenterhooks. Raffle House can already be seen among the trees at the end of the footpath.

A coin minted... last year! "Oh dear, what's the matter with you, doctor? You've gone quite red. Have you swallowed a midge?"

While Preston is thumping Trees on the back to help him spit out the imaginary insect, there's a cry that attracts Edward's attention. "Madam! Madam!" He recognises the voice as being Effie's, the maid's, and he also hears another sound, like the chirruping of a bird repeated infinitely: 'Tutitutitutituti'. In order to get there more quickly, he leaves the path and makes a beeline for the house, through high bracken. What he sees as he comes out of the trees doesn't seem to make sense to him, it's like a scene from a grotesque dream, with no relation to reality. To the left is the familiar summerhouse, to the right the two old elm trees and the little wall round the kitchen garden. The scene is set, everything seems normal. But what are Effie and Garrett, the old gardener doing? They look as if they're performing a bizarre dance, or that they're playing some children's game and trying to catch something that keeps on slipping away. You can hear the crunch of their footsteps on the stretch of gravel outside the back door.

"Oh, *please* Madam."

"Tutitutitutituti..."

Edward can't really see Margaret. It's as if he was being dazzled by the sun so that all he can see is vague shapes in a halo of bright light. Bare feet on the gravel, bare legs as well, bare thighs... the others emerge from the path a few steps behind him. Mrs Preston puts her hand to her mouth: "Oh my God!"

It is only now that Edward becomes aware of his wife's nakedness. How long is it since he saw her like that? He doesn't for one second think about the incongruity of the situation, nor about the embarrassment of the others or the gossip that it might cause, he doesn't notice how thin Margaret is, doesn't ask himself why she's exposing herself like this, no, he's simply overcome with the desire this woman sets off inside him, by the pointlessness of that desire. She stops because of the gravel that is hurting her feet, limps a bit, hops then sets off in the opposite direction. The two servants manage to stop her running away but not to get her under control, Effie because she's not strong enough, Garret because he can't bring himself to touch his mistress' naked body. Someone has left the farmyard gate open and four or five black hens approach in their cautious manner, looking on all sides, as if hesitant to join in the general confusion.

For Edward the vision goes on and on, but in reality it only lasts for a few seconds because the others haven't been slow to react; Preston runs up to Margaret, cutting off her retreat by holding his big arms wide, thus in a way throwing her into the arms of the doctor who, aided by Garrett, manages to get her under control. While Emily Preston puts a shawl over her shoulders, Snegg grasps her wrists and, looking deep into her eyes and speaking to her gently, manages, remarkably, to calm her down a little.

"Let's take her into the drawing room." Trees says, "I've got some laudanum in my bag."

"Titus!" she groans, tears in her eyes. "Where is Titus?"

Edward slowly recovers from his shock and suspecting that his presence in the drawing room won't make any difference, he decides to question the maid.

"It's the dog, sir…"

"Well, what about the dog?"

"He hasn't moved from his basket since yesterday. He hasn't stopped squealing. When he tried to stand up, his hindquarters wouldn't obey. He was stuck on the floor. But at some time or other he must have managed to get up on his feet, for when Madam asked for him, he was nowhere to be found. We searched the whole house. And that's when Madam went… the way you saw her."

"He can't have gone very far," Garrett says. "I would say he's gone to die under a tree, over there. That's where he buries his bones. I'll go and have a look…"

"No," Edward says, "you go and round up the hens."

Then he sets off for the woods, taking long strides. Once under the trees he picks up a stick and starts to explore the undergrowth, going round in wider and wider circles.

"Titus!"

He can't say why these tall, dark trees, creaking like crows in the breeze and appearing to be stuck in the sky rather than rooted in the ground, should always make him think of Byron.

> *The Tree of Knowledge is not that of Life.*
> *Philosophy and science, and the springs*
> *Of wonder, and the wisdom of the world,*
> *I have essay'd, and in my mind there is*
> *A power to make these subject to itself –*
> *But they avail not.*

"Oh come on, don't do this to me, Titus!"

Solomon wrote to him in January. He was planning a pilgrimage for the first anniversary of the poet's death, at Hucknall Torkard, and suggested Edward should be there, half way between London and Darlington. Out of the question. Edward had made up a reason why he couldn't be there and hadn't even invited him to carry on up north and visit him. His Holborn period was over. Sometimes some of Byron's lines came back to mind and he couldn't avoid finding them beautiful, but he's thrown away all his books.

Woof woof! Idiot! It looks as if Byron managed to understand her better in a few hours than you did in ten years... this woman is an elf, a fairy. She needed the pure air of the wide-open spaces. But instead of taking her far away, you kept her confined here among the stench of her father's farts and her mother's array of little tables with their pot plants... And when they died, you replaced them with your spurious air of a rebel preserved in madeira! You wrapped your way of life round her like a tomb. Now she's lost her only friend and is all alone... are you pleased with yourself?

With the end of his stick Edward clears away the dead leaves that have already gathered over the dog's belly and paws. Unbelievable. Unbelievable that such a grotesque creature when alive could end up as such a dignified corpse! Enveloped in the shroud of his fur, his bright eye gazing into the distance, Titus looks like a Stoic philosopher trying to impart a little more of his wisdom to us after death. The birds are silent, as if in mourning.

It's not too late.

It's always too late! There's no before and after, just the

*here and now. Just look at the world... watch those new ideas,
the way they fall into the ditch to rot away there with the old
ones... look at hope, that old owl nailed to the door of the
future! Only beings such as Byron and Margaret deserve to
live. The others are just stones you throw into the swamps.*

That's wrong. There's man's willpower. I will change the
world. The world will change. I will see to it that...

Woof woof! Oh do stop it, or I'll die of laughter!

Edward has no idea how long he spent talking to the dog's
corpse – a few minutes, an hour? Later on he found himself
stretched out, leaning against a tree, his eyes all puffy, his
head aching, and with each breath he lifts up Titus, lying
across his chest. It's started to rain. The drops sound different
depending on whether they land on his clothes or the dog's fur.
Somewhere in the treetops Byron is cawing:

> *All I see in other beings*
> *Have been to me as rain unto the sands,*
> *Since that all-nameless hour*

He lies there without moving, until a hand is placed on his
shoulder.

"Come on, cousin Edward, it's time to go in now..."

Mr Dick or The Tenth Book – Jean-Pierre Ohl

'Mr Dick is a character from *David Copperfield* and Ohl's book is in many ways a homage to Dickens. It is the story of two young Frenchmen whose lives are consumed by their obsession with Dickens' life and books and in particular his final, unfinished novel: *The Mystery of Edwin Drood*. It's a playful and highly literary detective story, like a Gallic mélange of *Flaubert's Parrot* by Julian Barnes and AS Byatt's *Possession.*'   Sam Taylor in *The Observer*

'*Mr Dick* is an odd and hugely entertaining novel, full of mock-scholarship, ghosts, impersonations, forgery and murder. Dickens, both a conventional man and wild poetic spirit, would have admired the skilful mixture.'

William Palmer in *The Independent*

'The narrative Jean-Pierre Ohl's novel is flashily post-modern in technique and reminiscent of Umberto Eco's *The Name of the Rose*.'   John Sutherland in *The Financial Times*

'*Mr Dick* – to whose resourceful translator I doff my hat – is an immensely playful *jeu d'esprit* stuffed full of Dickensian jokes and with some sharp things to say about literary obsession.'

DJ Taylor

'Ohl has mastered a blend of parody and vengeance that few writers can do. Except, of course, for Dickens.'

Miranda Carter in *Three Percent Review*

£9.99 ISBN 978 1 903517 68 0 224p B. Format

The Lairds of Cromarty – Jean-Pierre Ohl

'*The Lairds of Cromarty* presents us with a thoroughly engrossing mystery as well as an intriguing collection of supporting characters such as Par the butler, or Mary's Aunt Catriona, who watches the citizens of Edinburgh through a telescope, exclaiming loudly at their behaviour. There's even a cameo of George Orwell, for reasons we won't go into here. An absorbing page-turner that defies all attempts to put it down.'

Alastair Mabbott in *The Herald's Paperback of the Week*

'Jean-Pierre Ohl's *The Lairds of Cromarty* is a bulging carrier bag of a novel, a bibliophilic *jeu d'esprit*, containing the best literary rugby match since *Tom Brown's Schooldays*, a homage to the International Brigades and a convoluted love story.'

Catriona Graham in *The Guardian's Books of the Year*

'Some books are real surprise and this is one of them. What is at heart a detective story becomes in turn a love story, a tribute to friendship and courage, an ode to books and booksellers and to nineteenth-century literature… For all its Gothic twists, this is a book filled with humour, acute observations of character and place, and literary citations worthy of a professional bookseller – Ohl's other career. It has been flawlessly translated by Mike Mitchell in what deserves to become another of the latter's award-winning works.'   *The Historical Novel Review*

'Mike Mitchell's translation has depth and reach, with Ohl, he creates the density of a Victorian novel, but leavened constantly as the disparate parts of the complicated plot are pulled together. This wonderful, humorous, book should be displayed in all good bookshops.'

Scarlett MccGwire in *Tribune*

£9.99 ISBN 9781 907650 74 1 286p B. Format